SUMMER ROOMMATES

HOLLY CHAMBERLIN

KENSINGTON
PUBLISHING CORP.

www.kensingtonbooks.com

KENSINGTON BOOKS are published by

Kensington Publishing Corp.
119 West 40th Street
New York, NY 10018

ISBN: 978-1-4967-1365-0 (ebook)

ISBN: 978-1-4967-1363-6

First Kensington Trade Paperback Printing: July 2023

10 9 8 7 6 5 4 3 2 1

Printed in the United States of America

Books by Holly Chamberlin

LIVING SINGLE

THE SUMMER OF US

BABYLAND

BACK IN THE GAME

THE FRIENDS WE KEEP

TUSCAN HOLIDAY

ONE WEEK IN DECEMBER

THE FAMILY BEACH HOUSE

SUMMER FRIENDS

LAST SUMMER

THE SUMMER EVERYTHING CHANGED

THE BEACH QUILT

SUMMER WITH MY SISTERS

SEASHELL SEASON

THE SEASON OF US

HOME FOR THE SUMMER

HOME FOR CHRISTMAS

THE SUMMER NANNY

A WEDDING ON THE BEACH

ALL OUR SUMMERS

BAREFOOT IN THE SAND

A SUMMER LOVE AFFAIR

SUMMER ROOMMATES

Published by Kensington Publishing Corp.

As always, for Stephen
And this time, also for Dr. Jacqueline Olds

You only live once. But if you do it right, once is enough.
—Mae West

Chapter 1

"When will they get here, Clovis?"

Clovis, not being of the human species, didn't reply in words but bumped his large feline head against Sandra's calf.

"Oh, I know," Sandra said with a smile. "They'll get here when they get here. But I can't help being impatient."

Sandra Pennington stood at one of the windows in the living room, watching the road, awaiting the arrival of three total strangers. Three total strangers who were to spend the summer living in her home. Even though contracts had been signed weeks ago, everything settled and prepared, the idea still seemed strange to Sandra. Strange and somewhat frightening.

The two-story house, number 12 Spruce Street in Yorktide, Maine, was certainly large enough to accommodate four women comfortably. It was of a type commonly seen throughout New England. White clapboard, dark green shutters, front porch large enough for four wicker armchairs, two small tables perfect for setting down drinks or books, and a big ceramic pot of seasonal flowers. In the winter, a wreath made of pine boughs hung on the front door, surrounding the brass knocker. In the summer, a wreath made from dried flowers took its

place. Behind the house spread a green lawn with an herb and
flower garden in one corner. There was a small gardening shed
and a two-car garage, both added during Sandra's long marriage.

Indeed, Sandra Pennington had lived at number 12 Spruce
Street for most of her life, first as a young bride, then as
mother of two children, and now, as a widow.

At seventy-four, Sandra still stood at a slim five feet eight
inches tall. Her hair, naturally blond though helped along by a
L'Oréal product, was cut in a neat bob that came to about an
inch below her ears. Her eyes were dark blue. After successful
cataract surgery when she was in her early sixties, she had
been able to put aside the glasses she had worn since the age
of nine.

Her clothing style was classic and simple, though she loved
to wear color, especially blues and greens. Her jewelry collection, though not extensive, contained a few very good pieces
that had been passed down through her husband's family. She
always wore her wedding ring, a wide yellow-gold eternity
band set with colorless diamonds. Sandra had a native dignity;
her bearing was almost regal. People often compared her to
Grace Kelly, or Slim Keith, one of Truman Capote's so-called
swans. Sandra had never paid much attention to the implied
compliments, unless they had been delivered by her beloved
husband, John.

Sandra and John had had a very happy marriage. Sandra
knew that she was one of the lucky ones. She had, in fact, married her best friend. They had been true partners in life, never
really imagining that they would ever be apart. That is, not
until John was diagnosed with heart disease only months before his death from a massive coronary. His unsuspected illness, and of course the fear of an impending death, had come
as a brutal shock to the couple. They had made it a point to
talk about what lay ahead for Sandra when her husband was
gone, and together they had come to terms (at least, they had

tried to) with the situation. Still, five years after John's death, his absence could feel surprisingly cruel.

In fact, loneliness had become a too constant companion these past few months, and Sandra's mood had only been intensified by the ridiculously long Maine winter. March came in like a lion and went out like a tiger. April might be called the cruelest month, with its surprise snowfalls and sharp as a knife winds, but May could be unpleasant, too, with the temperature refusing to rise above the low fifties and occasionally dipping down to freezing point.

Sandra knew she wasn't alone in feeling depressed by the weather conditions. Each year, desperate for light and warmth, friends reported to friends their sightings of the first robin, the first forsythia bushes in bloom, the first scent of wild mayflowers in the air. The appearance of a snowdrop, or of a yellow crocus poking through the dark soil could bring a tear to the eye. It was difficult to describe to a person who didn't live in a northern clime the excitement surrounding the switching out of wool sweaters for cotton sweaters; the putting away of mittens if not yet of gloves; the trading in of one's fur-lined wool hat for a baseball-style cap. It was a genuinely giddy feeling, the realization that winter was finally over—at least for now—and that spring, that great tease, had truly arrived.

It was during this grim and dreary time before the hint of warmer temperatures and brighter days that Sandra, already lonely for John's companionship, had also badly felt the loss of her dearest friend of many years, Emma Nelson. Two years earlier, Emma had been diagnosed with dementia. The disease had progressed rapidly. The previous autumn, Emma, no longer able to care for herself, had gone to live with her daughter in a suburb of Chicago. In January, Millie had had no choice but to install her mother in a nursing facility with a memory care unit. These days, when Sandra spoke to her old friend via FaceTime, sessions arranged and organized by Millie, it was most likely that Emma wouldn't know Sandra, or that Emma would ask after old friends and neighbors long gone. Sometimes she exhibited symptoms of extreme frustration and at other times, terrible, directionless anger. To witness Emma in this state was heartbreaking. It was worse than heartbreaking, Sandra had decided. It was terrifying.

Who were you, Sandra wondered, when the people who knew you best were gone, dead or trapped in a living hell? Where or what was the self when it was no longer known by others? Did a person only really or fully exist in relation to other people? How much was self-knowledge worth if there was no one with whom you could *be* yourself?

Questions like these, unanswerable and exhausting, had troubled Sandra too often during the past, dreary months.

And then, one day in mid-April, she had happened upon an article in a national newspaper about a growing phenomenon in the United States as well as in parts of Europe. It was called co-living. Adults taking on roommates or housemates after divorce or after having lost a partner or even after years of having lived on their own. Co-living, it had been proved, had both financial and emotional benefits.

The idea had struck a chord with Sandra, and without much hesitation she had decided to undertake an experiment of her own in the realm of co-living. She would rent out her three extra bedrooms for the summer and see how she felt about living under the same roof with strangers, who, it was to be hoped, might not remain strangers as the summer progressed. She would try to get to know these three women—they would have to be women—and maybe even mention the idea of a permanent household of women, see if anyone was enthusiastic about the possibilities.

If the experiment was a disaster, if dissension among the women was a constant rather than an occasional thing, well, so be it. She could survive the summer. She had survived far worse than squabbling. Besides, trial and error was the only way to learn. And loneliness was not fun.

With some trepidation, Sandra had told her son and daughter about her projected summer experiment. Jack had been keen; he didn't relish the idea of his mother being alone so much and thought the benefit of companionship would outweigh most anything negative that might occur.

Kate, however, a lawyer as her father had been, had reservations. She was worried that strangers might take advantage of her mother. Sandra didn't need the additional income. Why would she choose to take on the responsibilities involved in being the host of what was essentially a sort of bed-and-breakfast? And by the way, was she properly insured against injuries to the renters caused by, say, a broken stair rail or faulty wiring? Sandra should speak to her homeowner's insurance representative. To Kate, welcoming strangers into one's home seemed like an unnecessary and potentially dangerous undertaking. If Sandra did, however, insist on going ahead with her scheme, she should at the very least get herself a good real estate agent who specialized in short-term rentals and other such arrangements.

A bit reluctantly, Sandra had admitted that she had no idea of what she was doing in terms of the business end of things. For example, as a landlord, even a short-term landlord, could she legally stipulate that a renter had to be over the age of fifty? Of course, there would have to be a screening process, for the safety of everyone involved. Did summer renters have specific legal rights that differed from the rights of renters who signed long-term lease agreements? Was she allowed to set rules as specific as "must use a coaster" and "person who finishes roll of toilet paper must replace it"? The renters would not be children; how much could or should she assume about their domestic habits? No hot plates in bedrooms. Kitchen off-limits at certain times. Food in fridge must be labeled. Was it wise to count on a certain level of maturity in the women who would be sharing her home? Maybe it was best not to assume anything.

The questions went on. Was it legal to reject someone with a criminal record? Was it legal to reject someone because she smoked? Sandra was pretty sure that as the homeowner she could ban smoking in the house and on the property, but was it okay on a *moral* basis to refuse to let someone who smoked live in her home? Certainly, she could allow no recreational drug use on the property. It was just too risky. Everyone would agree with that. But wait. The use of cannabis for pleasure or to help relieve pain was legal in Maine. Still, as the homeowner, didn't she have the final say?

Finally, after a week of fretting, Sandra had gathered her wits, and marshaled her courage. *She* was in charge. *She* owned the house. She was intelligent and strong and resourceful. And, she knew without a doubt that John was encouraging her to take this chance. John had believed in her a hundred percent, and he still did. Sandra was sure of that.

Taking Kate's advice, Sandra had found a real estate agent, a woman with an excellent reputation in Yorktide, and scheduled a preliminary meeting. Marcia Livingston was a no-nonsense sort of person who had imparted information as well as advice in a clear and straightforward manner. Sandra was impressed. Marcia put out the word. Applications began to flow in. With her expertise, Marcia handled the initial vetting of the applications received and presented Sandra with strong candidates for review. "My screening process is rigorous," Marcia had assured her. "Any of these women would be a safe bet."

At first, Sandra had found it difficult to choose among the potential roommates. Somehow, the process felt discriminatory; indeed, it *was* a matter of passing judgment. Several times she had to remind herself that first and foremost this was a business venture, if also, hopefully, the planting of the seeds of friendship.

Finally, the selection had been made.

Mary Fraser was a recently retired lawyer, single, in her

early sixties, from New York City. Her credit was impeccable. Her references, one from a former partner in her firm, another from an attorney with whom she had teamed up on occasion, were glowing. She would be occupying the largest bedroom.

Amanda Irving, in her late fifties, was from the Boston area where she taught history and social studies at a private school. Her references emphasized her reliability and trustworthiness and general amiability. She would be in the second largest room.

The third woman who would be sharing Sandra's home this summer had not been one of her initial choices. When the woman Sandra had chosen to occupy the smallest and therefore the least expensive of the bedrooms had canceled at the last minute due to ill health, somehow Patty Porter's application had slipped through Marcia's usually vigilant screening process and landed in Sandra's hands.

Something about the woman's application had touched Sandra. She couldn't say why, exactly, but her gut instinct told her that Patty Porter, a single, retired low-level office assistant from a small town in Massachusetts, who gave her age as "sixty-plus," should be the third guest. Marcia Livingston had strongly advised Sandra not to accept Ms. Porter—her credit history was not good and her references were both from family members, and therefore not entirely to be trusted—but Sandra had held firm. "I hope you know what you're doing," Marcia had said with a frown.

Sandra hoped so, too. She hadn't felt so excited, in a nervous sort of way, in years.

In preparation for her summer roommates, Sandra had hired a local cleaning service to scour the house top to bottom. That morning she had placed fresh flowers in each woman's bedroom. There were new sheets on the beds and new towels in the bathrooms. Maybe fresh flowers and new bedding weren't strictly necessary, but Sandra wanted to show her summer companions that they were indeed welcome. She wanted to introduce them to a house that might come to feel a bit like a home before long.

Sandra leaned closer to the window. A car had turned onto Spruce Street and was moving toward number 12. She could just make out the New York plates. It must be Mary Fraser.

"Here we go, Clovis," she said to her loyal feline companion, still standing at her side. "Get ready to say hello to our summer roommates."

Chapter 2

One hour earlier . . .

Sixty-three-year-old Mary Fraser sat with her hands firmly on the wheel of her car, heading north. She had reached her full height of five feet and eleven inches by the time she was fifteen. Since the age of forty she had worn her hair in a smart pixie cut. She loved jewelry, and her collection, amassed over years, was fairly eclectic. Her clothes were expensive and well made; she preferred black, white, tan, and taupe but wasn't opposed to an occasional pop of Kelly green or red or, lately, lilac.

Mary was not unaware of her sagging jawline but was too proud to go for plastic surgery. Some of the greatest people through history had sported jowls. Winston Churchill. Alfred Hitchcock. Queen Victoria. The wonderful British actress Margaret Rutherford. Who was Mary to complain of being in such august company? Besides, she was physically fit. She carried her own groceries, did her own housework, and every afternoon she took a two-hour walk.

Fifteen years earlier, she had bought a small but charming apartment in New York's West Village. The best thing about the ground-floor apartment was its backyard, which Mary enjoyed in all weathers. She was a regular at the secondhand bookshops in the neighborhood and spent a good deal of time at art galleries throughout the city. Over the years, Mary had amassed a small but important collection of paintings by contemporary artists. One of her most prized possessions was a painting by Jacqueline Humphries, an American abstract painter whose work was in the collection of the Museum of Modern Art in New York as well as the San Francisco Museum of Modern Art.

The very opposite of a competent cook, Mary subsisted on takeout and also had her favorite restaurants. She had dinner at Chez Etienne every Wednesday evening—they did a wonderful *moules et frites*—and every Saturday morning she had her breakfast at a classic coffee shop just around the corner from her home. Her cell phone kept her company at these solitary meals. Mary was a bit of an information addict, if one could be a bit of an addict.

Since retiring a few months earlier, Mary had found herself having nothing to *do*. Nothing important, that was. It was a perfect moment to trade an unpleasant summer in the city for a pleasant summer by the sea. The Hamptons were out; Mary couldn't stand the pretense rampant in that part of New York. She had been to Cape Cod and to Martha's Vineyard several times in her life—both also overrun in tourist season—but she had never been to Maine. This summer seemed like a perfect time to remedy that.

On a website that specialized in vacations for single adult women, Mary had found what seemed to be a very nice situation. She had heard back from the rental agent, a Marcia Livingston at the Sutter-Black Agency, only two days after having sent her references and credit history. Mrs. Sandra Pennington of Yorktide, a small town in southern Maine, would be happy to share her home with Ms. Fraser.

Mary, who had been married once for about a minute, had otherwise never had a housemate. The arrangement this summer would be a challenge, but she had faced much larger challenges in her life. Much larger. Besides, she could afford to break the nonrefundable rental agreement if she was really and truly miserable, and retreat back to her apartment in the West Village.

At the moment, Mary was seated comfortably behind the wheel of her car, a Subaru Legacy, on her way to Yorktide, that small coastal town where she was booked to spend the summer at Ms. Pennington's hybrid bed-and-breakfast. A summer that, she hoped, might help to restore at least some of her former get-up-and-go which had, in no uncertain terms, gotten up and gone.

Mary Fraser had always known herself to be pretty tough and unflappable; she had been that way since childhood. But since her dear friend Judy's sudden and tragic death almost a year ago, right after the trauma of Mary's firm being sued for malpractice, she had been feeling decidedly tired, emotional, on edge. And dare she admit it? Vulnerable.

The strain of the lawsuit had taken its toll on everyone involved, from Mary's partners to the administrative staff. Mary had been worried that they would lose everything they had worked to achieve. Knowing you were innocent, even having it proved in a court of law, didn't mean that other people were necessarily going to believe in your innocence.

In the end, the firm was fully exonerated, but the emotional damage she had suffered as a result of her friend's terrible death, added to the stress that had been occasioned by the lawsuit, had made it easy to decide that it was time to retire. To sneak away and lick her wounds? Maybe, a little.

Literally, every one of her colleagues had been surprised and puzzled by her retiring, and some continued to question her decision, months after Mary Fraser had walked out of the office for the last time.

I just can't see you retired! What are you going to do all day? Watch television?

You, of all people. I always assumed you'd die at your desk one day, probably in your late nineties, pen clutched in your bony fingers.

Oh, my God, you are going to be beyond bored. You'll have to get yourself a few serious hobbies, pronto!

This questioning and commenting annoyed Mary, largely because she had quickly come to realize that she was in fact not a hundred percent certain she had made the right choice in retiring. Her colleagues' questions were merely echoing her own unasked questions or, rather, questions she might have answered unsatisfactorily.

One of those unnecessarily large SUVs shot into Mary's lane just ahead of her.

"Where did you get your license? Sears?" she muttered, leaning on her horn. "Idiot."

She looked at the digital clock on the dashboard. If traffic didn't unexpectedly snarl, she would reach the state of Maine in about an hour. *The Way Life Should Be.*

That was still to be seen.

Chapter 3

Patty Porter was about five feet four inches; at least, that was what she had been at her last visit to her primary care physician. When had a person's GP become their PCP? Anyway, she might have shrunk since then as that appointment had been more than four years ago. Patty hated going to the doctor. They always found something wrong with you, something you would never have known was a problem otherwise, and once you knew you were sick, how could you avoid worrying? Worrying meant stress, which led to being unhappy. Patty liked to be happy, though increasingly being happy was a struggle.

She knew that she was a bit plump, but it suited her. It always had, though she had spent much of her life carefully watching her weight. She also knew that she was pretty, or that she had been. She had what people called "good bones," and her skin was still unlined. Her eyes were bright blue, the kind that got attention. Her hair was naturally almost black though for the past ten years or so gray had been creeping in, so she had taken to dyeing it. She couldn't afford visits to a hair salon, not these days, so she used a product she got at the supermarket. She didn't think her hair looked too bad, though every so often the flat blackness of it startled her.

Patty liked to dress up and loved wearing bright colors. Her nails were always painted hot pink or vivid purple or, at Christmas time, deep red. Sadly, she couldn't walk in heels anymore, but what could you do about that?

Anyway, heels weren't the best choice for driving, especially not all the way to Yorktide, Maine. The car was a twelve-year-old Honda Civic. It belonged to her brother-in-law Kevin, and he had kept it in excellent condition. Just before Patty had headed out on her adventure, Bridget, her older sister, had once again reminded Patty that she needed to take good care of the car she was borrowing from Teri and Kevin for the summer. As if Patty could forget. Patty was a good driver, in spite of the fact that she had never owned a car.

Maybe that made Patty unusual these days, like the fact that she had never owned a smartphone, either. Her pay-as-you-go phone was getting on three years old. Patty tried to be careful with her minutes. As her sisters, Bridget and Teri, never tired of reminding her, minutes cost money. The problem was that Patty tended to forget to buy more minutes before she had totally depleted the ones she currently had. She would have to be very careful not to mess up this summer. She was going to be living with strangers; she could hardly ask to borrow a stranger's phone.

Living with strangers. In all of her life Patty had never imagined that she would decide to set out on her own for an entire summer in a place she didn't know and with people she had never met! But in a way, she had had no choice.

Earlier that year, Patty had been compelled for financial reasons to leave her life in a lively suburb near Boston for the small town in New Hampshire where she knew barely anyone. It was true that she had been visiting her sisters for years, but visiting a place was very different from living in it. Sleeping night after night in Bridget and Ed's tiny spare bedroom, with her clothes stuffed into the tiny closet, and her collection of fairy figurines in cardboard boxes in the basement, well, it all made Patty feel like an outsider, an unwelcome guest, like every minute she had to apologize for being an inconvenience.

Life at her sister's house quickly became very depressing. Patty knew she had to get away or she would burst. She didn't like using the Internet, but figured that it was probably the best if not the only way she could find the sort of thing she was looking for. An escape. And she had, on a website that advertised vacation ideas for older women. One option in particular had jumped out at Patty, and she had sent off her application with high hopes. But almost immediately, she had heard from the Sutter-Black Agency that her application had been rejected. The agent said that the owner had already filled the house, but Patty had known in her gut that she had been turned down because her credit was so bad. Her references were from her sisters—she had no one else to ask—so it couldn't have been the references that got her rejected. *She's a very nice person, always pleasant. Nice to be around. Nice personality.*

Patty had felt seriously disappointed. She had so been hoping to be accepted by Mrs. Sandra Pennington as a summer renter. Mrs. Sandra Pennington. It sounded like the name of someone important, not like Patty Porter. Patricia Porter sounded better, more serious, but no one called her by her full name. She herself hadn't used it in years.

And then came the afternoon when everything had suddenly changed for the better. Only that morning there had been yet another tense conversation with Bridget about Patty's future.

"How do you propose to contribute to the expenses here?" Bridget had demanded. "We can't afford to pay for everything, you know. You have to stop spending what little money you have on clothes and silly things like that sparkly pocket mirror you came home with yesterday. You have to grow up. For God's sake, Patty, you're going to be seventy years old in December. Isn't it about time you stopped playing around with your life?"

Patty never liked to be reminded of her age. The approaching seventieth birthday had taken on the characteristics of a death knell. It seemed to signal the absolute end of every hope she had ever cherished.

Suddenly, the landline had rung, and Patty had dashed for it, grateful for the interruption.

It was the real estate agent in charge of Mrs. Pennington's summer rental in Yorktide. There had been a last-minute cancellation and, if Patty was still interested, there was a place for her at the house. Marcia Livingston had paused for a moment before telling Patty that Mrs. Pennington had suggested that Patty might pay per week, rather than in total up front, as the other women were doing. Patty had almost cried. Mrs. Pennington must be a very nice person, Patty thought, to offer such a manageable payment schedule.

Patty happily accepted the offer. She didn't mind being second choice. She was used to it.

As Patty set out from New Hampshire for her Maine adventure a week after that wonderful phone call, she had felt a surge of pure excitement. She had managed to escape! Oh, her sisters weren't evil or anything, not like Cinderella's sisters. They had agreed to write references for her, after all. It was just that they didn't understand someone like Patty. Both Bridget and Teri had married young to men they had been dating since high school. They lived modestly but well, saved more money than they spent, and were generally content with their lot.

But Patty had never fit in with her sisters' world. She had never considered marrying a man like her brothers-in-law, decent, hardworking, down-to-earth men with little pretensions to sophistication or worldliness. And why? Because her parents had groomed her for marriage to a rich professional man, a man who would want from Patty only what she could give—a pretty face, a good figure, and an amenable character. A man who would give her a fairy-tale ending.

Things hadn't gone as planned.

But things might still turn around. Right? The car was handling nicely. The traffic wasn't too bad. She had stopped for a coffee and a pastry about an hour earlier, and both had been delicious. All boded well for a happy summer in Yorktide.

Patty really, really hated to be unhappy.

Chapter 4

Amanda Irving made one last inspection of the medicine cabinet to be certain she had packed everything she had intended to pack. She had, but before she closed the cabinet she glanced at the plastic bottles on the top shelf. Those were Liam's. She hoped that he didn't forget to take his pills that evening. He could be forgetful. She could leave a note for him, reminding him to take the pills, but decided against it. After all, the pills weren't to help control or cure a life-threatening illness. They were supplements, probably ineffective. And Liam was an adult. He could take care of himself.

Next, Amanda went to the kitchen of her well-appointed apartment in Merrivale, a suburb of Boston. There, she retrieved her packed lunch from the fridge and filled her water bottle. She noted that there was only one banana in the fruit bowl on the counter. She wondered if Liam would eat any fruit or vegetables while she was gone. It was doubtful. He would probably survive on chips and dip.

Amanda was on her way to spend the summer in Yorktide, Maine. She would be living in a hybrid bed-and-breakfast situation with the owner of the house, Sandra Pennington, and two other women about whom Amanda had no idea. She had found the Sutter-Black Agency's advertisement on a website that catered to women seeking to vacation on their own or with other middle-aged women. The photograph of the house, number 12 Spruce Street, had hit a chord with Amanda—it looked like such a serene place—and she had immediately set about gathering references.

The references had been solid. *Hard-working. Dedicated. Down to earth.* Amanda had felt proud when the three colleagues she had asked to vouch for her had shared with her their remarks.

Her colleagues' assessments fit with Amanda's own perception of herself as firmly and reliably average. She was in fact above average in intelligence though not an especially creative thinker. She preferred to get on with her life without drawing unnecessary attention to herself. That seemed a mature way to go about things.

Amanda's physical appearance matched her personality quite nicely. She was of average height and build. When not at work, her wardrobe consisted of leggings, cargo pants, trainers, sporty tops and T-shirts, and sweatshirts. When at work, she wore blazers and slacks, flats, and tailored blouses. The only jewelry she wore consistently was a pair of small silver hoops. She kept her nails short and unpolished and rarely wore makeup. In short, she tended to blend into the background. She liked it that way.

Now back in the living room where her black travel bags were neatly lined up, Amanda reviewed her mental checklist. Phone charger and backup charger. Laptop. Books. Cash. New thick cotton socks. She had left instructions regarding the care of their one plant for Liam, along with, of course, Sandra Pennington's address in Yorktide. Not that she wanted him to visit. The whole point of her going off on her own was to, well, to be on her own so that she could think about her life without the interruptions of home.

So, Liam was an interruption?

Amanda hadn't told him the real reason behind her taking off in the abrupt way that she was. All she had said was that she realized she had never taken a vacation on her own and that the time had come.

They hadn't said an official good-bye. Liam had gone to bed early the night before. And that morning, he had left the apartment before Amanda was awake. He had been doing that a lot in the past few months, going to the gym before heading into his office.

Amanda supposed that a person could be excused for assuming that her leaving home for the summer indicated that she was on a quest for romance and adventure, but in truth, romance and adventure were the very last things she was hoping to find this summer. So, what *was* she hoping to find? Peace of mind? An answer to a tricky question? If so, what was the question?

Had she remembered to turn off the light in the bedroom? Amanda checked. Yes, she had. And she had put clean sheets on the bed that morning, too. Not that Liam would notice. As Amanda walked back to the living room she thought about her mother's reaction to Amanda's plans for the summer. At first, Mrs. Irving had said nothing. Her silence had annoyed Amanda.

"What?" she had demanded. "What aren't you saying?"

"Nothing," her mother had replied calmly. "If it's what you need to do, then it's not my place to give an opinion."

Interestingly, Mrs. Irving's response to her daughter's news hadn't been all that different from Liam's. Neither had said "I think going away is a good idea." Nor had they said it was a bad one. Both had, in effect, failed to express anything more than a studied neutrality. "Hey, if it's what you want to do," Liam had said, "then you should do it."

Well, all that mattered was that she, Amanda, had made the decision she considered best for herself. As for the other women who were renting rooms in Sandra Pennington's house, well, Amanda would never see them after summer had ended, so what they thought or suspected of her motives for being in Yorktide didn't matter in the least. She owed them nothing, not even the fact that she had left her boyfriend behind.

Amanda gathered her travel bags, took one last glance around the apartment, and left, shutting the door firmly behind her.

Chapter 5

Sandra had spent the morning moving from room to room, making a last-minute inspection and reinspection of the house. She had been so nervous before meeting her summer roommates for the first time, people she had chosen somewhat blindly to share her home. References and credit checks were all well and good, but they were limited measures of a person's character and personality. And there was nothing quite like being in the physical presence of a person; it was without a doubt the best way to get to know them.

Then, one by one, her summer roommates had arrived.

Mary Fraser, a New Yorker, had been the first to arrive. She exuded confidence and competency and was dressed smartly in taupe-colored linen pants with a relaxed matching blazer. Around her neck, she wore a stunning gold necklace composed of long, slim links. She had greeted Sandra with a handshake and a smile.

Next had been Amanda Irving. Sandra had been a bit surprised by the woman's almost military bearing. She held herself so very upright that for a moment Sandra wondered if she were wearing a brace. Amanda had said that she taught school. Sandra wondered if her students were afraid of her.

As for Patty Porter, the last to arrive, well, it had been a long time since Sandra had encountered a woman of Patty's age—which might be close to seventy—wearing clothes that seemed more suited to a much younger woman. Still, her face was a friendly one, under the heavily applied makeup.

Now the four of them were gathered in the kitchen, drinking lemonade Sandra had prepared and nibbling on shortbread cookies. Sandra thought her summer roommates had seemed comfortable enough as she had gone over the few house rules, all of which had been clearly stated in the contracts they had signed. Rules like: Each woman was responsible for doing her own laundry, including towels and bedding; she could use the machines in the basement or take her laundry to the laundry and dry-cleaning service in town. Each woman was responsible for the upkeep of her room; she was free to use Sandra's cleaning appliances and supplies. As for the bathrooms, Sandra would handle their maintenance with the proviso that each woman was expected to tidy up after herself on a daily basis.

"About the use of the kitchen," Sandra went on. "I know I left things vague in your contracts, but that's because it doesn't feel right to dictate when a person can make or have a meal, and I trust the four of us to be civil to one another. This is not a prison or a boarding school. We're here of our own accord, not under duress."

"I agree," Amanda said promptly.

Mary nodded. "I think we can rely on common courtesy to see us through. And I assume we'll each clean up after ourselves."

Patty nodded.

Sandra realized that she was a bit nervous about how the women would react to the idea she was about to propose. "I was thinking," she said, "that we might all have one meal a week together, maybe share the cooking and cleanup. Say,

Wednesday evenings, but really it could be any day of the week."

Amanda nodded briskly. "Sure. I'm okay with that."

Patty nodded and said: "Um, okay. That sounds nice."

"Fine by me," Mary said with a laugh, "but I'm a lousy cook. I'd be happy to pay for takeout if anyone is interested. Fish and chips. Pizza, Chinese."

Sandra smiled, relieved that the women were amenable to her idea. She hoped that the weekly communal meal might prove a good time for the women to discuss any "house business" there might be. But she wouldn't force the conversations or attempt to lead them in a certain direction. And if the gatherings petered out over the course of the summer, well then, so be it.

"If that's all," Mary said, "I'm going to finish unpacking. Great lemonade, Sandra. Thanks. Can I help you clear up?"

"No, no, it's fine. You all go and settle in."

One by one the women went off to their rooms. Sandra heard them chatting as they climbed the stairs. She busied herself with tidying up, and, as she did, she thought about what a strange experience it had been, reading references, something she had never before done. In effect, she had been acting like a judge, determining the fate—if only for one summer—of a person unknown to her.

Sandra put the leftover lemonade into the fridge. What, she wondered, would people say about her if she were asked to provide a reference? How was she perceived in Yorktide, the town in which she had lived for her entire life? Did some people see her as merely an old woman, beyond the point of having an influence on the town, beyond being of real value?

Did people, Sandra wondered, genuinely like her? She hoped that they did; she was pretty sure she had never made any real enemies in the course of her life. True, she had fallen out with a person here and there, or someone had fallen out with her, but not because of a malicious word or deed. Sometimes things just happened.

And what initial impression had she made on her summer roommates? Sandra almost didn't want to know.

"Clovis!" she called. A furry lump came trotting to join her, and, together, they went upstairs to Sandra's room.

Chapter 6

Mary was pleased with her room. It was the largest of the bedrooms after Sandra's master suite, with windows that faced both the street and the backyard. It had been decorated with an eye to both style and comfort but didn't have the feel of a curated hotel room. Personal touches betrayed her landlady's tastes, like the colorful prints of wildflowers in fields. And the vase of fresh flowers was a very welcome and colorful touch.

Mary was determined to enjoy herself this summer, the first summer of the rest of her life, the first summer in too many years with no pressing duties and looming deadlines. She should, she told herself, be luxuriating in a new sense of freedom, though luxuriating might be out of her skill set. It sounded a bit messy, and Mary wasn't comfortable with mess.

Anyway, freedom wasn't always what it was cut out to be. As Janis Joplin knew all too well, freedom could mean having nothing left to lose.

As Mary peeled off her clothes and changed into her nightgown, her thoughts turned to her summer roommates. They were quite a motley crew. Patty Porter looked like an old bit character out of central casting, the slightly blowsy unmarried neighbor who was too long in the tooth for the clothing and makeup she wore. Still, she seemed nice enough, if a bit dim. Or maybe she was just shy.

Amanda Irving was a puzzle. Mary had never quite trusted people who presented in so determinedly bland a manner. She thought they were probably hiding something pretty juicy. Well, who wasn't hiding something about themselves? At least Amanda seemed intelligent and not likely to make waves. That was a good thing.

Now, Sandra Pennington, Mary thought, was a happy surprise. There was a natural elegance about her. She was good-natured and seemed even-tempered. Ha! Sandra would probably turn out to be the seriously crazy one of the bunch! Mary knew that she really shouldn't make snap judgments. But it was hard not to, and, most often, she was correct in her assessment of people.

Mary slipped beneath the cotton sheet, plumped the pillows behind her back, and picked up from the bedside table the list she had compiled of "things to do" while in southern Maine this summer. Notably, there was no mention of canoe excursions and other dangerous outdoor adventures that enticed so many people on vacation. Long walks and easy hikes, however, had made the list, as had museums—the Portland Museum of Art; the Ogunquit Museum of American Art; maybe even the Farnsworth. Art galleries, too, held an attraction for Mary, as did antique markets where she just might discover an overlooked treasure. "Find good French fries" was also on the list. A woman had her priorities.

Mary put the list in the drawer of the bedside table, next to a small bottle of white pills. She had always been a good sleeper, but since the lawsuit she had found the act of falling asleep a bit of a chore. Her PCP had given her a prescription for a sleeping pill, but Mary had used it only once, after an uncommonly stressful day. She had, of course, castigated herself for "giving in," for not toughing out the night awake and miserable. In the morning, however, after a solid eight hours of restorative sleep, she had eased up on herself a bit. Still, she hadn't taken a pill since.

And something told her she probably wouldn't need a pill that night, either. She felt bone tired after the long drive and suspected she would be asleep moments after her head hit the pillow.

At least, she hoped that she would.

Chapter 7

Patty hadn't completely unpacked yet, but there was no rush, was there, and no one to tell her what to do and when and how to do it, not like at her sister's house. She knew she would have to find a job soon, but for the moment she still felt a bit of the sense of freedom she had felt when she set out that morning on her journey.

Her room at Sandra's house was the smallest of the bedrooms but still larger than the room back at Bridget's. The walls were painted a pale yellow that Patty found soothing, and the bedding and curtains were a flowery pattern in shades of yellow, mint green, and peach. It was a very feminine room, Patty thought, and it suited her. She, after all, was a very traditionally feminine person.

The mattress was nice, Patty thought, not too soft, like the old mattress in her room at Bridget's house. She wondered if she could ask Bridget and Ed for a new mattress. But mattresses were expensive, so probably not.

Patty thought again of how her family had tried to talk her out of going away. Bridget had said: "You've got to watch your money very carefully; there's no room in your budget for big vacations." Teri had commented that Patty's insistence on taking a summer vacation demonstrated yet again her childish habit of closing her eyes and hoping that the bad things—in other words, reality—would go away by the time she opened them again.

When Patty's application had been turned down, her family had rejoiced. Well, maybe they hadn't rejoiced, but they hadn't been able to hide their pleasure at the death of their irresponsible sister's ridiculous plans.

Well, Patty thought, here she was, in a lovely old house in Maine after all, in spite of what her sisters thought of her, and she was determined to enjoy herself. Because if no miracle occurred this summer—and what, Patty wondered, would that look like, other than a man sweeping her off her feet, and *that* wasn't going to happen!—she would be forced to move in permanently with Bridget. No one was pleased about the situation, especially not Patty. The idea of being totally dependent on and beholden to her family was mortifying.

Lately, Patty had been thinking a lot about the infamous Uncle Teddy, the black sheep of the family. The story was that he had been a drifter, a gambler, a con man, and a petty thief. Maybe he had been all of those things and maybe he had been none of them. What Patty did know for sure was that Uncle Teddy was notorious for never being able to keep a job for more than a few months and always scrounging off siblings, cousins, and especially his parents. Patty dreaded acquiring a similar reputation. Though she was a good person, she was in need. People who were *not* in need resented being faced with people who were in need. It rattled their sense of security and challenged their sense of superiority.

Patty went over to the window. It faced the path that led along the side of the house to the backyard. She couldn't see much. It was dark outside by now, and Sandra's neighbor to the right had recently turned out the porch light. Patty turned back to her room. She wasn't particularly happy about the idea of the Wednesday dinners. She had no intention of becoming too friendly with her roommates. But she wasn't under any legal obligation to attend the dinners. There wasn't anything in the contract she had signed. At least, she didn't think that there was. She hadn't really read the contract word for word.

If it turned out she *had* to attend the dinners, she supposed she could get by all right. Back in the old days she used to enjoy making dinner for her boyfriends, that is, when they could get away from their wives for a few hours. So many of them had had wives. If her specialties were a bit old-fashioned, they were expertly prepared and no one had complained, especially not about her chocolate triple-layer cake. Patty had always been sure to eat just a small slice of the cake so as not to get too fat. Her mother had told her time and again that important men didn't like fat women as wives.

Well, she had watched her figure and look where it had gotten her. Nowhere.

Suddenly, Patty realized that the sense of happiness she had felt driving away from Bridget's house that morning was gone. In its place squatted a sense of unease and anxiety. She crawled into the bed and took a long look at the bouquet of fresh flowers on top of the dresser. She couldn't remember the last time anyone had bought her a bouquet of flowers. Probably it had been a man, apologizing for some transgression. She turned off the light and scooted into a comfortable position.

It was all her parents had wanted for her, to secure a husband, and she had failed. But maybe that wasn't entirely her fault. Why hadn't her parents been able to believe that she might be happy on her own, or married to a simple, decent man, one unspectacular on the outside but sound on the inside?

In some ways, Patty didn't know at all who she was anymore, who she had ever been. The only thing she did know for sure was that she had been acting a part for most of her life.

She had smiled brightly when she felt like crying, gazed adoringly when she wanted to scream in anger, pretended to ignorance when her gut instinct knew just what was going on. The acting had become the reality, burying the increasingly tiny bits of the real Patty that remained. If any bits did remain.

Patty Porter willed herself not to cry. If she cried now, her face would be ugly and puffy the next morning. And she always tried to show the world her best face.

Chapter 8

Amanda put her hands on her hips and observed the room she had rented for the summer. It was a nice enough room, smaller than the one Mary Fraser was inhabiting, larger than Patty Porter's room. (Earlier, Sandra had led them on a tour of the house.) The mattress was pretty good, almost as firm as the mattress Amanda slept on at home. And the room was spotless, which was super important. There were just enough hangers for her clothes, and the drawers of the tall dresser were lined with fresh paper. A few prints and one watercolor painting hung on the walls, but Amanda didn't pay them much attention. In general, the visual arts left her cold. Except for blockbuster movies. And, of course, filmed versions of the novels by her favorite mystery writers. She had seen every Agatha Christie movie ever made so far and had watched every episode of the Sherlock Holmes television show starring Jeremy Brett at least six or seven times.

Amanda fetched her pajamas from the drawer in which she had stowed them earlier, and shed her travel clothes. She was pleased there was a washing machine and a dryer on the premises. In fact, Sandra's house had every convenience Amanda could hope for. So far, so good. And the idea of a shared weekly meal with her summer roommates didn't bother her. She had to eat dinner, she enjoyed cooking, and how bad could it be to spend half an hour or so with the other women once a week? Well, Sandra and Mary seemed intelligent enough, though Patty Porter might prove a bit of a challenge. She had a sort of out-of-date floozy air, which of course didn't necessarily mean that she was stupid, but . . .

Amanda felt relatively sure that this arrangement, here at Sandra Pennington's, would make no real demands on her. That was important because Amanda was in Maine with a purpose: to think about her relationship with Liam, and, in a larger sense, about her life. This summer was to be sort of a sabbatical, a retreat without the God part. Amanda had never been very good with the God part of things.

But she didn't need the God part of things. She never had. She was a highly capable person; she believed in her strength. In fact, on the journey north to Maine, in her Toyota Camry, Amanda had felt proud of herself for having escaped something or someone that would have kept her a prisoner if she hadn't been so strong and so clever. The moment she had shut her apartment door behind her, she had already achieved a sort of freedom.

A prisoner?

Maybe that was going too far.

Freedom from whom or from what?

Amanda felt herself frowning. Maybe she was being silly for doubting her relationship with Liam at this late date. Maybe it was ridiculous to consider throwing away a steady thing for . . . for what?

No, Amanda was not a shallow or a frivolous person in the least, just . . . just genuinely unhappy with her life. Just genuinely confused. She knew that she had acted in a cowardly manner by running off to Maine to ponder a situation that might have been addressed more honestly had she stayed home with Liam. But she hadn't wanted a confrontation. She hated confrontations. She was a master of avoidance. She knew that.

What would she have done if Liam had begged her not to go away that summer? What if, in desperation, he had asked her to marry him? Would she have said yes? She honestly didn't know. She hated being pressed for an answer. Well, thankfully, Liam had *not* proposed.

Liam Sexton wasn't the only source of Amanda's present state of discontent. She had been teaching social studies and history at the same private high school for fifteen years. She enjoyed her work as an educator, though in the past year she had sensed something change inside her, felt some source of focus and enthusiasm start to wither. She was afraid that she was irrevocably losing her mojo. If that were the case, her students would suffer. They—or, rather, their parents—were paying for a good education, and they deserved teachers who were dedicated and truly present.

But what was to be done? Briefly, Amanda had considered looking for another job. Maybe a change of environment would reinvigorate her. But a change of job might be risky at her age. She had decided that she would stay where she was and hope that she didn't get laid off before she could retire on her full teacher's pension.

Amanda frowned into the empty room. The feeling of freedom she had experienced earlier on the drive north was gone. She thought about calling Liam; he was a night owl and would most likely be awake. But hadn't she already sent him a text telling him that she had arrived safely? Yes, she had. And Liam had texted back. **Good. Have fun**. Smiley face emoji.

So, she didn't really have a reason for calling him now, at ten thirty. But did she really need a reason to call the person with whom she had been living for the past eight years? No, of course not. Amanda reached for her phone; she had plugged it in to recharge.

Liam didn't answer. After five rings his voice told her to

leave a message. Amanda didn't bother. Maybe calling without having something specific to say hadn't been a particularly good idea anyway.

She plugged the phone in again, got into the bed, and settled against the pillows. She hoped that she would be able to fall asleep quickly. She was suddenly aware that she was very tired, more tired than she had felt in a long time, but that was all right. There was no place she had to be first thing in the morning. She could sleep as late as she wanted to. There was no one to care what she did or did not do.

That felt like a big relief.

Chapter 9

Clovis was stretched out against Sandra's left leg in the bed, all five miles of him from front paws to tip of tail. It was fascinating how cats could change their size and shape from moment to moment. Of course, they didn't actually become five miles long or thirty-five pounds in the blink of an eye, but they could fool you into thinking they had.

For over a year after John's death, Sandra had kept their bedroom just as it had been. The goose-down comforter they had chosen together ten years earlier. The handmade wooden bench at the foot of the bed where John had sat every morning to put on his socks. The tall bureau of drawers that housed John's foldable clothing. The large oil painting on the wall across from the bed, the last thing Sandra and John had seen each night before turning off the lights.

But then, one day, she had suddenly begun to notice things about the room that bothered her. For one, the comforter was becoming threadbare in sections, and the colorful pattern had faded with time and many washings. It really should be replaced.

For another, it was silly that John's clothing was going unused. Someone might be able to get good use out of John's suits, shirts, the new summer shorts he had never had a chance to wear, even the shoes he had kept so carefully polished. One of the local churches might be able to help with that project. The bureau could stay; extra storage was always a good thing.

The wooden bench had become a nuisance. Not a day went by that Sandra didn't trip over one of its legs. Now, this was not the fault of the bench, of course, but a bedroom with fewer items that might cause a fall was probably a good idea. The church might help her pass that on, too.

And that painting. That absolutely awful painting across from the bed! It had been given to John by one of his very first clients, a man who had no money with which to pay his legal fees. John had taken the man's case for payment in kind, say, one of Mr. Blake's paintings, something small for the den maybe—something that might be partly hidden behind a door or a lamp. But this massive seascape had been delivered instead by a very grateful and very untalented Mr. Blake after John had won his case. So, the painting went up in a place of honor, and John had never had the heart to take it down. Sandra found that she did have the heart. The painting now resided in the attic, covered in a blanket.

The changes didn't take place all at once, but they did take place, and now the room felt a bit more like hers and not entirely like theirs, which was both a good and a necessary thing.

Sandra sighed and let her thoughts drift back over the day. So far so good, she concluded. Clovis hadn't shown any particular dislike of the women who would be sharing the house this summer, though with cats you could never be sure of anything. By morning Clovis might have decided—in whatever way that cats made their decisions—to take an intense dislike to one of Sandra's housemates, and all hell would break loose.

For the moment, though, peace reigned. The others had seemed receptive to the idea of a shared weekly meal, so that was a good sign of potential harmony. Although maybe one or more of the women had agreed just to be polite. Oh well, Sandra thought, time would tell.

At least the house wouldn't be empty all summer. Only that morning Kate had called to say that her wife Carrie's family was planning a lengthy visit from their home in southern California, a highly unusual thing as the Sommersons hated to travel. With limited time to spare away from their desks—Kate was a lawyer and Carrie a freelance marketing writer—the annual week-long visit to Maine would have to be canceled, though Kate did promise that she would dash up to her mother's place for a few days when she could. She could bunk down in the den where she and Carrie usually bunked down when they visited together, or she could couple up with her mother. Whatever Sandra wanted was fine.

Sandra wondered if having the women here—Mary, Amanda, and Patty—would help counter the disappointment of not being able to spend a week with Kate and Carrie. Again, only time would tell. Intimacy could not be forced, and it was something that developed at its own pace. And, some people weren't cut out for the sort of intimacy that this particular situation would require. Maybe she herself would prove to be one of those people.

Recently, Sandra had read that nearly one in three adults in the United States lived with a roommate or a parent, and that almost a quarter of people over forty sought out a roommate after being divorced or after the death of a spouse. What was going on, she wondered? What was fueling this trend, if it could be called that, toward a non-solitary domestic life? Loneliness alone? Or were economic factors just as important?

People in religious orders, those who lived in convents or monasteries, functioned well as a group in part due to a shared belief in a God they were serving through communal living. But what would hold together a group of people who didn't share a common religion? Would a legal contract be all that would protect the union from dissolution?

Sandra yawned. At the moment, the answer to that question wasn't important. She held herself very still and listened for sounds from the other rooms. The house was quiet. She realized she was hoping to hear evidence of the other women's presence, a snore or a sneeze, a cell phone alerting someone to a text, the trace of a lyric being sung under one's breath.

It felt odd to have these strangers sleeping in such close proximity to her bedroom. A bit unsettling. Not frightening, exactly, just . . . odd.

Sandra turned off the lamp on her bedside table, placed her hand on Clovis's warm and furry back, and was very soon asleep.

Chapter 10

The dining room nicely accommodated a table that could comfortably seat eight for dinner. Along one wall was a sideboard with a long and low mirror at the back. The walls were a tomato red. Long ago, Mary had read that the color red stimulated the appetite, but, personally, she had never needed any sort of prompt to aid in her desire for food.

Mary thought that Sandra seemed a bit nervous this evening, perhaps because this was the first Wednesday gathering of her summer guests. That was to be expected. Sandra appeared to be a sensitive though also a levelheaded woman, a combination Mary found congenial.

"I thought I'd provide the first meal as it was my idea to have dinner together once a week," Sandra explained when the women had taken seats at the table. "I kept it simple. There's pasta primavera, salad, and for dessert, well, I thought you might enjoy tasting genuine Maine whoopie pies."

"What," Mary asked, "is a whoopie pie? Of course, I'm thinking of a whoopie cushion, but . . ."

"It's a Maine classic," Sandra explained. "It's a sandwich really, marshmallow cream between two slices of chocolate cake. I didn't make these myself; our local bakery does a fine job. In autumn, the cake part is flavored with pumpkin spice. Frankly, I wish the pumpkin spice version was available all year round!"

To drink there was a choice of wine, water, or lemonade. And Sandra had even provided a chunk of Parmesan cheese to be grated over one's dish of pasta if desired. No shredded cheese in a can. Impressive, Mary thought.

"How are you settling in?" Sandra asked. "Are you happy with your rooms?"

The answer was a universal yes.

"I have a very important question, though. What's the best place to get French fries?" Mary asked. "I have a weakness."

"Thick cut or thin?" Sandra inquired.

"Definitely thin."

Sandra rattled off a list of restaurants, and Mary made note of them on her phone.

"Where's the closest movie theater?" Patty asked.

"Movies are so expensive these days," Amanda said. "I never bother to go to the theater. I wait until I can watch it online. Unless it's one of the big franchise science fiction or action hero flicks. They should be seen on a giant screen."

Sandra nodded. "I'm the same when it comes to waiting for movies to come online. But if you want to see a movie on a big screen, Patty, then you'll need to drive some distance, I'm afraid."

"I don't even know what's playing in the theaters," Mary admitted. "These days my interest in pop culture is limited to—well, to nothing, I suppose."

"Not all movies in theaters are pop culture movies," Sandra noted.

"Oh, I know. I guess I've just lost my taste for seeing movies outside of the comfort of my own home. That's probably too bad in a way. The experience of watching a movie in a room full of strangers also interested in what's happening on the screen does lend a certain excitement. Oh," Mary went on, "by the way, when I was in town this morning I ran into a woman who told me her name was Mildred Jackson. She came right up to me on the sidewalk and introduced herself, and then asked me if I was one of your summer houseguests. I didn't think I stood out that much as a stranger!"

Sandra shook her head. "That woman is a notorious busybody. I don't know why she needs to know everyone's business but she does."

"She probably has no life of her own," Mary noted. "Instead of taking the time to build a meaningful life she grasps at the lives of others, like a—like a leech or some other unpleasant creature."

"You're probably right. Anyway, I meant to tell you all that there are several wonderful farm stands within minutes of the house. You'll enjoy visiting them over the course of the summer."

"Thanks," Amanda said. "When are strawberries in season? I was thinking of making a strawberry galette for dessert one Wednesday night, if that's all right with everyone."

"What's a galette?" Patty asked.

"It's sort of a free-form pie, or even a pancake, over which you can spread a fruit compote or anything else you'd like, I guess."

Patty frowned. "So, it's like a pie without a top crust?"

"Sort of. Yeah."

"I like crust on the top and the bottom. I don't mean that as a criticism," Patty added hurriedly.

"Not taken that way," Amanda assured her.

"Strawberries should be here in early July," Sandra said. "Blueberries after that."

"I'm sure your galette will be wonderful," Mary said to Amanda, "but like Patty, I've always been partial to a top crust as well. You know, the more carbs the merrier."

Patty smiled. Mary hadn't intended the remark to make Patty feel better about having voiced her opinion, but it seemed to have had that result.

"So," Sandra said then, "shall we each tell a bit about ourselves?"

Sandra's tone was pleasant, almost incurious, as if, Mary thought, she knew the suggestion might not sit well with the others at the table and would be willing to let it drop.

Mary glanced at her fellow summer roommates. Amanda and Patty were looking down at their dinner plates as if some very important truth might be found among the strands of pasta.

"Amanda?" Sandra went on, mildly.

Amanda looked up and cleared her throat before speaking. "Well, I'm fifty-six, and I teach social studies and history at the high school level."

"Better woman than I'll ever be!" Mary laughed. "Trying to drill information into the typically dull minds and thick skulls of a room full of teenagers sounds like torture."

Amanda smiled briefly.

"Do you have a boyfriend?" Patty asked.

"Yes," Amanda said after a moment.

"What's his name?"

"Liam."

"What's he doing this summer while you're here in Yorktide?" Patty continued.

"He's on a very big project at work," Amanda replied quickly. "He's very focused on his career."

Nothing more seemed to be forthcoming from Amanda, not a word as to the nature of her boyfriend's career, not even his last name. Mary was certain that Amanda was hiding something. Maybe all was not well in paradise and Amanda was taking a much-needed break from domestic routine with her ambitious life partner. Well, if that was the case, good for her.

"What about your career?" Mary asked. "Are you happy being a teacher?"

"Yes," Amanda said. "I always knew I wanted to be an educator. Part of being an effective teacher is being able to perform, to get and keep the audience interested." Amanda smiled briefly. "I'm the least dramatic person you'll probably ever meet, but I know how to get information across in interesting ways."

"How long have you been teaching?" Patty asked.

"Since I got my first job out of graduate school. I was twenty-four, so that means I've been working steadily for about thirty-two years."

"Impressive," Sandra said.

"Thanks."

"What about you, Patty?" Sandra asked. "What would you like to tell us about yourself?"

Patty flushed through her heavy makeup. "There's not much to tell. I've been retired for a few years now, so . . ."

"What did you do?" Mary asked.

Patty shrugged. "Nothing very interesting. Mostly office work, you know."

"Administrative work?" Mary prodded.

Patty nodded. "Like that."

"Where do you live?" Amanda asked.

"In New Hampshire. You wouldn't know the town."

"Probably not," Amanda admitted. "I don't know New Hampshire at all. Are you in a romantic relationship? And if so, with a man or a woman or someone who doesn't identify as gender specific?"

"Me?" Patty laughed a bit wildly. "No. No. No one."

"So, that's it?" Mary asked.

"I guess so," Patty said quickly. "Yes. That's it. That's me. Not very interesting."

Mary wondered if Sandra knew much more about Patty

than the little bit Patty had just shared. Presumably there had been an application and references. But Patty's life, no matter how interesting or not, was none of Mary's business. Though she had noted that Patty hadn't mentioned her age. Maybe that meant something; maybe it meant nothing.

"Sandra," Mary said, turning to their landlord or host or whatever she was, "tell us about yourself. I mean, what sort of work did you do?"

"Except for a few not very interesting jobs I had before my marriage," Sandra replied, "I never really worked outside the home. Sure, I did volunteer work at the school, and for a time at the library. Primarily I was a homemaker, even though I came of age in the sixties—I'm seventy-four—when women were being encouraged to step up and be heard. I took care of the children while John went out to make the money to keep us well-housed, fed, and dressed. And, I served as my husband's hostess. Business dinners and cocktail parties were the 'done thing' in those days, and someone needed to be in charge of those potentially important social occasions. I must say, I was a very good hostess. John and I used to joke about my being the Jackie Kennedy of Yorktide."

"Without the glaringly awful political spotlight," Mary commented.

"Yes," Sandra said with a smile, "without that, thankfully. My daughter, though, had a problem with my decision to be a homemaker. Kate was always scolding me about how I had allowed myself to be demeaned by agreeing to take on the role of 'wifey' and 'hostess with the mostest.' She said I was a figure straight out of a nineteen-fifties sitcom, Mrs. Cleaver to Mr. Cleaver, or Samantha Stephens to Darrin, a powerful woman in subjugation to a bumbling man. Not that she thought her father was a bumbler. No, she always respected her father, except when she was accusing him of keeping me down."

"What did your husband say to that accusation?" Mary asked.

Sandra laughed. "He gave as good as he got. John and Kate loved to argue. Anyway, as Kate gained more maturity, she stopped judging my life and finally acknowledged the fact that I had made my own choices and that her father had always respected my intelligence. In fact," Sandra went on, "John and I always made all major decisions together, from where to travel, to what color to paint the front door, to how and when to discipline our son and daughter. He never made me feel that a decision about the house or the family was in any way less important than one involving his career."

"He sounds perfect," Amanda said.

Sandra smiled. "He was, nearly."

"How did your son feel about the domestic situation you and your husband had set up?" Mary asked.

Sandra laughed. "I don't think Jack noticed one way or the other, as long as food was on the table and his baseball uniform was clean for every game."

"Hmm. Does he do his own laundry now?" Amanda asked with a frown.

Sandra smiled. "Yes. His second wife has shaken him into shape. Gosh, I don't know what made me tell you all that, but there it is. Your turn, Mary. Tell us a bit about yourself."

"I'm sixty-three," Mary began promptly, "and recently re-tired from a long career in the law. My area of expertise is— was—tax law. Don't yawn; it's a lot more exciting than you think. I live in New York City, the West Village to be precise. I grew up in a neighborhood called Rivervale, in Queens. I like to walk, I have a great interest in art, especially painting, and, as mentioned, I am addicted to French fries. And I'm single, if it matters."

The meal ended soon after the four summer housemates had enjoyed the whoopie pies, which, to Mary's immense satisfaction, were absolutely delicious in an unpretentious sort of way, akin to the processed snack cakes of her childhood.

Sandra accepted the offer of help in cleaning up. As Mary ferried empty plates and glasses to the kitchen, she reflected on what they had—and had not—shared over dinner. Did everyone at the table, she wondered, have major secrets they felt it imperative to keep hidden? Well, so what if they did? She herself wasn't prepared to divulge certain painful aspects of her life to a group of strangers. Anyway, there was no law stating that the four women living under this roof had to become genuine friends this summer. Friendly strangers or even pleasant acquaintances would suffice.

Yes, Mary thought. That would more than suffice.

Chapter 11

"We'll see you tomorrow morning at ten o'clock. Good-bye."

"Good-bye," Patty said with one of her best smiles. "And thanks, again."

Patty walked out of the shop on Main Street into a beautiful early summer morning. She decided to stroll around a bit before going back to Sandra's.

The shop at which she had just been granted a job was called Crystal Breeze, and it was owned and managed by a woman named Michelle Chopin. Crystal Breeze, Michelle had informed Patty proudly, was the third high-end gift and arts-and-crafts shop she had owned in the course of her career.

Patty had been honest about having a relatively small amount of retail experience and was surprised she had gotten the job so easily, but maybe Michelle was desperate for an employee who could be trained before the real summer tourist rush began. Sort of like how Sandra had needed a third person to make up a full house when her first choice of tenant had backed out at the last minute.

Anyway, Patty was pretty sure she was the only one of Sandra's summer roommates who had to get a job to help pay for the privilege of staying at number 12 Spruce Street. Not that she was going to admit to Mary or to Amanda—Sandra, she assumed, knew—that she was working for any other reason than that she thought retail was enjoyable. And Patty was definitely going to continue to keep to herself any specifics about her past life as a sort of mid-level secretary. It didn't sound in the least bit interesting, and it hadn't been. Maybe she could have had a more interesting so-called career if she had bothered to keep up with advances in computer technology. But she hadn't, and, as a result, for the last fifteen years or so she had been basically unhireable for even low-level office work.

In fact, her last significant office job had ended in a particularly messy way. The office had been scheduled for a major technological upgrade, and, rather than attempt to train the existing staff, management had laid off many of the employees, all over the age of fifty. Immediately, several of the newly unemployed had found a lawyer with a specialty in workplace discrimination, and, before long, they had filed a lawsuit against the company.

Patty had chosen not to participate in the lawsuit. It seemed so risky; all legal matters frightened her. Her father had felt the same way about lawyers and courts and the police. The less you had to do with any of them, the better.

She had found another job that didn't require upgraded skills. The pay wasn't good, nor were the benefits, but it was a job she could perform.

In the end, her former colleagues won their case of age discrimination. Because Patty hadn't wanted any part of the lawsuit, she missed out on the compensation. Worse, her former colleagues had cut her off socially when she refused to join their cause. One had even gone so far as to accuse her of being sympathetic to "the oppressors." This accusation had upset Patty deeply. All she had tried to do was keep out of trouble. Didn't she have a right to make her own decisions?

One of her nephews had suggested that Patty take a computer class, update her skills so that she could be seen as a genuine contender in a competitive job market. No, Patty had decided, after very little consideration. She simply couldn't imagine herself as any kind of contender in the job market.

In recent years, Patty had found employment where she could. Retail was usually a decent option. Occasionally, a pleasant job turned up, in a shop like Crystal Breeze, with pretty things to look at all day while you waited around for customers to come in. But a lot of those shops, the high-end ones, didn't stick around for very long. Bridget said it was because they were vanity projects, a way for women with wealthy husbands to fill their time. If only those wealthy husbands had given their bored wives solid business advice along with a blank check, then maybe Patty would have found herself settled for a few years.

About those wealthy men. Patty wondered if any single wealthy men would come into Crystal Breeze, or if the men who did come in would be married men dragged in by their wives. In general, men didn't really go for shops like Crystal Breeze. At least, not the men Patty had known.

Still, it was lucky she had stumbled on that website where she had found the listing by the Sutter-Black Agency. The fact that Sandra Pennington's sort of guesthouse situation was located in Maine had seemed seriously significant. Patty had always wanted to visit Maine again, ever since that first and only time she had been there back when she was in her early thirties. The man she was seeing, separated from his wife, had taken her on a three-day vacation to Kennebunkport. It was the start of summer, before the heavy tourist season, so they had had the town largely to themselves. They had stayed at a big resort; their room had a king-sized bed, a real luxury. Burt had wined and dined her (she had eaten a lot of lobster) and bought her a cute silver bracelet with a dolphin charm. They had taken sunset strolls on the beach and lingered over breakfast on the little terrace off their room, looking out over docked boats, watching the antics of soaring seagulls, and talking about the future. Their future.

A week after they had returned to Massachusetts, Burt got back together with his wife. Patty never heard from him again. She remembered feeling really upset. The few days they had spent together in Maine had been so magical. At least, they had been magical for Patty. How could Burt just walk away? She remembered wondering if he was thinking of her as he lay next to his wife at night, regretting his return to his family. She had stared for hours at the one photograph she had managed to take of Burt during their idyll, a photograph Burt hadn't wanted her to take. Photographs were evidence.

After a few weeks, her pain started to ease. Eventually, the relationship and its ending became just a memory, like the vacation in Kennebunkport. Gone. Then the photograph went missing. It didn't matter.

Now, Patty Porter was in Maine again, taking a chance on . . . on something.

But anything was better than facing her sisters' worried looks every day this summer as they contemplated the grim future. Patty needing financial support. Patty being a burden. And while her brothers-in-law had never let on that they would rather be living alone with their wives, Patty was no fool and could sense the men's unhappiness about the situation. Ed and Kevin had worked hard all their lives in unglamorous and maybe even dangerous conditions, and they deserved a quiet retirement alone with their wives.

Well, Patty thought, as she headed back to the car after her short stroll, at least by going away that summer she was giving her family what they wanted for a little while.

No Patty.

The optimism Patty had felt after leaving Crystal Breeze in firm possession of a job had waned, to be replaced by the sort of nervous depression that could only be eased by keeping busy. So, Patty was cleaning and straightening her room. She was a neat person and liked an ordered environment.

When the lampshade and furniture surfaces had been dusted, she turned to the two fairy figurines she had brought to Maine with her. She had started collecting the figurines almost thirty years before and had amassed close to one hundred of them. The Fairy with Willow was one of the prettiest figurines, and, carefully, Patty wiped it with a damp cloth. The fairy's hair was yellow and curly and she was dressed in a pale green flowing garment. Her wings were streaked a slightly darker green. The willow tree itself arched over her head; the leaves actually looked like they were fluttering.

Next, she turned to The Fairy with Crystal Ball. This figurine was really impressive. Her hair was black and hung like a shiny curtain down to her waist. The ball was made of genuine rock crystal, and the fairy held it in both hands. Her flowing dress was pale blue.

It was strange how none of Patty's boyfriends, not one of them, had ever liked her collection. In fact, many of them had sort of made fun of her for collecting what they called knick-knacks. One had even gone so far as to say that the figurines were just junk. That had hurt Patty deeply. She couldn't remember now if Stan had ever apologized for his remark. Probably, he hadn't.

Patty sank onto the edge of the bed. It was also strange, now that she thought about it, that she had never actually lived with a man. Occasionally, a boyfriend had been able to spend the night away from his wife. She remembered feeling so excited on those occasions. She could hardly sleep, kept awake by fantasies of making coffee for two in the morning, caring for someone else's clothes, sharing the small intimacies reserved for people who lived together. She believed she would make a good wife. Her parents had told her as much. She would strive to be a partner. A loyal friend. She would always be sexy and not allow herself to morph into a slovenly, middle-aged frump. She would be ready to put her own needs and desires second to those of her husband.

Unlike her sisters. Sometimes, observing her sisters' behavior toward their husbands, Patty had found herself mentally criticizing them for being too harsh and not appreciative enough. That was before she had come to realize that the domestic dynamic was a complicated and largely private one. For all of her experience with men she was terribly naïve about relationships.

Patty got up from the bed and ran the dust cloth over the headboard, even though she had already done so. It made her very sad that she had never had her own household, her own husband and kids, her own dining room and patio, her own pantry and walk-in closet. There was a sort of prestige to that, old-fashioned as it might now seem. She had been raised to aspire to a "home of her own," to being the lady of the manor, to have the right to set her own rules for her own home. "There'll be no bad language in my house!" she could say if she wanted to. "In my house, you take your shoes off in the front hall."

Over time, as the possibility of her marrying began to fade away, Patty had begun to feel inferior to her sisters. Bridget and Teri owned their homes. They had husbands, children, and presumably, would one day have grandchildren. What did Patty have? Nothing.

And now, on the cusp of her seventieth birthday, to be reduced to—

"May I come in?"

Patty was startled by the knock.

"Yes, of course," she called out.

Sandra opened the door and came into the room. "Are you settling in okay?" she asked pleasantly.

"Yes, thanks." Patty waved the dust cloth in the direction of the dresser. "I just like to keep things clean."

"Those are pretty, the figurines. Are they fairies?"

Patty smiled. "Yes. I collect them. They're from this company in Germany. They issue new figurines a few times a year. Some are individual, and some are part of a set, like The Four Seasons and The Sun, Moon, and Stars, and Flowers and Trees. I've got close to one hundred fairies now."

"Wow. That's impressive. So, how do you display them?" Sandra asked.

Patty hesitated before answering Sandra's question. "I *used* to display them," she said, "but . . . All but these two pieces I brought with me are in boxes in my sister's basement. There's no room in her house for the entire collection."

"That's too bad," Sandra said, and Patty thought she sounded sincere. "These two are lovely, though."

"Thanks. The one on the left is called Fairy with Willow. It's one of my favorites. The one on the right is one of the first figurines I bought, about thirty years ago. Fairy with Crystal Ball. I dropped her once by accident but somehow, she didn't break."

Sandra smiled. "A miracle."

Patty had thought so, too. "To be honest," she said, "once or twice I've considered selling the collection, though I have no idea how to go about it."

"Why would you want to sell it?" Sandra asked.

"Well, it might be worth something . . ." What Patty couldn't say was that one day not too long from then she might have no choice but to sell her beloved collection.

"That's true," Sandra said, "but the money would get spent and the collection, which seems to bring you joy, is forever gone. If I were you, I'd think carefully about parting with something so meaningful."

Patty was touched by Sandra's words. She could tell they were sincere. "I will," she said. "Anyway, the figurines aren't as valuable as, I don't know, Lladró figurines."

"All that matters is that you like them," Sandra insisted. "Unless you're amassing the collection as an investment. Was it always your intention to build a collection in order to sell it?"

"Oh, no!" Patty cried. "The collecting part is fun, you know, waiting for a new figurine to be released, the holiday specials, even getting together for coffee with other collectors who live in your area. It's nice."

"It sounds nice. Well, I'll let you get on with your dusting. I'm sure there's some dusting I should be doing as well."

Sandra left then, and Patty sat on the edge of the bed. She was grateful for Sandra's genuine interest in her collection of fairy figurines. It had become such a bone of contention at Bridget's house; Bridget insisted that there was simply no room for the collection to be displayed. In truth, Bridget and Ed's home was pretty small, but if they were willing to, say, get rid of one of the oversized armchairs in the living room, for which there was no real need as far as Patty could see, and give over that space to Patty so that she could install a small, glass-fronted cabinet . . .

But it seemed she was to have nothing of her own, not a home, not a car, not her favorite pictures on the wall, not her usual brand of creamy peanut butter in the fridge—Bridget said she was not having two jars of peanut butter cluttering up the fridge and since Ed preferred chunky, chunky it would be—not even her treasured collection of fairy figurines on display.

Patty got up from the bed, walked over to the door of her room, and closed it. She didn't want the others to see her cry.

Chapter 12

Amanda had spoken to Liam only once since she had left home. They had exchanged several texts, but everybody exchanged texts with everybody all of the time. Texts meant nothing.

She didn't feel bothered by this paucity of communication. But she did wonder why she had lied to the others at dinner the other night, telling them that Liam was busy with a big project and very focused on his career. Truth be told, Liam was kind of lazy when it came to his career, preferring to just go with the flow rather than steer a course to a certain level of success. It hadn't bothered her at first but over time, being so close a witness to his behaviors and attitudes, Amanda had come to feel critical and even judgmental of her partner's approach to life. It didn't really affect *her* life in any major way—their finances were kept apart—but somehow, she had begun to feel tainted by Liam's habits.

Anyway, she had no intention of revealing the real reason she had come to Maine on her own this summer, that she had left behind her partner of eight years in order to think about the current state of the relationship and about the current state of her life. So far, she knew, she had accomplished little if any-thing in the way of her goal.

Amanda picked up her pace and swung her arms in a longer arc. Nothing beat the feeling of moving rapidly through space under her own steam. When she was behind the wheel of her car, Amanda tended to drive just below the speed limit. That just meant that she was not a rule-breaker.

Did it matter, she wondered now, striding along the shore, heels sinking into the sand with each step, that she didn't miss Liam? Out of sight, out of mind. For hours at a time she virtu-ally forgot that he existed. Could that possibly be normal? Or was it a sign of a defect in her character, and of a serious flaw in the relationship?

So many relationships had cluttered up her life. So many re-lationships had interfered with the smooth running of her days. Relationships were messy, but there was probably no way to get around that, except not to have them in the first place. Why wasn't that option presented to people early on as something valid and legitimate? Why was being consciously single still stigmatized?

Amanda had been engaged once, when she was twenty-five. The engagement ended when she discovered that Sam had cheated on her with a mutual friend. Once she had gotten past the first flush of anger and humiliation, Amanda had moved on without a backward glance. Sam and Sue had gone on to marry, and Amanda had heard through the grapevine that they were still together. She wasn't happy for Sam and Sue. Why should she be? Neither did she wish them harm. They just didn't matter.

Then, in her early thirties, there had been Jerry. They had met at a party given by one of Amanda's colleagues at the school where she was teaching at the time. He was some-body's cousin, tagging along for something to do. Amanda and Jerry had hit it off. They exchanged numbers, began to date, and quickly fell into a comfortable rhythm.

When they had been living together for four years, Jerry's company offered him a six-month gig in Los Angeles. It was something he had been hoping for; he had always been open about that.

Jerry had asked Amanda to go with him. That wasn't quite right. He had *expected* Amanda to quit her job to go with him. He would take care of them. He would be making big money, after all, and if all went well, the job might turn out to be permanent. Even if the job didn't last longer than six months, maybe they could stay on in the "city of angels." They were young. Why not?

Amanda could think of a million reasons why not; leading the list was the fact that she really didn't love Jerry. Poor Jerry was shocked when she told him that, while she was happy for him, she had no interest in moving to California, and, since long-distance relationships usually didn't work, there was no reason for them not to end their relationship right then. He could start his life in Los Angeles with a clean slate.

Jerry had pointed out—a bit angrily—that they had talked about getting married. He was right; they had talked, vaguely, about getting married. Why in God's name was Amanda suggesting they break up?

Things got more complicated as Jerry grew more upset. He said he would turn down the promotion, stay in Boston, because Amanda meant more to him than his career. The last thing Amanda wanted was anyone making such a ridiculous sacrifice for her. She feared that if she allowed him to make such a sacrifice she would owe him marriage, and she didn't want to marry Jerry.

In the end, because Jerry was so genuinely upset and Amanda not an entirely unfeeling person, she agreed to keep the relationship going for the initial six months of the gig. They would reconsider things when the six months were up. It was postponing the inevitable, Amanda knew that, but it was a way to stop the uncomfortable conversations. Jerry wasn't thrilled, but he accepted the compromise.

At the end of the six months, having earned the full-time gig, Jerry came back east to fetch Amanda and the rest of his belongings. That was how Amanda felt about it. That Jerry considered her one of his belongings.

Now, there could be no more stalling.

I don't love you. I won't uproot my life for you. That was the truth. But Amanda couldn't quite come out and say it. She was a coward. She had always hated confrontations.

Jerry pressed for answers she couldn't give—answers she didn't know how to give—and finally, angry, confused, and wounded, he had washed his hands of her. Amanda stayed with her parents for a few days in order to give Jerry time alone to clear his belongings out of their apartment. Amanda told her parents only that things hadn't worked out. They had asked no questions.

She hadn't felt even a sliver of regret, but neither had she felt triumphant. Freed, released? Yes. But not happy.

Now, at the age of fifty-six, Amanda could barely remember the relationship itself, only the messy end. Should she care about what had happened to Jerry in the years since she had last seen him? She had never been tempted to Google him, see if he was still with his company, if he had married, if he had had children. At moments, she couldn't even recall his last name. Connell or McConnell? No, it was Connelly.

A couple was coming toward Amanda, from a bit further up the beach. She knew they were a couple because they were holding hands. She felt herself frowning. She had never been able to hold hands with anyone and walk at the same time. Her gait was unique; it just didn't match with that of anyone else, and she was unwilling to alter it.

Both members of the couple smiled at her as they passed. Amanda nodded.

Her next relationship had taken place when she was in her early forties. She hadn't bothered to tell her parents about Marc. It might only have gotten their hopes up. Maybe their single daughter wouldn't be single forever. That sort of thing.

Marc, who was separated from his wife at the time of his relationship with Amanda, had kept his own apartment. Though he never talked about plans for a divorce, it hadn't bothered Amanda, nor had the possibility that Marc might still be sleeping with his not-quite-ex. After all, she had no intention of marrying Marc. And she had never promised to be faithful to him, though in fact she had been. Juggling multiple partners wasn't Amanda's cup of tea. It seemed an awful lot of work. She just couldn't be bothered.

The relationship, lasting about nine months, had just sort of petered out. In the end, Amanda and Marc had agreed to be friends. In fact, they never saw each other after that walk in the park on a spring evening. Not a bad way for things to end. Neat and clean.

Suddenly, Amanda came to a halt. Her breathing had become painful. She leaned forward and put her hands on her knees. After a moment or two, she straightened and turned to walk back to the parking lot.

She hadn't spent such a long time reviewing her romantic life—well, ever. Had it been worth it? Or had it been a waste of the afternoon?

Amanda, quickening her pace, realized that she couldn't really say.

Chapter 13

Bending over was not easy, nor was kneeling for any length of time, in spite of the kneepads Sandra wore whenever she was working in the front or the back garden. It was true that she could afford a gardening service for simple tasks like the one she was finishing now—she hired one for the large jobs, like raking up the leaves in late autumn (she refused to allow a noisy leaf blower)—but she was determined to keep up with daily gardening tasks for as long as she possibly could.

Sandra stood slowly and with a groan. She made her way up the stairs to the porch where she sank gratefully into one of the comfortable padded chairs and removed her gardening gloves and the kneepads. Later, she would return the gloves, kneepads, and gardening implements to their proper place in the shed.

Emma had been a keen gardener. For several years in a row she had won or placed in Yorktide's Summer Garden Spectacle. Sandra recalled her friend's ever so slightly smug smile as she stood on the makeshift podium to accept yet another engraved plaque. When it came to her gardening skills, Emma didn't do humility.

That morning, Sandra had called Emma's daughter for an

update, though she knew that any news was likely to be of the negative sort. Millie hadn't answered, so Sandra had left a message on her voice mail.

When Emma had first gone into the nursing home, Sandra had hoped that Emma would be able to make a friend there, someone with whom she could chat in her lucid moments. But Emma hadn't made a friend. Now, she seemed to be beyond the conscious need for other people. Surely, *some* people in care facilities must be able to connect with one another in meaningful ways, Sandra thought. Otherwise, loneliness would be rampant in those places. Maybe it was.

And maybe her idea of creating a genuinely humane and nurturing communal living situation, no matter the physical or mental health of the residents, was all just pie in the sky, like Marcia Livingston, the real estate agent, had declared that it was. After all, it couldn't be easy living day after day with others who weren't family or friends. You couldn't compel compliance to a system without a legal contract. Even prior, long-term friendships could be strained by living together. What about exit strategies? What if one of the members of the household decided to leave or suddenly died; how would that affect the others financially? How would they choose a replacement member for their community?

Certainly, advanced dementia couldn't be handled in the sort of community Sandra had been thinking about. That was another big question: How did you legislate regarding illnesses that were not pre-existing, and how could you declare some pre-existing illnesses as "not allowed" while accepting other illnesses? What if a longtime member of the group developed dementia, how could you possibly tell her to leave, even if the best thing for her was to go into a care facility?

There was just so much to consider! One thing was for sure, there was nothing romantic about constructing a successful living community. How many of the communities that had been hatched actually succeeded in the long term? If a community did succeed in surviving over the course of several decades, how far had it traveled from the original bright and shining idea that had given it birth?

Sandra sighed. Maybe the idea of communal living was too big for her to get her head around.

If only Emma was sitting by her side at that moment!

Emma Nelson was fifty-five years old when her husband, a brilliant math professor and the love of her life, died. Those first few years after Steven's passing were very difficult for Emma. He had handled the business of their marriage—the bills, investments, home repairs—and, faced with those challenges, Emma had suffered a crisis of confidence. But John had helped her get a handle on the paperwork, and it wasn't long before she began to feel competent enough to know what decisions needed immediate attention and what could be set aside for a time. All the while Sandra focused on being an emotional support to her friend and to Emma's daughter, as well.

The two women also had shared good times over the years. Twelve years back they had taken a trip to London, during which they had caught a glimpse of the queen, a definite highlight; booked a side trip to Stratford-upon-Avon where they saw a performance of *Romeo and Juliet*; and had taken another side trip to Oxford where they had toured the Bodleian Library. They had drunk more cups of tea in those ten days than they had in the previous five years, and had eaten scones with clotted cream until they groaned.

And then, five years ago, Emma had helped Sandra deal with the practical as well as the emotional aspects of John's passing. Emma had organized the catering for the gathering after the funeral. She had shared with Sandra lessons from her own experience on how to adjust to living alone in the house once shared with a spouse. Mostly, she had sat quietly and listened as Sandra talked of John, revisited memories of their years together, or simply cried.

A friendship of more than fifty years was now reduced to a memory in the mind of only one person, even though both friends were living. The situation created a particular sort of grief for Sandra. Emma had left her friend and had no idea that she had. At moments, Sandra's sadness felt unbearable. There was anger, too, anger at an unfair world in which there was no such thing as justice for the good and punishment for the bad. Instead, everything was so random. Not that it had ever been otherwise.

But you couldn't let that sort of thinking destroy you, and it easily could. Dwelling on the negative could prevent all possibility of joy in the present as well as the future.

Sandra, always alert to what was happing on Spruce Street, spotted a car just turning onto the road. A moment later she saw that it was Amanda's car. As her summer roommate drew closer to the house, Sandra waved. Sometimes all it took to raise one's spirits was the physical presence of another person.

Pretty simple, really.

Chapter 14

The day was warm, but Mary had dressed for the weather in lightweight cottons and a sun hat that made her look downright goofy. Still, it protected not only her head but also her forehead and the back of her neck. Sunblock covered every inch of visible skin. She wore her white cotton socks over her pant legs in an effort to prevent ticks from clamping on to her ankles. She had read somewhere that ticks had been found in Central Park. The countryside was encroaching upon the city. What next?

Sandra had told her about a system of trails about an hour north of Yorktide. At the visitor's center, Mary got herself a map and chose the trail marked "easiest." When she got to the trail's starting point she noted that it looked well-groomed, but that it was not without protruding roots and jagged rocks and all that other inconvenient stuff you found in Nature. She would have to step carefully. She had not come to Maine to break a limb.

Mary began her walk.

The scenery was beautiful. The path wound its way atop a rocky cliff, far below which was a narrow strip of beach. On the other side of the path was a wooded area, not so dense that sunlight was prevented from penetrating through the branches of trees, allowing for the rich growth of mosses and ferns. Occasional birdsong pierced the air, though Mary was unable to spot the singers in the dense greenery. Every once in a while, another hiker came along going in the opposite direction. Mary appreciated the fact that she wasn't entirely alone in this little patch of wilderness.

As Mary tramped along, she found herself thinking again about the somewhat startling fact that she had chosen to retire from a career that had meant so very much to her. Perhaps the decision had been ill considered. Maybe she should have just taken a sabbatical rather than give up her partnership. But there had been a few years of nonstop high-stress cases, the lawsuit against the firm, and then her old friend being suddenly killed. The combination of it all had crushed Mary badly enough that she had felt the need to take a giant step away from the world.

After the death of her parents, Mary had never lost anyone close to her. Until Judy, one of her dear childhood friends, had been killed in a hit-and-run while on her way to visit her brand-new grandchild in the hospital. Mary had tried hard to get over the grief in a timely manner. Life was random. Bad things happened to good people. No one was guaranteed a happy ending. Death was inevitable.

But none of the platitudes meant to convince a person that death was to be accepted calmly helped in the least. The grief would not budge, and, for a while, Mary wondered if she was having a good old-fashioned nervous breakdown. Eventually, time worked its magic, and Mary's grief, while not disappearing completely, became manageable. Mostly.

It was a fact that after the funeral, Mary and her other childhood friends had never talked with one another about their grieving experiences. Their mutual reticence was a result of the way they had been raised, children of lower-middle class Irish and German Catholics, many of whom were first generation Americans. Sentiment was for the weak. Life was tough, and there was nothing to do but to get on with it. Overt expressions of emotion were not allowed. Maybe if the women had felt free to talk honestly with one another, each would find the grief more bearable.

Maybe.

Like Mary, Maureen, Barbara, and Sheila still lived in New York, though they had moved out of the Queens neighborhood in which they had all been raised. Barbara was married to a man seven years her junior. Sheila was married to a man her own age and had five children. Maureen was married to a man fifteen years older, a priest in a former life. Judy, of course, had been married to Joe. Mary was the only one of the old gang who hadn't been able to make a marriage work. It was no surprise to anyone when her youthful marriage failed. There had been nothing wrong with Fred. It was Mary who was fundamentally unsuited to marriage. For a few years after the divorce, she and Fred had tried to keep in touch with each other, but that, too, hadn't lasted. Mary hadn't heard from Fred for about twenty-five years.

Later, there had been a few other relationships with men, nothing long-lasting, nothing important. In fact, Mary hadn't had sex in more than ten years and didn't miss it one little bit. If that made her odd in the eyes of some people, so be it. She considered herself lucky to be free of the demon called lust. It was nothing but trouble.

A woman rounded a bend in the path ahead of Mary, coming the opposite way. A large, fluffy white dog paced at her side, tongue lolling.

"Beautiful dog," Mary said with a smile as the women passed each other.

The woman beamed. "Thanks! I think so, too!"

Mary snuck a look over her shoulder at the retreating pair. Since retiring, she had given the thought of getting a dog some consideration. Animals were wonderful companions. Take Sandra's cat, Clovis. Clovis was a great comfort to Sandra, that was easy to see. But the same reason that had always stopped Mary from going ahead with the notion of adopting a dog continued to stop her now. Animals didn't live as long as human beings. It was likely that any dog Mary took in would die before she would; he might even need to be sent to Heaven, and Mary just knew she didn't have it in her to make that monumentally difficult decision. She was a coward in no other way but in this way. The death of a human loved one was disastrous enough. The death of an animal companion . . .

Mary stepped off the path and into a small clearing that allowed a view of the water and a heavily wooded island in the distance. The view was beautifully calming. Overhead, a large bird seemed to drift along the coastline. A bird of prey? A seabird? Mary didn't know. She knew next to nothing about wildlife. Whatever sort of bird it was, it was magnificent.

After a moment, she continued along the path, and before long she had come full circle, back to the parking lot. It had been about a forty-minute trek, and she had enjoyed it very much. She would be sure to thank Sandra for the suggestion.

As Mary climbed into her car, her phone pinged, announcing a text. It was from a former colleague.

Surviving life in Maine? Hope you haven't been attacked by a moose or a bear.

Or a tick, Mary thought grimly, glancing down at her ankles, hidden beneath socks and pants. A tick check would be the first order of business when she got back to Sandra's house.

Nature was okay. If only it weren't rife with stupid, blood-sucking bugs.

Chapter 15

For dinner Patty had made a roast beef, green beans, and baked potatoes with sour cream and butter and chopped chives. The meat had been expensive, too expensive for her budget, really, but she had wanted to impress her housemates in some way, and, luckily, the others all ate red meat.

"I know it's probably not a typical summer meal," she said, hearing the note of apology in her voice. "But, well, it is pretty classic. I hope you like it."

"Classic is good by me," Mary said. "Although frankly, I'll eat pretty much anything at any time. Living on my own makes that easy."

"Do you know, I've never lived on my own," Sandra said. "Well, until my husband's passing, that is. I went from my parents' home to a home with John and then the children. Sometimes I've wondered if my situation isn't a bit unusual for my age group. I mean, I came of age in the nineteen sixties and seventies. It wouldn't have been at all odd for a woman of my generation to get an apartment on her own or with a friend. And yet, somehow, I seem to have missed out on the zeitgeist of those years, marrying not long after I graduated from college, having my children, forgoing a career of my own. Not that I've ever regretted the choices I made," Sandra added hastily. "Honestly, even in my most introspective moments I've felt nothing but gratitude for what my life has been."

Mary grimaced. "I think I'm constitutionally unfit for living with another person, in terms of a romantic partner, at least, and probably also a roommate. Obviously, this situation we have here is an exception. It's only for the summer, and we don't have to be making joint decisions about the running of the household. I guess I'm a loner by nature. And I'm difficult, I know that."

"Everyone is difficult," Sandra pointed out.

"I've spent a fair amount of my post-college years living with someone," Amanda said, "a man I mean, a partner. I don't remember feeling unhappy during the times I lived on my own, though. It was fine. Well, more than fine, it was good."

Patty, though not usually open about her life, felt compelled to contribute something to the conversation. Especially since the other women were all looking at her in an expectant sort of way.

"Once I left my parents' house after high school," she began, "I was on my own. Well, I did have a roommate, but that was for, like, a few months. I didn't like sharing an apartment with someone I didn't really know. Living alone is okay, though. Mostly."

Not that she was living alone at the moment, and she probably would never be able to live on her own again. She had failed at that, too. Patty didn't want to think about that. In fact, she wished someone would change the topic.

"I've been seeing a lot written about what's sometimes called collaborative living," Sandra said then. "It's a form of cohousing that originated in Denmark. Often, it's based on themes like sustainability and environmentalism."

Mary was once again on her phone. Patty thought that she, too, might use her phone to look things up if she had a smartphone. But she didn't.

"Did you know there's something called the Cohousing Association of America?" Mary said, glancing up at the others. "Seems it's a national nonprofit that supports newly forming and existing communities. Huh. That's a new one on me."

"Me too," Amanda said.

"This says there are something like one hundred and seventy cohousing communities in the country. I had no idea there were so many. Residents own their own homes and share community space, which might include a kitchen, dining and lounging area, a workshop, laundry facilities. And, there are established rules of caring communication." Mary smiled. "I'm guessing calling your neighbor a selfish bastard for not mowing his lawn isn't considered caring communication."

"People in communities like that probably don't mow their lawns," Amanda said. "I think mowing has fallen out of favor with a lot of environmentally minded people."

Mary nodded. "Good point."

"I think groups like that try to function as a sociocracy," Sandra noted. "If I'm remembering correctly from what I've read. A sociocracy organizes people into various circles to make decisions consensually. It's a form of self-governance."

"Sociocracy can go wrong just as any form of government can go wrong," Amanda pointed out. "Even democracy isn't doing too well these days, sad to say. Sometimes I wonder if there will ever be a form of government that works well for every member of the society over a significant length of time."

"Some of these communities fail before they're even fully functional," Mary told them. "There's an article here about one community that recently foundered on all sorts of decision-making and financial issues. The bank foreclosed on them, and a bunch of the members lost their life savings. A few of the people interviewed for the article admitted to being naïve about various matters, and yet they still hoped to start again. Crazy, if you ask me."

Patty poked at her baked potato. She didn't think she could live in a community like the sort the others were talking about. All she had ever wanted was her own home to share with a husband. But that hadn't happened, and here she was spending the summer with three almost total strangers. Things were working out okay so far, she guessed, but she certainly wouldn't want to live like this for the rest of her life. In a—a commune.

Patty Porter living in a commune!

"Patty, this meal is outstanding, really."

Patty blushed, thankful not only for Sandra's compliment but also for its timing. It had served to interrupt Patty's darkening thoughts. "Thank you," she said. "My mother taught me to cook, she taught all three of us, that is. She wanted her daughters to have the skills we'd need as—"

"As wives and mothers." Mary nodded. "I never did pick up any of those skills, try as my mother did—and she did—to train me."

"Were you ever married, Patty?" Amanda asked.

Patty willed her cheeks not to flush again, but they disobeyed. "No," she said, attempting a smile. "I guess I just never met Mr. Right."

As the others began to chat about something or other, Patty's thoughts insisted on returning to the topic of living situations. Living with one of her sisters might be a better choice for her than living with a group of strangers, she supposed, but there would still be the money issue to deal with. Without money, you weren't able to do much of anything. It wasn't right but that's the way it was and always had been, she supposed.

Money. Minutes meant money. Patty realized that she

needed to buy more minutes on her phone. She hoped she had enough money in her account to do so. She hadn't really looked at her finances in a while, and there was the piece of meat she had splurged on for tonight's dinner.

"Whew, I'm stuffed. Stuffed and happy," Mary said with a smile.

Patty smiled in return. At least the others had enjoyed the meal she had prepared. At least, Patty thought, she was good at something.

Chapter 16

Someone had once commented that watching Amanda Irving walk was like watching someone determinedly trying to leave someone or something behind.

Amanda still didn't know quite what that person, a neighbor she had hardly known, meant. Or maybe she did know. It didn't matter.

As she strode along the sand that morning, arms swinging, she remembered what she had told the others at dinner the night before, that while she had spent a good deal of her adult life cohabitating with a romantic partner, the years she had spent living on her own had been good ones as well. She had never felt chronically unhappy or lonely, or even overwhelmed by the responsibilities of living on one's own. But maybe she was being nostalgic about those days of being single. It was possible.

Anyway, she didn't really want to live on her own again. Well, maybe she did. Just a little. The idea felt frightening, but also, if she was honest, a tiny bit enticing. A tiny bit.

Suddenly, Amanda felt annoyed with herself. Her thoughts about her relationship, as well as about her life as an individual, hadn't progressed one jot since she had landed in Yorktide. She had reviewed her past but come to no conclusions and had experienced no epiphanies.

Amanda kicked at the sand as she took the next step. Maybe she should just go home and tell Liam—tell him what? That she had made a mistake by leaving him that summer? Or that she had made a mistake by being with him in the first place?

No, Amanda thought. She would not go running back home. She would start at this very moment, alone on the beach, to give some serious attention to the issues that were troubling her.

First, her eight-year relationship with Liam Sexton. The truth was that much of their mutual affection and absolutely all of their romantic life had fallen away. In the beginning and for some time after, they had enjoyed so many small pleasures together. Sending out for pizza every Friday night. Roasting a chicken every Saturday. Watching television shows together. Playing card games over coffee. Somewhere along the line, all of those comfortable habits and more had dropped away. Some days, they barely looked at each other. There was no open animosity. There was just—nothing.

So, if there was nothing, how could Amanda expect Liam to be there for her if she got really sick? Would she resent having to care for him if *he* were to develop heart disease or cancer or some other chronic health problem? Could they possibly continue to grow old together in this way, living parallel lives, possibly full of resentment, possibly full of anger?

Amanda sighed out loud. It seemed more than possible. How many couples already in middle age decided without deciding that they would stay together? After all, they had put so much into the relationship, spent so many years together; it would be crazy to toss it all away. For what? To start over again with someone else? Too much work. Too much uncertainty.

Still, a mere lack of pain or misery was not happiness. On the other hand, Amanda thought, happiness wasn't something guaranteed to anyone, and every person's definition of happiness was so personal, so idiosyncratic; how could one version of happiness ever be measured against another version? Maybe it was better not to think in terms of happiness at all. Contentment might be the healthier goal. A general sense of satisfaction with the way things were in one's life. Maybe it was best to cultivate a life of reasonable expectation rather than a life of unlikely or impossible fantasies.

Amanda's attention was momentarily caught by the sight of two women about her age walking toward her a few yards up the beach. They were talking and laughing as they strode along in their colorful athletic wear. As the women came abreast of Amanda, she suddenly realized that not one of her friends back home had ever expressed an opinion about her relationship with Liam. Ever.

Why not? If her friends felt that she was in a good place in her life, wouldn't they say so? But maybe they were silent because they didn't think that Amanda was in a good place, but rather thought that her relationship with Liam was destructive in some way. If you can't say anything nice, don't say anything at all.

It was true that Amanda didn't invite shared confidences in any of her friendships, all of which, if she was being brutally honest, were not really friendships at all. On some level, she just didn't care about the lives of other individuals. She had always been uncomfortable with intimacy, confused by it. She had never been tested when young for autism, but she had often wondered if she was "on the spectrum," unable to fully understand or connect with people who were neurotypical. But in every other way she was a highly functioning person, so what did it matter if she was diagnosed as autistic or not? More important, who in her life would care?

Sandra Pennington might.

The thought startled Amanda. Their host? Landlady? What was she exactly? Whatever her role, Amanda found Sandra interesting. She seemed a matriarchal figure, someone you could go to for advice and not be disappointed. She exuded a sort of serenity, too, somehow not at odds with her practical, nurturing persona.

Of course, maybe Sandra was playing a role; maybe she had long ago donned a mask to fool the world and protect herself from its scrutiny. Amanda knew that she herself presented as content, self-confident, and calm, but what people didn't know was that the public Amanda was largely a role she had adopted many years before. The real Amanda was . . .

Amanda literally came to a halt and stood absolutely unmoving on the sand. She had no idea who the real Amanda Irving was. Maybe the public Amanda was and always had been synonymous with the private Amanda . . . or maybe not. How was she supposed to know after all these years?

She looked at her watch and saw that she had been walking swiftly and determinedly for an hour and a half. That meant it would take her approximately ninety minutes to walk back to the parking lot where she had left her car. A total of one hundred and eighty minutes. Three hours.

Suddenly, it seemed too much. Amanda wasn't sure she could make it back on her own. She was so tired. But she had no choice, did she? Sure, she could sink to the sand and rest for a while, but the journey home would still await.

With a deep and determined breath, Amanda turned and started the trek back.

Chapter 17

Sandra Pennington found it encouraging that each of her summer roommates had been interested in discussing the idea of communal living. Patty had been the least engaged in the conversation, but even she had contributed a bit of personal information, about how she had briefly shared an apartment with another woman many years before.

As if summoned by Sandra's thoughts, Patty walked into the kitchen and came to an abrupt halt. Her eyes were red, and she was twitching her nose as if it itched.

"Are you feeling unwell?" Sandra asked.

Patty sneezed into a tissue that had been balled up in her right hand.

"No," she said. "I think I might be allergic to something in the air, pollen or dust maybe." Patty sneezed again. "Excuse me! It's odd. I've never had allergies before. Oh well."

"Supposedly you can develop allergies at any point in your life," Sandra noted. "My son developed an allergy to certain fruits and vegetables in their raw state when he was about fifteen."

"That's not very comforting, is it?" Patty said with a frown. "I mean, the idea that you can get sick at any time."

"Well, that's true of life in general, isn't it? Anything can happen, good or bad, at any time."

The look of unhappiness that had suddenly come over Patty's face told Sandra that she had said the wrong thing.

"I'm sure you'll be fine," she added, hurriedly. "I'm sure it's nothing."

Without replying, Patty walked out of the kitchen. Sandra wondered why she had come into the room in the first place. Maybe her assumed allergies were affecting her brain. A congested head could be disorienting.

It was only several minutes later that it occurred to Sandra that maybe Patty had developed an allergy to cats, specifically, to Clovis. A person in a formal, legal commitment to a communal living situation might be forced to abandon her cat if a housemate developed an allergy. Well, that would never happen to Sandra. She would *never* sign an agreement that compelled her to abandon her cat under any circumstances. She had adopted Clovis shortly after John's death, and Clovis had quickly become her constant and beloved companion. Even her friend.

But it was yet another thing to consider about communal living. One had to be very sure of one's priorities, of what one could or could not, would or would not accept. Of course, underneath all of the questions about practical matters was the assumption that a person was making a *choice* to live with another person or group of people, and not being somehow forced to accept a situation on someone else's terms.

Suddenly, Sandra realized that she was hungry and decided to make herself a light lunch. As she put out two slices of whole-wheat bread and fetched the jar of peanut butter and the jar of strawberry preserves, she found herself reminiscing about the years in which her father's older sister had lived with Sandra's family. Kitty had cooked and cleaned along with Sandra's mother, sharing all household duties with vigor. She had enjoyed weeding the back garden and often took care of hanging the wet laundry on the line that stretched from the back wall of the house to the oak tree several yards away. When Sandra's brother Jacob was born, Kitty had proved to be an expert diaper changer and baby bather.

Sandra had never asked why Aunt Kitty had come to live with them. She believed that Kitty had felt truly welcomed in her brother's home, but children didn't see everything that went on in their homes, even a bright, sensitive child such as Sandra had been.

Kitty died after only four years with the family. Sandra was told that her heart had given out. Maybe ill health was what had brought Kitty to live with the family in the first place. Sandra, who had been not quite ten at the time, remembered feeling very sad. Every member of the family had felt Kitty's loss; Sandra was sure of it. Her mother had kept a photograph of Kitty as a young woman in an elaborate silver-plated frame on the mantel in the living room. Her father had spoken of her often, sometimes as if she were still alive.

There had been several other local kids whose relatives other than parents and siblings had lived with them. It wasn't unusual in those days to enter a friend's house and find a grandparent or an aunt or a cousin there as well, passing through or a permanent resident. Sandra would never forget her friend Matt's Uncle Tommy. Uncle Tommy was not much older than Sandra when he came to stay with his family in Yorktide, maybe about nineteen or twenty. It was said that there was something "wrong" with him. Something had happened to him while he was serving in the army that made it impossible for him to live on his own. He was skittish, withdrawn, solitary. Sandra remembered his eyes. They were so blue, so haunted. His eyes had frightened her, but she had also found them beautiful. After Uncle Tommy had been living with his sister's family for just over two years, he broke down completely. There was a public incident, quickly hushed. Uncle Tommy went away after that, to some sort of mental care facility, Sandra presumed. The details were kept from the neighbors. By the time Sandra was old enough to understand the facts of Uncle Tommy's case, she had lost most interest in knowing them.

Now, all these years later, Sandra felt ashamed. By ceasing to care about Tommy's fate, she had in some way abandoned that troubled young man. Was he alive or dead? To whom did it matter now? His sister was gone. Matt was old, Sandra's age, with kids and grandkids. Did Matt ever think about the damaged young man who had shared a home with him so long ago?

Not all people in need of a room in which to lay their head at night were lucky enough to have a welcoming family. When Sandra was a young girl in Yorktide, there had been a boardinghouse run by a woman named Mrs. Barber. A sign on the building announced that only respectable men and women were allowed a residence. Sandra had never understood how Mrs. Barber determined if a prospective resident was respectable. It was doubtful she had actually paid for formal background checks. Maybe she had made her decisions based on gut instinct, much as Sandra had done with Patty.

Sandra had often wondered if Mrs. Barber ever developed genuine friendships with her boarders. Perhaps she had made it a policy to keep business and pleasure distinctly apart. Sandra did vaguely remember one ancient man—what was his name?—who seemed to have been a resident at Mrs. Barber's establishment forever. He was a dapper man, quiet, polite. Perhaps Mrs. Barber had allowed him to take tea with her in her private parlor. Perhaps there had been a discreet romance. Well, that bit of history was lost to time. Both Mrs. Barber and the dapper man were long gone from this world.

Had Mrs. Barber ever kicked anyone out of her home? Had anyone ever complained about the meal they were given each evening, a meal Mrs. Barber herself cooked and served? Not that there would have been much point in complaining, Sandra realized. Residents probably didn't have the money to pay for meals in restaurants. They would be grateful for what they were given. Beggars, it was said, could not afford to be choosers. Mrs. Barber's boarders had likely never felt truly secure. Residents in the old-style boardinghouses might not have had legal rights like those of long-term renters. They might never have signed a written agreement with their landlady. Perhaps a handshake had sufficed, not a very reliable method to seal a deal.

"Hey."

It was Mary, come into the kitchen. Sandra was grateful for the company and the diversion it would bring.

"I ran into Patty earlier," Mary went on. "She was muttering about allergies sneaking up on a person. She seemed pretty distressed. I had no idea what to say to her so I said nothing. Any idea what's going on?"

Sandra smiled. "I'm afraid I put the idea of sudden allergies into her head. I never thought it would make her so upset. Look," she said, "I was just about to have some lunch. Will you join me?"

"Yes, thanks," Mary said. "I stashed half of a chicken salad sandwich in the fridge. As long as I don't develop a sudden allergy to mayonnaise I'll be a happy camper."

"You and me both! I'll never go over to the dark side."

Mary grimaced. "Miracle Whip? Don't get me started."

Chapter 18

Mary was at the beach. She was wearing the same large, floppy sun hat that she had worn while hiking, a hat as silly looking as it was successful in keeping the sun off her neck, face, and head. Again, she had heaped sunblock onto any bit of skin that might become exposed in spite of her protective gear. Today, she was wearing a designer caftan she had bought at Hirshleifers. Princess Margaret had rocked caftans, many in prints as wild as the one Mary was currently wearing. On her feet, Mary wore a pair of expensive woven leather sandals. She refused to be seen in a pair of flip-flops. Ever. No one needed to expose that much foot.

As she strode along, Mary found herself thinking about the odd living situation in which she had chosen to spend her summer. Sharing a house with three total strangers? What had she been thinking? True, things were going pretty well, but that was partly because she was being cautious. Thus far, though she had spoken fairly freely, she hadn't revealed anything of real importance about herself. When you were an adult there was a constant process of decision-making about what and how much to share with others, whether friends, colleagues, or strangers who happened for a time to be living under the same roof. She once had been silly as all young people were, but over time she had learned to share prudently, even warily.

Mary's eye was suddenly caught by a young woman in a neon-yellow string bikini. The woman was not in good physical shape. Honestly, Mary thought, she looked downright unhealthy. Something about this young woman screamed, "I haven't eaten a vegetable in my entire life, and I live on soda."

The string bikini. The concept, the reality, both were so . . . unseemly. So . . . unnecessary. Of course, the woman was perfectly within her rights to wear whatever she wanted to wear. Even if it did absolutely nothing for her.

Mary cringed. Since when had she become such a prude and so overly critical? No, she decided quickly, she wasn't a prude or overly critical. She was just someone with a highly developed aesthetic sense. Even if the woman had a beautifully proportioned and toned figure, Mary would still find the sight of her in one of those floss things not at all pleasing to the eye.

Ugh, Mary thought. After all the years of education she had acquired, *this* was the sort of topic that absorbed her thoughts?

No doubt her parents would be amused. *See? We told you all that education was a waste.*

Neither of Mary's parents had gone to college; there was some doubt as to whether her mother had ever graduated from high school. It had been pretty clear to Mary from the start that her parents hadn't really known what to do with their brilliant daughter and, subsequently, that they were unable to guide or encourage her. Mary had succeeded largely on her own, with the occasional help of professors and mentors along the way. She had continued to puzzle her parents as she went from strength to strength, leaving them further and further behind.

To this day, her parents long gone, Mary felt resentment re-garding her upbringing. She knew that harboring resentment was a waste of her precious time and resources, but there it was. Sometimes she wondered if her brother, Bill, now fifty-two, still allowed his parents to darken his life. Bill had gotten along better with their parents than Mary had, but not much better. He had married relatively young and had settled in Chicago, where he had gone to college. His son, Bill Junior, was . . . Mary couldn't remember how old Bill Junior might be. Occasionally, Mary felt bad that she had never made much of an effort to get to know her brother and his family.

To be honest, the few times that Mary had met her sister-in-law, Stacy, she had found her to be a dull woman. And it was clear that Stacy was suspicious of Mary, maybe even intimi-dated by her. Had Mary done anything to make Stacy feel in-ferior? And if she had done so, why? What had she been hoping to achieve?

Her phone, in a pocket of her beach bag, alerted her to the arrival of a text. Habit, mostly, made Mary dig out the phone, though it was very likely the message was one of no impor-tance. She was no longer in demand. Her time was her own.

Mary frowned. This text was from a former colleague she had faced off against on more than one case, an unpleasant woman by all accounts. She had no taste in clothes, either.

Rumor has it you went north. Why? Can't get far enough away from the scene of the crime? Oops. Faux pas. Seriously, don't get trampled by a moose.

Such a stupid, antagonistic message. *Scene of the crime* clearly referenced the lawsuit Mary's firm had struggled to survive. Well, the text didn't merit a response. If Mary never saw or heard from Blanche Brown, Attorney at Law again, it would be too soon.

Suddenly, Mary realized that she had walked past the area where the majority of vacationers at the beach that afternoon had set up their blankets and umbrellas. Now she found herself alone but for one old man wielding a metal detector, eyes trained on the sand. She stopped and looked out over the small, white-crested waves slapping the shore and felt a blanket of sadness descend upon her.

What *was* this New York City gal doing so far from home for an entire summer?

Chapter 19

Patty was bored. So far, there had only been two customers in the shop, and Theresa, the other woman who worked at Crystal Breeze, had rushed to assist both of them, leaving Patty to wander aimlessly past the piles of baseball-style caps and logo sweatshirts; the glass case of jewelry, some of it pretty expensive (that would be the pieces in gold with pink and green Maine tourmalines), some of it not so much (that would be the pieces in silver with green, blue, and pink sea glass); and the large selection of notecards printed with photographs of lighthouses, boats at sea, and trees in full autumn color.

That day, Patty had worn her cobalt Capri pants and a pink, short-sleeved blouse. She had noticed that her boss, Michelle, and Theresa dressed in clothes that were mostly beige, taupe, olive green, and navy, but neither had mentioned a dress code, and it wasn't as if Patty were coming into work wearing outfits she might wear to a nightclub, so she didn't think they had any objection to what she wore.

Not that she had been to a nightclub in years. In fact, she had no idea what sort of clothing people wore to nightclubs or even out to dinner these days. Her social life had become seriously circumscribed, limited to the occasional dinner with her sisters and brothers-in-law at Olive Garden, where Patty, acutely conscious of the miserable state of her finances, always made do with just the unlimited salad and breadstick deal.

The bell over the door tinkled, announcing a customer. Patty scurried to see who had entered; when she was in view of the door she saw that it was a man between sixty-five and seventy. It was hard to say. Everyone aged so very differently. Get together five sixty-year-olds and there was a very good chance that one would look no older than forty-five and one would look as if he or she were turning the corner to sixty-five.

Anyway, this man was handsome no matter his age. He still had a full head of hair. He was trim and nicely dressed. His shoes were obviously expensive, maybe designed and made in Italy. Good things came from Italy. His watch might be a Rolex; Patty couldn't get a good look due to the long-sleeved, blue Oxford-cloth shirt the man was wearing. He wore no rings that Patty could see.

Theresa was nowhere in sight, so Patty sidled close to the man, who was idly twirling a circular rack of postcards.

"These magnets over here are popular," she said, pointing to a shelf display. She spoke brightly, helpfully.

The man made no response; he didn't even turn to look at her. Then, he walked further into the shop.

Patty followed him, undeterred. Maybe he just hadn't heard her.

"Maybe you'd like to see our collection of souvenir mugs," she said, speaking more loudly.

But again, the man made no indication that he had heard her and turned toward the section of the shop where colorful T-shirts were stacked on several long shelves.

"The *MAINE* T-shirt is the most popular," Patty said, moving close enough to the man to make herself unavoidable. He really was very handsome. "It comes in blue, red, and white. I think the blue would look good on—"

Suddenly, the man turned to face her. He looked annoyed.

"I'm sorry," he said, "did you want something?"

Patty took a step back. Her stomach was fluttering uncomfortably. "Want something?" she said, attempting one of her fabulous smiles. "No, I just . . . I was just being helpful."

"Honestly," he said, with a frown, "you're not being helpful. And I'm here with my wife, so if you wouldn't mind."

Wife, Patty thought? She hadn't seen anyone else enter the shop.

Abruptly, the man started toward the front of the shop. A tall, slim woman, very nicely dressed, stood there considering the rack of expensive, hand-printed cards. Patty watched as the man touched his wife's arm and leaned in to speak to her. The woman quickly glanced over her shoulder, no doubt in hopes of catching a glimpse of the pesky woman who had been harassing her husband.

A moment later husband and wife were gone. They hadn't bought a thing. Patty didn't work on commission, but still. She had lost the shop a sale. She felt stupid.

And then she saw her boss, Michelle, approaching, her face set with a slight frown.

"Patty," Michelle said evenly, "I need to speak with you. Can you step into the back for a moment? Theresa can keep an eye on the shop."

Patty felt sick to her stomach. Michelle was probably going to fire her. If Patty hadn't exactly flirted with the handsome man, she had done everything but, and her behavior had been totally unprofessional. Patty knew this.

"I watched how you—how you handled that man a few minutes ago," Michelle began. "It's important you learn the difference between being of help to a customer and being a nuisance. It's a lesson all of us in retail have to learn, and the sooner the better."

"Yes," Patty said. "Of course. I'm sorry. It won't happen again."

Michelle nodded. "Good. I know you meant well but . . . Now, let's get back to work."

Michelle moved off—Theresa was still out of sight; thankfully she hadn't witnessed Patty's humiliation—and Patty took a steadying breath. She was grateful for Michelle's tact and kindness. Still, Patty felt awful. Had she honestly thought something good would come of her pestering that man? Had she honestly believed there was a chance the man would ask her out? Or had she acted the way that she had purely out of habit?

She was almost seventy years old. Would she *never* stop acting like a silly, brainless teenager, thinking only of the moment and never of the consequences of her actions? It was ridiculous. *She* was ridiculous, and she felt mortified. That was a dark word, *mortified*; she thought she might have heard it in church, or was she thinking of mortification, maybe self-mortification, or maybe even mortician? Whatever the case, feeling the way she did at that moment was not a good thing.

Not a good thing at all.

Patty had gone up to her room right after dinner that night, politely refusing Sandra's invitation to join her in the living room to watch *Tootsie*. Mary and Amanda had accepted, and, as Patty climbed the stairs to the second floor, her summer roommates were settling in, a bowl of popcorn ready at hand.

Now, Patty was tucked into her bed under Sandra's good, high-thread cotton sheets. She wanted to sleep, but her mind refused to shut down. The incident at the shop earlier was weighing heavily on her, taunting her even. It was bringing up some very troubling memories.

Patty's mother had taught her to regard her virginity as a valuable commodity only to be traded for marriage. Her virginity was a prize to be earned. Patty had listened to her mother.

About a year after she had moved into an apartment of her own, Patty was sure that the man she was seeing was about to propose. One night, she decided to nudge him along by going almost all the way. The idea was that he would be so eager to finish what they had begun that he would promise marriage. That was what men did. But not this man. Instead, over her desperate protests, he had raped her. She had never heard from him again after that. He had gotten what he wanted.

Patty was left in a deep state of embarrassment and shame. She had bungled. She felt responsible for what had happened. Only at odd moments did she feel anger toward the man. Patty didn't blame her mother for what had happened, either.

After that awful incident, Patty became more cautious. She realized that she was playing a serious game. She told herself to be careful, to be smart. Still, things never seemed to work out the way she hoped they would. Probably because she was in the game in the first place. She had never been good at games requiring strategy. She was impulsive. She didn't know how to think ahead. She was trusting. She was naïve.

After a while, Patty had found that she was willing to trade sex for things other than an emotional commitment. It never really felt right, but she was willing. A short vacation to somewhere warm and sunny. Occasional help with the rent when she had overspent on new clothes. A piece of jewelry, like the Tiffany and Company diamond solitaire necklace one man had given her at Christmas after she had dropped a bunch of hints. The fact that he ended the relationship with her a few days later, so that the necklace could be seen as his way of ensuring that Patty would not make waves by doing something stupid like calling his wife, made little difference to Patty. She was in possession of a diamond, even if the diamond weighed less than a carat and wasn't set in a gold ring.

Did it matter that years later, seriously strapped for cash, she had been forced to sell the necklace? She hadn't gotten all that much for it, probably far less than what it had originally cost. Maybe if she had researched how to sell the necklace online via some website or other, eBay maybe, she might have gotten more for it, but the idea of trying to learn something new had seemed—as it so often did—too daunting and not at all fun.

Suddenly, Patty became aware of the sound of laughter floating up from the living room. Maybe she should have joined the others. She liked *Tootsie*. It was a really fun movie.

Too late.

Chapter 20

Amanda was in her room getting dressed for dinner. She had been out walking all that afternoon and had come home—well, to Sandra's house—soaked with sweat. After a quick shower—she was always careful not to waste water—she had returned to her room to find a new text from Liam on her phone.

Can't wait to talk about last night's episode. Lord Rexor is toast if Cyril doesn't come thru. See you later.

Lord Rexor? Clearly, Amanda thought, he had sent the message to her by mistake. That was odd. Liam was a tech guy through and through. He never made mistakes with his phone or computer; he was the whiz who never failed to fix problems with every piece of machinery in their home.

The real question was, Amanda thought, as she put on a fresh T-shirt and pair of shorts, who was the message meant for? And then she remembered that Liam had a friend from college who shared his passion for fantasy-themed video games and television series. That must be it. The message had been meant for Gary. They must be meeting up for dinner or drinks. They didn't get together often, but maybe since Amanda had been away they were spending more time together. Amanda picked up her phone.

Hey. Glad you liked whatever fantasy thing you saw but think you meant this for Gary. Slipping up in your old age?

Not more than three minutes later, Liam responded.

Must be. Sorry. Hope yr having fun.

Questions answered. But for some reason, Amanda couldn't let the matter drop. That was the trouble with text. It was a poor means of communicating anything but the most simple and direct message.

Amanda decided that she would just call Liam. That would clear up any confusion, assuming there was any real confusion, assuming she wasn't simply uncharacteristically creating drama where there was none. Liam had made a mistake. That was all.

But her call went to voice mail. Why hadn't Liam answered? She knew he was with his phone.

Annoyed now, Amanda canceled the call without leaving a message.

It was funny, Amanda thought as she finished dressing. In a way, her relationship with Liam had just—happened. They had been dating for about seven months when Liam's landlord decided to kick out his tenants because he was going to renovate and sell the building. Liam was in a pickle and asked if he could stay with Amanda for a bit while he looked for a place of his own. Soon, they had realized that things were kind of okay with them both living at Amanda's, sharing expenses and a daily life. They agreed that Liam should stop looking for a new apartment. He got rid of most of his furniture that was in storage, and together they bought a few items—like, for example, a big screen television and a Japanese rice cooker.

Suddenly, in a thunderclap moment, Amanda realized how often she spoke in the conditional, approximate, the tentative, or the indefinite when she described her relationship with Liam. Kind of. Sort of. Fell into. Just happened.

Had it been that way with her other relationships, as well? With Sam, Jerry, Marc?

Enough thinking for now. She was hungry after all the exercise she had gotten that afternoon. The moment she entered the kitchen, Patty said: "So, Amanda, what are we having for dinner?"

For a moment, Amanda just stood there. Talk about slipping up in old age. "I'm so sorry," she said finally. "It's Wednesday, and I promised to make dinner. I can't believe I totally spaced. It's so not like me."

Patty laughed. "It's so like *me*!"

"As long as I'm not asked to cook, we'll make do," Mary said.

"Where there's a can of tuna," Sandra said, "there's soon a meal on the table. Anyone object to tuna salad sandwiches? I've got good bread from the bakery."

No one objected.

Mary opened the bread box on the counter and pulled out the large loaf of bread. "I'll slice this. Anyone want their bread toasted?"

Sandra opened the fridge. "Here's the mayonnaise. Now for a stalk or two of celery. Onions? Consensus?"

"Not too many, please," Patty said. "My tummy can't handle onions as well as it used to."

"And two cans of soup!" Mary announced, turning from an open cupboard. "Tomato and chicken noodle, perfect. Who's better than us?"

"Anything for dessert?" Amanda asked. "If there isn't I'll run out and get something. It's the least I can do."

"Check the cupboard over the stove," Sandra instructed Mary. "There should be a box of gingerbread mix. I can whip that up quickly, and there's some vanilla ice cream in the freezer."

In less time than it would have taken to call out for a food delivery, a simple meal was on the table. Before long, the spicy smell of baking gingerbread began to fill the kitchen. Amanda felt a tiny trickle of nostalgia for her childhood. Her mother had often made gingerbread.

"I don't think I've ever had wine with a tuna salad sandwich," Mary noted. "But I'm not complaining."

"Did anyone see the latest issue of *People* magazine?" Patty asked. "I saw it today at work. Oh, my God, they have the cutest pictures of the new royal baby with his big sister."

"What country are we talking about?" Mary asked.

Patty frowned. "Sweden, I think. No, one of those other countries . . ."

Amanda refrained from rolling her eyes. "A Scandinavian country?"

"Yes, that's it. Those royal children are all so adorable in their little matching outfits!"

"Not adorable enough to make me want one," Amanda said quietly.

"I *always* wanted children, ever since I was a little girl. I never questioned that desire, and I have no regrets." Sandra shrugged. "It's true that in my world it was assumed that women would marry, have children, and stay at home to raise them. I know it wasn't right for everyone, but it worked for me. My only sadness is that I have no grandchildren. Neither my son nor my daughter has children. Honestly, I'm not sure why, and it's not a question I can ask."

"I agree," Amanda said. "I find it incredibly rude when people ask about a person's plans for procreation. I mean, it's nobody's business."

"When I was much younger," Mary said suddenly, "in my early thirties, I considered becoming a single mother. I did lots of soul-searching, and, ultimately, I decided against the idea. I haven't for a moment regretted that decision."

"So, you thought about using a sperm donor?" Amanda asked.

Mary nodded. "I did but I decided that it wasn't right for me. Anyway, then I focused on adoption, which felt far more comfortable. But finally, I came to admit that I was too wrapped up in my own concerns to make the sacrifices I would have to make to be a good parent."

"I think your decision not to have a child you might not be equipped to care for properly was an act of generosity. At least, an act of reason and self-knowledge."

"Thanks, Sandra," Mary said. "I appreciate your understanding."

"I never had any interest in being a mother," Amanda told the others. "I didn't even play with dolls as a kid. Long ago I came to realize that the 'family dynamic' never intrigued me all that much. Like, I'm not a fan of novels or movies about families, happy or unhappy. I love mysteries, and sometimes the plot involves a death or some other disaster in a family but the primary focus is on the solving of the case. And I do enjoy reading about historical family dynamics in biographies, but I'm less concerned with the emotional matters than I am with the dynastic and political issues."

"So, maternal instinct never reared its warm and fuzzy head?" Mary said.

"Not once. I believe that the idea of a universal 'maternal instinct' is a damaging myth used to control and subjugate women."

"Well, there is biology," Sandra noted. "I mean, science can explain a lot."

Amanda shrugged. "Whatever. I guess I just don't have the maternal gene then. Non-scientifically speaking, of course."

Briefly, she thought about Liam. Having a child had always been a nonissue in their relationship. There had been no tortured discussions, no second guesses. Liam liked spending time with other people's children, as did Amanda, but that wasn't the same as being a parent.

"What about you, Patty?" Mary asked.

Patty laughed a bit shrilly. "My nieces and nephews kept me busy enough! Besides, I didn't want to have children unless I was married, so . . ."

Amanda thought that Patty looked seriously uncomfortable.

The oven timer dinged, indicating that the gingerbread was ready.

"Gosh, I love the smell of warm gingerbread!" Patty exclaimed—recovered, it seemed—as Sandra brought the cake still in its square baking pan to the table and placed it on a trivet.

Mary had fetched the carton of ice cream from the fridge, as well as a scoop, knife, and spoons.

"My mother used to make this very gingerbread," Amanda told her summer roommates. "Same brand. We ate it with Cool Whip, though, not with ice cream. Still, this takes me back."

"A nice memory, then," Sandra said as she began to slice the cake.

"Yes," Amanda said. "A very nice memory."

Chapter 21

It looked like it was going to be a beautiful day, Sandra thought, glancing once again through the large window of her bedroom suite. The sun was shining and the air looked free of humidity; it was clear and without a touch of haze.

As she finished getting dressed, Sandra found herself recalling the conversation she and the others had engaged in at dinner the night before about children, having them, not having them, regrets, and no regrets. From the way in which Patty had so quickly and so awkwardly shrugged off the question, Sandra surmised that she felt bad about not having had a family.

On the other hand, Amanda seemed thoroughly content in her decision to remain childless. If Sandra were being honest, she thought that a smart choice. She had trouble imagining Amanda as a mother. Well, it didn't matter what Sandra thought about the matter. Amanda was content.

As for Mary, in spite of her claiming to be inadequate parent material, Sandra thought she would have made a very good mother indeed. Loving, fair, even fun. But she seemed to have given the matter serious thought; Sandra felt sure that Mary, too, had made the right choice for her.

But again, her opinion didn't matter.

Ready for the day ahead, Sandra headed downstairs to the kitchen. At the doorway, she came to a horrified halt.

Patty was bending down to give Clovis a small dish filled with what could only be heavy cream. Sandra knew there was a container in the fridge. She had put it there herself. She liked heavy cream on her oatmeal.

"What are you doing?" Sandra cried.

Quickly, Patty stood. Her face was flushed; she knew she had been caught in the act. "I saw the heavy cream in the fridge," she said, "and Clovis was here and he was meowing at me so I just thought—"

"You just thought you would give him some cream when I expressly instructed each of you living here in my home this summer never to feed Clovis anything, especially not food meant for humans."

Sandra felt absolutely furious. She was shocked by the intensity of her anger. And, she realized, at the depth of her guilt. By bringing strangers into the house she had put Clovis at risk. She blamed herself for the near disaster almost as much as she blamed Patty for not having honored her promise.

Patty's face was scarlet now. She rushed to the fridge, retrieved the carton, and began to pour the heavy cream back into it. The cream spilled over the sides of the bowl and pooled on the counter.

"Leave it," Sandra said, still shaking. "I'll clean it up."

She had *told* the women not to give Clovis anything to eat. She had stressed that he had a sensitive tummy and could only safely tolerate the medical diet prescribed by the doctor. In Sandra's opinion, to give him something that was bad for him was tantamount to a crime.

Suddenly, Sandra recalled Patty's sneezing attack a few days before. Clearly, Clovis had not been the culprit, not if Patty could get so close to him this morning without incident.

"I'm really, really sorry," Patty said then. "I just thought, well, all cats like cream, don't they? It's in almost every story about cats. You see those cute old-fashioned prints where a farmer is milking a cow and squirting milk into a cat's mouth."

Sandra restrained a sigh of frustration. "It doesn't matter if Clovis likes cream. What matters is that it doesn't like him, and I told you not to give him anything to eat. You agreed that you wouldn't. You broke your word."

Patty clasped her hands in front of her. She looked as if she might cry. "I'm sorry," she said, "I really am. And I won't do it again, I swear. I'd apologize to him if I thought he'd understand me."

"All right," Sandra said, wearily. "No harm done. Just, please, in the future—"

"I promise not to go near Clovis ever again."

Sandra nodded, and Patty hurried from the room.

When Patty had gone, Sandra sank into a chair at the table. Clovis came to sit on her right foot. If he was disappointed he hadn't gotten his treat, he didn't let on.

How wise had it been, this notion of filling the house with summer roommates? Maybe not very wise. At that moment, Sandra felt that she had been invaded by the others, even though they were there with her permission, even, in a way, by her invitation. She wished she could shut the door on them all and be alone with Clovis. The idea of an "intentional community" was ridiculous, as Marcia Livingston had said. There was no way Sandra could handle such an arrangement, not unless it was with family members. But neither of her children nor their spouses had ever expressed an interest in living with her as she aged. . . .

How she missed John! If only he hadn't died. Even if John were sick at least he would be *present*, and that would be better than his being absent.

Sandra sighed. It would be good to have someone with whom she could talk! If only Emma was still here in Yorktide. Sandra leaned over and lifted Clovis into her lap. She held him tightly, and he rubbed his face against hers, purring. After a few moments, Sandra felt soothed.

She would have to make things up with Patty if the woman was going to stay on as a housemate. This was something Sandra hadn't considered in the many hours of thinking she had done before embarking on this scheme. Tension between two members of the little summer community would inevitably damage the mood of all members. Sandra felt a responsibility as—as what? as housemother? as the eldest?—to ensure that all of the women living under her roof were content.

She didn't think Patty would resist making peace. Patty didn't seem the type to foolishly hold a grudge or to enjoy negative drama.

At least, Sandra hoped that Patty wasn't the type.

Chapter 22

Mary had settled in the living room with her latest find, a copy of T.G. Rosenthal's *L.S. Lowry, The Art and the Artist*. It had been sitting at the very bottom of a four-foot-high pile of art books in a dark corner of a fabulous old books and antiques shop she had stumbled across on an afternoon drive. She had been looking for a copy of the book for ages, and, while she knew she could buy one via Amazon, she had had her heart set on discovering the volume just as she had. Retrieving the book from its resting place hadn't been easy—a lot of bending and lifting was involved—but it had been worth every sore muscle and creaking joint.

Now, though eager to explore the pages of Rosenthal's work, she found her mind wandering back to the conversation she and her summer roommates had shared the other evening. Frankly, Mary had surprised herself by being so open with the others about her decision not to be a parent. She wondered if she was getting mushy in her old age. Careless with her secrets. Still she didn't really regret having shared what she had. There was nothing shameful in her story.

Poor Patty though. The topic had unsettled her. Well, hav-

ing a child was a major—perhaps the most major—experience
in a person's life, and, no matter the situation, it was bound to
elicit strong emotional reactions even years after the possibility of having a child had become an impossibility.

As for Amanda, she had unequivocally declared that she
had never had any interest in being a mother, and had gone on
to state her belief that the notion of a maternal instinct was in
fact a damaging myth meant to control the lives of women.
Mary thought that Amanda might have a point, but at this
time of her life, she wasn't really interested in arguing for or
against it.

Sandra came into the living room then. Mary noted that she
looked worried.

"Anything the matter?" she asked.

"We're in for a storm," Sandra said. "The tail end of a hurri-
cane in the south."

Mary nodded. "I saw that on the news."

"The last time Yorktide was hit with the tail end of a hur-
ricane there was a fair amount of damage. People lost window shutters, and roofs were torn off, and a number of lovely
old trees didn't make it through. Some boats were unmoored,
and one was destroyed. There were even a few injuries as a
result of flying debris. In all my years, I'd never seen anything like it."

"Anything I can do to help make the house secure?" Mary
asked, eager to be of assistance to Sandra, who clearly had
good reason for being worried.

"Yes, as a matter of fact, if you wouldn't mind. Thank you,
Mary."

"Not at all," Mary said, rising from her seat. "I think the
others are around somewhere. I'll round them up. If we work
together, all should be well."

Moments later, Mary returned to the living room with Patty
and Amanda in tow.

"How much time do we have before the storm hits?" Patty asked. "I didn't see anything about it on the news. But sometimes I forget to check the weather."

"The storm is supposed to make landfall in about ninety minutes," Sandra told them. "We'll need to close all of the windows and lock all of the wooden shutters upstairs, and make sure that all the outdoor furniture and flowerpots and any stray gardening tools are put away in the shed and that the shed door, and the garage door, are securely locked. We'll need to prepare for a blackout as well."

Amanda went off to the closet under the stairs as directed to fetch flashlights and candles and a box of matches.

"Do you have a backup generator?" she asked when she returned, loaded with supplies.

"Yes, and it should work just fine," Sandra said. "I had it checked at the end of last winter. And Kate got me a battery for charging my cell phone should I lose power."

Patty returned from her examination of the fridge and cupboards. "There's plenty of food in the house for several days." She turned to Sandra. "But I'd be happy to run out now and bring in anything you think we might need."

Sandra shook her head and smiled at Patty. "I'm sure we'll be just fine. Thank you."

"Well, come on," Mary said. "Let's go secure the windows and clear up anything outside that's not bolted down."

About half an hour later, mission accomplished, Mary and the others were to be found gathered in the living room to await the storm.

"I'll never forget a magnificent storm I witnessed over Lake Winnow," Sandra said, cradling a cup of tea in her hands. "We were visiting relatives up north. I must have been about nine or ten; my brother was just a baby. My mother and father and I stood holding hands and watching the spectacular bolts of lightning over the water. I wasn't frightened at all. I remember laughing in my excitement."

"I've always been a bit afraid of lightning," Amanda admitted. "I'm not sure why. I mean, I've never known anyone who was struck by lightning. It's just so—I don't know—sudden and violent."

"I don't mind lightning but I hate thunder," Patty told the others. "When I was a little girl it really terrified me. I'd hide in the back of my closet with my hands over my ears and my eyes squeezed shut. My sisters thought it was funny, my being such a fraidycat. They barricaded the door to the closet once, I remember, so that I couldn't get out. That made me really frightened!"

Mary declined to comment on the nasty behavior of Patty's sisters. It was none of her business, other people's sibling dynamics. "I'm pretty neutral on the subject of thunder and lightning," she said. "I mean, I'm not particularly scared of the noise and light, but neither do I particularly enjoy a storm."

"Well, no matter how each of us feels about storms, at least we've done what we can to protect ourselves and the house from this one."

"What about Clovis?" Amanda asked suddenly. "I haven't seen him in a while."

Sandra smiled. "Being a cat, he senses the change in atmospheric pressure long before any of us mere humans do. He's been under my bed since morning. He'll come out when it's all over."

"Oh, my!" Patty exclaimed. "Look at how dark it's gotten all of a sudden!"

"The sky is that weird grayish-green." Amanda shuddered. "It's like the end of the world."

A vivid display of forked lightning illuminated the sky, followed by a crash of thunder.

Patty yelped, Amanda jumped, and Sandra went to the window to watch the rain come beating down.

Very Mary Shelley's *Frankenstein*, Mary thought, thunderstorms. Had Mrs. Shelley only known what a lasting impression her tale would make!

For the next hour, a heavy rain fell, but there was relatively little wind. And there had been no further episodes of thunder or lightning after the one that had announced the storm, for which Patty and Amanda were no doubt grateful.

"Well, that was much ado about nothing," Amanda noted when all was calm again and the sky had resumed a more welcoming tone. "Some heavy rain and it was over."

"It was kind of a letdown, wasn't it?" Mary said. "Not that I was hoping for damage, but a bit more drama might have been nice."

Patty grimaced. "That was plenty of drama for me, thanks."

Suddenly, the loud meow of a hungry feline resounded through the house.

"Clovis agrees with you, Patty!" Mary laughed. "Enough with the drama, how about some food?"

Sandra smiled. "Thank you all for pitching in today. Tomorrow we'll return the place to normal. I'm pooped. It used to be that I'd never leave a mess until the next day or walk away from a chore that needed doing."

"It's called getting old and realizing that your priority is your health," Mary said, "not the dishes in the sink or the flowerpots that need to be brought out into the yard."

"But you can never put off feeding your animal companion," Sandra said. "Clovis, Mommy's coming!"

As her summer roommates went their separate ways, Mary picked up the book she had still not opened and headed up to her room. The four of them had been a good team that afternoon, coming together in a moment of potential crisis, almost like colleagues in a well-organized office. As she climbed the stairs to the second floor of Sandra's house, Mary realized that she missed that collegial dynamic now that she was retired. She missed her partners, the administrative staff, the guy from the mailroom, the kid at the café in the lobby who handed her a cup of black coffee every morning.

Mary closed the door of her room behind her, feeling suddenly low. What she needed was a big dose of Lowry's charming matchstick figures. They never failed to lift her spirits.

Chapter 23

Michelle had told Patty to go around the shop collecting items that customers had put back in the wrong place. There were an awful lot of such items, Patty discovered, as the basket she was carrying got heavier. People could be very careless.

As she herself had been when she had attempted to give Clovis that bowl of heavy cream. Sandra had been so nice to her since that awful incident, almost as if she was going out of her way to make Patty feel that all was forgiven and forgotten. Patty hadn't often met people like Sandra, kind and so, well, so real. Sandra's children were lucky to have her as their mother.

Who in their right mind would stick a package of lobster-shaped gummies in a pile of T-shirts? Patty shook her head and dropped the package into her basket. Maybe it had been a child, in which case you couldn't really get mad.

Patty sighed, and hoped that no one in the shop had heard her. Like she had kind of told the others, she had once thought she was on the path to marriage and children, but she had been wrong. And she had never at all considered the idea of becoming a single parent. Her family would have seen it as a very odd choice. Thinking about it now, Patty doubted she would have had any emotional support from them, and she doubted the child would have been fully accepted into the Porter family. Patty sighed again. Well, it was too late now to worry about such things.

Patty heard the tinkling of the bells over the door to the shop and turned to see who had come in. It was a man in work clothes, carrying a large box filled with tall jars of something amber colored. Maybe honey or syrup, Patty thought. She saw Michelle greet him with a welcoming smile, and, after the man had set the box on the front counter, the two chatted for several minutes.

Finally, they parted. As he headed toward the door, the man caught Patty's eye.

"Nice out there today," he said with a smile.

"Yes," Patty replied, determined to say no more. She had to be careful not to appear too friendly. After all, she had been scolded for flirting with that good-looking man. As if she would flirt with *this* man! He didn't look like he had much money. He was clean, as were his clothes, that much Patty could tell, but nothing about him said style or sophistication or, well, money. He wasn't bad-looking or anything, just not . . . not what? Patty thought about it. Not worth risking her job for, that was for sure!

In the end, she supposed that no man was.

Only when Patty was back at Sandra's house did she check her phone for messages. She had missed a call from Bridget. She supposed she should listen to the voice mail her sister had left.

Where are you? My Maura is visiting and she just cannot believe that you're in Maine for the entire summer. Where did Aunt Patty get the money for a vacation, she wants to know. Didn't anyone try to talk her out of such a ridiculous scheme? What was Aunt Patty thinking?

Here Bridget laughed.

Anyway, call me when you get this. Bye.

Patty sat heavily on the edge of the bed. She wished she hadn't listened to her sister's message. Now she knew for sure that her niece Maura, and probably all the other nieces and nephews—Colleen and Ian, and Teri's kids: Frank, Jim, and Cathy—thought she was ridiculous.

Well, Patty kind of knew that already.

When her sisters' children were young, Patty had loved to shower them with gifts, many she could ill afford, some that had been paid for by one of her gentleman friends. It was clear that the children adored their glamorous aunt, looked forward to her visits as something special and exciting. Aunt Patty was so *different*. Her clothes were so fun. She was so bubbly.

But as they aged, those bright children had begun to ask questions of their parents. What does Aunt Patty do for a living? Why isn't she married? Does she have a boyfriend? Does she live alone? Patty heard all about these questions from her sisters, who seemed to enjoy relating their children's puzzlement.

Eventually, when the children were teenagers, they were told that Patty didn't bring her boyfriends for Sunday dinner or Thanksgiving or Christmas because, mostly, the boyfriends were married to other people. Aunt Patty did nothing much for a living. She didn't really have any money. Aunt Patty wasn't very interesting at all.

As the years went by, the expensive gifts stopped coming. There was no one to pay for them as the men in Patty's life began to drift away and Patty's so-called career faltered.

Once, Teri's daughter Cathy had tried to talk to her aunt about self-respect, about not relying on a man to give her a meaningful life, about cultivating female friendships. Patty had felt hurt by Cathy's assumption that she needed help.

Now the nieces and nephews were on their own, working in good jobs, and totally independent of their parents. There was an awkwardness when Patty was with them. They had long ago been disabused of any notion that she was a glamorous or a fascinating person, and that fact embarrassed her. Still, Patty believed that her sisters' children loved her, if in a slightly condescending or patronizing way.

Patty's stomach gurgled loudly. She had missed lunch, and dinner was at least three hours away. As she made her way down to Sandra's kitchen for a snack, an image of the man who had delivered jars of something amber colored to Crystal Breeze earlier popped into her head. What had Michelle later said his name was? Peter? No. Phil? Maybe Phil.

Patty had no idea why she should be thinking about the delivery man. Hunger, Patty decided, was probably making her light-headed.

Chapter 24

Early morning was, in Amanda's opinion, the best time for a walk on the beach, even if the tide was super high, leaving only a narrow strip of sand on which to walk. Most important, there were only a few other early risers enjoying a constitutional, and, aside from a wave or a brief nod, no one seemed inclined to communicate. This suited Amanda perfectly.

Briefly, Amanda wondered if Liam was out of bed yet. She knew he didn't have to be in his office until nine thirty, though for the past six months or so he had been out of the house at the crack of dawn to get to the gym. They had exchanged texts the night before. Liam had apologized for not being in touch more often but he had given no reason as to why he hadn't been in touch. Amanda hadn't asked.

Since the conversation about children with her roommates the other night, Amanda had been doing some thinking. She liked children. She enjoyed spending her days with her students, in spite of their being teenagers or, in other words, human beings not yet fully developed but absolutely certain that they were. For a short time at the start of her career she had taught second graders and had enjoyed them, too. Babies were cute. Toddlers were funny. You would have to be a monster not to be devastated by the death or even the mistreatment of a child.

She had spoken lightly to the others about not having even a shred of maternal instinct, but the truth was that there had been and still were moments when Amanda was bothered by what she thought might be a deep flaw in her character. Mary, at least, had given serious consideration to the idea of having a child before deciding that it wasn't for her. She, Amanda, had never bothered to give the idea any real thought at all. Maybe it was something to worry about, an inability to feel as other human beings felt, an inability to care enough, to love enough . . .

Maybe these flaws were behind the failures—the whimpering ends—of her romantic relationships thus far. And her relationship with Liam? Was that, too, at a whimpering end? If not, why had she walked away from him, from them, for an entire summer?

Amanda literally shook her head. She didn't want to think about what she had come away from home to think about.

Suddenly, something on the sand caught her eye. It was an almost perfectly round disc with some sort of faint markings. Amanda peered more closely. It was an intact sand dollar. Gently, she picked it up. She seemed to recall that there was some superstition surrounding sand dollars. She thought they were supposed to be a sign of something positive, of good luck. Not that she bought into superstitions and things like signs and symbols. Still, if she was really interested she could see what the Internet had to say about the mythical significance of sand dollars. Either way, she felt glad that she had found it. Carefully, she wrapped the natural treasure in a tissue and put it in a zippered pocket of her fanny pack.

Amanda walked on. The sun was not fully risen and there was still a chill to the air, which Amanda found bracing, even a bit uncomfortable but not unwelcome. She stuck her hands deeper into the pockets of her jacket. In the distance, she could see another early morning walker coming toward her. She couldn't tell if it was a man or a woman, a young person or an old person. Whatever the case, when the person got closer, she would lower the brim of her baseball cap and keep her eyes on the ground. Maybe that way the person wouldn't bother to greet her and she could continue on her way alone.

Chapter 25

Sandra had come to the library in the hopes of finding more information about the history of intentional communities in the United States. She was a bit tired of using her computer for her research. Reading online was all right if it was limited to short articles or even to headlines, but nothing beat the tactile experience of turning the pages of a book.

Sadly, though, Yorktide's little library had done away with the old-fashioned card catalogue, forcing Sandra to use one of their computers to find call numbers of books that might offer the information she was seeking. Without too much effort, she found a few appropriate titles and went in search of them.

A few minutes later, she was settled at a table with a hefty book and a journal from a university out in Montana. She opened the book first, a history of nineteenth century Utopian communities in the United States, and realized that she remembered much of what she had learned about the topic in a high school course. The communities were based on transcendentalist beliefs, namely, that institutions like organized religions and the political process corrupted the purity of both humans and of Nature. Insight and intuition, the transcendentalists professed, rather than logic and experience, revealed the most important and essential truths, perhaps the most important of which was that all creation was one.

Nathaniel Hawthorne, Sandra read, was a founding member of Brook Farm, established in 1841 and arguably the most famous of the communities. The information came as a bit of a surprise to her, as for some reason she thought of Hawthorne as not particularly into promoting gender equality, which, it seems, was one of the community's ideals, along with an equitable division of labor, the abolishment of the class system, and the promotion of self-improvement. By self-improvement the founders meant learning how to follow one's moral compass no matter how it might differ from that of the outside world.

Sadly, the Brook Farm community had come to an end in 1847 due to debt, smallpox, and a devastating fire. You could read a message into that if you were so inclined, that the pie in the sky venture had been doomed from the start. Or, Sandra thought, you could simply call the ignominious end a bit of very bad luck or very poor timing. Maybe both.

Today, it seemed, intentional communities in the vein of Brook Farm and its ilk were popular with millennials seeking a sanctuary from materialism and modernity. That was all well and good, though Sandra Pennington, at the age of seventy-four, wasn't seeking a sanctuary. It was not her intention or her desire to escape from the world at large, or from her little corner of the world. While she certainly thought that both materialism and modernity were seriously faulty, she wasn't enough of a revolutionary or of a reactionary to want to turn her back on what were the realities of her culture. For better or worse, she had made a separate peace with the world, as she suspected most people did at any given time in history.

Sandra turned next to the university journal. The article, published earlier that year, focused on the concept of sustainability. You heard the term everywhere, in all sorts of contexts. In order to be respected as an individual, it was vital now to claim that one's business was sustainable, that one's clothing was sustainable, that one was "all about" sustainability.

From a brief perusal of the article—the writing style was turgid and at times impenetrable—Sandra came away with the idea that sustainability was about balance, about humans coexisting, or learning how to coexist, with the planet and with consideration of future generations. Humans hadn't done a very good job thus far; seemingly, some were attempting to make up for their more awful actions. But was it too late to make a measurable difference? Some said no, and that intentional communities were a step in the right direction. Others said yes, it was too late, there was no point, the end was near; why not just continue destroying the planet?

With a sigh, Sandra closed the journal. One of the things that had struck her the most in all of the reading about intentional communities she had done since spring was the absolute importance of a shared sense of meaning, the sense that members were living according to their shared beliefs and morals.

Not for the first time, Sarah wondered what purpose a group of adult housemates could claim. What would bind the housemates one to the other? No shared children. No economic enterprise in common. No shared religious belief. No memories held in common, at least, not necessarily. It would all be down to intention, a daily decision to recommit, to say, yes, I agree to this arrangement. But human nature was fickle, unreliable, prone to moods and whims. Could any community survive without a shared ideal to live up to?

Related to this question was the issue of self-governance. Everyone in an intentional community would have to agree to a set of laws, as well as to a system of punishment. So, Sandra wondered, what would constitute a crime requiring that a person be exiled from the household? An act of violence, of course. Consistent failure to pay rent or to keep to other agreements essential to the smooth running of the household. The use of illegal drugs.

Traditionally, Sandra considered, family members weren't kicked out of a home for bad behavior. They were often sheltered, given second, third, even fourth chances. Sometimes, that turned out to be a bad thing, but still, with family there was a sense of security there never could be in a housemate situation. Could a person who was a mere housemate be given a second chance? It didn't seem terribly likely.

Then again, Patty had been just about to break an important rule of the household by feeding Clovis, but Sandra had given her a second chance. The incident had been smoothed over, and there were no bad feelings as far as Sandra could tell.

Sandra put a hand to her head. She had a suspicion she might be overthinking the subject of intentional community. She got up from the table and returned the book and the journal to their proper places.

She needed a sweet treat. She would go to the bakery for a blondie. If they were out of blondies then she would have a brownie. Or maybe a cupcake. Or a giant cookie. Anything sugary would do.

Thinking was hard work.

Chapter 26

Mary had fought with herself all morning. She had told herself to suck it up, to let it go. But something perverse in her nature was forcing her to go ahead with her complaint.

She was standing in the hall outside the bathroom on the first floor, waiting for Patty to emerge so that she could have her say. What in the world was taking Patty so long in there? Mary's own morning routine was a streamlined affair. She was in and out of the bathroom with impressive speed. Her college roommates had found it almost amusing.

Finally, after another eight or nine minutes, Patty emerged, clutching a large purple zip bag stuffed with, Mary assumed, "product." She was wearing a pink frilly robe and open-backed slippers with heels that clacked against the floor as she walked. Mary sniffed. Yup. There it was.

"Patty," Mary said, "I have a favor to ask of you."

"Okay," Patty said with a smile. "Sure. Ask away."

"Could you not put on your perfume in one of the shared bathrooms? Could you maybe wait until you're back in your room?"

Patty looked perplexed. "I don't understand. Why?"

Mary sighed. "Because the scent you wear is kind of overwhelming. It gives me a headache."

Patty laughed. "A scent can't give you a headache."

"Yes," Mary said deliberately, "it can, and this one does. I'm not asking that you refrain from wearing any perfume, just that you not apply it in a common bathroom."

"But it's part of my morning routine," Patty protested, shaking her head. "I get washed and then put on deodorant and powder and perfume. And sometimes I like putting on more perfume in the afternoon. It makes me feel good."

Mary restrained another sigh. Talking to Patty could be like talking to the wall. "All I'm asking is that maybe you could wait until you're in your room before the perfume bit."

"I . . ." Patty frowned. "Why don't you just use another bathroom if my perfume bothers you?"

"Just do me a favor and think about it, okay?"

Without waiting for a reply, Mary marched off to her room, leaving Patty standing in the hall with a puzzled expression on her face.

Mary threw herself into the armchair she had moved to a position by the window, overlooking the backyard and garden. She felt seriously displeased with herself. Disappointed. Why had she felt the need to make such a big deal of things with Patty? Why had she felt the need to make her own minor discomfort someone else's problem or responsibility? Why hadn't her better self stepped up and admonished her to keep her mouth shut?

Confronting Patty had been childish. Impulsive. If a grievance really needed to be aired, it should only be aired after careful consideration. And really, Mary shouldn't have said anything at all. What a ridiculous argument over something that would never have been a problem if she had booked into a hotel rather than a hybrid bed-and-breakfast or whatever this place was meant to be. It had been her decision to spend the summer at Sandra Pennington's house on Spruce Street and so it was her responsibility to accept any consequences that might arise from such a situation.

Well, Mary thought, rising from the chair with a sigh, she had better apologize to Patty before too much time passed. She went downstairs and found Patty in the living room, sitting on the couch and looking through a fashion magazine.

"Hey," she said.

Patty looked up from her reading. "Hi." Her tone was hesitant, wary.

"Look," Mary went on, "I'm sorry for making a big thing about the perfume earlier. The fact is that it does give me a headache, but that's my problem, not yours. There's no need for me to use a particular bathroom right after you've been using it. Like you said, I can use another bathroom."

Patty smiled, though Mary thought she still looked a bit wary. "Thanks. I'm sorry, too. I mean, I'm so used to doing things the same way every day; I don't even think about what it is I'm doing. It's just that I've lived alone for so long. . . . I'm not used to people. I'm not used to sharing—well, to sharing anything, really."

Mary nodded. "Neither am I, to be honest. Living alone has made me particular about things. Maybe even a bit fussy. It's hard to avoid that happening. When there's no one around with whom you're forced to negotiate, well, you're always in the right, aren't you? You always get your own way."

"That's a good way to put it," Patty said. "We always get our own way."

"Maybe that's not always a good thing. Though it might be compensation for the challenges of living on one's own. I don't know. Anyway, sorry again."

"Sure," Patty said. "Thanks."

Mary left Patty to her magazine and went back upstairs to her room. She definitely felt better for having apologized. In fact, the entire incident might have helped to bring Mary and Patty a wee bit closer.

Whether or not that was a good thing was still to be seen.

Chapter 27

Patty was sitting on the edge of her bed. In her right hand, she held one of the two collectibles she had brought with her to Maine, the Fairy with Crystal Ball. It might not be a cuddly toy, a plush bear or bunny, but it helped to comfort her. Just a little.

The confrontation with Mary, coming so soon after the confrontation with Sandra over Clovis, had given Patty pause. True, Mary had apologized to her, and Patty had apologized to Mary, but she didn't like confrontations, she didn't seek them out the way some people did, and yet, somehow, she had managed to be the cause of two confrontations with her housemates. In the first instance, okay, she had been at fault. But in the second instance, what, really, had she done wrong? Well, maybe she had been self-centered, failing to consider how her actions might affect those around her, but . . .

Yes, now that Patty thought about it, she realized that in both situations she had failed to consider the consequences of her actions.

This bothered her. Maybe there was something very wrong with her. Maybe she wasn't capable of getting along with other people. Why? Because she didn't care about other people? Could that be true?

Maybe she *did* wear too much perfume. No one had ever mentioned it before, but then again it might be a difficult topic to broach. A criticism of one's smell was pretty personal. Mary had had the guts to say something, but lots of people probably didn't.

Patty got up from the bed, leaving the Crystal Ball Fairy next to the pillow, and went to the dresser. One by one she opened the drawers and sniffed hard. Was there a lingering odor of perfume on her underwear, T-shirts, socks? She couldn't tell.

Patty shut the final drawer. Now that she thought about it, she remembered her mother teaching her that wearing too much perfume showed an insensitivity to other people. Had Patty been acting selfishly all these years? If so she certainly hadn't meant to be! Had she turned off men in the past because she wore too much perfume? Was her makeup too bright? Her clothes too garish? Had she come across as cheap or stupid?

Patty put a hand to her forehead and tried to take a deep breath. She hadn't gone down this road in a while. It was nothing new, this experience of self-criticism, even loathing, but it was painful nonetheless.

Patty sighed. She knew she wasn't supposed to waste money, but she needed to hear a voice from home. Surely that was a good enough reason to spend a few dollars or however much it cost to call New Hampshire.

She dialed Teri's number. She didn't know why she had chosen Teri rather than Bridget. But a sister was a sister, and Patty was in sore need of some measure of consolation.

"Hi," she said, in reply to Teri's hello. "It's me. Patty."

"I know." Teri's reply was clipped. "Your number comes up when you call, remember?"

Patty attempted a laugh. "Right. It's just a habit, saying 'it's me.' So, how are you?"

"Okay. Can't complain."

But you always do, Patty said silently, beginning to think that this call had been a mistake. "How's Kevin?"

"He's as well as can be expected. That man needs a break. I'll be surprised if he makes it to retirement without keeling over."

"Yes," Patty said carefully. "Kevin works hard."

"You know," Teri went on, "it's funny. I was saying to Kevin just last night that I haven't had a vacation in years, and here you are spending the entire summer in a resort town, lazing on the beach all day."

A sick sort of whirring started in Patty's stomach. "I'm not lazing on the beach all day, Teri," she said. "I'm working. I told you that."

"At a part-time job," Teri snapped. "There's no way your salary can cover the expense of your rent or . . . Look, never mind. You have your fun while you can. I've got errands to run. I'll tell Bridget you called. Make sure you take good care of Kevin's car. Bye."

Patty put her phone on the bedside table. She sat very still, her hands flat on her thighs. She knew what Teri had meant by that remark. *You have your fun while you can.* She had meant that this summer was Patty's last hurrah because once she was back in New Hampshire come the end of summer, her life was going to become very constricted, her freedom to make her own choices severely limited, her status as a dependent confirmed.

She would be the poor relation.

Patty also knew that Teri had been going to say that whatever money Patty might earn, now and in the future, little though it was, should be given to Bridget in compensation for Bridget's having taken Patty in back in February. Teri thought that Patty was selfish. Probably she was right. But Teri just didn't understand, no one understood, what Patty was feeling, what she was going through and had been going through for so long now.

Maybe what she needed after all was a friend, a real friend, maybe someone like Sandra or Mary, someone who might be able to understand her without judgment and maybe even with sympathy. But all her life she had turned away from friendship with women. Female friendship was not something that was essential for well-being. It might exist alongside a marriage, but it would never be as important as a marriage.

Probably, she had been wrong about all that, too. And now, on the cusp of turning seventy, she had nothing at all, no husband, no children, no friends. All she had was a silly collection of fairy figurines and . . .

She should have called Bridget. Bridget was more forgiving than Teri. But Bridget, too, wouldn't think to ask if Patty was feeling sad or lonely or depressed. She, too, would fail to see her sister as a full human being, not just a type or a character.

The badly spoiled daughter who had grown up to be an inadequate adult. The family failure.

Patty lay down on the bed next to the Crystal Ball Fairy and curled up on her side. Tears began to trickle down her face.

Chapter 28

"This is fantastic, Amanda." Mary sighed with pleasure.

Amanda nodded. "I'm glad you like it."

For dinner, she had made cream of broccoli soup from scratch, and a cold chicken salad flavored with tarragon.

"Where did you learn to cook?" Sandra asked. "You really are very good."

"No place special, really," Amanda replied. "I taught myself, I suppose, once I finished school and had a place of my own. I have a fair collection of classic cookbooks. They're great teaching guides and inspiration."

Mary laughed. "There have been long periods of my adult life when my dinner consisted of either a peanut butter and jelly sandwich or a pizza from the corner shop. For a few months, I was obsessed with sesame noodles from my local Chinese place."

"You really never cook for yourself?" Sandra asked Mary.

"On occasion, I boil pasta and dump half a stick of butter on top when it's done."

"I love butter," Patty said. "I don't believe it's bad for you like some people say."

Amanda didn't bother to respond to that statement. Could Patty really be so ignorant, or did she just assume an air of ignorance? Why in the world would someone do such a thing?

"You know what I witnessed today in town? A blatant act of disrespect. I swear it made me so mad I could have—"

"What happened, Mary?" Sandra asked.

"This little shit—excuse me, this young girl, maybe about fifteen—pushed right past this older woman, and I mean older, like in her eighties, who was trying to go into the bakery. The poor woman was jostled almost off her feet. I grabbed for her arm and steadied her, for which she was grateful. She didn't seem annoyed with the kid; she was just very polite to me. Better woman than I am! I mean, when I was a kid back in the old days I was taught to respect my elders. It was one of the basics, like hold the door for the other person to go ahead. Step aside to let the other person pass when you're walking along a narrow sidewalk. It's the basic stuff of a civilized society!"

"Me too," Patty said. "I mean, I was taught the same stuff. Not that they were the old days . . ."

Amanda refrained from rolling her eyes. It was clear to everyone that Patty was in her late sixties or early seventies. Why wouldn't she acknowledge her age? What was the big deal?

"Getting old sucks," Mary suddenly pronounced. "Pardon my French. Again. The only thing that makes it tolerable, from what I can tell so far, is that you're given a kind of license to be a little nutty or wacky. Not too out there, otherwise people think you need to be in a nursing facility. Just . . . colorful. I mean, if I took to wearing my makeup like Lynn Yaeger wears hers—more power to her, by the way—hardly anyone would blink an eye. Look at that batty old woman with the bizarre makeup! End of. There's a license to being 'a certain age,' if you choose to go the oddball route. I'm not saying that

I, personally, do choose that route, but if I did decide to wear bells on my toes and paint my nails neon yellow and dress only in polka-dotted clothing, I would be bothering nobody."

"You don't have to be old to present yourself in a unique way through your clothes or hair or makeup," Sandra pointed out.

"Of course not," Mary agreed. "But it's difficult to be nutty as an adult when you've made your priority a career in the law, like I did, or when you have to present as a responsible parent, someone who doesn't totally embarrass her kids at school functions. For those of us for whom an 'acceptable appearance' mattered, no longer having to show up for the people you once had to impress is kind of cool."

Sandra laughed. "I can just imagine what Jack or Kate would have said if I dropped them off at school wearing purple harem pants and bangles up and down my arms and black lipstick. In some places, that would be run of the mill. But not in Yorktide."

"People also assume that older people are going to say whatever's on their mind," Mary went on, "no matter how outrageous or insulting it is, because older people just don't care what other people think of them. I mean, aging shouldn't be a license for bad behavior, but on the other hand, I can understand that if you've been around for sixty, seventy, eighty years, you've accepted that not everyone you meet is going to like you and that you're under no obligation to like everyone you meet. So, just being yourself is finally easier than it has been since you were a child, before you got molded into a polite, socially acceptable citizen."

"Okay, anything else that's good or at least bearable about getting old?" Amanda asked with a bit of a smile. Mary was entertaining once she got going.

"Nope," Mary said stoutly. "Do you know that when I was thirty I was still able to eat a pint of ice cream in one sitting without any ill effects? By the time I was forty, I'd had to go off ice cream because of the disgusting things it did with my lower intestines, not to mention the fact that if I even looked at a pint of ice cream I'd immediately gain five pounds. Good times, those early days. An entire pint. Damn."

"Yeah, but what about all the wisdom you've acquired from years of experience?" Amanda said. "Doesn't that make being an older person valuable?"

Mary shook her head. "Whatever wisdom we garner is countered by the havoc wreaked by years of heartbreak and disappointment."

"What doesn't kill you makes you stronger," Patty added. "My father always said that."

Mary laughed. "What doesn't kill you leaves you scarred, wary, and weary."

"You need another glass of wine," Amanda suggested. "That might lift your spirits."

"And that's another thing!" Mary cried. "Do you know how much I could drink without ever having a hangover? I could easily manage a bottle of wine over the course of an evening. Now? Well, not so much."

"Hardly the end of the world," Sandra pointed out.

"Of course not," Mary agreed with a shrug. "I'm just saying."

Amanda shook her head. "I think I'm the one who needs another glass of wine," she said. "You guys are making me depressed. I'm fifty-six. I know I'm not young, but neither am I ancient, and yet, right now I feel like throwing in the proverbial towel. If there's nothing positive about getting old, why bother?"

Patty's eyes widened. "You're not—"

"Of course not," Amanda scolded. "But come on, there's *life* to consider. I mean, breathing, eating, sleeping, listening to bird song and playing music, going to movies or reading or whatever it is you like to do, taking care of your cats and dogs, talking to your friends—"

"The ones still alive!"

"Mary!" Sandra frowned and turned to Amanda. "I agree

with you, Amanda. Life itself is still there for the enjoying until the spirit is ready to move on."

Mary shrugged. "Yeah, okay, Amanda has a point. Hey, this was just me being cantankerous. There are lots of things I still enjoy and am in no hurry to let go of. Reading. Watching old black-and-white movies. Taking long walks, no matter the time of the year. One day I won't be able to walk for as long or as far as I can now but . . . And here I am again, back to the theme of loss and diminishment! Where's that glass of wine Amanda suggested?"

"A glass of wine won't solve anything," Sandra pointed out.

"I know. But it will make the problem seem less thorny."

"That's true. I'll get a fresh bottle." Sandra rose from the table. "And I think we should toast the chef."

Amanda felt inordinately pleased by the compliments about her food, and realized that she had enjoyed the spirited conversation around the dinner table. Life with Liam had become awfully quiet. Silence was fine, mostly; when you were on your own it could even be soothing. But so often when you were with another person, silence could be unpleasant and even, strangely, loud.

"Here we are," Sandra said as she returned to the table and filled each glass for a toast. "To the chef!"

"To the chef!"

Amanda raised her glass, as well. "And to my summer roommates," she said.

Chapter 29

Sandra had gone into town to buy stamps at the post office. She knew she could buy stamps online, but she liked going to the old post office. Even as a child she had found the experience a bit of an adventure. The postmaster at the time had been in his position for more years than anyone could remember. It was a position of trust and responsibility, and he had a certain dignified place in Yorktide. Mr. Glass was an important man in the community.

All that was changed, of course. There was little if any prestige in being a federal employee these days, at least, from what Sandra could tell. Well, nothing stayed the same and there was nothing much to be done about it.

When she came out of the post office, she was happy to see Phil James standing on the sidewalk almost as if waiting for her.

"Sandra, hello," he said, stepping closer, a smile on his handsome, weatherworn face. "It's good to see you."

"And you," she said genuinely. "How are you, Phil?"

Phil James, seventy-five, was a local man, respected and well liked. His family had lived in Maine since the early nineteenth century, and while the family fortunes had gone up and down over the years, not one member had left the state for the chance of a better life elsewhere. Phil was one of the more successful members of the family. He had made his living as an engineer at the power plant about an hour north of Yorktide. He had done well and lived in some comfort. For most of his life he had served as a volunteer fireman, joining the force while still in his teens and only giving up the work when a knee injury made it impossible for him to be of real value on the site of an emergency.

Phil was a widower of many years. He and his wife, Nancy, had had no children. To Sandra's knowledge, Phil had never been tempted to remarry. And yet, Sandra knew of several women in Yorktide who would happily accept an invitation to dinner from such a kind, intelligent, and nice-looking man.

"As well as can be expected," Phil replied, "maybe a bit better than that. I hear you've a few ladies living with you this summer."

"Yes. I've rented out the extra bedrooms. So far, things are going well."

"I'm glad to hear it. I saw that one of your boarders, if that's the right word to use, Patty Porter, has taken a job at Crystal Breeze. I'm friendly with the owner, you know. She carries my candles and honey."

Sandra nodded. "Yes, Patty took the job shortly after she moved in."

"From where does she hail, do you know? Just my curiosity," he added hurriedly. "Used to drive my mother crazy, always asking questions."

Sandra hesitated. It wasn't her place to reveal Patty's address. But she saw no harm in saying: "I believe she's currently living in New Hampshire. She has family there."

"Hmm. Well, Michelle says she's a nice person. A bit old-fashioned."

Sandra bit back a smile. It was clear that Phil was interested in Patty in a romantic sort of way and was hoping for some tidbit of information about her that he might use to encourage her interest in return. Well, Sandra didn't want to stand in the way of a possible friendship.

"Patty is a nice person," Sandra said with a smile. "And it's true about her being a bit old-fashioned. It's not a bad thing."

"No. Yes. Yes, well, I'd better be off. Take care, Sandra."

Sandra promised him that she would.

There was no doubt about it, she thought. Phil James had it bad for Patty Porter.

When she arrived home, Sandra found that she had missed a call from Kate, who had left a message saying that she would be able to visit soon, and would call back with details.

Sandra was pleased. Her children meant so much to her, especially now that her parents, brother, and husband were gone. As she made herself a cup of tea, Sandra remembered how blindsided she had felt when Jack and his first wife had announced they were divorcing, even though right from the start Sandra had worried that the two were fundamentally unsuited. Jack was carefree and often careless; Helen, in contrast, was a very mature and sensible person. Helen had often made excuses for Jack's irresponsible behavior and downright babied him. Such a dynamic in a relationship might not be all that unusual, but Sandra had strongly suspected that at some point both would tire of it.

Sadly, she had been proved right. Sandra had witnessed Jack becoming more mature over time, but maybe the early years had set a bad precedent for the pair. It was near impossible to completely reverse or restructure a relationship's dynamic.

The final meeting between Sandra and Helen, just before the divorce was finalized, had been brief and tearful. Neither woman had promised to stay in touch. How could they have promised? Two years later, Sandra received a note from Helen saying that she was engaged. She hoped the family was well and thanked Sandra for having been a supportive mother-in-law. That was the last time Sandra had heard from Helen.

Not long after Sandra's having received Helen's letter, Jack met Robbi, the woman who would become his second wife. Like Jack, Robbi had also been married before and had no children. Sandra couldn't really say if she liked her second daughter-in-law. She didn't really know her. They had spent very little time together since her wedding to Jack. But there was no denying that Jack and Robbi seemed happy.

As were Kate and Carrie. Carrie, who was in her early thirties, was one of those people who everyone loved pretty much immediately. She was open without being an over-sharer, straightforward without being tactless, and empathetic without being condescending. Whenever the couple visited Maine, Sandra and her daughter-in-law spent a significant amount of time on their own together, sometimes at the beach, sometimes window-shopping in a nearby town, oftentimes cooking.

If only Kate and Carrie didn't live so far away. Rochester, New York, was not a hop, skip, and a jump from Yorktide. And if only the women would decide to start a family! Kate had always been good with children. She had been a very popular babysitter when she was young. Sandra had just assumed that Kate would want children of her own one day. But Sandra had learned the hard way never to assume you really knew your children.

Sandra took the last sip of her tea and put the empty mug into the dishwasher.

She was glad she had run into Phil James earlier. He was such a nice man. It would be good if he and Patty hit it off. Then again, even if they did, Patty was going back to her family in New Hampshire come the end of the summer. Sandra felt very sure that there was no way Phil would ever leave Maine, not even for love. But maybe a short-term romance, even if it consisted of just a few lunch dates and evening strolls along the beach over the course of three or four weeks, might just be what both Patty and Phil needed at this moment in their lives.

Sandra hoped that was the case.

Chapter 30

"Stupid art class," Mary muttered as she strode toward her car.

The class had been held in the basement of Yorktide's community center. Not exactly a great place for painting if you were hoping for good natural light, but Mary could imagine worse settings.

There were seven students that morning, including Mary, all female, ranging in age from mid-twenties to mid-seventies. Clearly, the other women knew one another either as friends or as familiar faces from around Yorktide. Oh, well, Mary had thought. She didn't need to be anyone's buddy, and she wasn't afraid to be the outsider. She was there to learn.

The instructor, who told the students to call her by her first name, Louisa, explained that she worked at the local grade school as the art teacher. She was excited, she said, to be working with adults. Teaching children how to draw and paint was satisfying in its own way, but it was a bit like trying to herd cats. Everyone, including Mary, laughed politely. Louisa looked to be in her forties, and, while she was pert and pretty, her hands certainly looked like the hands of a working artist—strong, nails cut short, and stained with pigment. Mary was heartened.

The first lesson in drawing, Louisa told her students, would concentrate on learning how to sketch. How hard could it be to sketch? Mary had thought. Louisa said to work swiftly, to not be afraid of making mistakes, to try to capture the overall look of the simple still-life composition she had arranged: an earthenware jug, an apple, a crystal goblet.

It took all of a few seconds for Mary to realize that sketching was far more difficult than she had imagined. She had glanced at the others, every one of whom was working swiftly as instructed. Recognizable images were appearing on their sketch pads.

Again, Mary touched her pencil to the paper, looked intently at the objects presented on the table before her, and . . .

Nothing. She simply could not move the pencil. Louisa had come over to her then, had placed her hand on Mary's and tried to guide the pencil to create a few lines that would suggest the jug, but it was as if a perverse imp had taken possession of Mary's motor skills. The result was a disaster. Louisa had quietly moved away.

"Don't give up," Louisa had advised Mary at the end of the class, in one of those obnoxiously cheery voices that even her grade school students had probably come to loathe. Mary thought that if Louisa went on to say something like, "Tomorrow is another day," she would scream.

Mary had left the room quickly, hoping to avoid the chatting women and their proper sketches. She had paid in advance for the course, which consisted of five two-hour lessons. There was no refund. Well, that money was gone, but Mary didn't really care. She was not going back ever again. She was not going to knowingly put herself in a situation where she was the laughingstock. (An outsider, no problem. A laughingstock, no way.) Okay, no one had actually laughed at her ruinous efforts at sketching, but Mary just knew they had wanted to laugh. A five-year-old could have produced a better picture using a fat crayon than Mary had with a drawing pencil that had cost her ten dollars.

It was a mystery. She had taken art history classes through-out college. Since then, she had been in the habit of buying and actually reading books of art criticism and art history. She owned many original works of art, and she treasured them. She knew she had a good eye, an instinct for what was truly worth-while, and what was genuinely valuable. Her color sense was enviable.

Then why the hell couldn't she draw, let alone sketch? It was frustrating in the extreme. It was mortifying. But in truth she had never attempted to draw or to paint before now. Maybe she simply had missed her opportunity. Maybe if she had taken lessons early on in her life she might have achieved some small mastery of the basics.

It was too late to know.

Mary got into her car and tossed her bag of materials into the back seat. And then she sat behind the wheel, staring ahead at nothing.

What in the world was she going to do with herself for the next ten, fifteen, or even twenty years? Was it legitimate to just hang around all morning, to read for a while in the after-noon, to walk a bit in the evening, to let one's mind wander, to take a nap at an odd hour? Was it morally acceptable to be a human slug?

If you were just "living your life," harming no one (at least, not to your knowledge), minding your own business, well, was that enough? Didn't everyone owe a duty to others to do more than not harm or annoy them? Weren't you supposed to *do* good, be active, be involved in making the lives of others somehow better?

It was what Mary had been trying to do for the past four decades in her career, but now, she was tired. She wanted to rest, to turn her back on certain emotionally draining dynam-ics, but something about doing so seemed wrong. Her parents had been dead for a long time but still, Mary could hear their voices in her head, telling her to get out of bed, to stop wasting time, to make herself useful. Human beings were not meant to stagnate. Decompressing could lead to decomposing. She who was not busy changing was busy dying. The New Testament clearly stated that you were not supposed to hide your light under a bushel.

With a sigh of frustration, Mary started the car. She didn't feel like going straight back to Sandra's house. Instead, she would just drive around for a while. Maybe she would stumble upon something interesting, a flea market or a garage sale, something to take her mind off the large and looming question of what to do with her future.

Chapter 31

Patty had retrieved a broom from the shop's storeroom and was pushing sand, a few small scraps of paper, and bits of broken leaves to the curb and from there, into the street, as Michelle had instructed her to do. She had never used a push broom before and felt a bit embarrassed, like a character in an old movie. Maybe she should be wearing a boiler suit and cap or something. But in fact, there was no shame in what she had been asked to do by her employer. She just had to remind herself of that fact.

Besides, it was a really nice day and being outside in the fresh air was pleasant. If only she could stop thinking about the voice mail from her sister Bridget that she had ignored. Patty knew she would have to return the call soon. She was sure that Teri had mentioned Patty's recent call, and equally as sure that the sisters had indulged in a catty chat in which they bemoaned the bad luck that had left them saddled with their errant sister just at the time of their lives when they were ready to enjoy a well-earned rest. No doubt they would feel self-satisfied and morally superior.

"Hello."

Patty startled at the sound of a voice just over her shoulder and whirled around. She felt herself blush. Now she definitely felt embarrassed about being caught wielding a broom. It was the man she had seen in the shop before, delivering boxes of candles and honey.

"Hi," she said.

"I don't know if you remember me, but we saw each other in the shop once," the man went on. "My name is Phil, Phil James."

He extended his hand and Patty took it. It was a nice hand, strong, but Mr. James didn't use his hand to crush hers like some men did. Too many men.

And he was kind of handsome actually, not the type she had always been attracted to, but that was all in the past anyway. He was wiry of build and not tall, but not short, either. He had kind eyes. His hair was silver, and there was quite a bit of it. He was wearing jeans and a lightweight plaid shirt with the sleeves rolled up. His brown boots looked well-worn. She wondered how old he was.

"I'm Patty Porter," she said. "I'm staying at Sandra Pennington's house this summer."

"I know. What I mean is," Phil went on hastily, "I know Sandra, and she mentioned she was running a sort of bed-and-breakfast or what have you."

"Yes. I'm not sure what it is, really. But it's nice. I mean, Sandra's really nice and the house is . . . really nice."

"I hope you're not working all hours," Phil said, with a glance toward the shop. "There's a lot to enjoy in these parts."

Patty smiled. "I've been to the beach a few times. I went with Sandra one evening after dinner. It was really nice then. Peaceful."

"I like to take my boat out in the evenings when I have the chance."

"You have a boat?" Patty hoped her excitement hadn't been too obvious. She loved being on a boat.

"Nothing fancy," Phil explained, "but she's seaworthy. Her name is Dolly."

"I haven't been on a boat in years. I think boats are great. What I mean is . . ." Patty laughed a bit shyly. "Well, you know."

Phil smiled and nodded to the box he was carrying. "Well, I'd better be on my way and deliver these. I guess I'll see you around."

"I guess you will."

Patty watched as he strode down the sidewalk. She hoped that they would meet again. He really was very nice.

The door to the shop opened behind her.

"Patty!"

Patty turned abruptly to find her boss, Michelle, standing in the doorway. "As soon as you're finished sweeping, could you open the delivery that came this morning, check it's what we ordered? We've had some trouble with the vendor in the past."

"Sure," Patty said, managing a smile. "Right away."

Chapter 32

Amanda stirred the sauce for the vegetarian curry dish she was preparing. It was a variation of something called Undhiyu, made with fried vegetables and chickpea dumplings. She enjoyed cooking for herself though she preferred to cook for others. In the early years of her relationship with Liam, she had prepared his favorite meals several times a week. After a time, this habit had sort of faded away so that currently, Amanda prepared Liam one of his favorite dishes only on his birthday. Come to think of it, he hadn't actually *asked* for her to cook something special for him in ages.

An odd thought struck Amanda then. Had she really enjoyed the act of preparing the meals for Liam's sake, to make him happy, or had preparing the meals been more of a performance, a way of showing off her culinary skills, even a way of exercising a bit of control over her partner?

Amanda frowned. Where were these ridiculous thoughts coming from?

Patty suddenly appeared in the entrance to the kitchen. Her face was screwed up in an almost cartoon-like grimace.

"Hi," Amanda said, a bit taken aback at the extremity of her housemate's appearance. "What's wrong?"

"What are you making?" Patty asked, grimace still in place.

"An Indian dish called Undhiyu."

"It's got curry in it, doesn't it?"

Amanda bit back a snippy reply. Did Patty really not know that *curry* was a generic term for a combination of spices? "There's a curry mixture involved, yes. This particular one has cumin, turmeric, coriander, and ginger."

Patty put her hand over her mouth and nose now. "The smell has always made me sick, ever since I was a little girl. One of our neighbors made curry dishes, and the smell came right across her yard and into our house."

"I'm sorry," Amanda said. "I didn't know." She wondered briefly if she felt offended by Patty's comment. But why should she be offended? It wasn't like Patty was saying that Amanda herself made Patty feel sick.

"Could you stop cooking?" Patty's tone was becoming desperate. "I mean, clear it all away or something. I really feel nauseous."

Amanda shook her head. "But I'm . . . No, I can't just stop cooking. The dish is almost prepared. And I'm not going to throw out a perfectly good meal just because you don't like the way it smells. Can't you, I don't know, go outside and get some fresh air?"

"It's eighty-five degrees and humid out there! No, I can't just go outside and get some fresh air!"

"I'm sorry," Amanda said, "but I really don't know what to do."

Suddenly, Patty turned and dashed from the kitchen. Amanda shook her head and turned back to the stove.

"What's going on?" It was Sandra, come into the kitchen. "I just saw Patty dashing up the stairs. She looked a bit green around the gills."

Amanda sighed and explained the situation. "I've got the fan on high," she said. "I feel bad for her, but really, how is this my problem? If I had known she had such an aversion to curry spices I wouldn't have made this dish, or I would have left out the spice she finds most offensive. Anyway, I'm almost done and the smell should dissipate before too long."

"I think it smells yummy," Sandra said. "Yorktide used to have an Indian restaurant but that was ages ago. I'm afraid we're not a very diverse community in this neck of the woods. You have to go to Portland for Indian or Thai or good Mexican cuisine. Anyway, I'm sure Patty will be fine. Don't worry about it."

"Thanks," Amanda said. "Sorry for the fuss."

Sandra got herself a glass of lemonade and went off.

Amanda put the finishing touches on the dish and put it aside. It would taste better after having sat for a while. She proceeded then to clean up. For some reason she couldn't quite name, the incident with Patty had really bothered her. She tried to imagine how she would feel if she was the one who was made sick by an odor caused by her roommate's cooking. She suspected that she would feel frustrated, maybe even angry. She would expect—or at least, she would want—the person who had unwittingly offended to respond to her complaint with compassion. And if the offender didn't sincerely apologize she would be hurt.

Suddenly, Amanda recalled how, a few days earlier, Mary had asked Patty not to spritz on her perfume in one of the shared bathrooms. (Amanda had overheard the confrontation. Mary didn't speak softly.) Patty seemed to have forgotten that just recently she had unwittingly caused discomfort to one of her housemates. If she had remembered, she might not have made such a fuss about the smell of Amanda's cooking.

Still, wasn't she, Amanda, a bit to blame? Maybe she should have checked with the other women about any sensitivities to food smells or textures. Lots of people didn't like oysters just because they were slimy. But why was that her responsibility? Still, it would have been a polite thing to do.

Maybe, Amanda suddenly thought, she wasn't very respectful of Liam's likes and dislikes, either. He certainly was respectful of hers. There was no point in denying that.

There was an obvious case in point. Liam was allergic to roses, but roses were Amanda's favorite flower, and two or three times a year she treated herself to a dozen freshly cut blooms. Liam suffered on these occasions—there was lots of sneezing—but he told her that he didn't mind the inconvenience, not as long as the flowers pleased Amanda. But now, standing on her own in Sandra's kitchen, Amanda wondered if Liam *did* really mind. Maybe he was just being nice to her, accommodating of her desires.

Amanda's conscience squirmed. Was it really necessary for her to have the roses in the apartment? Was she really incapable of making the small sacrifice of keeping the apartment rose-free for the sake of the man she was supposed to love?

If that was the case, Amanda thought, if she was indeed so deeply selfish, then maybe it was better if she lived on her own. She didn't think that she was exactly toxic to other people, but maybe she wasn't exactly good for them, either. If that were the case, how did she get this way? Had she been born with a deficiency of whatever it was that allowed a person to develop the talent of empathy? Of sympathy? Had she always lacked the capacity to properly connect to others? Or had something—or a series of somethings—happened to her over the course of her life to bring her to this point in time, questioning her fitness for human companionship?

Amanda glanced at the pot of Undhiyu she had made with such enjoyment. She had absolutely no appetite for it now.

Chapter 33

Sandra was seated at the kitchen table, leafing through a home decorating magazine. Even though she had no desire to redecorate her own house at this point in her life, she loved seeing what others were doing with their homes.

As she leafed past ads for high-end bath fixtures and carpets that cost a veritable fortune, she thought about the little contretemps that had occurred between Patty and Amanda the other day. If the four of them—Sandra, Mary, Amanda, and Patty—were a permanent household, not just summer roommates, she supposed they would be compelled to establish rules about certain foods that could not be cooked, certain perfumes that could not be applied, certain types of music that could not be played at certain hours on certain days.

But what if a person just didn't care enough about her roommates to stick to the rules of the house? How could you successfully legislate behavior?

In a romantic partnership, Sandra thought, mutual respect was—or should be—a given. One partner is a vegan; the other is an omnivore. They agree not to attempt to convert the other to their way of eating/thinking. The omnivore promises not to eat red meat in the house and the vegan swears they won't impose a vegetarian diet on the cat. Some solution is found. And if an equitable solution can't be found, then the couple either splits, or one party gives in and grows resentful and then the relationship dribbles on miserably, useless to all involved.

But in a permanent housemate situation? Sandra frowned. Maybe it was a good thing she was sharing her home for the summer only!

The doorbell rang just then and Sandra sprang from her chair. Kate had arrived!

Sandra hurried to open the front door. Her daughter looked good, Sandra thought, healthy if a bit tired, but that might be due to the long drive from Rochester, New York, to Yorktide, Maine. Kate was wearing a pair of cargo shorts, wrinkled from sitting behind the wheel, and a dark, short-sleeved T-shirt. Apart from her simple platinum wedding ring and a large Swiss Army-brand watch Carrie had given her for her forty-fifth birthday, Kate wore no jewelry. Her hair—Kate had her father's hair—was light brown, streaked golden at the moment thanks to the summer sun. Kate traveled lightly, all of her gear, including, Sandra assumed, a pair of sturdy walking shoes—Kate liked to ramble—tucked into one medium-sized wheelie bag.

Kate gave her mother a tight hug and then, stepping back, looked at her intently from head to toe.

"What on earth are you doing?" Sandra asked with a laugh.

"Inspecting you. You look good. Healthy. Not like you're under any undue strain. Am I right?"

"You're right. I'm fine, Kate. Really. Now, come in and get settled."

During the course of the afternoon, Kate briefly met all three of her mother's roommates and, much to Sandra's relief, Kate hadn't quizzed any of them on the state of their finances or any hidden criminal past. Conveniently, Sandra thought, Mary, Patty, and Amanda each had plans for dinner out, allowing Sandra and Kate to dine alone together. They feasted on swordfish steaks, green beans, and baked potatoes, with raspberry sherbet for dessert. During dinner, Kate reverted once again to her overprotective mode, probing into details of her mother's physical health, asking questions about the condition of the house—when was the last time the roof had been inspected?—and reminding Sandra that, with Emma now largely removed from her life, Sandra might want to talk through the grieving process with a therapist.

"Stop!" Sandra laughed finally. "I'm fine, really. You remind me of myself when you came out all those years ago. Remember how I fussed and hovered and basically drove you mad with my worrying?"

Kate looked stunned. "Sheesh, I hope I'm not that bad!"

"You are. Almost. Look, I appreciate your concern, I do, but it's not really necessary. At least, not yet."

Kate agreed to attempt to control her overprotective impulses where her mother was concerned.

They had gone up to bed at around ten o'clock, not long after the other women had returned from wherever it was they had been. Sandra noted with some amusement that Kate still wore to bed what she had been wearing since she was a teen, light pajama pants and a T-shirt. This T-shirt had the word *Peacenik* splashed across it in neon green; the pajama pants were bright purple. Sandra, on the other hand, had always preferred to sleep in a long nightgown, plaid flannel or white cotton, depending on the time of the year. Interestingly to Sandra, she and her daughter, so different in so many ways, preferred the same type of slipper, a closed-toe slide that could be worn with socks in winter. It was one of the very few surface characteristics, if that was the right word, they had in common.

"I like Mary," Kate announced, when she had lain down on what had been her father's side of the bed. "She's solid. You get the feeling she's been through a lot but isn't at all interested in throwing a pity party."

"Yes," Sandra agreed. "She's a perfect houseguest or roommate. A few weeks back she and Patty had a momentary tussle about Patty's wearing so much perfume. I don't know exactly how they left it, but I did notice that the bathrooms haven't smelled quite so heavily of gardenias since then."

Kate laughed. "I'm with Mary. People need to be aware of announcing their presence from a mile off. Anyway, Amanda seems kind of lost or something. Do you get that sense from her?"

Sandra shook her head. "I'm not sure. I can't quite figure her out. She doesn't reveal much about herself. But that doesn't mean she's lost."

"Maybe *lost* isn't the right word, then. But she doesn't seem solid, like Mary. She seems sort of hazy, unformed or something. Maybe the way she dresses is coloring my perception of her personality. So—bland."

"Well," Sandra said, "I know that she left her partner back home in Massachusetts for the summer. They've been together for eight years, I think she said. I don't know why she's spending the summer away from him, something about his being really busy with work, I think. She rarely mentions him, and for some reason I don't think they've spoken often since she got here. But maybe this is a normal dynamic for them, periodic separations, a way to revive things."

"Hmm. Something's definitely up in that relationship. Well, I hope they figure it out. Not our concern."

"Oh," Sandra went on, "and there was a bit of a conflict between Amanda and Patty, but this time Patty was the one with the complaint. Amanda was making a curry dish and Patty claimed the smell was making her sick." Sandra shook her head. "We seem to be a bunch with more than the usual odor sensitivities!"

"On to Patty, then." Kate frowned. "She strikes me as kind of sad. I see her as someone who never really grew up, some-one who's continually being surprised by the hard facts of life most of us have come to accept by the time we're in our twenties. I mean, she's nice enough, just . . . Let's put it this way. There's no possible world in which she and I could be friends. And it's not just about the perfume and the makeup."

Sandra smiled. "Yes. You two are about as opposite as people can get. And I think she keeps a lot about her life to herself, which of course is her right. Sometimes I get the sense that she feels inferior or . . . I don't know. In the end, she's harmless." Except when attempting to feed cream to Clovis, Sandra thought. But Kate didn't need to know about that incident.

"You know," Kate said suddenly, "it's weird seeing strangers in the house. It's unsettling. A person's childhood home is sacro-sanct or something. Maybe that's just nostalgia talking. But I feel like Mary, Amanda, and Patty are intruders in some way."

Sandra was surprised by Kate's words. Her daughter had never expressed any strong tie to the house before now.

"I'm sorry," she said. "I didn't think it would be so upset-ting for you."

"It's not a problem," Kate said quickly. "The house is yours, not mine. Anyway, I'm glad I grew up here."

"I'm glad that you're glad. Do you think your brother ap-preciates having grown up in Yorktide?"

Kate shrugged. "I don't know. We've never spoken about it."

The women were silent for a long moment. It wasn't at all unpleasant, Sandra thought, to be sharing a bed with her daughter, but it was unusual. She and John hadn't been the sort of parents who welcomed their children sleeping with them. Maybe that was a societal habit that had come later, after Jack and Kate were grown. Whatever the reason, the only times that Jack or Kate had ever shared their parents' bed had been when one or the other had woken from a nightmare and come running for comfort. Maybe the family had missed out on something good. Too late now to say.

"What are you thinking about?" Sandra asked after a while, noting Kate's pensive expression.

Kate sighed. "The few times that Carrie's been away, say to visit her family, and I've been in our bed on my own, it's so . . . so not right. Not the way it should be. My sleep is totally disrupted. Her place is by my side and my place is by hers. I know she's feeling the same way tonight."

"It was like that with your father and me," Sandra told her. "It still is, five years after his death. Sometimes I think I'll never get past missing his bodily presence, who he was as a physical person, let alone his spirit."

Kate reached for her mother's hand. "I'm sorry, Mom. I miss Dad, too. I really do. I'm sure I became a lawyer because of the example he set and his genuine love of the law. He cared about what he was doing. That counts for something, I think."

"It counts for a lot. He helped so many people in the course of his career."

Kate shifted onto her side so that she was facing her mother. "I know I've asked you this before," she said, "in a belligerent sort of way, but now I'm asking with respect. Did you really never want a career of your own?"

Sandra smiled "Honestly, no. Oh, there were times over the years when I'd find myself wondering what it would be like to be an educator, or a librarian, maybe even a lawyer. But I never felt the need to pursue those paths. I don't think it was fear or laziness that held me back. I was genuinely content in my chosen roles as mother and wife, neither of which is all that easy. I mean, lots of people get married and have children, but to make a real go of it takes luck, certainly, but also a fair amount of skill."

"I remember when your answer would send me wild with anger, when I'd chastise you for not making a mark in the wider world. Now, I admire you for living your own life, for being your authentic self."

"Thank you," Sandra said. "Not everyone has the opportunity to live the way that feels right to them. I know that I'm extremely lucky. Now, let's turn out the lights. I'm tired."

Within moments, Kate was asleep, her breathing slow and even. Sandra looked at her grown daughter with a tenderness that hadn't faded or lessened in intensity since Kate had been an infant sleeping in her crib.

Chapter 34

Mary had spent a good deal of the day rereading—for the third time—one of her favorite novels. It was titled *The Historian*, and it was the first novel of writer Elizabeth Kostova. She didn't understand people who read a book once and were done with it. Of course, that was understandable if the book hadn't really been worth reading even the first time, but to put aside a good book after an initial read seemed downright nuts to Mary. You didn't listen to a song once, enjoy it, and never listen to it again. You didn't watch a movie or look at a painting and then walk away forever, not if you had found the movie or painting moving.

Now, it was early evening. Mary glanced in the mirror that hung over her dresser. She looked presentable enough, she decided, for the evening to come. She would be having dinner with Sandra and her daughter, Kate, who had arrived the day before for a short visit. The other houseguests were unavailable to join them.

Supposedly, Patty was helping her boss take inventory. Mary assumed that Patty was getting paid for her efforts. At least, she hoped that Patty wasn't being taken advantage of; Patty struck her as the sort of person an unscrupulous boss might easily dupe. There wasn't really a way for her to ask Patty if she was being compensated for the extra hours without sounding like she was prying. After all, she hardly knew Patty Porter. It was not her responsibility to teach Patty how to get the respect a good employee deserved from her employer. But if Patty did come to her seeking advice, Mary would be more than pleased to give it.

Amanda had gone off to see one of those big summer action flicks with robots for heroes and lots of gadgets to help the heroes kill the bad guys, who also might be robots or maybe distorted figures from someone's mythology, or perhaps comic book figures in skintight rubber costumes that exaggerated body parts in truly disgusting ways. In short, not the sort of movie Mary could tolerate. What had Amanda said was the title? Whatever the title, the movie was part four or five or six in a franchise that was, presumably, making certain people in Hollywood very rich.

Mary had offered to leave mother and daughter alone together that evening, but both had insisted she join them for dinner, and Mary had accepted the invitation. Now, she joined the Penningtons in the kitchen. Sandra had made chicken piccata, a dish Mary hadn't had in years. There was broccoli from one of the local farms and bread from the local bakery. Mary contributed a bottle of the Sauvignon Blanc she knew her host liked.

Kate Pennington was what Mary's mother used to call a smart cookie, though Mrs. Fraser had always used the expression with a note of criticism in her tone. Mary, however, saw nothing to criticize in Sandra's daughter. Kate was intelligent and straightforward, and, if some of her comments could occasionally be sharp, other comments proved that her heart was in the right place.

Mother and daughter didn't look much alike in terms of physical characteristics like overall build, shape of face, hair and eye color, but Mary could see evidence of a genetic link in the way they used their hands when speaking, how they crossed their legs, the manner in which they tilted their heads when listening to another person speak.

Once the three women were seated at the kitchen table, Mary and Kate chatted briefly about their life in law, and while Mary was indeed grateful for the conversation, she had no intention of mentioning the lawsuit that had been filed against her firm. It was still too painful a topic for her to discuss. But it was good to talk, however briefly, to another person who shared to some extent the thrills and the pressures of a career in the law.

Eventually, as might be expected, talk turned to the subject of Sandra's summer roommate experiment.

"I have to admit," Kate told Mary, "I wasn't keen on Mom's idea of using this place as a sort of bed-and-breakfast for the summer. I was worried it would be too much work and stress for her." She turned then to her mother and smiled. "But I'm glad to have been proved wrong. At least, I think I have been."

"I can't speak for Sandra, of course, but I think we have a pleasant household here." Mary laughed. "Maybe we generally get along because we know we won't be stuck together under one roof forever. Whatever the case, we're compatible enough. And we're not in one another's pockets all day. We go off and do our own thing. Well, that's my take. So, Sandra, what do you think about this little community?"

Sandra nodded. "I think this is a pretty peaceful house at the moment. And I still think the idea of adults, whatever their age, sharing a household, is a strong and a viable idea that might solve a lot of problems surrounding the aging population and their right to live comfortably."

"And affordably," Mary added. "It's all well and good that people are living longer than ever before but not so great if the cost of living prevents having quality of life."

Kate nodded. "Hear, hear. I think lots of people are realizing that the ultimate goal isn't necessarily to be entirely independent but, rather, to be interdependent."

"Easier to accomplish when in an established relationship." Mary stopped to think a moment before adding: "Unless, of course, one member of the relationship assumes from the start that the other member is the one who should do the caregiving."

"Mostly, that's been men," Kate noted, "at least, in a heterosexual union."

"Or self-centered people," Sandra noted. "And there are plenty of women who fall into that category, too. Or a partner who's a good deal older than the other partner. Then, the assumption of who will be caretaker is at least understandable, maybe even reasonable."

After that, the conversation turned to less fraught topics. The state of Sandra's garden. The most recent hilarious rant of one of the late-night talk show hosts. The artist who had designed and crafted Mary's necklace. Suddenly, for no particular reason, Mary glanced at the clock on the kitchen wall and was astonished to see that it was already nine thirty.

"Wow, I didn't realize it was so late. I'll leave you two alone now," she said, getting up from her chair. "Let me just bring the rest of the dishes to the sink."

Sandra refused her offer, thanked her again for the wine, and shooed her housemate up to her room. As she prepared for bed, Mary reflected on how pleased she was to have spent the evening with Sandra and Kate Pennington. Companionship, particularly of the uncomplicated kind, and conversation when it was among similarly intelligent people, were both necessary for a healthy life.

Sometimes, Mary thought, both could be very hard to find.

Chapter 35

Patty sat on the edge of the bed in her room at Sandra's house, her hands tightly clasped.

She had patched things up with Amanda after the curry incident. Really, there had been no need for her to run from the kitchen; she hadn't felt *that* ill, just a bit queasy. And she had remembered how Mary had apologized for complaining about Patty's perfume giving her a headache. Together, Mary and Patty had admitted that living with other people took some social skills that neither of them had ever had the opportunity to hone.

But social skills had nothing to with the trouble Patty was in now. That morning she had discovered that there wasn't enough money in her checking account to pay the next week's rent. It wasn't the first time in her life she had made a mistake when trying to balance her checkbook or read her bank statements. She doubted that it would be the last.

Patty sighed. Maybe she shouldn't have bought more minutes on her phone until her paycheck had been deposited and had cleared. Maybe she shouldn't have spent twenty-five dollars on that T-shirt she didn't need. She already owned two pink T-shirts!

This was the second big mistake she had made in as many weeks, missing a rent payment after attempting to feed Clovis food that might make him ill. Her sisters were right. She was a stupid woman. Maybe they had never actually said so, but they certainly had implied as much.

Memories suddenly surfaced, uncomfortable memories of times in her life when men, boyfriends, had helped her out, given her money for expenses she hadn't counted on, or for items she wanted but couldn't otherwise afford. She didn't recall ever feeling uncomfortable about the transactions. Mostly, she had just felt grateful.

She could, she supposed, ask Bridget for a short-term loan. Teri would say no outright; she was always claiming near-poverty even when she and Kevin were spending money on a fancy new microwave they didn't really need. But Bridget might agree, though to ask would be humiliating and no doubt bring with it yet another lecture from her older sister about responsibility.

No, Patty decided. She would deal with this situation on her own. There was nothing to do but to tell Sandra, and the sooner the better. And she would hope and pray that Sandra didn't tell her daughter about the rent being late. Something about Kate frightened Patty. She didn't have her mother's softness.

Patty found Sandra in the living room. She was reading a book. Patty was struck as she always was by Sandra's air of maturity. She was always so calm and collected. Patty was pretty sure nobody had ever considered *her* calm and collected. Patty Porter was a lot of things, but calm and collected she had never been.

"Sandra?" she ventured. "I have to speak with you."

Sandra smiled and nodded.

"My rent is going to be late this week," Patty said in a rush. "I'm very sorry. I made a mistake when I was doing my checkbook and . . . I'm sorry. I swear I'll pay you the moment I get my next paycheck from the gift shop."

Patty literally held her breath while she waited for Sandra to say something. Sandra's expression—almost passive—hadn't changed at all, and somehow that was worse than if her face had made it clear what she was thinking or feeling. After what seemed like an endless moment, Sandra spoke.

"Thank you for telling me in advance," she said. "I appreciate that. When, exactly, do you expect your next paycheck? So that I can make a note in my own accounts."

Patty literally breathed a sigh of relief. "Thank you. I get paid again next Tuesday. I know what it says in the contract I signed, and I'm so very sorry for causing trouble. I—"

"Patty," Sandra interrupted, "it's all right. I know you'll pay what you owe as soon as possible. We all make mistakes or miscalculations from time to time."

Patty struggled not to cry. "Thank you. Do you think that we could keep this from the others?" She meant, most especially, that her failure might be kept from Kate.

Sandra nodded. "Of course. It's nobody's business but our own."

"Thank you," Patty breathed. "Thank you."

She left the living room hurriedly. She was deeply relieved that Sandra hadn't scolded her or worse, told her to leave, as she had the right to do as the owner of the house. Patty also felt embarrassed. And stupid. She needed to get out of the house and to be alone with her shame.

Patty wasn't a great fan of walking but she found herself heading off in the direction of downtown Yorktide. The sun was strong and she regretted not having worn a hat, but she couldn't bear to go back into the house. Not just yet.

As Patty trod along, down to the end of Spruce Street, and then onto Pine Street, she reviewed her life since she had retired from full-time work in mid-level administrative roles.

She had been a sales assistant in a stationery shop as well as in a clothing store, a lunchtime waitress at a diner, and, for a very brief time, she had been paid, under the table, to sit with an elderly woman while her daughter went to work. There had been a few times when Patty hadn't told her family about a particular job so that she could spend the money she earned as she liked, without having to listen to Bridget and Teri reminding her to put a few dollars in her savings account rather than waste money on a frivolous purchase. Patty had known—she had always known—that she was being childish, but, somehow, she could never seem to stop carelessly spending her money. She needed pretty things and new things. Her belongings, collectibles, clothing, jewelry, all of these made her happy.

But things don't pay the rent, do they? That could be Bridget or Teri speaking.

No, things didn't pay the rent. Money did. But was it good to live without pretty things or little pleasures? Didn't everyone have a right to the not-strictly-necessary? Patty had already had to relinquish so many small luxuries—professional hair coloring, manicures, massages—luxuries that had helped to define her in the world.

It wasn't fair! No, it wasn't, but that was life. Did anyone really care about her and the sacrifices she had been forced to make? Did her sisters secretly rejoice that the beautiful, celebrated Patty was now beholden to them?

Please, Patty prayed, let that not be true. She had never set out to hurt anyone in her entire life! If she had hurt anyone inadvertently then she was truly sorry and would make up for it if she could.

A car whizzed by, and Patty let out a cry. She had been lost in her thoughts and hadn't even heard the car approaching. She felt close to tears. Suddenly, the fact that she had not been one of Sandra's first choices as a summer guest seemed monumental, an ugly reminder that Patty Porter was always a bridesmaid—or a mistress—and never a bride. Patty Porter was always second best.

The sun continued to beat down. Patty felt sticky and teary. She was sweating. Girls don't sweat, her father used to say. They glow. Patty pulled the bottom of her shirt away from her body. She was not glowing. She was sweating.

Abruptly, she turned around and began to walk back to the house. Sandra's house. It was the only place she had to go.

And she really wished she had taken her car.

Not her car. Her sister's husband's car.

Chapter 36

Amanda found Sandra and Mary in the kitchen having coffee together.

Kate, Sandra's daughter, had gone home. Amanda was glad of this. She had felt uncomfortable around Kate. Once or twice she had caught Kate studying her—Amanda didn't think it had been her imagination—and it had made her feel both annoyed and vaguely embarrassed. She didn't know if Kate was a criminal lawyer—she hadn't bothered to ask—but she knew she would hate to face cross-questioning under that penetrating stare.

Still, it had been nice to see how well Sandra and Kate got along. Not every mother and adult daughter enjoyed each other's company. Her relationship to her own mother was close enough, Amanda thought, but they had never been friends as well as family. Maybe that was regrettable but it was too late now to change the relationship. Probably too late.

"There's fresh coffee in the pot," Sandra told her. "Help yourself."

"I'm good, but thanks. I was wondering if it would it be okay for me to do a jigsaw puzzle on the coffee table in the living room?" she asked. "I brought a puzzle with me without thinking about the possibility that there'd be no place for me to lay it out. The coffee table seems the right size."

"Sure," Sandra said. "That would be fine. The table is rarely used. As a matter of fact, I can't remember the last time I had anyone in for a sit-around-the-living-room visit. But I have to point out that Clovis might interfere. At the very least he'll be curious. You might find yourself chasing chewed up bits of cardboard."

"I'll take that risk," Amanda said with a smile. "And thanks."

"May I participate?" Mary asked. "Or do you like to do a puzzle on your own?"

"I don't know, really," Amanda admitted, joining the others at the table. "I've never done a puzzle with anyone else. When I was a kid my mother and I used to work on separate puzzles, side by side. I don't remember us helping each other. It was a bit of a contest, actually, who could finish first. But sure, why not do this puzzle as a team?"

"It'll be a first for the both of us," Mary said. "I haven't worked a jigsaw puzzle since I was a kid, and it was always alone. I was pretty good, too. I wonder why it's never occurred to me to get back into doing them."

"We can cover the puzzle at night so Clovis can't have a go at it," Amanda suggested.

Sandra smiled. "Though he'll probably try. Cats are compelled to open closed doors and uncover anything that's covered."

"What's going on?" It was Patty, standing in the doorway.

"We're going to do a jigsaw puzzle," Mary said. "Want to join in?"

"Sure," Patty said, taking the fourth seat at the table.

"I forgot to ask, did Kate get home all right?" Mary asked Sandra.

"Yes, thanks, she did. She's only been gone a day, but I already miss her."

"Did you experience empty-nest syndrome when your kids went off the college?" Amanda asked. "Were you depressed or, I don't know, did you feel at sixes and sevens?"

Sandra took another sip of her coffee before speaking. "I'd say that John was hit hard by Kate's leaving for college. Jack had gone off a few years before that, and John seemed hardly to blink an eye. Maybe it was a daddy and daughter thing; John and Kate were always very close. I suppose I felt a greater sense of sadness when Jack left home. He was my firstborn; we were alone with each other for three years before my daughter was born. Still, the experience wasn't crippling. And John and I had each other. I've heard that a fair number of couples break up when the kids leave for good. They realize they'd been staying together for the sake of the family, that they'd fallen out of love along the way. But John and I had always remained very close, so we were okay when the children left."

"My experience is of a mother who couldn't let go," Amanda told the others. "When I left home for college—and mind you, I was only two hours away—my mother called every single day to ask if I was eating properly—of course I wasn't—and dressing appropriately for the weather and getting to bed at a reasonable hour. It drove me nuts, and after a while I stopped taking her calls. Not all of them, but I cut it down to once every two or three days. It finally dawned on me that it wasn't so much that my mother didn't trust me to behave like an adult, but that she was worried she hadn't properly prepared me to be on my own. Those calls weren't really about me as much as they were about her feeling that maybe she'd failed. She needed me to prove to her that she had succeeded in raising a child capable of being independent. Once I figured out what was happening, I had more patience with her."

"Did you ever confront her with what you'd surmised about her calls?" Sandra asked.

Amanda laughed. "Gosh, no! She would have totally denied

having had any sense of failure. And maybe that's *not* what was prompting her incessant phone calls. Maybe she really didn't think I had it in me to survive without her. Maybe she just didn't have faith in me. Which would be odd, really, as I was always a pretty independent person. There was no way she couldn't have known that."

"My mother was happy to see the back of me," Mary said. "She was not a coddling type with either me or my brother, and certainly never failed to let us know how much work we were for her, how we'd ruined her figure—a lie, and I have the photos to prove that she was rotund before we were born—how she couldn't wait for us to grow up and have kids of our own so we'd know what we put her through."

Patty frowned. "It doesn't sound like you had a very loving home. Oh, I'm sorry. I didn't mean to offend you."

"No offense taken," Mary assured her. "Anyway, I guess my home was loving enough. It's just that my mom wasn't gooey and my dad and all the other fathers I knew weren't expected to be too involved in the lives of their kids, so it was our normal, having these two distant parents. Anyway, I couldn't wait to get away from home and never come back. I'm sure my mother was just as eager for me to go."

"Are you certain about that?" Sandra asked. "You were, after all, her flesh and blood."

"One hundred percent certain," Mary said grimly.

"I read somewhere that it can take up to two years for a woman to make the transition from seeing herself as primarily a mother, to a point where she can see herself as an independent woman first and a mother second." Amanda shook her head. "That's kind of awful."

"What about those of us whose nest was never full?" Mary said musingly. "We still go through periods of loss and disorientation as we age. Friends fall away, parents die, careers falter. All of those experiences can make you doubt your worth in the world. They can make you feel terribly lonely, even make you dangerously nostalgic for the good old days, which probably weren't so good in the first place."

Sandra nodded. "Loss is universal. Is it just me or does it feel more difficult to bounce back from losses than it was when we were in our thirties or forties? Am I getting more sensitive? Is life just wearing me down? Aren't we supposed to care less about loss as we age? Aren't we supposed to let go of earthly matters and concentrate on the hereafter?"

"Assuming one believes in a hereafter," Mary noted.

"I've always assumed that the older you get, the more you become inured to loss. Your defenses become stronger or your expectations become lower. Either way, you're protected to some extent from the ravages of grief." Amanda shrugged. "At least, I hope that's the way it is. It would be awful to think that we don't learn enough from our earlier years to help us cope in our later years."

"In some ways," Mary admitted, "I'm a way bigger sap now than I was, and in other ways, I'm much tougher. Things are often black or white to me these days, when everything used to be varying shades of gray. On the one hand, I find it harder than ever to make excuses for someone's bad behavior, but, two hours later, I find myself reacting with enormous sympathy to another person's troubled actions. It's very strange."

"What do you mean by strange?" Sandra urged.

Mary hesitated for a moment before speaking. "Well," she said finally, "lately I go very squishy about babies and young children and find myself feeling enormous pity for teenagers in general, even rude ones. When I was younger, I don't think I gave other people's children a second thought. Now, if I'm anywhere in the vicinity of a child, even a stranger's child, I'm likely to be overcome with a fiercely protective feeling, a desire to eliminate all threats, to fight to the death to save that child from harm. It's weird."

"That's not weird," Sandra argued. "That's evidence of an increased awareness that life is very precious and that young life needs to be nurtured and nourished. Patty? What are your thoughts about handling loss and, well, about how our ways of experiencing the world change as we age?"

Amanda thought that Patty looked as if she had suddenly realized she had been trapped in a corner by some very scary creature, possibly one with fangs.

"Um," Patty said, very obviously not meeting anyone's eye and with a little nervous laugh, "I don't know, I guess. It's not something I think much about, really."

Amanda wondered if there was anything Patty thought much about, other than her makeup, then scolded herself. It was not her place to determine or to judge Patty Porter's mental capacity. Anyway, had she, Amanda, done any serious thinking about how her relationship to loss might help her cope as she grew old? Had she ever really fully engaged with the losses she had experienced? There hadn't been that many of them actually, just one broken engagement that had rendered her upset for a few weeks. Had that really been the greatest loss she had ever endured? If that was the case, then she was seriously ill-prepared to deal with the trials involved with aging.

"Amanda? You're looking thoughtful."

Amanda looked quickly to Sandra. "Just thinking about the puzzle," she said. "I mean, I hope we can get it finished before Clovis makes his mark."

"It'll be fun," Patty said. "What's the picture on the puzzle, anyway?"

"It's a photo taken by the Hubble Space Telescope," Amanda told the others.

Patty looked crestfallen. No doubt she had hoped for an image of romping Labrador puppies wearing pink and blue bows around their necks. Again, Amanda scolded herself for making an assumption.

"Sounds like it's going to be a challenge," Mary said. "Good."

"Sounds intimidating," Sandra said with a laugh. "But I'm game."

Amanda rose from her seat. She realized that she was glad the others had expressed an interest in an activity she had assumed would be a solitary one.

"Great," she said to her summer roommates. "And thanks."

Chapter 37

The women were having dinner at one of the local clam shacks. The servers seemed to Sandra to be about twelve or thirteen years of age. Of course, they were several years older than that, but these days, anyone under the age of fifty looked like a kid. And how old did Sandra seem to these servers, she wondered. Ancient, no doubt.

Amanda had been the one to suggest this little outing. "I'm told," she had said, "that you can't live through a summer in Maine without eating a lobster or, at least, a lobster roll."

The others had agreed, and now, this evening, they found themselves enjoying traditional summer vacation food. On the round table before them was a basket of French fries and another basket of onion rings. Mary had ordered steamers. Amanda had ordered a lobster, and both Sandra and Patty had chosen a crab roll. While not inexpensive, a crab roll cost less than many of the other items on the menu. Sandra wondered if that was why Patty had chosen it for her dinner.

In all honesty, Sandra doubted that Patty could afford this meal out at all. She had paid her rent as soon as her next paycheck had cleared, as promised. But it was clear to Sandra that Patty was still a bit embarrassed by the incident.

Back at the start of the summer it had been Sandra's idea that Patty pay the rent on a weekly basis. She had correctly made the assumption that Patty, unlike the others, didn't have the money to pay for the full summer rental in advance. When, only days after arriving in Yorktide, Patty took a job at Crystal Breeze, Sandra knew she had been right. She had kept this arrangement from the other women; it wasn't any of their business how she chose to deal with her houseguests. Her clients, it might be said. Sandra had never imagined herself as being "in business," though she supposed that now she was.

"It was a total mistake on my part that she got past the first stage of the screening process," Sandra recalled Marcia Livingston saying about Patty Porter. "Her financial information is sketchy at best. Her references are from her sisters, both likely prejudiced in her favor. According to the application she's living with one of them at the moment. You really can't choose this woman."

But Sandra had held firm. She had acted from her heart and not from her head, though the decision had been a deliberate one, one she had considered before allowing it to become final.

As promised, Sandra hadn't told anyone, least of all Kate, about Patty's inability to pay her rent on time. Kate would have demanded her mother send Patty packing at once. Sandra knew that by allowing Patty slack she was breaking one of the rules she had established in the formal contract. But rules were made to be broken. If it happened a second time . . . Best not to think about that.

Just then, Sandra's attention was caught by a group of three adult men, two adult women, and four children probably between the ages of four and six, passing along the road just beyond the clam shack. The men wore white shirts, dark vests, and what Sandra knew to be the traditional style of pants for members of Mennonite and Amish communities to wear. On their heads, they sported wide-brimmed straw hats. The women, including the female children, wore cape-dresses, modest affairs with high necklines, loose bodices, fitted waists, and long, full skirts. On their heads the women wore white head coverings called, Sandra believed, kapps.

"Could they be Amish?" Amanda wondered quietly as the group passed out of sight.

"I don't know," Mary said. "I'm afraid I'm pretty ignorant about the various communities we used to lump together under the name of 'the Amish.' You know, those quaint people with suspenders and funky beards, riding around in horse-drawn carts."

"I think they might be Mennonites," Sandra told them. "I knew a family when I was growing up, the Hertzlers, who had relatives in the Mennonite community. I didn't encounter them often, but I remember very clearly how exotic they seemed to me, so set apart from the rest of us. I found them fascinating in some way. I just hope I didn't stare at them, but you know how kids can be."

"So, the entire Hertzler family wasn't Mennonite?" Amanda asked.

"No. I seem to recall my parents talking about the Hertzlers. The ones who lived in Yorktide, Aaron and Susanna, had left the community some years before."

"I thought there wasn't supposed to be any contact between members who stay and members who leave," Mary noted. "It's called being shunned."

Sandra shrugged. "All I know is that our neighbors were still in touch with a few of the family members who remained with the community."

"I've always been bothered by—as well as fascinated with—religious sects and well, religions themselves," Mary said then. "I mean, is it really fair that a child is brought into a community by his parent, indoctrinated even, while being too young for intelligent consent?"

"In the Catholic church, godparents are assigned to speak

on behalf of the child at a baptism," Patty said. "They're like surrogates."

"Isn't that the case with any child and his parents or caregivers?" Sandra noted. "All children need other people, adults, to make informed choices for them until they're old enough to do so on their own. I'm not sure there's any way around that. The assumption has to be that the parents or caregivers truly want what's best for the child."

"It's a risky assumption to make, though," Amanda pointed out. "I suppose the real trouble comes when—if—the parents object to the child's rejecting the choices they made for her once she's old enough to think for herself. If the parents fight the child's opinions, maybe even reject the child for choosing a different path in life, well, that's a problem."

"That's why all kids eventually hate their parents," Mary said, "or, if not actually hate them, resent certain choices their parents made for them when they were young. Like being raised Catholic or living in a rural community off the grid, or being hauled from one army base to another all in the cause of a parent's career, or even being forced to wear uncool clothes. But there's no getting around the fact that a kid needs an adult for the first chunk of his life."

"What do you wish your parents had done differently?" Amanda asked. "Sandra?"

"I know I must once have resented certain decisions my parents made for me, but now, I truly can't remember those resentments. Now, it doesn't seem to matter if my parents made mistakes in raising me." Sandra smiled. "Let's face it, I don't have all that many good years left—I know I'm not ancient, but still—so why spend them dwelling on old grievances?"

Mary shook her head. "You're a better woman than I am, Sandra. I still feel angry about having been raised in a family that didn't properly value education. My parents almost actively stood in my way as I tried to pursue a path that would lead away from their world, a world I saw as narrow, ill-informed, dull.

Their attitude damaged me, and I'm not entirely ready to release my anger." Mary shrugged. "Of course, now that my
parents are dead, there's really no place for the anger to be
released into, so it just festers inside me. Nice. Maybe I need
to see a therapist."

"I'm not sure there's anything my parents did or didn't do
that bothers me today," Amanda said then. "I mean, back
when I was growing up I wasn't thrilled that my mother was always urging me to make friends and bring them around to the
house and all that. I mean, I got along just fine with kids my
own age, I just never really needed the sort of close friendships my mother seemed to think I should have. But her pushing me to be more social certainly didn't do any lasting
damage."

"Patty?" Sandra asked. "Anything to add?"

Patty shook her head. "No. I mean, I got along just fine
with my parents. They were great. You know."

"Lucky you," Mary murmured.

Sandra cleared her throat. "I think another order of French
fries would be an excellent idea," she announced. "Everyone
agree? My treat. And then we might talk a bit about the Independence Day celebrations going on in town. The holiday is
almost upon us."

"I love holidays," Patty said excitedly.

Mary shrugged. "With the exception of Christmas, I could
take them or leave them. Especially the commercially created
holidays, like Grandparents' Day. Really?"

"Generally speaking," Amanda said, "I find holidays a
waste of time. Why should we all be forced to stop working
and 'enjoy time off'? How can a person 'enjoy time off' if it's
mandated?"

Sandra watched for their waitress to come in sight. This
Fourth of July would be interesting with this particular group
of housemates, she thought. Maybe not entirely pleasant, but
interesting.

Chapter 38

Why had she come to this shindig, Mary wondered? It was a nice day and all weather-wise, and the backyard in which the party was being held was pretty enough, and, okay, the food was really good, but . . .

But in truth Mary had only accepted Sandra's invitation to the party at the house of someone she knew from her book group out of politeness. Sandra had seemed so invested in showing her houseguests a good time this Fourth of July that Mary hadn't wanted to appear a killjoy.

That morning, Sandra and Patty had gone to watch the Independence Day parade. Both had been as excited about the event as a child might be, though how they could really believe that something magical might occur between the passing of the bedraggled marching band and the members of the town council draped in shiny sashes, Mary had no idea.

Mary hated parades and there was a good reason for this. The summer Mary was twelve and her brother, Bill, was two, their parents had commanded Mary to take the little boy to a small local parade. Mary had long forgotten what the parade was in occasion of, but she would never forget how Bill had been badly frightened by a guy in a clown get–up. The idiot had come bounding toward the children, crazy red wig flopping, wide red mouth gaping, gloved hands flapping. Bill had quickly become hysterical, and Mary, unable to stop the little boy from crying and screaming, had herself begun to panic. Luckily, a neighbor, seeing the siblings in distress, had come to their rescue and driven them home. Mrs. Fraser had consoled her son but had turned to her daughter in anger. Somehow, Mary was to blame for Bill's hysteria. Mary remembered her father trying, albeit weakly, to defend Mary against her mother's anger. Unsurprisingly, he failed and Mary was punished.

Yet another unpleasant memory Mary wished she could forget.

Amanda, clearly having no fear of appearing a killjoy, had announced to the others that she had absolutely no interest in parades due to her long-standing distaste for spectacle and attention-seeking behavior. Why, she had wondered aloud, do marchers in a parade, people of virtually no consequence in the world, wave to the cheering spectators, and why do the cheering spectators wave back? She knew, she said, that parades made people feel things like patriotism or a love for their community. She just didn't understand *why* they did.

Mary admired Amanda for being so candid. Still, she was a bit wary of her roommate's ability to disassociate herself from common human experience. But maybe Amanda protested too much. Maybe she pretended to be more coldly reasonable than she really was. But why pretend to such a thing? A protective device? Whatever. It wasn't Mary's job to decipher the enigma that was Amanda Irving.

Mary was only half listening to the talk among the group of people, including Sandra, with whom she was standing. She had never been great at making small talk at parties or chitchat around the water cooler. Not that her office had ever had a water cooler.

"I'll never forget the Fourth of July when John agreed to dress up as Uncle Sam for the parade."

Mary tuned into the chat again. The man who had just spoken, a friendly looking guy, went on. "When he opened the box in which his costume had been shipped from that shop up in Portland, oh boy, did he get a surprise! We all did."

"Why?" Mary found herself asking. She noted that Sandra's smile had gone a bit fixed. "What was wrong with it?"

The storyteller laughed. "First, you have to remember that the box only arrived the evening before the big day, so there was no time to return it, and it should have been returned, because it contained the wrong costume entirely! The shop had sent a Yosemite Sam costume instead of an Uncle Sam costume! Next morning, John, being the good sport that he was, got himself into it, popguns and massive mustache and all, and marched along with the others. Everyone got a laugh out of the mix-up. Right, Sandra?"

"Right," Sandra said, attempting a less fixed smile.

Mary looked closely at Sandra. "Are you okay when people talk about your husband?" she asked quietly when the others had moved off.

"Yes and no," Sandra told her. "It's been five years since I lost John, and most days now I'm okay. But then there are moments, out of the blue, when I feel devastated. The trigger can be the way the light is hitting the water at dusk, his favorite time of the day, or I might hear a turn of phrase he often used, and I'm right back into the grief. It's like I'm never really safe from the impact of his death. Maybe I never will be. I suppose that's just the way it is for all of us who lose a loved one. A death is a trauma, really, whether it's sudden or lingering. At least, that's what I think."

"Yes," Mary said. "I think you're absolutely right."

"Oh," Sandra said then, "there's a woman I used to know

from the PTA back when Jack was in school. I haven't seen her in years. I'm going to go and say hello."

With Sandra gone, Mary felt glaringly alone. She couldn't fail to notice that the majority of people at the party were, or seemed to be, in male-female couples. She wondered if she would feel any less of a standout if some of the couples were of the same sex. Probably not. A couple was a couple and a single was a single. What really bothered her was that until this very moment she had never been in the least concerned with her single status. So why now?

An answer came to her with disorienting speed. The reason why she felt glaringly alone at this late date was because the thing that had almost entirely defined her, the chosen companion in her life, had been her career, and she didn't have her career anymore. She and her career had parted ways. More accurately, she had abandoned her career, and why? Because she had grown tired. Exhausted, even. Was that good reason enough to have walked away?

If her career had been a person, would he have ever forgiven her for her disloyalty?

Mary grimaced. Crazy thoughts. And yet, they made a dismal sort of sense to her.

It was at this moment that she became aware of a man standing quite close to her. He looked to be around her age, give or take five years or so. But she had always been bad at guessing people's ages. She couldn't see his eyes; he was wearing sunglasses, classic aviators. To look cool? Maybe just to protect his eyes from the strong sun of a July afternoon. He was wearing a polo shirt, untucked, and cargo shorts. Also, a watch, nothing too large or pretentious.

"Hi," he said. "I haven't seen you around these parts before."

"I'm not from these parts," Mary replied quickly.

"So, what brings you to Yorktide?"

"I'm on vacation."

"From?" The man smiled. "I mean, are you taking time off work or something?"

"Or something."

Why was he still standing there? Mary wondered. Wasn't it clear she had no interest in talking to him? But on he went.

"Are you here, at the party, I mean, with someone?" he asked.

"I'm a friend of Sandra Pennington."

The man's face brightened. "Oh, Sandra. She's great. I've known her forever. I knew her husband too, of course. Terrible thing, his dying. I'm Pete, by the way. Pete Richardson."

Pete put out his hand for Mary to shake. She didn't see a way to avoid the handshake without being unspeakably rude to a friend of Sandra's.

"Mary Fraser," she said, snatching her hand back as quickly as was possible.

There followed a silence that bothered Mary not a bit but that clearly began to make Pete Richardson feel increasingly uncomfortable. Mary looked up into the leaves of the oak tree over their heads, then glanced to her right, where the food had been set up on the edge of the property. Someone was putting more meats on the big grill.

"Well, nice meeting you."

Mary turned back to see Mr. Richardson walking quickly away. She sighed in relief. She hoped she hadn't been too harsh with him, though he didn't look the type to fall apart just because a woman rejected his advances. If his attempt at conversation had been an advance and not just an incident of polite party behavior. Still, you never knew with men and their notoriously fragile egos.

And then a weird thing happened in Mary's head. She realized she felt kind of flattered that Pete Richardson had chosen her to talk to. It was pathetic, but old ways of thinking, the habits loaded onto you by your parents and your early childhood environment, were notoriously hard to break. Why should a woman feel flattered to have been singled out by a man because he liked the looks of her? What if the man was a jerk? How could his flattery be anything to be proud of? What made a man the subject to be pleased and the woman the object to do the pleasing? It was all so stupid.

Truth be told, romance—the desire for it and the actuality of it—had never played a big part in Mary's life. Maybe this was the reason she was so fascinated by Patty and her total obsession with men. Okay, Patty hadn't announced that romance was the focus of her life, but to Mary, it was pretty obvious.

Mary ran her eyes across the yard and spotted Pete standing with a group of other men by the grills. How bad would it have been to chat with him for a few minutes? What would it have cost her?

Mary turned away. She was becoming a crazy person, someone who was nasty just for the sake of being nasty. She didn't want to become that person. Why was it happening? Maybe because she had too much time on her hands. *The devil finds work for idle hands.* Her mother used to say that whenever she came upon Mary doing "nothing," like reading a book.

Maybe Mrs. Fraser had been on to something, Mary thought, wishing she had stayed back at Sandra's house. Though Mary was loath to give her mother credit for possessing any wisdom, in this instance, Mary thought, she might just have to do so.

Chapter 39

Patty had read in the local Yorktide paper that the Laughing Clam, a restaurant right off Main Street, was offering discount drinks all night in recognition of the Independence Day holiday. She had decided to give it a try. There would be dancing, and Patty liked to dance. And maybe Phil James would be there. She could say hello.

She hadn't told her summer roommates her plan, having the idea that none of them would be interested in joining her. She had simply waved good-bye and gotten into the cab she had called. She was at the restaurant within minutes. Before she even got out of the cab she was almost deafened by the noise of the sound system blaring classic rock songs into the night. People had spilled out onto the sidewalk to smoke. Patty made her way through the crowd and into the hot and even more crowded interior.

How long, she wondered, glancing around the packed room, would it take her to make her way to the bar to get a drink? Maybe she would just do without one, though if she was going to dance, she would definitely need a glass of water.

But no one seemed to pay any attention to her as she stood on the edge of the dancing crowd. She tried to smile and make eye contact with a few people, both men and women, but no one returned the greeting. Maybe, Patty thought, they were all locals, in which case, they might not have any interest in talking to a stranger tonight.

And as far as Patty could tell, Phil James was not one of the partygoers.

Her spirits a bit dampened, Patty still determined to make her way toward the bar. It took even longer than she thought it might—her feet were stepped on more than once—and when she finally reached her destination, who should she find but Amanda.

"Oh," Patty said, truly surprised. "Hi."

"Hi." Amanda looked disturbed to see Patty.

"I didn't know you would be here."

"Same."

In contrast to Patty's colorful outfit, Amanda was dressed much as she always was. Her only concession to the fact that it was a holiday was a blouse rather than a T-shirt or sweatshirt. Patty supposed it didn't really matter. Very few people at the Laughing Clam that night were dressed up.

"I didn't think it would be so crowded," Patty said.

Amanda nodded. "Do you want something to drink? I can flag the bartender."

Patty asked for a cosmo—Amanda was drinking a beer—and handed Amanda some cash.

When Amanda passed along Patty's drink, the two women stood together, watching the scene on the improvised dance floor, a scene that seemed to grow more frenzied by the moment. It wasn't long before Patty's attention was caught by a woman who looked to be in her fifties, wearing a pair of skintight jeans, leopard-print ankle boots, and a zebra-print top. She was clearly very drunk, stumbling about more than dancing, hooting and hollering. Honestly, Patty thought, the woman seemed to be having a lot of fun. She felt a very tiny bit jealous of the woman's ability to let go and enjoy the party.

"That woman in the leopard print is making a spectacle of herself," Amanda said, her tone critical.

"No one seems to mind," Patty noted, though now taking a bit of a critical look herself at the woman.

From just behind Patty and Amanda came a voice. It was the bartender, and Patty and Amanda moved close to the edge of the bar to hear her.

"That's our Sharon Doyle," she said, her own tone neutral.

"She's certainly enjoying herself," Amanda said with a frown.

"She thinks she has a right to. She's been married three times, if you can you believe that. The first husband dropped dead in his thirties, a heart thing I think. The second one drove his car off a bridge. Suicide. The third guy ran off, just like that. One day he was just gone. That was about a year ago now. For all anyone knows, Sharon might still be legally married." The bartender shook her head. "I don't think even she knows, and I'm sure she cares less. Our Sharon likes a good time, and as long as she's having one, not much else matters."

"I hope she's not driving home later," Amanda said, glancing around to where Sharon was dancing in a circle of men and women.

"Lord no," the bartender said with a laugh. "No one would let her drive in that condition. There's always someone willing to take her back to her place and pour her into bed. We look after one another around here."

The bartender moved off to serve a customer.

"I'll be right back," Patty said to Amanda, placing her drink on the bar. "I'm going to the ladies' room."

"There'll be a long line," Amanda noted.

Patty frowned. "No choice."

She fought her way to the back of the restaurant where the bathrooms were located and got on a line that was even longer than she had supposed it would be. Suddenly, being out and about that night seemed a very bad idea indeed.

So, why had she done it? The answer was obvious. Patty

had felt lonely. Loneliness had driven her from a safe space—her summer home—into an environment loud with strangers doing their frantic best to "have fun." How many of the people at the Laughing Clam that night, Patty wondered, were lonely and miserable and using the holiday celebration—dancing! discount drinks!—as a possibly effective way to forget about their troubles for a few hours?

A lot of people, Patty thought, looking under her lashes at the men and woman squeezing through the crowd outside of the bathrooms. A lot of lonely and miserable people.

Just like her.

Chapter 40

Patty had been gone for almost fifteen minutes. Amanda was thankful for having a strong bladder. But maybe that, too, would fail as she grew older. There was one thing for sure. When she was Patty's age, whatever that was exactly, she would not be caught dead in a place like the Laughing Clam on discount drink night.

Amanda sighed. Why had she come out to the Laughing Clam in the first place? Certainly not to meet a guy or to dance. She had a guy back in Massachusetts, and that was more than enough trouble. And she hated dancing. Then what had driven her from her comfortable summer home this evening and into a scene of frenzied fun? The truth was that she had needed not to be alone with her thoughts.

I hope she's not driving home later.

Amanda felt her conscience squirm. She knew that when she had said those words to the bartender, she had been less concerned with Sharon Doyle's welfare than she had been critical of the woman's choice to drink so much. Why was it that she could be so critical of other women? Why couldn't an older woman choose to be loud and to wear a zebra-print top and tight jeans? Women, Amanda knew, could be their own worst enemies. She felt ashamed. She had spoken from an assumed position of moral superiority. It was what she had done when she first met Patty.

"Want to dance?"

Amanda was startled by the words spoken so close to her ear and turned abruptly to find a tall man about the age of forty leaning in to her. His breath stank of booze, and his eyes were slightly unfocused.

"No," Amanda said, leaning back as best she could from the man. "Thanks." She turned to face the bar again, hoping that was the end of it.

But it wasn't. Suddenly, Amanda felt a hand roughly grab her upper arm. With strength made sterner by anger, she yanked her arm from the man's grasp, causing him to lose his balance and stumble into a group just behind him.

"Whoa!" he cried. "What the hell?"

Amanda clenched her fists at her side. There was no point in getting arrested, not because of this loser. "I said no," she hissed.

Muttering to himself, no doubt about the gross injustice of life, the man shoved off into the throng of partygoers. Amanda turned back to the bar.

"You okay?" the bartender asked. "There's always one, isn't there?"

"I'm fine," Amanda replied tersely. "But thanks."

Patty appeared just then, a frown of concern on her face. "Are you okay?" she asked. "Was that guy bothering you?"

"I'm fine," Amanda said again. "Why did I come here? I hate places like this. Why did I do this to myself?"

"It's not your fault," Patty said sternly. "Anyway, let's go home. By the way, thank your lucky stars you didn't need to use the ladies' room tonight. It's a mess. You would think adults would know how to put garbage actually *into* the garbage cans. Sheesh."

The two women battled their way through the crowd of revelers, including Sharon Doyle, looking even worse for wear, out into the night of downtown Yorktide. Patty had taken a cab to the restaurant; Amanda had driven her car and now offered Patty a ride back to Sandra's house.

"So, why did you come out tonight?" Patty asked as they began the journey back to Spruce Street to the sound of distant fireworks.

Amanda attempted a smile. "Honestly? To avoid my own company. Why did you come out?"

"The same. That and, well, I thought that maybe . . ." Patty shook her head. "Never mind. It was a bad idea."

A long moment of silence followed.

"That woman," Patty said finally. "The drunk one."

"Sharon. What about her?" Amanda asked.

"I don't know. She made me feel really sad."

Amanda was silent for a moment. Then, she said: "Me too, actually."

"But maybe there's no reason to feel sad, I mean, for her. Maybe she's happy with her life."

"Yeah. Maybe."

"Still, to have such bad luck with husbands. That could really wear you down."

"You wonder why she kept getting married."

"Maybe she was lonely," Patty suggested quietly.

"Yeah. Well, this was a night not to remember," Amanda murmured as she turned onto Spruce Street at last.

"Yeah," Patty said. "Definitely a night to forget."

Chapter 41

The four summer roommates were gathered on the front porch. In the distance, there were sounds of people laughing and fireworks going off in backyards. Sandra could just make out a few stars in the night sky.

She had the strong impression that they all were feeling a bit unsettled or melancholy; she certainly was feeling that way. Holidays, even those like Independence Day that were relatively impersonal, could be difficult. So many ridiculous expectations. So much forced good spirits. So many memories.

"So," Mary asked, "where were you two earlier?"

Amanda glanced at Patty and then smiled a wry smile. "We might as well come clean. Small town like this. Patty and I found ourselves at the Laughing Clam. And before you can pass judgment on our choice of entertainment, yes, we know we made a mistake."

Patty made a face. "I'll say. It was way too crowded, and people were getting pretty rowdy. Besides, you could hardly hear yourself talk."

"But there was an interesting moment," Amanda went on. "We encountered—we didn't actually meet—a woman named

Sharon at the party. The bartender was only too happy to tell us a bit about her."

"She certainly was enjoying herself," Patty said. "Sharon, I mean. She was dancing up a storm with anyone and everyone. I think she was pretty drunk."

"I know exactly who you mean." Sandra sighed. "Sharon Doyle. That poor woman," she said, "has had the rottenest luck. You heard that her first two husbands died and that the third one skipped town not long ago?"

"Yeah," Amanda said. "We got the outline."

"Well, it doesn't end there. Sharon Miller grew up in an alcoholic household. Both parents were wrecks, leaving Sharon and her younger sister pretty much to fend for themselves. Sharon did the best she could, but she couldn't prevent her sister from becoming one of those kids who's always in trouble one way or another. I don't recall exactly what happened, but Evie wound up in juvenile detention, and, after that, things got worse and worse for the family. The parents died young, Evie had been back in Yorktide for less than a month before she took off for who knows where, and poor Sharon was the only one left, all on her own, just out of high school." Sandra paused for a moment, thinking about that long-ago time. "A few months later, Sharon married her first husband. He was no great catch in some ways but I suppose he was better than nothing as far as Sharon was concerned."

"But he died young?" Mary said.

"Yes, he had an undetected heart problem," Sandra explained. "The second husband was a strange duck. He wasn't from around here; in fact, no one seemed to know where Sharon had met him. He used to go wandering in the middle of the night, frightening the life out of people by peering into windows. He was pleasant though, always had a smile on his face, poor man. Then, there was the accident which was determined not to be an accident after all when police found a suicide note."

Amanda shook her head. "What a nightmare."

"Dare we ask about husband number three?" Mary said.

Sandra literally shuddered. "By the time Sharon married him, she was worse for the wear with drink. Her judgment, if there was any left, was shabbier than it had ever been. The guy was slightly known around Yorktide, though he hadn't grown up here. One of those ne'er-do-well types, with a vaguely threatening way about him. No one trusted him, but Sharon found something in him to love, I suppose. When he skipped town, he cleaned out her bank account. I doubt there was much in it, but whatever there had been was gone. And now, Sharon is on her own again."

"Better off without the bum," Mary said with a frown.

"Maybe," Patty said quietly. "I suppose only Sharon can say for sure."

"What a life. Did she ever have children?" Amanda asked.

Sandra shook her head. "No, and I know for a fact she really wanted a family. I don't know why it never happened, but it's too bad. She was really good with kids. I can't help but think that if she had been able to have a family she might not be in such a, well, such a sorry state now. But that's just conjecture."

"Stories like that make you realize just how ridiculously lucky you've been." Mary sighed. "Well, I'm off to bed. It's been a long day. And parties totally take it out of me, even civilized ones like the party Sandra and I went to this afternoon."

"I'm off, too," Amanda said, rising.

"I could sleep for days." Patty stretched her arms over her head and yawned. "I think standing out in the sun this morning at the parade got to me."

Sandra followed the others inside, locked the front and back door, and amid a chorus of good nights punctuated by yawns, went up to her room.

As she undressed for bed, with Clovis attending, she thought back with a smile to the amusing story Hal Rolleri had told about John and the Yosemite Sam costume. She had thought her husband looked cute as the cartoon character. She had always thought he looked cute. John Pennington was the only man with whom she had ever gone to bed. She had been so very happy with John. If now she had only the memories, well, memories were better than nothing.

"Come on, Clovis," Sandra said softly to her feline companion as she settled into her bed. "It's time for sleep."

Chapter 42

Amanda had grilled hamburgers for dinner, proving that she was proficient at that cooking skill, too. It was too early for local corn on the cob but they did manage a caprese salad with locally grown tomatoes and basil, and there was a homemade pickle relish that Sandra had bought at a farm stand.

It hadn't passed Mary's notice that the summer roommates were tending to have dinner together more than once a week, as if by silent agreement. And there had been the spontaneous gathering on the front porch the night of the Fourth. It seemed that they were growing more comfortable with one another as the summer went on.

"I can't get that woman Sharon out of my head," Patty admitted when they had all settled at the table. "The one Amanda and I saw at the Laughing Clam the other night."

Amanda nodded. "Me too. I don't know why."

"Her story could put anyone in her right mind off men for good," Mary said.

"Well," Patty said, "I don't know. Not all men are bad, and Sharon's first husband died of natural causes and her second husband was a suicide. . . . But I see what you mean."

"Other people," Mary said. "Relationships. Entanglements. They're what's really the problem."

"Any relationship is risky," Sandra noted. "There's no way around that. But who would want to live entirely without involvement with other human beings? Certainly, not me."

"You can choose to keep other people at a distance, though," Amanda pointed out. "Keep your involvement to a minimum or on a fairly superficial level. That way, you've protected yourself from hurt."

"And from pleasure." Sandra shook her head. "No, I'll take relationships over aloneness any day."

"I'm okay with the idea of being alone," Mary said. "Then again, maybe I have no real choice about it. A man hasn't looked at me with desire since I was forty. Well, maybe a bit later than that but not much later. Okay, there was a guy at the party the other day, Pete, a friend of Sandra's, who spoke to me for a minute or two, but he was probably crazy."

"Now, Mary," Sandra admonished. "I know Pete quite well and he's perfectly sane. You just weren't interested."

Mary didn't reply.

"We've become generally invisible to men." Amanda frowned. "It's unfair, I suppose, but it happens."

"I never really thought about the situation," Sandra admitted. "I had John in my life for so long, and he gave me all the attention I needed, which had very little to do with telling me I looked pretty. Since he died, well, I guess I've just never noticed if a man is looking at me or not. Besides, I'm no spring chicken! The only men around Yorktide who would give me the time of day are in their eighties!"

"Don't be so sure," Mary argued. "Some men are perfectly happy to be with a woman five, ten, even fifteen years older than they are. They might be rare but they do exist."

"Oh, I know. But I haven't encountered any of those men in Yorktide."

"Like what happened with you, Mary," Amanda said, "I noticed when I was about forty-five that I'd become invisible to most men. Suddenly, I wasn't getting harassed while walking down the street. I certainly don't miss that! Honestly, I don't miss any of it, all that exhausting push and pull when men are involved."

"But you're involved with a man, right?" Mary noted. "Unless after eight years the nonsense has worn itself out and things are nice and calm."

Amanda didn't reply.

"Young, so-called woke men wouldn't dream of calling out to a woman on the street, would they?" Sandra said musingly. "I mean the sort of young men who support abortion rights and equal pay for women aren't the sort who routinely objectify women, are they?"

Amanda shrugged. "Let's hope not. But there will always be plenty of cretins who claim not to have gotten the memo that women aren't in existence solely for their pleasure."

Mary nodded. "Probably true. You know, it occurs to me that being a sexist pig has to be exhausting. Always on the make, always having to go it alone in some ways because you don't trust women to be true partners. Of course, buddies do rely on each other—male bonding can be unbreakable—but how many buddies do you see growing old together under the same roof like women friends are more prone to do?"

"I remember when people first started to use the expression male chauvinist pig, back in the late sixties and early seventies," Sandra said. "Before that a man was a cad or a lothario, or, simply a man. Predatory and superior. We've come a long way and yet, we've barely taken a step."

"And let's face it," Mary said. "The likelihood of one of us finding a guy and getting married at this point isn't good. The numbers are against us. Not that it matters to me. I mean that."

"You're such a pessimist!" Patty cried. Mary noted that until that moment, Patty had been mostly silent.

"It doesn't matter to me, either," Sandra admitted. "I can't conceive of marrying again, I really can't, not to a sixty-year-old or to an eighty-year-old. Why would I want to?"

"Love?" Patty suggested. "You might fall in love again."

Sandra looked doubtful. "I've had my fair share of love. I don't need to be greedy."

"The capacity to love doesn't end when you reach a certain age," Mary pointed out.

"I don't dispute that," Sandra said. "It's just . . . I highly doubt I'll be walking down the aisle ever again."

"Well, no one says you have to," Amanda pointed out.

Sandra laughed. "No one says I have to do anything, not even get out of bed in the morning. At this point I'm the sole decider in my life. Well, except for the government. The government says I have to pay my taxes."

"You choose to obey that rule of citizenship," Amanda said. "So, you do decide for yourself."

"You're right, I do choose. Taxes are necessary. Anyone who doesn't understand that needs a course in how government works."

"Women have been defined and confined by the male gaze for way too long," Mary said suddenly, aware that she had spoken the words almost as an announcement or a call to arms.

"What do you mean by the male gaze?" Patty asked.

"It's a term used when talking about a sexualized way of looking that empowers men while objectifying women," Mary explained. "For example, it's always been the assumption in the art world—painting, movies, what have you—that the core, important audience is the heterosexual male. Therefore, women, who are meant by their nature to be attractive to that audience, are shown as weak, available for sex and for being rescued, and, even if a woman is portrayed as a heroine, her 'weak' point is sex, her pathetic need for a man's approval. Her costume, her attitude, all are chosen to remind the audience that deep down, no matter how bravely she behaves, she is a woman, meant for sex with men and nothing more."

Patty nodded. "Oh," she said. "I never really thought about that sort of stuff. Not much, anyway."

"Take a look at a fashion magazine or website," Amanda said, "or scroll through the Instagram feeds of It-girls. Count how many blank stares and open mouths you see. To this day women are posed—and choose to pose, even for other women it seems—as innocent Bambi-like figures, too dumb to know they're prey."

Sandra frowned. "Surely not every heterosexual male automatically objectifies women, at least, not individual women, the ones in his life, his mother, sister, daughter? I simply can't imagine my John doing such a thing. Or my son, for that matter."

"I can't answer that question," Mary said. "I mean, personally, I've known some pretty wonderful guys. In terms of behavior, the way they lived their lives, these men genuinely liked women, were respectful, didn't put women on a pedestal or crush them underfoot. They treated women like the equals we are."

"Not that I don't find this conversation interesting," Sandra said suddenly, "but I did make brownies. And there's vanilla ice cream, too."

"Yes, please," Patty said promptly, rising from her chair. "I'll help you bring everything to the table."

As the others cleared the table in preparation for coffee and dessert, Mary realized that she would miss this sort of light but interesting conversation over dinner when she was back home in New York. But if she did, it wouldn't be the end of the world. She had always done just fine living on her own, and she would continue to do so for as long as she possibly could.

Yes, Mary thought. She believed she had what it took to always be just fine.

Chapter 43

Like she had told the others at dinner, try as she might, Patty could simply not get thoughts of Sharon Doyle, the woman she and Amanda had watched at the bar the night of the Fourth, out of her head. In so many ways Patty's life had been different from Sharon's, and yet, neither had come to a happy place due to poor choices in men, sheer bad luck, or maybe, a combination of both. Somehow, and maybe it was a failure of imagination on her part, Patty couldn't envision Sharon finding real love and stability with someone, not after what she had been through. Maybe, though, Sharon could reach a place of contentment without the presence of a man who might die or disappear. People were unreliable even when they didn't set out to be.

Better to be alone?

Patty knew that she would always choose to be in a relationship with someone rather than to be on her own. That is, assuming she had a choice in the matter. And that was the problem. The time of choice was gone, like Mary had said about her own situation. Patty was almost seventy years old. Nothing would really change, for the better or the worse, if she didn't have the opportunity to choose that change. That was a fact.

Why had she never really thought through the role in which she had positioned herself all those years ago? Why, somewhere along the line, hadn't it occurred to her that she was making a big mistake catering to men's desires and ignoring her own emotional needs, the result of which was her being left on her own with nothing?

It was like what Mary had been saying about the male gaze, and what Amanda had said about women posing like prey or willing victims. She had allowed herself to be a victim.

Patty felt frustrated. She hated thinking so much. She wasn't good at it. Thoughts and ideas got all muddled up and she was left feeling deflated, tired, sad. And worst of all, lonely.

Hurriedly, Patty left her room and went downstairs in search of the others. She found them in the living room, gathered around the coffee table, on which there was a pile of puzzle pieces.

Amanda had changed her mind about the Hubble telescope image when she saw this puzzle in a local shop. She said she thought it might be more popular with the others. As far as Patty was concerned, Amanda was right. Not that Patty had ever read a novel by Jane Austen, but she had seen a few of the movies made from her stories, and they were really good. And the clothes were so pretty.

The puzzle showed a man and a woman—maybe Elizabeth and what was the name of the guy she wound up with in the movie? Yes, Mr. Darcy—standing facing each other in a pretty garden. On the backside of the picture was printed a page from the chapter in which the scene supposedly occurred.

"What side do you think will be easier?" Patty asked.

"I don't know," Amanda admitted.

Patty frowned. "Do you think we can manage to turn it over once we've finished, without having the whole thing fall apart?"

"Not a chance," Amanda said. "Not unless we had one of those mats that roll the puzzle safely, and I didn't think to look for one."

"Has everyone read Jane Austen?" Patty asked. "I haven't, but I've seen some movies."

Mary raised an eyebrow. "Really? You don't know what you're missing."

"I hate when someone asks me this sort of question," Amanda said, "but here goes. Sandra, do you have a favorite book?"

"Well," Sandra said, "As it happens, Jane Austen is my favorite writer, so I'd have to say one of her novels. I'll choose *Pride and Prejudice* as my all-time favorite, followed closely by *Emma*. Mary?"

"It's impossible for me to choose one favorite book. I'd have to break it down into categories, and there would be several books in each category. As far as fiction, *Bleak House*. *The Name of the Rose*. *Wuthering Heights*. *My Cousin Rachel*. Anything by Iris Murdoch and Patrick McGrath. But the list goes on. As for nonfiction, I'd say that *Landscape and Memory*, by Simon Schama, and Peter Ackroyd's biography of London are two of my all-time favorites."

"A biography of a city?" Patty asked with a frown.

"Yes. Why not? He's also written a biography of the river Thames. How about you? What are some of your favorite books?"

"Oh," Patty said, "I guess I like some of Louise Penny's books. But I actually don't read that much, if you don't count magazines. What about you, Amanda?"

"I'm addicted to so-called cozy mysteries," Amanda said promptly, "though what's cozy about murder I'll never know. Agatha Christie, of course, is my hero, but I also enjoy not so cozy mysteries by P.D. James, and Ruth Rendell, and Ann Cleeves."

Suddenly, Patty became aware of Clovis, watching the women from his post atop a highboy.

"He's been so good about leaving us alone," Patty noted. "So far, anyway."

Sandra eyed him carefully. "I think he's plotting something. Cats are subtle creatures. When they're not being outright insane creatures."

"Oh, I forgot to tell you guys this!" Patty suddenly exclaimed. "Yesterday I stopped into that other gift shop in town, you know, just to poke around, and there was a big display of stuff like notepads and mugs and visors all about *The Golden Girls*, that old television show. Everything was stamped with the words *Stay Golden*, and there were these cartoon-like pictures of the four women. I had no idea people were into the show all these years later."

"There was a convention not too long ago," Sandra said. "I saw something about it online. If I remember correctly, it was called Golden-Con: Thank You For Being a Fan. There were pictures with the article, a lot of guys in drag, dressed up like the characters, but the majority of the attendees looked to be women."

"I've never seen the show," Amanda admitted.

"I wasn't a big television watcher when John was alive; neither of us was. When we did watch, it was mostly dramas and mysteries on PBS and, in later years, on BritBox. That and news programs. But I know about *The Golden Girls*, of course. Everyone does. It's part of the pop culture now."

"I got a kick out of the show," Mary said, "especially out of Dorothy and her mother, Sophia. I can't say I watched the show religiously, but when I did catch it I thought it was fun."

Patty nodded. "I liked it, too. I think Blanche dressed nicely. I mean, she was always well-dressed." Patty would not, however, tell the others that a few people she had worked with used to call her Blanche because she was "man hungry." Patty hadn't liked being called Blanche; it certainly hadn't been meant as a compliment.

Mary shrugged. "I think every character's style was horrible, given the time period."

"I seem to remember that Dorothy and Rose responded to an ad Blanche had put up on a bulletin board at a local grocery store," Sandra said. "It was how a lot of things got done in the past. Now so many deals are made via online venues, and there are agents who specialize in helping to find compatible housemates. It seems to me there's a general sense of suspicion, an assumption that people are often not what they seem and that it's best to protect yourself just in case. To be honest, when I decided to open up the house for the summer I had absolutely no idea of how to go about finding suitable housemates. My daughter wasn't at all happy about the idea, mostly, I think, because she was worried I'd be scammed."

"She was right to be worried," Mary said. "And you were right to hire a professional."

"Looking back," Sandra went on, "there was a real narrowness to *The Golden Girls*. Back in the mid-to-late eighties and early nineties, there were fairly hard and fast ideas about retired or older women, widows and divorcees, who they should be and what they should look like, what role they should play, if any, in the world."

Mary laughed. "And what sort of hairstyles they should have. Clearly, puffiness was a requirement. Lots of hairspray."

"Does the show still hold up, I wonder?" Sandra asked. "I mean, with young people."

Mary nodded. "I've heard that it does. Hence the fan conventions and souvenir products. Of course, a lot of that is a sort of gentle making-fun. But that's okay."

"I suppose I should give it a go at some point," Amanda said. "At least watch a few episodes so that I know what I've been missing."

"In a way," Patty said, "we're sort of Golden Girls, even if it's only for the summer."

"I'm Dorothy!" Mary declared with a laugh. "Now, let's get started on this puzzle. Picture side and border first?"

Amanda nodded. "Sounds like a plan."

As the others began to hunt for border pieces, Patty realized that she wished her life could go on as it was this summer. She liked her room at Sandra's house, and she enjoyed her job at Crystal Breeze. Her roommates were nice, too. At least they didn't watch her every move and find something wrong with what she was doing or saying, like Bridget did, like she always had, ever since they were kids. Bridget never seemed to find fault with Teri, though, and it worked the other way around, too. Teri was always saying how great Bridget was, at least when Patty was around. Sometimes, Patty wondered if they planned it that way, to always show a united front against their silly, useless sister.

It was a waste of time to obsess about a stupid family dynamic that had existed forever and that was never going to change, no matter how Patty's life might turn around.

"That's one edge completed!"

Patty realized her thoughts had drifted away from the puzzle. "Hey," she cried, "let me have a go!"

Chapter 44

Yorktide's chain grocery store was one of the cleanest and most well-organized Amanda had ever encountered. And the staff was inordinately friendly and helpful. Well, this was a small town in southern Maine, the state that proclaimed it offered life the way it should be.

Amanda had awoken that morning from a night of strange dreams she now couldn't recall. She thought they might have had to do with Liam somehow. Since then, she had been wondering what Liam would think if he knew she had gone to a place like the Laughing Clam on discount drink night. He probably would say that she had been out of her mind. It was totally out of character for Amanda to go out at night on her own, not even to a coffee place, let alone a rowdy bar. Well, there was no reason he had to know.

Amanda was, though, a bit curious to know if Liam had ventured out to a Fourth of July party. He, too, wasn't in the habit of going out on his own, but anything was possible. If he had gone to a party, she hoped he had enjoyed himself more than she had, which was not at all.

As she turned into the spice aisle, Amanda wondered if the man who had grabbed her had also tried to assault Sharon

Doyle. There seemed a good chance that Sharon knew the guy, assuming he was a local, but maybe the idiot only hit on women from out of town.

Sharon Doyle, the dancing woman, as she had come to be called in Amanda's mind, the woman Amanda, after only a moment or two of observation, had judged as lesser. But why? Because the woman was dancing at a party? If you were going to dance, a party was a good place to do it. The same held with drinking. Better to drink at a party, in the company of friends who would look after you, than to drink alone in some strange, seedy bar.

It was an unpleasant truth that she had a tendency to judge other women. What was to say her own life couldn't have been as miserable as Sharon's life seemed to have been? After all, her three major romantic relationships before Liam had been failures, and she wasn't stupid enough to blame those failures entirely on the men involved, even Sam, the man who had cheated on her. Hadn't she perhaps given Sam a reason to look elsewhere for affection, for intimacy?

Amanda's phone dinged, alerting her to a text. She ignored it. A few moments later, the phone dinged again. With a sigh of annoyance, Amanda dug the phone out of her fanny pack. The text was from Liam.

No easy way to say this. I've met someone else. I've moved out. Don't be mad. You know it hasn't been right for a long time.

Amanda stared at her phone for a long moment. Then, she put it back into her fanny pack.

Don't be mad.

She reached for a small tin of saffron.

Really? Oh, okay, I won't be mad. You just ripped my world apart but hey, that's okay.

She put the tin of saffron back onto the shelf.

Why did people say that sort of thing? *Don't be mad.* It was so stupid. People were so stupid.

Liam was so stupid.

She wouldn't give his text the dignity of a response. Not yet, anyway.

Amanda dropped the red plastic basket onto the floor, ignoring the sudden stare of the man across from her in the aisle, and walked unseeingly to the front of the store, out through the automatic sliding doors, and into the parking lot.

Don't be mad.

Amanda got into her car and pulled onto the road. She had no idea of where she was going. She simply went.

Suddenly, she remembered the conversation at dinner the other night, when Sandra—had it been her?—had said that all relationships were risky but worth it. And she remembered what she, herself, had replied. *You can choose to keep other people at a distance. That way, you've protected yourself from hurt.*

Had that been what Amanda had done with Liam, kept him at arm's length in order to protect herself? Was that why things had withered? Was that why Liam had walked away, because she had never really let him in?

Whatever the truth, Amanda decided, she would take this turn of events logically, calmly, rationally. She was simply being required to make another adjustment to one of life's surprises. That was all.

As an exercise to that end, Amanda tried to visualize herself walking back into the apartment at the end of the summer—or, sooner, as there was no real reason for her to stay on in Maine, now that Liam was gone from their home.

Their home. A place they had shared for roughly eight years. A shelter, a base, a haven. That's what a home was, or was supposed to be.

She tried then to imagine how she might *feel* the moment she opened the door and stepped inside that newly changed space. Would she *feel* Liam's absence?

Amanda's imagination failed her. She had no idea how she might feel. She could, however, more easily imagine certain facts of the situation, like, for example, the fact that the espresso machine would no longer be stationed on the kitchen counter. Liam had bought the expensive machine; he had used it daily; of course, he would have taken it with him when he moved on.

What about the painting she had given Liam for his birthday not long into their relationship? Would that, too, be gone? Amanda liked that small oil painting, the image of an old oak tree swathed in autumn mist, its leaves a mellow golden color, more than Liam had ever cared for it, but technically, the painting was his. He had a right to do whatever he wanted to do with it.

As Amanda drove unseeingly past green fields and classic New England farmhouses, she remembered something else. Liam had once given her a silver chain from which hung a round, peridot pendant. Peridot was her birthstone. She liked the necklace, but she had worn it only once or twice, and it had been sitting in her underwear drawer since.

Now Amanda wondered if Liam had been hurt that she rarely wore his gift. And *why* hadn't she worn it? Had she felt that wearing it gave Liam a hold over her? Had she not wanted him to know that he really meant something to her?

Amanda pushed those questions from her mind. Maybe, like the espresso machine, the peridot necklace would be gone. Technically, it belonged to her—as the small oil painting belonged to Liam—but maybe Liam had a right to take it back. If not a legal right, or even a moral right, it might at least be understandable that he would want to reclaim the necklace. Amanda decided that if she found the necklace missing she would hold her tongue. It wasn't worth a confrontation. She would take the high road, claim the superior moral stance. Forget all about the necklace.

And to be honest, Amanda told herself, the dividing up of property, the portioning out of physical objects, utilitarian or otherwise, that had once been shared by both people in the relationship was all so *distasteful*.

Amanda frowned. Shouldn't she feel that the dividing up of a couple's possessions was more than merely distasteful? Shouldn't she feel as if she had been torn open by giant claws, that her guts had been spilled onto the street, that her world was at an end? And yet, at that moment at least, she felt none of these things.

Maybe she was in shock.

Texts meant nothing. Ha. This latest text from Liam wasn't in the least bit meaningless. She should pull to the side of the road right then and send him a shocking text of her own.

But the idea frightened her in some way. She had no idea what she would say, shocking or otherwise.

Suddenly, Amanda realized that she felt bone tired. Exhausted. It was time she headed home. Not home, but to Sandra's house, Sandra's home and haven.

She would not tell the others that Liam had dumped her. It was none of their business, and it was likely that they would offer unwanted advice or worse, sympathy. Amanda didn't need any advice.

And she wasn't quite sure that she deserved any sympathy.

Chapter 45

The puzzle on the coffee table was carefully covered with a folded tablecloth held down at the four corners by heavy, silver-plated candlesticks. Sandra was itching to get back to the puzzle, but each woman had promised not to work on it without the others. She tried to ignore the temptation as she went about dusting and polishing the furniture and knick-knacks in the living room.

As Sandra flicked dust off the lampshades and brought back a shine to the end tables, her thoughts turned to her summer roommates, as her thoughts so often did. She was pleased that Patty seemed to like living at number 12 Spruce Street, in spite of the minor conflicts in which she had been embroiled.

Something had seemed to be troubling Amanda in the past few days. Maybe something unpleasant was going on in her relationship with her workaholic partner. But Sandra would not pry.

And then there was Mary. The other morning, Sandra had come upon Mary sitting in the living room, a book opened on her lap, gazing into space. The look of sadness on her face had stopped Sandra cold. For the rest of the day she couldn't stop wondering about the nature of Mary's sorrow. She didn't know

Mary well enough to ask what was bothering her or to offer herself as a sympathetic listener. Anyway, Sandra had no doubt that Mary was capable of taking care of herself.

Sandra moved to the mantelpiece over the fireplace where two framed photos stood side by side, one of Kate and Carrie on their wedding day, and one of Jack and Robbi on theirs. Carefully, Sandra ran the dust cloth over the frames.

Poor Jack. She had never imagined that one of her children would suffer through a divorce, but thankfully, in the end Jack had landed on his feet. Kate, too, had been involved in a romance doomed to failure. Grace Norton had been thirty-one to Kate's twenty-two when they met. Only weeks after they had started dating, Kate had brought Grace home to Yorktide to meet Sandra and John. It was abundantly clear that Kate was head over heels in love or lust or obsession or whatever you wanted to call it. If Kate had been hoping that her new girlfriend would impress her parents, she had been badly mistaken. Both Sandra and John had found Grace decidedly less than spectacular, ill-mannered, and not particularly bright. But how did you tell your besotted child, an otherwise sane and levelheaded being, that you just couldn't see what she saw in her paramour? You didn't.

The relationship had gone on for almost two years. Kate, not exactly flush with cash in those student days, had nevertheless supported the two of them. Kate had even paid for Grace's solo vacations with her friends. But it was the daily, casual carelessness with which Grace treated Kate that had infuriated Kate's friends and had led a few of them, tired of their warnings falling on deaf ears, to distance themselves for the duration.

The final straw for Kate came when Grace disappeared for almost two weeks. She left no note telling Kate where or why she had gone. And then one afternoon, when Kate was at home studying, trying desperately to quench her fears and concerns for her partner, the door to the apartment had opened, and

Grace had walked in, smiling, without apology, expecting understanding and even forgiveness for the cruel thing she had done.

Kate did not understand and would not forgive. Afterwards, Kate never spoke of the experience, and her parents had been wise enough not to ask even well-meaning questions like, "how are you holding up?" Wipe the slate clean. Out of sight, out of mind. It was what Kate wanted. And it was years before she showed any interest in dating again. When she finally met Carrie, it had seemed like a miracle. Kate's family and friends had breathed a collective sigh of relief.

Sandra had no idea if Carrie knew about Kate's long-ago disastrous romance, and for all Sandra knew, Carrie, too, had gone through a relationship from hell. It was not uncommon. Sandra felt herself unusual in that she had been spared romantic heartache, that is, until John's passing.

But his passing hadn't eradicated the fact that Sandra was a caretaker, by nature and by practice. She might no longer have a husband and children under her roof to care for and to pamper, but she did have Clovis. And, for a time, she had her summer roommates to worry about and fuss over.

Sandra turned from the mantel to see that Clovis was eyeing the covered puzzle from his seat on his favorite armchair.

"Clovis," she said, "are you getting ideas about Mommy's puzzle?"

Clovis looked up to Sandra, languidly blinked both of his golden eyes, and then yawned. It seemed he was not, in fact, getting ideas.

Or, maybe he was.

Chapter 46

"Damn it!"

Mary pulled her car to the side of the road, accompanied by a loud clunk-clunk-clunk. No doubt about it. Whatever it was she had driven over a moment ago had busted her tire.

Mary was a good driver. She was certain of that fact. But she wasn't used to driving on country roads. City potholes she could negotiate. Crazy cabbies she could out-maneuver. Careless pedestrians she could—well, she could make sure not to hit them. But a lousy rock the color of the dirt it sat on had defeated her.

She called AAA, and within fifteen minutes, a man and his truck were on the scene. He took a look at the car, assessed the damage as a busted tire caused by her having driven over a particularly pointy rock (duh, Mary thought), took her contact and other information, and prepared to haul the car off to a local repair shop. Though he admitted he was in no position to promise, he assured Mary that the shop was the best around as well as fast in producing results. Mary was in no position to doubt him.

She stood now on the side of the road, waiting for Sandra, hoping she didn't look like a vulnerable hitchhiker and attract the unwanted attention of some creepy driver. If someone did stop and attempt to lure or to coerce her into his car, he would meet a very unpleasant situation indeed. Mary was not skilled in hand-to-hand combat, and she certainly didn't carry a concealed weapon, but her temper could be terrifying (so she had been told) and her tongue could be vicious (she knew this herself, though it wasn't something she bragged about).

The sun was strong. Mary was tired of standing. She wished there was a bench, but she had never seen benches along a country road, so why should there be one here? Even a large boulder would serve; she could lean against it if not sit on it. But there was no boulder, either. Just dirt, and scraggly green things poking through the dirt, and then fields empty of people or animals, and behind the fields, trees. Lots and lots of trees.

A wave of melancholy swept through her, so strong she literally swayed on her feet. Recently, thoughts of her friend Judy had been plaguing her, thoughts of Judy's life, as well as of her death. There was no great mystery about the appearance of those thoughts. The anniversary of Judy's death was fast approaching. Memories, long assumed forgotten, had been streaming into Mary's consciousness, memories of all her childhood friends, the things they had done as kids, the silly clubs they had formed when they were nine or ten, the physical dares with which they had challenged each other, the sleepovers, the movies they had seen together, trick-or-treating, antics in gym class. Her childhood was flashing before her eyes. Was it a sign of her own impending death? It had better not be. Mary wasn't ready to die. But she might go stark raving mad if Sandra didn't show up soon.

As if summoned by Mary's lousy mood, Sandra's car came into view. Mary waved as it approached, though Sandra could clearly see her on that otherwise empty stretch.

Sandra pulled the car to a stop, and Mary opened the

passenger-side door and slid in. "Thanks again for doing this," she said.

"No worries. I'm glad to be of help."

"Country life is full of dangers," Mary declared as Sandra headed back to the house, "the sort of dangers you never expect and then, wham, they're upon you in the form of fire and flood and rampaging wild animals. Or pointy rocks. Whatever the future holds, I swear right now that I will never live anywhere other than a city. Nature is just too unpredictable."

"What about human nature?" Sandra inquired mildly. "Human nature can be unpredictable, too, or, at least, dangerously surprising."

"Sure, but people, I understand. Nature, on the other hand, puzzles me. It looks all pretty and harmless . . ." Mary sighed. "Ignore me. I'm talking gibberish. Thanks again for giving me a lift back to the house."

"You've thanked me often enough. I'm sure you'd return the favor if I were the one stranded."

"I would. To be fair, there are potholes on city streets. You might have gullies and ticks, but I have potholes and cockroaches."

Sandra glanced at her and smiled.

"Do you ever think," Mary said after a moment, "about what you would take with you if, I don't know, we got the word that someone was going to drop a bomb on us and we would only manage to survive if we hurried ourselves into an underground bomb shelter for, say, a year or so until things calmed down?"

Sandra raised her eyebrows. "I can't say that I've given such a scenario much thought, if any. Of course, I would take Clovis; that goes without saying. And photos of John and my children. I'm assuming in your scenario this shelter is stocked with food and the other necessary supplies?"

"Yeah. You'd want to take a few books, right?"

"Of course. And music, assuming batteries or Internet reception was available. Mary, do you think about such gloomy things a lot?"

Mary laughed. "No, not often. Just sometimes. It's like an exercise to pass the time, make a list of what's currently most important to my emotional or psychic well-being, I suppose."

"Okay. So, what's something you would take with you to this hypothetical bomb shelter, if, God forbid, you had to get yourself there today?"

Mary rested her head against the back of the seat and sighed. "Oh, I don't know. The usual books, the Bible, Shakespeare's collected poems and plays, good stuff that would keep me interested even if I had to read them over and over again. And a whack-a-mole game. I think I would grab a whack-a-mole game, you know, for stress relief."

"Mary, are you sure you didn't hit your head when you went over that rock? Because I'm pretty certain that your fellow bomb shelter inmates would not be thrilled sharing a space with someone wielding a weapon."

"Didn't I say? I'd have my own bomb shelter. You could have your own, too, if you want. Remember, this is just a game. A fantasy."

"Okay then. You take your whack-a-mole and I'll take my old tennis racket and a ball. As long as there's no one to mind."

Mary smiled. She liked Sandra. She was a good sport. In fact, Mary bet that one of the most important keys to any long-term relationship was the ability to be a good sport. To show a positive attitude, to be good-natured even when the circumstances weren't all that great, to let the other person have their way without being obviously pissy or jealous.

Judy had been a good sport. God, Mary thought, how she missed her old friend.

Chapter 47

Patty didn't feel like leaving her room at all that day. She guessed there was no real reason why she had to. She didn't have to be at the shop. She had no appointments. All she really had to do was sit on her bed and think about her upcoming date with Phil James.

She had been more than surprised when she had found him waiting for her the day before at the end of her shift at Crystal Breeze. He told her he had just been passing by, but Patty knew that was a lie. She had been out with too many men not to know when a random meeting was not really a random meeting. Sure enough, as if the thought had just occurred to him, Phil James asked her to have dinner with him.

Patty had said yes. They were going to have dinner on his boat, which was moored or docked or whatever you called it at the Yorktide Marina. He had told her that it was a genuine Grady-White Pacific model from 1966. That information meant nothing to Patty, but she had tried to look impressed.

Not that she had had many opportunities in her life to hang out on boats. And she had never been in a rowboat or a canoe or, God forbid, a kayak. Kayaks looked like deathtraps to

Patty. They flipped over easily—so she had heard—and how did you ever get your legs out before you drowned? No, she would stay far away from kayaks, thank you very much.

Anyway, if Phil's boat was large enough for two people to enjoy dinner, it couldn't be scary small.

She didn't think that Michelle had seen them talking outside of the shop, but Patty wondered if Michelle would approve of one of her employees having dinner with one of her vendors or suppliers, whatever Phil was exactly to Michelle and Crystal Breeze.

One thing was for sure, Patty would not tell her sisters—or her roommates—about Phil, not unless something serious came of it, and there was very little likelihood for that. A man like Phil James was not the sort Patty had ever envisioned to be her salvation. Not that she knew much about him, but still.

And how old was Phil, anyway? She had never been in the habit of dating younger men. Men you dated were supposed to be older than you. Not terribly older—unless they were very, very rich—but at least four or five years older. That's what her mother had strongly advised. But if Phil turned out to be a bit younger than Patty, well, that was okay. What did it matter at this point in her life, anyway? Marriage was out of the question. And she was only in Yorktide until the end of August.

But here was another troubling thought. What if Phil thought she was younger than she was, say sixty or even sixty-five? Would he not want to see her if he knew the truth? He didn't *seem* like one of those men who rejected a woman because of her age, but you never could tell.

Suddenly, Patty wondered if Phil James lived on his own. Maybe he had a housemate or lived with a relative, maybe even with one of his children, assuming he had children.

Patty sighed. Her summer roommates talked about living with another person as if it was always a good thing and it wasn't, of course. Still, living alone until the day she died was the last thing Patty had ever wanted for herself. But now, when she thought about spending every morning for the rest of her life sitting at a kitchen table not her own, having coffee with Bridget and Ed, feeling guilty if she had a second cup or if she didn't leap to clear the table, filled her with dread. And what if she chose to have her coffee and cereal in her room or at a time other than the time Bridget and Ed ate? Would they think her rude or, worse, ungrateful?

The family had yet to talk about how much Patty would pay into the household expenses. Would her family increase the amount she was expected to contribute as the years went by, as landlords usually did? What if one day she could no longer afford to meet her financial responsibilities? She didn't believe that her sisters, either one of them, would throw her out; of course they wouldn't. They had all been raised to respect family. That was why Bridget had taken her in.

The whole situation was a mess! And it was a mess from which Patty just couldn't see her way out. The worst thing about it all was that she had only herself to blame. Did that make self-pity unforgivable? Could you only legitimately pity yourself if harm had been done to you by someone or something other than yourself? But wasn't self-pity a right of sorts? If it wasn't, Patty thought, then it should be. Everybody should have the right to feel sorry for him or herself. Maybe not all the time but sometimes.

She wondered if that woman, Sharon Doyle, the one Sandra had told them all about, ever sank into the depths of self-pity. Certainly, of all people, Sharon had the right to feel sorry for herself. But maybe she refused to succumb to self-pity. Maybe that was how she kept on going, maybe that was what allowed her to dance and laugh even though her life wasn't easy.

What did it matter how Sharon Doyle lived her life? What

mattered, Patty thought, was how Patty Porter lived her life. What was left of it.

Abruptly, Patty climbed out of the bed. She had to get out of the house. She had to get away from herself, find something to distract her from her thoughts.

She would go shopping. Shopping was always a good idea.

Sometimes it was a good idea.

Chapter 48

Amanda looked down at the sand dollar in the palm of her hand. To think that this round, rather beautiful sun-bleached item was the exoskeleton of what was once a living being, a sea urchin, in fact. *There are more things in heaven and earth, Horatio/Than are dreamt of in your philosophy.*

Inexplicable or puzzling things, Amanda thought, like the fact that Liam had actually left her. The situation was so . . . weird. Never once, not even for a second, had the possibility of Liam's ending their relationship crossed her mind. That was part of the problem. *Should* she have at least considered that Liam might want or need to walk away?

He had seemed almost relieved when she told him that she was going to Maine for the summer. Or had that been her imagination? Still, he hadn't fought for her to stay. He hadn't once mentioned the idea of his visiting her in Yorktide that summer. He hadn't even said that he would miss her, not in so many words. "This apartment is a big place for one person" didn't mean much of anything. It was a fact more than an opinion.

At the time, Amanda had felt relieved that Liam wasn't

making a fuss. She hadn't really expected him to, but one never knew.

Amanda still had not responded to Liam's text, or called him, or sent him an e-mail. Was she punishing him with her silence? No, not that. It was more . . . inertia, maybe. She hated confrontations. She had no desire to enter into a confrontation with Liam. Besides, she didn't really know what she was feeling, and that made it almost impossible to *say* anything.

You know it hasn't been right for a long time.

Those were Liam's words. But he had been wrong. Maybe. Well, not entirely wrong. Oh, it was all a mess. Amanda hated messes.

It suddenly occurred to her that, all those early mornings when Liam was supposed to be going to the gym before the office, he was in fact going to the woman's house. Or apartment. Or wherever it was she lived.

Amanda placed the delicate sand dollar on the top of her dresser and wondered. Had she stopped paying attention to Liam at some point along the way? There was her incapacity to feel deeply for another person to consider, her inability to really connect. Was that always a bad thing? Was it wrong that she didn't like talking before she had her morning coffee? It wasn't about waking up. The moment her eyes opened each morning, her mind was as sharp as the proverbial tack. It was more that she needed to come into the day on her own terms. Liam was similar in his habits. Morning after morning had found each silently going about his or her business with barely an acknowledgment of the other's presence. Had it been healthy? That was probably up for debate, but it had been functional; it had worked, and there was value in things working.

Until Liam had fallen in love with another woman. Would *they* spend their mornings chatting about the news of the day, eating breakfast together, planning what they would do with their evening or their weekend?

Suddenly, an awful thought struck Amanda. Had Liam ever brought this other woman to *their* apartment? She felt sick imagining the possibility. She could ask Liam if he had ever done so, but he might lie—or, he might tell her the truth. How would she know the difference? Either way, truth or lie, nothing would change the fact that there was another woman. And the thought of another woman in her space, in her bed, looking at and maybe judging her belongings—her clothing, her books, her face cream, her teakettle—and finding them pathetic or laughable, well, that hurt more than the loss of Liam.

Amanda crossed to the window and stared blindly at Sandra's well-kept yard. What did she really know about Liam Sexton? Had she ever really known the man she had been with for the last eight years? And if she hadn't ever really known him, who was to blame? Amanda just didn't know.

What she did know was that she was very tired. She considered avoiding dinner with the others that night but quickly determined that *not* showing up would bring more attention to her than any attention she might garner by showing up with a frown.

Reluctantly, Amanda made her way down to the kitchen. Dinner that evening consisted of pasta primavera, a salad, and bread. There were strawberry sorbet and shortbread cookies for dessert.

Once they had settled at the table, Sandra raised her glass of wine. "I'd like to propose a toast to my brother, Jacob," she said. "Today is his birthday. You've seen his picture around the house, I'm sure. He died some time ago now, but I never forget to acknowledge his birthday."

Mary lifted her glass; Amanda and Patty followed.

"To Jacob," the women chorused.

"Can you tell us about him?" Mary asked.

Sandra smiled. "I'd be happy to. I adored Jacob. Everybody did. He was so optimistic and kind and funny. But Jacob had Down syndrome, and, back in those days, finding good schooling for him wasn't easy for my parents. For a couple of years Jacob had to travel two towns away to a school that could meet his educational needs. It was a strain on my parents, financially I mean, but they never complained. Besides, there was no other option, and Jacob loved school; he really thrived."

"So, he lived at home?" Amanda asked. Interestingly, she found that she had an appetite. The pasta was really very good.

Sandra nodded. "Yes. I remember when I learned that so many people—doctors, mostly—had suggested my parents put Jacob in an institution. I was shocked, sickened. Jacob was different, but that didn't make him a problem. Okay, he had many of the usual challenges people born with Down syndrome can have. His heart wasn't in the best of shape, and his eyesight was poor, even after having cataract surgery when he was a baby. But nobody's perfect."

"Ain't that the truth!" Mary said with a laugh.

"It was only when my parents died that things got difficult," Sandra went on. "They were both killed in a terrible car accident one night about a week before Christmas. Two people in the other car were badly injured. One young woman lost a leg. The roads were slick with ice and . . . Anyway, Jacob was only seventeen. It was devastating, losing Mom and Dad like that, and so close to Christmas, which was always such a special time for our family."

"Oh, Sandra, I'm so very sorry." Patty reached across the table to pat Sandra's hand.

"Sheesh, Sandra, that's horrible." Mary shook her head. "I don't know what else to say."

"So, what happened then?" Amanda asked, gently.

"I wasn't yet married to John," Sandra explained, "though we were engaged and had taken a lease on a small apartment. I was busy getting it set up so that once we got married we could move right in. I couldn't take care of Jacob on my own. It had taken the three of us—my parents and me—to properly manage his care, and he couldn't stay in that big house we had grown up in all alone. I knew it would be in his best interest if John and I found a good care home for him. It broke my heart to make that decision, but Jacob handled this major change in his life beautifully. And we were very lucky to find such a good home with a wonderful staff. It was almost two hours from Yorktide but an easy drive, and I visited Jacob twice a week for the next five years. John and I would bring him to our place for Christmas and for his birthday, and he enjoyed being with us but was always happy to get back to what had become his home, a place where he had friends."

"Jacob was lucky to have such a caring sister and brother-in-law," Mary noted.

"And we were lucky to have him." Sandra smiled. "Jacob adored little Jack and was a very good uncle. He loved to help me feed and bathe Jack, to make him smile. Sadly, Jack has no memory of Jacob, he was so young when his uncle died."

"What happened to Jacob?" Patty asked. "I mean, he died, but . . ."

Sandra smiled fleetingly. "He was only twenty-two. There were complications resulting from an infection he contracted after a relatively minor surgery. For a while, it was like I had died, too. For weeks I couldn't stop crying, could hardly eat or sleep. I just felt so bereft. Only knowing that my son needed me brought me back to life, that and John's good care. Jacob was not only my brother; he was my friend. I really missed him in my life. I still do, in fact, even after all this time. There are still moments when something makes me smile and I think, I must tell Jacob about this. He lives on, somehow."

Mary shook her head. "It's awfully sad when a young person dies. It's such a waste. All that potential. All the good Jacob might have done, the happiness he might have experienced."

Sandra nodded. "As late as 1983 the average lifespan for someone with Down syndrome was only twenty-five, so back in 1979, when Jacob died, it didn't come as a total shock that he should pass so young. Still, it hurt."

Amanda felt a tingle behind her eyes. Her recent loss was nothing compared to Sandra's loss of a beloved brother. "I'm so sorry, Sandra," she said, her voice unexpectedly soft. "Really."

"Thank you. The good news is that the average lifespan of a person with Down syndrome is now around fifty years or so, thanks to a better understanding, I suppose, of the condition, and access to affordable health care. Fifty years still isn't a terribly long time, but at least now some people have the opportunity to have a career and a romance, maybe even a marriage." Sandra smiled and looked to Mary. "What about you, Mary?" she asked. "Any siblings?"

"Just one, my brother Bill," Mary told the others. "He's a little more than ten years younger than me, which is a huge gap when you're growing up. For the first years of Bill's life I was like an unpaid babysitter, someone he could be fobbed off on when our mother didn't want to deal with him. I resented it, a lot. All through high school I was stuck taking care of my little brother when what I really wanted was to be hanging out with my friends. Still, whenever I could I brought Bill along. My circle adored him, so that helped. But there were too many times when he was dumped on me when I really needed to study for an exam or finish writing an important paper. I swear, I used to wonder why my parents even bothered having Bill if they didn't want to spend time with him. Then, of course, it dawned on me that he was probably an accident—no birth control or abortion for my strict Catholic parents."

"So, what about when you and Bill got older?" Amanda asked.

Mary shrugged. "Once I left home for college, that was that. I was eighteen, Bill was eight, and for years we hardly saw each other. When we did, mostly on holidays, it was kind of weird, almost like we were strangers. I mean, we cared for each other, but it seemed we never had anything to talk about. To this day, we hardly speak. When we do it's civil, even pleasant, but beyond that? Not much."

"Is he married?" Amanda asked. "Does he have kids?"

"Yeah, he's been married for about twenty-five years I think, and he and his wife have a son, Bill Junior, who . . . Huh. He must be . . . I'm embarrassed to say this but I lost track of what he's up to. I think he's in law school. That was his intention at one point, but I'm not sure he actually went."

"What about your sister-in-law?" Patty asked. "Do you get along?"

"Not really," Mary admitted. "Our relationship isn't comfortable. I get the feeling she sees me as, I don't know, above her, or better than her. I don't know where she gets that view, but there it is."

"Could you be imagining that she feels inferior to you?" Sandra asked.

Mary paused for a long moment before answering. "The thought has crossed my mind, but why would I imagine such a thing? I don't care one way or the other who's smarter or more successful."

"Maybe she's upset that you haven't shown more interest in her son," Sandra suggested.

"I've thought about that as well," Mary admitted. "It's true, I haven't exactly been an attentive aunt. Of course, things would have been easier if Bill and his family didn't live halfway across the country. Still, I suppose I could have visited more often. It's not like I couldn't afford the airfare."

"How often *did* you visit when your nephew was growing up?" Patty asked.

"Not often," Mary said tersely. "Let's leave it at that."

"When was the last time you saw your brother?" Patty asked.

Amanda resisted the temptation to roll her eyes.

Mary laughed. "Really, Patty? You're going to make me admit to just how lousy a sister I am?"

"No," Patty said quickly. "Sorry."

"It was a while ago, if you must know."

"Oh."

"Was Bill close to your parents?" Sandra asked. "I mean, did he experience them as you did, as kind of cold and distant?"

"You mean, did they favor him because he was a boy?" Mary shook her head. "Not that I could tell. Bill got away from home in the same way I did, went off to college and never went back. I don't remember him being particularly broken up when our parents died. We were both sort of . . . Well, it was like 'that's that,' you know?"

"Not really," Patty said. "My sisters and I were devastated when my parents died. It was just awful. It felt like the world had gone upside down or something. Anyway, it's sad that you and Bill aren't closer, given the sort of home you grew up in. You could have been there for each other. That's not a judgment, just a . . . It's just too bad."

"Maybe Bill and I aren't close *because* of the sort of home in which we were raised," Mary suggested. "Maybe we just don't know how to be close to each other."

"I suppose that's a possibility," Patty conceded.

"You don't miss what you've never had, isn't that the saying?" Amanda said. "I enjoyed being an only child. I'm not sure I would have wanted someone else around all the time."

Mary laughed. "A sibling can be a lot more than just someone who's around all the time! They can be an ally, a comrade in arms, a coconspirator. Or, on the other hand, they can be a nuisance, a tyrant, or a burden."

"I'm sure you're right," Amanda acknowledged, "but like I said, I wouldn't know. And before you ask, no, I wasn't spoiled. In fact, I was always pretty self-reliant. I always liked to do things myself, even when it should have been clear to me that there was no way I could manage on my own."

"Like what?" Patty asked.

Amanda considered if there was a way she could duck out of this conversation before she revealed more about herself than she had ever planned to reveal. What was going on with her lately? She had been dumped, that's what was going on, and it hurt. It had changed her. It was making her ... different.

"Well," she said, "once when I was about eight my parents were at the neighbors' house for a cocktail party. I decided that I was going to put up the strings of Christmas lights around the living room windows. The lights were coiled in a box, ready for my father to get around to them. Of course, putting up the lights required a ladder, but I decided I'd just use one of the dining room chairs. It didn't give me enough height, though, so I stuck a couch cushion on the seat of the chair. With a hammer and nails stuffed into my pockets, and a coil of lights tucked under my arm, I climbed onto the makeshift ladder."

"So, what happened?" Mary asked.

Amanda shrugged. "I fell, of course. Right to the floor when the cushion slipped off the chair. Luckily, my head didn't collide with the sharp edge of the coffee table."

"Good thing!" Mary exclaimed. "Cripes, you could have been killed!"

"I know," Amanda admitted. "I wanted to put everything back the way it had been so that my parents would never know what I'd been up to. But instead, I started to cry, and I sat there on the floor crying until my parents came home. I was, after all, only eight."

"Did you see asking for help as a sign of weakness?" Mary wondered.

Amanda shrugged again. In for a penny, in for a pound, she thought. "I don't know. I don't think so. I remember my parents sometimes scolding me for biting off more than I could chew—my father loved using that expression—but . . ." Amanda paused for a moment before going on. "I know it's a cliché that only kids are dependent and spoiled, but I think they're no more spoiled than kids with siblings."

"I remember hearing when I was growing up that only children were lonely so they invented imaginary companions. Did you have an imaginary playmate?" Sandra asked.

"No," Amanda said. "Besides, I was never lonely. My childhood was very normal."

"I read once that not having to compete for the parents' attention is a real benefit for an only child. I have no idea if that's true," Mary added, "but it does make sense."

"I just remembered something," Sandra said. "I was at a party once, a long time ago, and this woman I'd just met asked me if I had a favorite child. I was appalled by her nerve in asking such a personal question. I don't know how my answer came so quickly, but the next thing you know I said to her, "No. I dislike both of my children equally." That got quite a laugh from the other guests, though the woman who asked the question didn't seem to find it amusing."

"Serves her right for asking such an idiotic question," Mary said.

"Still, I wonder if favoritism is inevitable," Amanda mused.

Sandra frowned. "I don't think that it is. If you love each child for who they uniquely are, how can one emerge as a favorite? At least, it wasn't possible in my case, I'm glad to say."

"Some kids must make it impossible for their parents to like them much," Amanda said. "Let's face it, some people are just not likable."

"Not many parents are going to admit to not liking their child!" Sandra said. "Sure, at times you want to throttle your teenager—not literally, of course—but that doesn't mean you don't love the child. To really not *like* your child . . . That's got to be tough."

"I'm pretty sure my mother didn't like me," Mary said, "but it was no big deal because I didn't like her, either. I know, it sounds awful to say, but I didn't. I loved her in the way that you love your mother because you know you have to rely on her."

"Were you ever actively afraid of her?" Amanda asked. "I mean, did you ever fear for your safety?"

Mary seemed to think about her answer before saying: "No, I don't think I was ever actually afraid of her. I remember her yelling a lot, always scolding me for something I'd done wrong or something bad I'd said, but words, even spoken at volume—and my mother was loud—didn't frighten me. I could give as good as I got. And after a time, I started to ignore her tirades. I think that annoyed her more than when I yelled back and told her that I hated her and that she was the worst mother ever."

"Disengagement," Sandra said, "is frustrating. I think your mother wanted you to fight back; otherwise she wouldn't have found so much to criticize. If she truly hadn't cared about you she would have ignored you, let you run wild without comment." Sandra smiled. "I'm sorry. It's just a thought. I might be totally wrong."

Mary sighed. "Do we ever stop being someone's kid? I'm in my sixties, for God's sake, and I'm still coming to terms with my parents who aren't even alive anymore. Family is a nightmare."

"And on the flip side—" Sandra began.

"Yeah, yeah, I know. Home is where the heart is and all that. So, Patty," Mary asked, "tell us about your childhood. You have two sisters, yes?"

Patty suddenly picked up the fork she had laid down and began to twirl it. "Um, right. One older and one younger. I'm the middle child. Well, obviously." Then she yawned. "Excuse me! I'm *so* tired. I think I'm going to go straight to bed after I help straighten up. The store was crazy today."

"Go on up," Sandra said. "We'll manage."

"Are you sure? Thanks a lot."

Patty left the table quickly.

"Is it just me or did anyone else think that Patty's yawning just then was an act?" Mary asked when Patty was gone from the room.

"It was a little convenient somehow," Sandra noted. "But that doesn't mean she isn't really tired."

As Amanda helped Sandra and Mary clear the table and load the dishwasher, she realized that she felt slightly exhausted by the conversation that had taken place over dinner. She wasn't used to sharing so much or to listening to others share so much of their personal histories. Maybe this sort of thing was par for the course with the majority of women. She just didn't know. She tried to recall if her mother had had close female friends over the years and realized that she just wasn't sure. Obviously, she hadn't paid enough attention to know.

At the same time, Amanda also realized that listening to the stories of others and allowing herself to imagine the pain they had experienced had taken her mind away from her own woes, which at the moment didn't seem so horrible after all, certainly not as bad as losing one's parents in a car crash just before Christmas, or losing one's beloved sibling at an early age, or being essentially estranged from one's only brother. And having shared a significant memory of her own, something she very rarely did . . .

Amanda didn't exactly regret having spoken, but everything lately was feeling just so—

Just so weird.

Chapter 49

Sandra was puttering around the house. Puttering. What an ugly word, she thought. But it was what she was doing. Earlier, she had finished the daily morning chores of cat maintenance—cleaning the litter, refreshing the water bowls, serving Clovis his breakfast—and then she had gone on to sweep the hardwood floors, give the bathrooms a quick check, make her bed, and de-hair as best she could the furniture on which Clovis preferred to spend his time. Now, though there were more interesting ways in which to occupy her time, she was— puttering.

With a sigh of frustration, Sandra went to the kitchen. She would have another cup of coffee. It would be something to do. As she poured ground coffee into the machine, her mind vaguely revisited the greetings each of her summer roommates had offered that morning, Mary in passing as she was racing toward the front door, off to a country auction; Patty in a hurry, too, afraid she would be late for work; and Amanda, on her own time and headed for a hike, backpack loaded with the essentials for health and safety.

Before this summer, the last person to have greeted Sandra over morning coffee had been her husband. After John retired, every morning had been a weekend morning, with a leisurely breakfast, the local paper and the *New York Times*, both delivered to the house, and chat about what each of them planned to do for the rest of the day. Only after John was gone did Sandra realize how comforting those shared mornings had been.

Nowadays, on her own, mornings still had a routine, if a less pleasant one. After a quick meal of toast and coffee, Sandra sent an e-mail to both of her children. It was more of a "check in"—hey, I'm alive—than anything substantive. Kate had requested this of her mother after her father died. "Now that you're living on your own," she had said, "it's important you let someone know that you're alive and well." Fair enough, Sandra thought, but what if moments after hitting the send button she fell out of her chair, broke a bone in the fall, and was unable to reach for her phone, which she knew she should always have on her but often didn't because it felt like an intrusive nuisance. Anyway, she could lie there on the floor, in pain, maybe dying, until the following morning when Kate or Jack, not hearing from their mother, called her, got no answer, and sent the police to the house.

Living alone, Sandra thought, and not for the first time, was not for sissies. If there was an aura of romance about being queen of one's own realm, beholden to no one, that aura of romance quickly faded when you encountered a chore that was clearly too difficult to be handled by one person alone—like the raking up of millions of leaves in the autumn—or when loneliness set in, which it could do at the oddest of times.

The landline suddenly rang and Sandra started. She had been so lost in her thoughts she had half forgotten there were such things as phone calls and doorbells. She dashed to the counter on which the phone sat and saw that the call was from her son. Sandra was surprised, and for a split second wondered if Jack was calling with bad news. Why her mind should leap to such a thought surprised her. She had never been a particularly panicky sort. What had changed?

"Hi," she said, when she had picked up the receiver. "It's good to hear from you."

"I realized we hadn't actually talked in a while," Jack said, "so I thought I'd give you a ring."

"I was just thinking of you, of you and of your sister, in fact," Sandra told him.

"And what were you thinking, exactly?" Jack asked.

"Nothing in particular. How's Robbi?" Sandra couldn't remember the last time she had spoken to her daughter-in-law. It might have been months.

"She's fine, busy with work, still doing Pilates. So, Mom," Jack went on, "how's the summer roommate experiment going?"

"Pretty well, I think," she said. "There have been a few minor bumps in the road but nothing worrying."

"Well, I'm glad to hear it. So, do you feel less lonely, having other people around?"

Sandra pondered that question for a moment. "Yes and no," she admitted finally. "It depends."

"On what?"

"On various things. Anyway, have you talked to your sister lately?"

"Not really. She seems busier than ever; I left her a few voice mails and never heard back. She did send me a text after her visit to Yorktide to say she thought things were going well there overall."

"I'm glad she thought so. She seemed pretty intent on analyzing each of the guests. You know how she is." At least, Sandra added silently, how Kate had become after those terrible years with Grace. Kate had always been generally observant; now she was a master of scrutiny.

Jack laughed. "Oh, yeah. She has to *know* things. She has to be absolutely certain that she *understands*."

"Not that that's a bad thing."

"No," Jack admitted, "but sometimes I think she would

have been more suited to the life of a scientist than a lawyer. Anyway, what's the situation with Emma? I don't suppose there's been any change for the better?"

"No," Sandra said, "and there won't ever be."

"I'm sorry, Mom," Jack said feelingly. "It's so unfair, isn't it? For a while, before Emma got sick, I hoped that maybe you two would move in together, maybe sell both houses and get something smaller, closer to the heart of town so you wouldn't need to drive so much."

Sandra felt a lump of emotion come to her throat. "We missed our moment, I guess. Even if we had set up house together it wouldn't have lasted long, not with the dementia."

"Yeah. That's true."

"Any thoughts about coming east in the fall?" Sandra asked suddenly. It was not a question she had planned to pose. "Not necessarily for Thanksgiving, I know Robbi's family likes to host a big event at Thanksgiving, but maybe some time in October? You know how pretty it is here in autumn."

Sandra waited for Jack's reply. She hoped she hadn't sounded pushy. And she certainly never wanted to lay a guilt trip on one of her children. But sometimes, people needed to be prodded before they would take action. Before they would do the right thing. And if visiting your widowed mother wasn't the right thing, then Sandra didn't know what was.

"To be honest, Mom," Jack said after a moment, "Robbi and I haven't given it any thought, but I promise we will. You know, you could always come here for Thanksgiving. I'm sure the Brownings wouldn't mind. What am I saying? I'm sure they'd love to have you."

Sandra wasn't at all sure that Robbi's parents—who Sandra had only met once, at Robbi's wedding to Jack—would welcome her into their home on their favorite holiday. They hadn't struck her as the most hospitable people, in spite of their reputation for throwing a Thanksgiving blowout. But all she said was, "Well, it's something to think about."

Jack and Sandra said good-bye shortly afterward, Sandra asking her son to give his wife her best. The moment Sandra replaced the receiver, she was overcome by a wave of melancholy so strong that she grabbed on to the counter for support. That golden time was so very far in the past, the time when there was never any doubt that she and John and their children would be together for the holidays and for many of the days in between. Of course, things changed; life never stayed the same for more than a moment. Sandra knew that, and often, change was a good and a necessary thing. Still, sometimes the memory of the precious gifts you had once possessed but had somehow lost along the way could hit you badly. Sandra took a few deep breaths, willing herself to come back to the moment, the reality of which wasn't so terrible at all. She had her health. She knew that her children loved her, even if they lived hours away. Soon, she felt recovered enough to release her grip on the counter.

Still, she wondered when her roommates would return. She hoped it would be soon. In the meantime, she would have that second cup of coffee.

Chapter 50

Mary sat in one of the wicker chairs on the front porch, reading *The Grotesque*, a novel by Patrick McGrath. It was one of the books she had brought with her to Maine. She had read it several times, as she had all of Patrick McGrath's titles. McGrath was the master of, what could she call it, maybe the literary psychiatric thriller, if that was a thing.

Everyone else was out that afternoon, allowing her, for the moment at least, to indulge a fantasy of being lady of the Maine manor. Not that she would really want the responsibility of maintaining such a large domicile. No, her Greenwich Village apartment was big enough for her purposes, if it lacked the sort of dignified, old-fashioned presence of Sandra's home.

No sooner had Mary opened her battered copy of the novel did her phone alert her to a call. Mary looked at the phone and frowned, annoyed at having been interrupted. The area code . . . It was Bill. Her brother was calling her. Now there was a surprise.

"Hey," she said, putting the book aside. "I was just talking about you."

"You were?" Bill laughed.

"Yeah. I'm spending the summer in Yorktide, Maine. I'm staying at a sort of hybrid bed-and-breakfast. Anyway, the other night at dinner the other guests and I had a conversation about our families."

"Yikes. Dare I ask what you said about your little brother?"

Mary smiled. "Nothing bad at all. Promise."

"Good." Bill sighed. "Not that there's anything juicy or even very interesting to say about me these days, anyway. I'm about as boringly middle-aged as a guy can get. Sometimes I think even Stacy finds me too dull."

Mary bit her tongue. She had never found her sister-in-law to be much of a bright spark, but it was all too possible that she had been judging Stacy too harshly.

"So, what's up?" she said.

"You mean, why did I call? Well, I bring tidings of great joy. At least, it's good news. Maybe I should have told you before now. Bill Junior graduated from law school in May and—"

"What?" Mary was genuinely shocked. "Already? But—"

Her brother laughed. "Yeah, already."

"Why didn't you tell me? I mean, remind me?" Mary put a hand to her forehead. How could she have been so negligent?

"Anyway, I didn't call to complain; I called to brag a little. Bill graduated summa cum laude, and I don't have to tell you what that means, do I?"

No, Mary thought. He didn't. She, too, had graduated from law school with the same honor.

"And he was awarded the Jeremiah Hirsch Prize," Mary's brother went on. "That's a hefty monetary gift given to someone going into public interest law and who's already shown a big commitment to pro bono work. Not bad, huh?"

"Not bad at all," she replied, aware that her voice was a bit husky with emotion.

"You know, Bill Junior reminds me of you. He's a hard worker and he's super bright. Not like his old man!"

"Thanks for the compliment," Mary said, more moved than she might have expected. "And congratulations are certainly in order. Where is he working?"

"He got a position in a legal aid office, you know, they deal with stuff like civil rights and social justice. They deal mostly with poor people."

"That's wonderful," Mary said earnestly. "I mean it, Bill. You and Stacy have done a fine job with your son."

"I don't know about that," Bill said with a laugh. "I think Bill Junior is mostly responsible for becoming the man he is."

"So," she asked, "what about Stacy? Is she well? What's she up to these days?"

There was a moment of silence, and Mary assumed that her brother had been stunned by her asking after his wife. It was not something Mary had ever been in the habit of doing.

"Yeah, she's good, thanks," Bill said finally. "She's been taking a painting course at the community college for the past few months. She minored in art history in college and keeps up with current market trends, and she finally thought she should get to understand more about painting by actually picking up a brush."

Now it was Mary's turn to be stunned into silence. She had had no idea that her sister-in-law had a serious interest in the visual arts. Stacy had never mentioned her passion to Mary. Then again, Mary had never asked Stacy about her interests.

"Well," Mary said finally. "That's great. I'd love to see some of her work if she's willing to let it be seen." She would not mention her own pitiful foray into the art world.

Bill laughed. "I didn't say she was any good! In fact, she's the first to admit she's pretty awful. But the experience is helping her better understand how art is actually made. At least, that's what she tells me. You know I've always been a cretin when it comes to art."

Mary smiled as she thought of how her brother had decorated the walls of his first apartment after college. A black-

and-white GUESS print ad of a young buxom woman in a pair
of cutoff jean shorts did not, in Mary's opinion, prove even a
tiny bit of good taste in art.

"So, retirement going all right?" Bill asked then. "I mean,
any regrets?"

"The jury is still out," Mary admitted.

"You could always go back to work at some point."

"I could."

"But you really should take some time just to do nothing.
You've been a workaholic since we were kids. At least, that's
how I remember you, always busy, never just, I don't know,
sitting down, relaxing."

Was she a workaholic? Yes. Had she always been a workaholic? Maybe. Was there anything wrong with needing to be
always busy? Also, maybe.

"I'm relaxing this summer," Mary said, a bit defensively.

"Good. You deserve the downtime. Well, I'll keep you
posted about Bill Junior. I mean, if you'd like to hear about his
adventures. Hey, and maybe we can see you sometime. It's
been way too long."

"Thanks," Mary said. "I'd like to see you, too. And yes,
please keep me posted about Bill."

Brother and sister said their good-byes, and Mary put her
cell phone back on the little side table. She wondered what
had prompted her brother to contact her at this particular moment in time. Sure, he was proud of his son, but was there
more to it than that? Was Bill feeling the need to connect with
his only sibling before it was too late? Before they were too old
to care? Before they died?

Well, she *would* enjoy catching up with her brother in person. And now, knowing of Stacy's keen interest in art—and
that she, too, was a terrible painter!—Mary realized that she
and her sister-in-law had something in common. Mary realized she had some serious rethinking to do concerning her
sister-in-law.

And as for her nephew . . . For a moment, Mary couldn't even recall his second name. Walter. That was it. She had a vague idea that Walter might be the name of Stacy's father. When had she last seen Bill Junior? Mary thought hard and couldn't exactly recall. He had still been a boy, not yet in high school . . .

Mary sighed. She realized that now she had cut herself off from daily, often intense interaction with others, there was a risk that she would come to experience a long-term, debilitating state of loneliness. She might even wake up one day to realize that she was terminally alone.

Loneliness as illness. Maybe loneliness *was* an illness of sorts. How did a person deal with that? Those small moments of loneliness were bad enough. The flashes of self-pity that came along with those moments were unpleasant at the time and painful in recollection. In short, there was nothing good about loneliness that Mary Fraser could see. Maybe a philosopher could argue that loneliness bore emotional benefits of a sort, but Mary wasn't buying whatever it was philosophers might be selling.

There was no doubt about it. She had work to do. She couldn't allow loneliness to creep into her life and distort her into a helpless, pathetic figure. She had to maintain ties with the world and with her childhood friends. She might even— and this sounded kind of dreadful—need to make new friends.

Most important, she would make an effort going forward to be more present in her nephew's life. Assuming he would accept her efforts. There really was no reason why he should.

Mary tried to imagine how she might feel if her nephew rejected her advances of friendship. She rested her head on the back of the chair and sighed. Not good, was what she concluded. She wouldn't feel good at all.

Chapter 51

Patty leaned closer to the mirror to inspect her makeup. She had been wearing less in the past few weeks than she usually did, and thought she might just look a little bit younger than she really was. Somehow, there didn't seem to be the need these days—if that made sense—for putting on a full face when she could easily get away with a powder foundation, a bit of peachy blush, one coat of dark brown mascara, and a slick of a slightly glossy (though not sticky!) coral lipstick.

Patty patted her lips with a tissue one final time to soften the color just a bit. She didn't think Phil was the sort who liked a woman to wear a lot of makeup. He seemed so very different from her former boyfriends, all of whom had liked the way she put on her face. At least, she thought that they had. No one had ever complained. Why should they have complained? Over the years, she had become very good at emphasizing her cheekbones and evening out her lips because the top lip was much thinner than the bottom. She had even taken a few lessons from a woman who had worked for years at a makeup counter in Macy's.

Suddenly, Patty frowned. She remembered her sister Bridget remarking on how much money Patty would save if she cut down on buying so much makeup and hair-care products.

Patty stepped back from the mirror so that she could see the upper part of her body as well as her neck and face. What in the world *did* Phil James find attractive about her? Why had he asked her out for dinner? Her looks were mostly gone; in spite of her skill with makeup there was no hiding that. There was her neck, for instance. There was nothing she could afford to do about her crinkly neck. She knew she was out of the habit of making sparkling conversation, if, in fact, she had ever possessed that skill. Her world had become pretty small and narrow. What could Phil James possibly see in her that interested him? What could any man?

With effort, Patty pushed aside those unhappy questions, picked up her makeup bag, and went back to her room. She would try to focus on the positive, such as the fact that she loved boats and would soon be spending the evening on one. She hadn't actually been anywhere near a boat in years, not since she had been invited to a dinner-dance cruise around Boston harbor by a colleague whose date had bailed on her at the last minute.

"I spent all this money on two tickets," Maria had told her with a frown. "It would be a shame to let them go to waste. Come with me, why don't you?" Patty had enjoyed the evening. It was an opportunity to dress up, and the food had been better than she had expected, and two men had asked her to dance. Poor Maria, Patty remembered. No one had asked her to dance, but maybe that was because she had sat there looking so gloomy. Men were sensitive creatures. Their egos were so easily bruised. They never wanted to risk being turned down.

Suddenly, a new idea popped up in Patty's mind. Would she get seasick on Phil's boat? She never had been seasick before but things changed. People developed allergies to foods they had always enjoyed. People who had always loved watching horror movies suddenly found them disgusting. That had happened to someone Patty had known at one of her jobs. Anyway, she told herself sternly, there was no way she could know ahead of time whether or not she would feel seasick so she would just have to show up and find out.

And then there was the question of what she should wear. Would it be chilly on a boat in the evening, especially after the sun went down? It was always cooler on the water, wasn't it? Would she need a hat, one with a brim in case the setting sun was blinding? Of course, she could just bring a pair of sunglasses.

After studying her clothes and accessories for well over an hour, Patty had finally opted for her cobalt-blue Capri pants, a white T-shirt worn under a pink jean jacket, and a pair of sneaker/sandals. She wasn't sure if there was a name for the hybrid-looking shoes. They were kind of ugly but everyone seemed to be wearing them and they had been on a super sale, so . . .

She was still committed to keeping Phil a secret from her housemates, so while she didn't exactly sneak out of the house, she left quietly and in a hurry, hoping that none of the others would see her. She wasn't committing a crime, having dinner with an unattached male, but somehow, it felt a bit forbidden.

The drive to the marina was uneventful. Once there, Patty parked in the lot, got out of her car—her sister's husband's car—and began to follow Phil's directions down the wooden pier to his boat. She hoped she looked as if she belonged. Lots of these boat owners were probably rich. They might see right away that she was an outsider. She tried hard not to appear nervous.

Phil had told her that his boat was named Dolly, after his mother. Mrs. James's real name had been Dorothy, but she had always gone by her childhood nickname. Patty thought it nice that Phil had christened his boat after his mother. Men who respected their mothers were good men. Sometimes.

He was waiting for her on the deck of his boat and waved to her as she approached. He was wearing much the same sort of clothes as he had been wearing each time Patty had seen him at Crystal Breeze. Not in the least fashionable but spotlessly clean.

Patty waved in return and felt a smile come to her face. "Hi," she said when she was near.

"Hello, I'm glad you made it," Phil replied, reaching for her hand to help her onto the boat. "On board," as boat people said. At least, Patty thought that was what they said.

Patty didn't have the vocabulary to describe Phil's boat, other than to say that it was beautiful, sort of streamlined, and the wood parts were lovely and shiny. Phil had set out two deck chairs for them and directed Patty to one.

"You're a natural," he said when she had taken a seat. "You've already got your sea legs."

Patty laughed. "Maybe in another life I was a lady pirate!"

"Now that's a thought! How do you feel about going around with a parrot on your shoulder?"

"Not good," Patty admitted. "I'll skip the parrot and the hook for a hand, and the peg leg while we're at it. But I can see myself in a fancy hat and buckled boots."

"I think you'd make a very fetching pirate," he said.

Patty felt herself blush. Would she ever be too old to blush? Did it matter?

Phil explained that he had brought in dinner from a local specialty food shop. "I didn't know what you'd like—I should have asked," he said, "I'm sorry for that—so I got a variety of things hoping there would be something you'd enjoy."

"I'm not very fussy when it comes to food," Patty told him. "Except I can't do curry or lots of onions."

There was cold pasta salad with peas, celery, carrots, and

parsley; crusty rolls with packets of butter; hard-boiled eggs sprinkled with paprika; and, best of all, hot dogs, wrapped in a silver foil to keep them warm, and packets of ketchup and mustard. For dessert, there were two giant cookies, one chocolate chip and the other cinnamon raisin.

"We should be nice and comfortable here," Phil said when he had laid out the food and eating utensils. "It's been a while since I've eaten my dinner on Dolly."

"Phil!"

Patty looked around to see a middle-aged man carrying fishing gear standing on the pier, waving in their direction. Phil waved back.

"You're popular," Patty noted, turning back to her host.

"Not popular so much as a fixture," he explained. "I've lived in Yorktide all of my life."

"And you like it here."

"I wouldn't live anywhere else, not if I could help it. It's a lovely place to call home, Patty."

At that moment, with the sun just beginning to set and a cool breeze coming off the water, Patty thought that Phil was probably right.

"You look very pretty in this light," Phil said suddenly. "I hope you don't mind my saying that."

"Oh, no," Patty assured him. "I mean, I don't mind. Thank you."

"Would you like some wine?" Phil opened the cooler that sat by his feet. "I have white and red. They're what you call table wines but I'm told they're nice."

"Thank you," Patty said with a smile. She knew virtually nothing about wine, in spite of having tried to learn about vintages and things like that over the years. Well, she hadn't actually *tried* to learn. She had thought about learning, but in the end, it had seemed too much effort. "I'll have some white, please."

While Phil opened the bottle and poured the wine, Patty

realized that even if their friendship consisted only of this, one summer meal of hot dogs and pasta salad before she had to leave Yorktide, that would be okay. This was good for her, sitting here on this boat with a really nice man, watching the sun going down.

"Cheers," Phil said, raising his glass to hers. "To a lovely evening with a lovely lady."

Patty smiled and raised her glass in return. Phil thought she looked pretty. He had called her a lady. For the first time in a very long time, Patty Porter felt happy.

Chapter 52

All three of Amanda's summer roommates were present for breakfast that early August morning when she found herself saying: "Today is my birthday."

Amanda was stunned that she had spoken. She had had no intention of telling the others. Could she un-speak the words? She took a fortifying sip of orange juice and told herself that it was best simply to accept that what was done was done.

"Hey, happy birthday," Mary said, pouring her second cup of black coffee. "Any special plans?"

Amanda laughed a bit. "No. No plans, special or otherwise. I never make a big deal out of my birthday."

"I do," Sandra said. "I think everyone should. Why not celebrate the fact that you're alive and have been for however many years?"

"I agree," Patty said. "I mean, about celebrating. Not the part about counting the years."

"You never did tell us how old you are," Mary commented with a smile.

"It's not . . . I don't like to talk about it," Patty said firmly.

Mary shrugged. "Anyway, I'm half with Amanda and half

with Sandra and Patty on this one. But as we're all here, why not do something special? It certainly can't hurt."

Amanda felt genuinely tongue-tied. She didn't see how she could get out of doing something 'special' without insulting or worse, alienating her roommates. And right now, Sandra, Mary, and Patty were pretty much the closest friends she had. The only friends?

Gosh, she thought, that sounded pitiful. But things could be worse. She liked her summer roommates, even Patty. Sort of.

"Okay," she said finally. "Thanks."

"You'll be in for dinner this evening?" Patty asked.

Where else would I be? Amanda thought. "Yes," she said. "I'll be here."

"Good."

Sandra nodded. "Then it's settled. We'll have dinner together and lift a glass to the birthday girl. I'll get the Prosecco."

"How old are you, anyway?" Patty asked.

That was just like Patty, Amanda thought. Not ready to tell anyone *her* age but feeling free to ask the question of others. "Fifty-seven," she said.

Mary sighed. "A mere youth."

Amanda had spent much of the day on her own; at one point, she had driven to the beach and walked for almost two hours along the shore. Largely, her mind had been a blank, which seemed a gift of sorts, given the fact that there were more than a few troublesome thoughts that might easily have disturbed her.

Late in the afternoon, her parents had called. Mrs. Irving apologized for having sent a birthday card only two days before. "Lately, I just can't keep track of dates the way I used to," she had said. Amanda had assured her mother that all was well. She had been grateful for the call.

There had been no call from Liam. Had she really expected him to reach out? No. Did she really care that he had ignored her birthday? As much as Amanda hated to admit it, yes, she did care, not a lot but some.

Amanda left her room and joined the others downstairs. For dinner, which they ate in the dining room as it was a special occasion, Sandra had made a pork and vegetable stir-fry and a large salad, and there was a delicious sourdough boule from the local bakery. She had also provided two bottles of Prosecco for toasting, and, of course, for drinking with the meal. Mary had picked up a lovely bouquet of dahlias to serve as a centerpiece.

Conversation largely revolved around humorous tales of birthdays gone wrong, of parties crashed by an ex-boyfriend, of pin-the-tail-on-the-donkey become pin-the-tail-on-the-daddy, of a fight breaking out between two supposed BFFs after one too many martinis. Long before dinner was over, Amanda realized that she was really enjoying the evening.

When the dinner plates had been removed and the coffee pot turned on, Patty rose from her seat.

"Are you ready for your surprise?" she asked, face beaming.

Ready as I'll ever be, Amanda thought. "Sure," she said.

Patty dashed out of the dining room and returned a few moments later holding before her a pink glass platter on which sat a perfectly formed triple-layer chocolate cake decorated with four candles. As she brought the cake to the table, the women sang the Happy Birthday song and Amanda, not one prone to easy tears, nevertheless was moved more than she had expected to be.

"I can't remember the last time anyone made me a birthday cake," she told the others when the candles had been extinguished and removed. "Really, it must have been when I was in grade school. Thank you, Patty."

"I know I took a chance on chocolate cake and icing but if

I had asked you what flavor you liked best then I'd have blown the surprise. Besides, I've seen you eat chocolate ice cream so . . ."

"I love chocolate. This is perfect, Patty, really. And, oh, it's delicious!"

Amanda was truly touched by her summer roommates' gesture of friendship, so touched that she made the sudden decision to tell them about the trouble in her private life. What could be the harm? And if the impulse to reveal Liam's desertion was due to the Prosecco, so be it. In vino veritas.

"I guess I should explain why I've been a bit, well, down lately," she began. "Not that you necessarily have noticed," she added hurriedly, "but if you have . . ."

"What's wrong, Amanda?" Sandra asked gently.

Amanda took a deep breath. "My boyfriend, Liam, sent me a text about a week ago telling me that he'd met another woman and that our relationship was over. He's moved out."

"He broke up via text!" Mary cried, accidentally dropping her fork in her astonishment. "What a weenie!"

Patty reached for Amanda's hand and gave it a pat. "Oh, Amanda, I'm so sorry. You must be very upset."

Amanda smiled a bit. "I was upset. I am. But not as much as maybe I should be. I don't know what I feel, to be honest. In his text, Liam told me not to be mad. I thought I could follow that advice—"

"What a ridiculously stupid thing for him to say," Mary declared.

"Yes. It was stupid. Anyway, I guess I am mad but not terribly. I'm not sure what that means."

"Finish your cake," Sandra urged. "And then tell us if there's anything we can do."

Amanda took another bite of the cake Patty had so generously made for her. It really was delicious. When she swallowed, she realized that she felt a bit better than she had all day.

"You could help me find the courage to call him," she told her roommates, "not exactly to confront him but, I don't know, maybe to get some answers. Like, why wasn't I right for him anymore?"

"You mean, you haven't been in touch with him since you got his text?" Sandra asked.

Amanda shook her head. "No," she admitted. "I guess I . . . Talking to him is not something I'm looking forward to."

"There's nothing to be afraid of," Mary said firmly. "He can no longer hurt you. He walked away; he set you free."

"Even if she didn't want to be set free," Patty said softly, almost to herself.

Amanda took another bite of the cake, and then her slice was gone. Mary was right, she thought. Liam had set her free. There was nothing of which to be afraid. Certainly, she would not be afraid of her newfound freedom. At least, not very afraid.

"I'll do it after dinner," she said to the others around the table. "I'll call Liam. But I think I need another piece of cake first."

Amanda was surprised that Liam had answered the phone. Surely, he had recognized her number; she had expected him to avoid her call. But maybe he had answered his phone by mistake. Amanda wondered if his new girlfriend was with him.

Her face felt hot.

She was determined not to mention her birthday.

"Why did you break up with me by text?" she said immediately. "Why couldn't you have called?"

"Hello, to you, too," Liam said, with an attempt at a laugh.

"It was disrespectful."

There was a weighted silence. Finally, Liam spoke. "You're right. I should have called. I don't know why I didn't."

But Amanda knew why. Liam hadn't wanted a "scene,"

even one over the phone, not that Amanda was the sort to make a scene. And he hadn't really apologized for his behavior, had he? He hadn't actually said that he was sorry.

"Why didn't you let me know before now that you got my text?" Liam asked then.

Amanda ignored his question. "Who is this other woman?" she said. "When did you meet her?"

Suddenly, Liam became animated. "Her name is Ana," he said. "I met her earlier in the year through someone at work. I've been seeing her since."

Amanda's stomach lurched. She regretted that second piece of cake. "I see," she said as blandly as she could. "How old is she?"

"Amanda, why do you care how old she is?" Liam sighed. "Forty-six."

About ten years younger than Amanda. Now, she thought, would be the time for Liam to mention her fifty-seventh birthday. He didn't.

"So, you fell in love with someone else. Okay. Did she know you were living with a woman at the time?"

"Yes. I told Ana straight away."

And Ana hadn't cared.

"Who started it?" she asked. "I mean, did you ask her out or did she pursue you?"

Again, Liam sighed. "It wasn't like that. Neither of us pursued the other. We just clicked, you know?"

Amanda wasn't sure that she did know.

"Is she married?" she asked. "Was she living with someone, like you were, when you met?"

"No," Liam replied. "She's divorced. She has a ten-year-old son from the marriage."

Amanda's stomach lurched again. Liam had always been very definite about the fact that he didn't want to raise children, his own or anyone else's. Something had happened to change Liam's mind. But why did his change of heart bother

her? Because maybe what he had really meant all along was that he hadn't wanted to raise children with *her*, Amanda Irving, a woman lacking in some essential emotional way.

"Does she have custody of the child?" Amanda asked finally. Or, was she perhaps a recovering drug addict, not allowed access to her child without supervision? Was Liam involved with someone potentially dangerous? Would he be so stupid, so foolish? Was he just having a midlife crisis? Was he—

"Yes," Liam replied. "She has sole custody. Jamie hardly ever sees his dad, which is fine with us."

Us. Amanda was no longer part of an "us." She had been given her freedom. Dubious gift.

"So, you've met the boy?" she said.

Liam laughed. "Of course. Jamie is a great kid. Really smart, a little shy at times, but he'll probably grow out of it."

"Not every shy kid grows out of being shy." Amanda had no idea why she had made that comment.

"I know that. It was just something to say."

"So, you're serious with this woman?"

"Of course, I am," Liam said, a bit impatiently. "There's a *kid* involved, Amanda. What a question."

What a question. "Right. So . . . you're moving in together?"

"Yeah. I'm staying with her at the moment, but we're looking for a new place big enough for the three of us. Now that I'm part of the family, we need more space."

Part of the family.

Wow.

Suddenly, Amanda had had enough, more than enough.

"Good-bye, Liam," she said, and before he could respond she had ended the call.

Amanda sat there on the edge of her bed, hands on her thighs, her back straight. Who was this person pretending to be Liam Sexton, Amanda wondered? It seemed that there were depths to him she had never imagined he possessed. *Why* hadn't she imagined those depths? Had Liam hid himself from her, or did the fault lie with Amanda and her lack of interest in the man with whom she was spending her life?

Still, how cowardly, his just disappearing after eight years together! But wasn't that kind of what she had done, run away, in her case to avoid facing the truth about her relationship with Liam? Her actions had to be acknowledged as a significant sign that the relationship had been doomed for some time.

And how had she not known he was cheating? Did her ignorance mean that they were already, in effect, living separate lives? Or, maybe she was just clueless by nature. Her long ago fiancé had cheated on her, and she had had no inkling of that infidelity, either. Had her other boyfriends cheated on her as well, Jerry, who had wanted to marry her, and Marc, who had not? It was probably too late now to discover the answer to that question, and even if she could learn the answer, what could she do with the information but brood on it and come to the decision never to get romantically involved again?

The thought struck Amanda now that if Liam had already been preparing to leave the relationship, and clearly, he had, then she had handed him a perfect opportunity by going away this summer. It was almost funny. Almost. Not quite tragic. Definitely ironic.

Amanda stood and stretched her arms over her head. She took a deep breath and lowered her arms. It was odd, she thought. She wasn't even all that mad at Liam. She really wasn't. Maybe he was right. She had known for a long time that the relationship wasn't working.

In fact, she thought, she didn't want Liam back in her life, at all. Not one little bit. Sure, she felt—messy. Bruised. Vulnerable. In need of healing.

But she didn't want or need Liam Sexton. Of that, she was a hundred percent sure.

Chapter 53

"Oof. Kneeling is not for anyone who's reached the age of reason."

Sandra was aware that she had spoken aloud though there was no one around to hear her. For the last fifteen minutes, she had been on her knees in the living room, gathering the scattered pieces of their Jane Austen puzzle. The pieces were all over the place, under the couch, on top of the coffee table, even across the room, by the windows that looked onto the street.

It had been easy to determine what had happened. Clovis had cleverly managed to unearth the puzzle from its protective contraption and had then set about breaking it down into pieces of one, two, or at most, five joined bits.

Sandra hoped he was pleased with himself. No doubt he was.

Suddenly, she became aware that she was no longer alone. Her roommates stood in the doorway. With a groan, and using the coffee table for support, Sandra got to her feet.

"What happened to the puzzle?" Patty asked, pointing to the open box heaped with puzzle pieces that sat on the couch. Sandra thought she sounded genuinely upset.

Mary frowned. "Let me guess. Clovis. He must be pretty strong to have knocked away those candlesticks."

"Cats don't have to be strong," Amanda said. "They're crafty. Cunning. They find a way around an obstacle. You have to admire them."

"Where is the little devil, anyway?" Mary asked.

Sandra shrugged and sank onto the couch, next to the jumble of puzzle pieces. "Gone off somewhere to gloat, no doubt. I've managed to find what I hope are all of the pieces," she told the others, "but there's no way to tell for sure unless I count every piece and see if I come up with a thousand. Which I'm happy to do because without all of the pieces, well, the puzzle is sort of worthless."

"Thanks, Sandra," Amanda said, "but don't bother. It's not a big deal, really."

"I saw him eyeing the puzzle the other day," Sandra told them, "and I had my suspicions. But he gave me that innocent look and I didn't think any more about it."

"Should we start over?" Patty wondered.

Amanda shook her head. "I say it's a lesson learned. Cats and jigsaw puzzles don't mix. Like I said, it's no big deal."

"There's a rumor that cats are jerks," Mary said. "Sorry, Sandra."

"It's all right. I've heard the rumor and it's not entirely untrue."

"There's also a hypothesis," Mary went on, "that cats are liquid, or at least boneless. You know how they make themselves fit the contours of whatever container they decide to occupy. A cardboard box. A salad bowl. A crevice in a wall."

Sandra laughed. "They're certainly mysterious. And mischievous."

The other women took seats around the room.

"Maybe we should play a board game instead," Patty suggested. "At least the game gets put away after every session so it will be safe from Clovis."

"Do you know," Mary noted, "I read somewhere that there are literally hundreds of versions of Monopoly, including one based on *Game of Thrones*."

"How does that work?" Patty asked. "I mean, what's the goal?"

Mary shrugged. "I have no idea. I never watched the show."

"The tokens must be dragons and ogres," Patty went on.

"Are there ogres in *Game of Thrones*?" Amanda asked.

"No idea. Like I said, I never watched it."

"Actually, neither have I," Patty admitted. "I'm not really into fantasy, though I like some of those old stories about knights in shining armor and people like Robin Hood who robbed from the rich to give to the poor."

Sandra smiled. "Do you think players of a *Game of Thrones* version of Monopoly are buying kingdoms and acquiring principalities?"

"Definitely more interesting than hotels and utilities," Mary noted.

"Speaking of Monopoly, the version I have predates the replacement of the boot, wheelbarrow, thimble, and iron."

"What do you mean?" Patty asked.

Sandra explained. "I was visiting a friend of mine from my book group, and she has a recent version of the game. That's where I found out about the new tokens—the cat, the bag of money, some dinosaur, I think it's a T. rex, the rubber ducky, and the penguin. Her grandkids love to play, which is a bit surprising. I mean, given it's a board game and not an online game. But maybe the fact that it's a board game gives it an old-fashioned appeal."

"Remember how everyone had their favorite token and had to play with it for good luck?" Mary asked. "My favorite was the boot. It was fun to stomp around the board. Drove my mother crazy. Do you have to be so loud, she'd ask? And I'd reply, yes, I'm a boot. That's what boots do. They stomp."

"My favorite was the iron," Sandra said. "It was a teeny version of the actual iron my grandmother used for years. Of course, if I were playing with a new version of the game I'd choose the cat as there is no iron."

"I think originally a few of the tokens were war-related," Mary went on. "I seem to remember a battleship, and no, I'm not confusing things with the game Battleship."

"I'm glad that was done away with. I say that as a history teacher who has to explain to kids, in an inoffensive, neutral sort of way, why people go to war. So, when did you get your copy of Monopoly, Sandra?"

Sandra shook her head. "I really can't remember. I think it might have been at one point early in my marriage. There's probably information on the box that would help date my particular version."

"My family never played board games," Patty said then. "They were card players, though. My mother tried to teach me how to play gin rummy and bridge; she said they were good games to know for social reasons. You know, as a hostess you could suggest a game of cards after dinner. I never could get the hang of card games, to be honest."

"Did your parents have a folding card table or did they sit around the kitchen table?" Amanda asked.

"A special card table," Patty said. "I don't know why they needed it when the kitchen or dining table would have served just as well. Maybe it was part of the fun? They had folding chairs, too. Everything was stored in the closet in the front hall. And they made cocktails when their friends came over for an evening of cards. I remember my mother serving highballs. The whole thing seemed very glamorous to me, especially since my mother would put on lipstick and her pearls."

"Whiskey sour," Mary said. "That was my mother's favorite drink. Foul stuff in my opinion. I prefer my whiskey neat."

"Neither of my parents drank," Sandra said. "I don't know why. I don't think they were actually opposed to alcohol. Anyway, my aunt Kitty lived with us for a few years before she died, and I remember that every evening she would pour a small glass of sherry and take it to her room. Sometimes she would invite me to sit with her while she sipped it and read whatever book she was reading at the time. I so loved those evenings spent in her cozy little room. I'd sit there quietly and watch her sipping and reading and I'd feel very grown-up. It's funny what we remember as being important to us. I think if she could know that at seventy-four I still consider those evenings special she would be pleased."

"Masterpiece," Mary said abruptly. "That was another board game I loved when I was young. A girl at school had it, and I'd go to her house after school to play. I was so tempted to steal one of the cards printed with the image of a famous painting. I can't remember now which famous painting it was that attracted me so intensely. And I can't remember the name of the girl, either. So many lives we live and so many lives we forget."

"It's scary when you think about your own past and find it surprising," Amanda said. "Like, did I really do that, go there, say that?"

"How anyone can write an autobiography is beyond me," Mary said. "I mean, who keeps notes about every person they ever met and every little experience they encountered? Okay, some people keep a journal but not consistently, not over the course of thirty or forty years. Or do they?"

"Most people who set out to write their autobiography are already pretty famous," Sandra said. "And they have the help of a ghostwriter who shapes the life story. Then there's all the information that's been made public over the years, who a famous person dated in tenth grade, why they were fired from their first real job. Everyone comes out of the woodwork to offer a tidbit about the person's life, true or false."

"But how does a biographer, even a really good one, ever manage to properly explain or even to suggest the life of his subject?" Mary shook her head. "It seems an impossible task.

In the end, what makes a biography of a living person, or a dead one at that, good or bad?"

Amanda smiled. "Ask a literary critic."

"I'd be afraid to." Mary turned to Patty. "I've been meaning to ask, where did you disappear to a few nights back?"

Patty blushed. "What? What night? Nowhere."

"The night you were wearing those retina-burning electric-blue Capris."

"I don't know. Just—out."

Sandra bit back a smile. She knew it could be dangerous to speculate; often putting two and two together resulted in an awkward five. But she had a hunch that Patty had been with Phil James the night in question. And if she had, well, good for her. But she could understand why Patty might want to keep silent about her relationship—in whatever form it existed—with Phil. Why mention a budding romance doomed to end in a few weeks' time?

Sandra glanced from one of her summer roommates to another. It was nice that the four of them could sit around together and chat pleasantly about nothing. Conversation helped time to pass and—

"Here's the culprit!" Mary announced.

Sandra looked up to find Clovis standing in the entryway to the living room. He stared straight ahead, completely unabashed by his crime. And then he plopped to the floor, lifted a hind leg, and began to wash his nether regions.

Chapter 54

"Rats!" Mary muttered as a harsh grinding noise issued from the food disposal.

"What happened?" It was Sandra, just come into the room.

Mary turned around from the kitchen sink. "Sometimes I can be such a klutz," she said. "I dropped the lid of the soup can I was rinsing and it went down into the food disposal and I can't get it out. Finally, I tried starting the disposal, but that just forced the lid to jam the mechanism somehow. Damn."

"Stop trying to dislodge it," Sandra said quickly. "You'll only get hurt. I'll call a plumber. Let me see, what was the name of that guy I had to call last year when the bathtub wouldn't drain? Oh, yes. Mike at Wonder Plumbing."

"I'll pay for his visit, of course," Mary said.

Sandra shook her head. "I couldn't allow you to do that. This is my house. I'm responsible for its maintenance."

"Look, you wouldn't have to call a plumber in the first place if not for me. I'm paying for the plumber and that's that."

Sandra nodded. "All right," she said after a moment. "Thank you. I'll go and get Mike's number."

Sandra went off and Mary stood there, wondering if old age was the reason for her clumsiness. Maybe, as a result of retirement, she was allowing herself to grow careless or lazy. Could she be giving up, losing her focus? Or, was she overreacting to a simple mistake that anyone at any age might have made? Things slipped down drains. It happened.

Not long after, the four women were gathered at the table to enjoy a classic summer meal of hot dogs, potato salad, and corn on the cob. Each of the women, Mary noted, chose a different condiment: ketchup for Patty; mayonnaise for Sandra; brown mustard for Amanda; and yellow mustard for Mary. What did this say about their different personalities? Nothing, Mary immediately concluded. Nothing at all. People read too much into things like condiments and the color of M&M's.

"Patty," she said, "I want to thank you for inadvertently making me feel guilty about ignoring my brother and his family. I got a call from Bill the other day. He tells me that my nephew just graduated law school with all sorts of honors and that he's working in the public sector, which is admirable any way you look at it. And I discovered that my sister-in-law isn't as dull as I made her out to be. Maybe she's not dull at all. She has a passion for art, same as I do. I guess I'd just never bothered to find out what makes her tick."

Patty smiled. "I'm glad things are working out."

Sandra looked to Patty. "You haven't told us about your family yet. Tell us a bit about your siblings."

"Well," Patty began, without hesitation, "as you know, I have two sisters, one older, that's Bridget, and one younger, that's Theresa, Teri for short. Since February I've been living with Bridget and her husband, Ed. I . . . I couldn't afford to pay rent on my own place any longer." Here, Patty paused and attempted a smile. "I guess you could say that I'm basically homeless."

This was unusual behavior for Patty, Mary thought, who to date had been reticent about her personal life. Maybe Amanda's having shared her romantic crisis had inspired Patty to open up. Whatever the reason, Mary had something to say.

"Don't say that you're homeless," she scolded. "Living with a relative or with a friend isn't the same as being homeless!"

"Mary is right, Patty. Even if the situation isn't perfect, you're not living on the streets." Amanda paused. "I'm sorry. That came out wrong. I didn't mean to sound unsympathetic."

"That's okay," Patty said. "I know what you mean, and I do realize how much worse off I could be. I mean, not everybody is lucky enough to have someone willing to let them move into the spare bedroom."

"But you're unhappy, aren't you?" Mary wasn't sure she should have asked the question, but she had.

Patty looked down at the untouched hot dog on her plate. "Yes. I know I have no right to be unhappy, but I am." Patty looked up again; her eyes were shining with tears. "It's just the situation. My sisters, they say things like, 'if you'd been smart and put away money all along, you wouldn't be in this mess now.' They're right about those things. But it hurts when they say them. I don't think they mean to be hurtful, not really, but they are."

"They mean it all right," Mary said angrily. "Look, if you're going to live with one or both of them from now on, you have to speak up right away and tell them how their saying or doing certain things makes you feel. Let them know you're fully aware this is not an ideal situation and that if you could change it now, you would, but since you can't, would they please show you the respect you deserve."

"I'm not sure I have a right to demand anything of my sisters," Patty said. "They have the upper hand. They own their homes. They can say who can live there or not. They can set the terms, and I have to abide by them."

Sandra shook her head. "It shouldn't be a matter of someone having the upper hand."

"Maybe not, but I know for sure Bridget resents my having to live with her and Ed. I understand. I never wanted this, either. I just never thought . . . I never thought I'd wind up this way. See, my parents always tried to steer me toward marriage to a successful man, like a doctor or a lawyer. There was never any question of my going to college and, to be honest, I had no interest in college. I was never a great student. Maybe I should have gone for a secretarial course, but no one suggested it and . . . I guess I was just lazy. The lazy, sweet, pretty sister."

Mary realized that she was fascinated by Patty's story.

Patty sighed and went on. "I was thinking about what we were talking about the other night, about sibling rivalry. The thing is, my parents' favoritism really hurt my sisters. Bridget and Teri tried to get our parents to notice them, but our parents just didn't. Or wouldn't. It was unfair of our parents not to recognize Bridget's school smarts and Teri's athletic ability. They didn't actually neglect my sisters, but they never showered attention on them, either. Of course, it was only later on I realized the favoritism our parents showed me was pretty extreme. Honestly, I think I would have been better off now if my parents hadn't doted on me, if they hadn't sent me into the world so . . . so ill-equipped."

"I didn't know your parents, of course," Sandra said after a moment, "but I can't help but think they would have changed their behavior if they'd been aware of the damage it was doing. Too often parents just don't see what's happening right under their noses. Well, I suppose that's true for all people, not just parents."

"When our parents died," Patty went on, as if, Mary thought, she hadn't heard what Sandra had said, "within a few months of each other, Bridget, as executor, was in charge of having to clean out their house and sell it. All she got in their wills was a small bequest. It was the same with Teri, who'd helped Bridget with the house as best she could, which wasn't a lot because at the time, her husband, Kevin, had a really bad broken leg. He was in a wheelchair for about six months, couldn't put any weight on the leg at all, so poor Teri was run ragged. Anyway, I got the bulk of the estate. It wasn't big, but it was far more than what my sisters were left. They weren't afraid of telling me how angry they were, either. It really *was* unfair, given the fact that it was Bridget and Teri who had been around to look after our parents as they got old. I was the one who had moved away."

Patty stopped speaking to take a long drink of water. "Anyway," she went on, "I didn't give any of the money to my sisters. I was on my own, things were tight, and after all, I reasoned, both of my sisters owned their own homes and were doing all right as far as I could see. My brothers-in-law had steady jobs, and the kids were always nicely turned out for Mass on Sunday, and they'd all gone to or were planning to go to college. I just . . ."

Amanda shook her head. "This is an awkward question and you certainly don't have to answer it, but is there anything left of the inheritance?"

"No. It's long gone." Patty laughed bitterly. Mary had never heard a note of bitterness in Patty's voice before.

"I'm sorry," Sandra said. "I really am."

Patty attempted a smile. "I remember when I told Bridget that the inheritance had run out. She was furious. She asked if I'd just assumed that she and Ed would be there to bail me out. But it wasn't like that, I told her. I hadn't planned anything. I hadn't been thinking at all. It wasn't what Bridget wanted to hear. 'That's your problem right there,' she said to me. 'You never *think*.'"

"A bit harsh," Sandra murmured.

Patty went on, her eyes fixed on her plate. "I remember saying to Bridget that maybe I *couldn't* think, that maybe I was just dumb. That seemed to make her even angrier. 'No,' she said, 'you're not dumb. You're lazy. You've always been lazy. Mom and Dad never pushed you to do anything; they never made you accomplish anything on your own. And you never took control of your own life, never said, I can make something of my life; you never even tried.' I felt like I'd been slapped across the face. I said something like, 'How do you know I didn't try?' But Bridget just laughed. The fact is that she was right. I never tried hard at anything. I pretty much coasted through most of my life. I guess I thought that would be enough. What a joke. Now I'm the poor sibling, the one asking for charity. I don't mean to sound pathetic, but maybe it serves me right."

There was a long silence then. Both Sandra and Amanda looked pensive. For herself, Mary realized that, while she couldn't applaud the way in which Patty had conducted her life—assuming Patty was telling the truth of the matter, but why would she lie?—Mary absolutely did not believe that Patty deserved to be made to feel ashamed of herself by anyone, least of all her sisters. But it was often family that managed to hurt a person the most deeply.

"I think it would be a good idea for you to talk honestly with your sisters when you get home at the end of the summer," Sandra said, breaking the uncomfortable silence at the dinner table. "Like Mary said, tell them how you feel, share your fears about becoming dependent on them."

Patty shook her head. "I'm not sure I'm brave enough, to be honest. Besides, Bridget and Teri have a right to feel resentful and angry. I can't deny that."

"Even if they have a right to be upset about your parents' behavior," Sandra conceded, "they don't have a right to blame *you* for the choices your parents made."

Amanda nodded. "I agree. What do you think, Mary?"

"It seems a complicated situation," Mary said after a moment. "In spite of everything, it sounds to me as if Patty and her sisters are actually pretty close. Which kind of confuses things and adds a lot of messy emotion."

Patty nodded. "We are close. And you're right, Mary. Everything is so very emotional. That's what makes this all so hard."

"I'm not sure Patty would gain anything by telling her sisters how she feels," Amanda said. "But I don't know them, do I? I don't know if they'd even listen to Patty, if they'd ever apologize for any hurtful behavior on their part."

"And there are the brothers-in-law to consider," Mary added musingly. "How do they feel about their wives having been virtually ignored in the parents' will? You can never really consider a married person as an individual, not in my experience, anyway. A spouse is always whispering in the ear of the partner. *This is what you should think or feel. This is what you should demand. This is what's owed to you.*"

Sandra shook her head. "That's a bit paranoid, Mary. While I acknowledge the fact that a married couple, any long-term couple, juggles three worlds, if it can be put like that—two individual lives and the third life, the life of the couple—that doesn't always mean that the individual lives take a back seat. With John, I never felt that my voice was going unheard or my opinions were being ignored. And I don't think that John ever felt hindered, either. But then, maybe we were lucky."

"It sounds like you were," Mary conceded. "And I don't begrudge you that."

Unprompted, Patty continued telling the others her story. "Bridget—she's seventy-three now—she told me once that when I was born she felt usurped, like I came along and stole her position as the apple of our parents' eye, and I guess that's exactly what happened. It's probably not all that unusual."

Sandra shook her head. "No matter how careful parents are to remind the firstborn that they're still loved, the oldest child is bound to resent the next sibling, at least for a while. I know Jack did, once Kate began to show us her personality. Luckily, his jealousy didn't last long."

"What about your younger sister?" Amanda asked.

"Teri, she's sixty-seven now, she says she felt ignored by our parents right from the start, which she says was good in a way. She got away with stuff Bridget wouldn't have been able to get away with when she was small because no one was paying attention to Teri. I certainly wasn't. I didn't dislike her or anything. I just didn't . . . I didn't care all that much. I was so caught up in . . . in myself."

"Look," Mary said, "we're not going to let this situation at home get you down. It's summer and you're here, we all are, to relax and enjoy some time off." Suddenly, Mary remembered that Patty had a job; her summer was not all vacation and downtime. But on she went, if lamely. "Please try to put it out of your mind."

Patty smiled a bit. "Thanks, Mary. Really. Thanks, everyone."

Mary struggled not to cringe. *We're not going to let this situation at home get you down.* It was a promise Mary knew that she couldn't keep, a promise that Sandra and Amanda were unlikely to be able to keep, either. She should have kept her mouth shut, not spouted silly pseudo-comforting platitudes.

Mary watched as Patty finally picked up her cold hot dog and took a bite. She felt an enormous wave of sympathy for Patty just then. And she sincerely hoped that Patty didn't come to regret having shared her story with her housemates.

Chapter 55

Patty went about her work without paying much attention to what she was doing. Luckily, counting the number and variety of fridge magnets-Maine license plates, lobster pots, fir trees-that remained on the spinning rack didn't require any great skill or she would be in trouble with her boss. Michelle was nice enough, but in the shop, she was a business owner first and foremost. Patty understood that. Sort of.

She was thinking about the other night. What in the world had made her tell the others the sorry story of her life? Well, parts of it. She hadn't mentioned the men. So many men. Anyway, it was certainly nothing she had planned to do! But she hadn't been met with criticism or judgment; at least, no one had said anything nasty or given her one of those shaming looks her sisters had perfected. Maybe, secretly, one or more of her summer roommates thought her ridiculous or stupid or worthless, but at least they had kept their feelings to themselves.

Since then, Patty hadn't been able to stop thinking about her parents. Had they just been such narrow-minded, stuck-in-their-ways sort of people that they had never even considered options for their daughter other than those they, their parents, and their grandparents before them had known? Why hadn't they been able to see past Patty's looks and appreciate her other positive attributes?

Assuming she had any. She certainly hadn't been an A, or even a consistent B student. She did have a nice personality; plenty of people had told her that. But how did you go about making money with only a good personality? Patty realized she had never given the question any thought.

And that was the problem, she realized, yet again. She had been stupid. She had been careless with her life. Maybe that was worse, being careless. Some people couldn't help acting stupidly, but there might be no excuse for acting carelessly. She didn't know for sure.

One thing she did know for sure, though. She would never tell Phil James the truth about her past. He was too . . . He was too nice. Patty had really enjoyed their dinner date. She thought that Phil had enjoyed it, as well. The problem was, he hadn't called her since then. What was she to make of his silence?

She had already begun to feel that she could trust Phil. But she had made so many mistakes before. What if he was playing her as all the others had, lying to her, wasting her time? How would she know until it was all too late, until she offered him something of herself and he took it and then walked away?

She supposed she could ask Sandra about Phil, carefully, without letting on that she might be interested in him in a, well, in a romantic way. She could ask questions about Phil's character, his popularity in Yorktide; maybe she could even ask about his former wife. He had mentioned, briefly, that he was a widower, but had said nothing more than that. Patty hadn't felt comfortable saying anything other than, "Oh, I'm sorry."

The bell over the door to the shop tinkled, and Patty looked over to see a couple entering. She knew better than to stare, but a quick glimpse told her that they were, she guessed, in their mid to late sixties. Both were tan. The woman was dressed in pink and white and the man was wearing sky blue and beige. They were about the same height as each other. They weren't holding hands, but Patty imagined that they enjoyed holding hands. She wondered how long they had been married. She assumed they were married, though she couldn't see if either was wearing a ring on the third finger of the left hand. They were probably staying in a swanky resort. Gosh, Patty thought, they looked so perfect together. They looked so happy.

Abruptly, Patty looked away. She was doing it again. Why did she always leap to the conclusion that a couple was happy when she *knew* that lots of couples weren't happy? Was she that jealous of people in a relationship that she couldn't even see them as real people with troubles as well as with joys? Silly. The sad fact was that over the years, she had managed to lose what little judgment she had ever possessed, not only about herself, but also about other people. Maybe these two, this woman in the pink baseball hat and this man in the sky-blue polo shirt, weren't happy at all.

She supposed the real question, the one at the bottom of the matter, was this: Was anyone ever happy with his or her lot? Were people even *supposed* to be happy?

There she was, *thinking* again. Thinking was depressing, even if it was something you were supposed to do. Patty liked to be happy.

And right now, there were still fridge magnets to be counted. Well, recounted. Patty had lost track.

Chapter 56

Amanda found Sandra in the kitchen, seated at the table with a cup of tea and a hardcover novel.

"Do you have an ice pack by any chance?" she asked, aware that her voice was wobbling a bit.

"What happened?" Sandra asked, hurriedly rising from her seat and coming over to where Amanda stood, just inside the door.

"I hurt my ankle. I was walking along the road down by that big farm, Wildewood or something, and I heard what sounded like a car coming too fast from behind. I turned to look over my shoulder and stumbled on the uneven surface of the verge. I twisted my ankle, pretty badly I think. The car just sped by, which was probably a good thing. No one driving that fast has good intentions."

"And you hobbled back to the house in pain. Why didn't you call me?" Sandra asked. "I would have come and brought you home."

"I didn't want to be a bother. I know, it was probably stupid. Walking back to the house probably made the injury worse."

"Well, never mind that now," Sandra said briskly. "Here,

lean on my arm. Let's get you into the den, and I'll get an ice pack and some ibuprofen or Tylenol, whatever you prefer."

Amanda looped her arm through Sandra's. It was the first time she had touched one of her summer roommates. Amanda wasn't big on touching; she had never been the sort to greet people—even her parents—with a hug and a kiss. Her aversion to human touch probably had something to do with her difficulty in asking others for help. Was it really too late to change the habits or psychological tendencies of a lifetime?

The den wasn't a room Amanda had visited often for some reason. Now she noted just how lovely a room it was, cozy in the extreme, right out of one of the classic British mystery novels she enjoyed. There was a broad, plush armchair upholstered in a pattern of pale pink cabbage roses against a mint green background. The couch, as plush as the armchair, was covered in the same pretty fabric. A tall bookcase was filled neatly with a wide variety of titles—a set of the works of Charles Dickens caught Amanda's attention, as did an oversized book of Audubon prints.

Windows on two sides of the room meant that the room probably got good sun for at least part of the day. The walls were painted a pale but cheery yellow. An old-fashioned standing lamp with a glass shade in the style of Louis Comfort Tiffany stood by the armchair. The design of the shade included gorgeously colorful dragonflies. Maybe the lamp was a genuine Tiffany.

Sandra helped Amanda to the couch and propped up her injured ankle under a large pillow.

"If you need any help at all, with anything," Sandra said, "don't hesitate to ask. There's no point in standing on ceremony in times of need."

Amanda felt close to tears. How humiliating it would be to cry in front of this woman who was really just a stranger, and over something as silly as a sprained ankle. But the tears weren't so much about the ankle as they were about an unwelcome sense of vulnerability. If the accident had happened back home, and she had had to take care of herself now that Liam was gone, how could she have managed? Well, how did anyone who lived alone manage? They just did, maybe with the help of a friend or family member who agreed to stop by and make meals or do a little housecleaning. Still, to be alone . . . Was it what she really wanted after all?

"I'm not comfortable being waited on," she managed to say, voice trembling.

Sandra smiled. "Don't worry. It won't go on forever. We'll expect you up and about pretty soon. But in the meantime, try to enjoy a little pampering. We all need it now and then."

A terrible wave of self-pity engulfed Amanda. Who *would* there be to help her if this sort of accident should happen back home? She barely knew the names of her neighbors in the building.

The sudden appearance of Mary and Patty came as a welcome distraction.

"Hey, what's going on?" Mary asked.

Sandra briefly explained the situation. "I was telling Amanda that she should ask for help with whatever she needs."

"I'll be right back," Patty said suddenly. "I won't be long."

"What was that about, I wonder," Sandra said, as Patty dashed down the hall.

"You'd better ask for help," Mary told Amanda, after glancing at Patty's retreating form. "You'd be nuts to try to get up and down the stairs before the swelling goes down. Give me a list of things you need from your room and I'll put your toiletries in the downstairs bathroom and we'll make up the couch as your bed."

Amanda gave Mary the information she had asked for and Mary dashed off, returning to the den to announce that Amanda's toiletries and pajamas and robe were now at home down the hall.

Another fifteen or twenty minutes had passed, during which time both Sandra and Mary had fussed over Amanda as if she were a child who had been found wandering on her own through a shopping mall, before Patty reappeared in the doorway of the den, her face flushed, holding a bouquet of fresh flowers in a clear glass vase and tied with a green satin ribbon.

"I thought these might cheer you up," she said to Amanda. "I'll put them on this little table so you can see them," she said.

"Thank you, Patty," Amanda said, feelingly. First the birthday cake and now a bouquet. "You shouldn't have."

"Why not? Flowers always lift the spirits, and right now I bet your spirits need lifting."

"You know, if I were you," Mary said with a grin, "I'd use this opportunity of being a temporary invalid to indulge in something you ordinarily don't allow yourself. Like, for example, cupcakes or, I don't know, a wheel of brie."

Patty's eyes brightened. "Cupcakes! That would be my indulgence for sure! With lots of icing and sugar sprinkles, too."

"It's always cheese for me," Mary said. "I've even been known to opt for Velveeta when desperate."

"Velveeta makes a very yummy grilled cheese sandwich," Patty told her.

"Hmm. I bet it does at that."

"So," Sandra asked Amanda, "what indulgence can we bring you?"

Amanda was almost puzzled by the question. An indulgence? She wasn't the sort to indulge, not really. She wasn't the sort to break any rules, her own or someone else's. She never had been. Except for the night of her birthday. Two slices of Patty's chocolate cake had done the trick. Not that she would ever eat two slices of cake in one day again.

"I'm not sure," she admitted. "Can I think about it?"

"Of course," Sandra told her. "Well, I've got to get on. I'm attending a concert at the library and I don't want to walk in late."

The others followed soon after, leaving Amanda on her own in the den, her injured foot propped on a large pillow, the pretty flowers from Patty in clear view. These women with whom she was sharing the summer were all so kind, Amanda thought, even Patty, who at first Amanda had thought one of those terminally self-centered people. She knew that Patty didn't have money to spend on anything not a necessity. The fact that she had bought what was obviously an expensive bouquet of flowers for Amanda had been foolish, perhaps, but also a very lovely gesture.

Suddenly, Amanda caught sight of a framed photograph on a small occasional table. It was of Sandra and her husband, John, on their wedding day, Sandra in a white dress, John in a tuxedo. The pair were undeniably attractive, but what most stood out was the look of genuine happiness on the faces of both the bride and the groom.

Amanda looked away from the image of the happy couple. It depressed her. She wondered if she had ever really been in love with Liam. She *must* have been; why else would she have allowed him to move in with her?

Had she been in effect sleepwalking through the past few years, maybe even through her entire adult life?

Maybe she had taken Liam for granted. Maybe he was justified in leaving her, if not in the way that he had.

Maybe she wasn't capable of love, at least, of the kind of love it took to sustain a healthy romantic commitment to a person. Had anyone ever really loved her? Had Liam? How could he ever have loved her if he had been able to dump her in the way that he had, so coldly and carelessly? He hadn't even remembered her birthday. Or, if he had remembered, he had chosen to ignore it. Amanda didn't know which was worse.

The idea that she might have been and might remain unloved was terrifying. Other than her parents, who pretty much had to love her, had anyone, man, woman, or child, felt genuine love for her?

Why couldn't she seem to feel beyond a certain depth? Was there anything she could do about that? Did she *have* to do anything? Was it okay to be a coward, to accept that your life wasn't what it might be and to also accept that you didn't have the energy or the skills to fix it?

Why was this happening to her, all these thoughts and disruptions and, and, and cars coming at her and—

Overcome, Amanda burst into tears.

Chapter 57

Why, Sandra wondered, did emptying the dishwasher feel like an annoying chore while filling the dishwasher felt like a mildly interesting chore? With a smile, she closed the door of the dishwasher. Emma used to pose silly questions like that in such a way as to cause Sandra to laugh out loud. There was nothing Emma hadn't been able to turn into fun.

Patty came into the kitchen then. She was wearing a bright yellow blouse; it wasn't, Sandra thought, the best color for her.

"Are you busy?" Patty asked.

Sandra thought that Patty looked nervous. "Not really," she said. "The dishwasher is emptied and everything's been put away. What's up?"

"Can I ask you something? It's about Phil James."

"Sure," Sandra said. Interesting. First Phil had approached her regarding Patty, and now Patty was asking questions about Phil. Something was definitely going on. "Fire away."

"You've known him for a long time, you said."

Sandra nodded. "Since forever. Phil and I were in school together."

"Then you knew his wife." Patty clasped her hands before

her, then unclasped them and stuffed them into the pockets of her pants.

"Yes. Nancy." And Eileen before her, but Sandra would not talk about Phil's first love, not that she had ever learned why it had ended the way that it had.

"What was she like?" Patty asked. "I mean, was she . . ."

Sandra refrained from smiling; she found Patty's obvious nervousness touching. "Is there a reason you're asking me these questions?" she said. "I take it you've spoken with Phil, maybe spent a little time together?"

Patty blushed. "Yes. We've spoken. That's why I'm curious, you know, to know, um, who it is I'm talking to. In a way."

"Right. Well," Sandra went on, determined to be as honest as she could about Phil James's wife. "Nancy was a very good person, very concerned with the welfare of her neighbors. She volunteered whenever and wherever she could. She was always dashing off to drive an elderly person to church, to bring a hot, home-cooked meal to a new mother, to shovel the front walk for a housebound relative. The catty types of Yorktide's population used to refer to her as Saint Nancy. Not to her face, of course. I don't condone name-calling, even when done jokingly, without malice, but honestly, in this case it was difficult not to think of Nancy James as someone very different from the rest of us mere mortals."

Patty looked as if she might cry. "Oh," she said. "I see."

Quickly, Sandra put Patty out of her misery. "Can you imagine living with that sort of person day in and day out, year after year? I certainly can't."

"What do you mean?" Patty asked, visibly brightening.

"I mean it must be exhausting! A lot of us here in Yorktide used to feel sorry for Phil. It really was like he came at the very end of Nancy's list of important causes. I can't tell you how many times she sent him off to a holiday concert or to a friend's birthday party on his own because she'd identified a needy person she just couldn't ignore for a moment longer."

"Do you think they were unhappy?" Patty asked. "Not that I'd want them to have been unhappy," she added hurriedly.

Sandra reflected before speaking. "I wouldn't say unhappy, exactly. As far as I know, Phil never said an unkind or a critical word about his wife. But after a time, he didn't seem all that happy, either. He seemed kind of lonely. And over the years, Nancy became more tiresome to be around. Frankly, I used to dread running into her because I knew it meant I'd be stuck listening to her go on about all the good she'd done for the community since I'd last seen her."

Patty looked genuinely perplexed. "Why did Phil stay with her then? I mean, if she was so . . . annoying."

"That's easy," Sandra said. "Phil took his marriage vows seriously. And I think he truly loved her. He seemed to have accepted the fact that Nancy was who she was and that nothing was going to change that. They rubbed along well enough, I guess you could say, as so many other married couples do, happy or not. When Nancy died, Phil grieved but from what I could tell, not for terribly long. In fact, since Nancy's been gone, Phil has been more, how can I say it, more lighthearted, more like he used to be before he got married."

"Marriage." Patty sighed. "I know so very little about it."

Sandra laughed. "No one knows all that much about it, not even those of us who were married for years. It really is a mysterious thing. It's important—and I hope you don't mind my saying this—it's important not to go into a marriage expecting this or that specifically. The marriage will take on its own shape and gather its own momentum because of the two individuals involved."

"Why would I mind your telling me that?" Patty asked.

"Well, I don't want to assume that you're contemplating a

marriage of your own any time soon. And if you were contemplating such a thing, it's really none of my business."

"Oh." Patty blushed and laughed. "Don't worry."

"Good. Now, how about joining me in a cup of tea?"

"One more thing. Did Phil ever, I mean, was there ever . . ."

"Another woman?" Sandra guessed. "No. Which is not to say that someone didn't try to grab his attention at one point, not long before Nancy died! I won't name names as she's still living in Yorktide, but she really did her best to catch Phil's eye while he completely ignored her attempts. There was no way he could have been oblivious to her efforts, believe me, but if he was ever tempted, he never acted on the impulse."

"Good," Patty said with a nod. "I mean, oh. And what about after Nancy died? Has he been on his own since then?"

"As far as I know, yes. But I don't think his not getting involved with another woman has anything to do with respect for Nancy's memory. I think . . . No, I shouldn't say this. It's just my opinion."

"Please, Sandra. I . . . I kind of need to know."

Sandra hesitated a moment longer before speaking. "Well, in my opinion, that marriage exhausted Phil. I think it soured him on the idea of finding a new relationship. But I also think that if the right woman comes along, well, things might very well change."

"Yes," Patty said quietly. "I mean, maybe. I hope. Phil seems like a really good man. I really . . . I really like him. And sure, I'll have a cup of tea. Thanks."

While Sandra prepared the tea, she thought again about the fact that she seemed to have become a bit of a surrogate mother to her summer roommates. She enjoyed the feeling of being wanted. If she could help nurture a friendship between Patty and Phil, then she was happy to do so.

"Here we go," she said, bringing the cups of tea to the table.

"Thank you," Patty said. "It's so nice here," she added suddenly. "So—warm. I don't mean hot. I mean—well, it's comfortable. This house. The people in it."

Sandra smiled. Patty's comment was the greatest compliment one of her summer roommates could have given her. "It's you I should be thanking," she said. "You and Mary and Amanda have made this house a home again."

At least, Sandra added silently, a home for the summer.

Chapter 58

Mary had been seething all day since she had read about the tragedy reported in the morning's online news. It was seven o'clock now, dinnertime at Sandra's house, and still, Mary's emotions were running just as high as they had been earlier.

"I promised myself I wasn't going to bring this up," she announced abruptly, "but I just have to break that promise. I'm sure you all heard about that lunatic with a gun who let loose in a congregation gathered for a worship service this morning. It was somewhere in the wilds of Utah, but it could easily have been anywhere, downtown Los Angeles, New Orleans, a suburb of D.C."

"According to the article I read," Amanda said, "the gunman had no clear idea of what the congregation even believed or professed. They just weren't *his* group, and that alone was reason enough for wanting to eliminate them."

"The 'other' has always been a problem for humans," Sandra said, shaking her head. "So terribly silly."

"Such contention around religion," Amanda added. "I suppose it's always been that way and probably always will be."

"Why can't everyone just get along? Leave one another

alone to be who they want to be. Oh," Patty said with a shake of her head, "I know that's all pie in the sky. But still. It seems so simple. Just be nice. Why do people have to complicate life by being angry and aggressive?"

"Human nature," Amanda said. "Sadly, it's not in us to live and let live for any length of time."

"Do unto others as you would have them do unto you. Why can't people abide by that commandment?" Sandra smiled sadly. "Sometimes it seems like so many people don't even try to be kind and accepting."

"And the fact that we live the way we do makes it all feel worse," Mary opined. "I mean, nowadays pretty much everyone anywhere knows about miseries and mayhem occurring in every corner of the world. There's no buffer. I mean, I know the world is messed up, but why do I need to have those realities thrust in my face twenty-four seven? I could turn off the television, walk away from the phone and the laptop. But it's not all that easy to forget about what you've already witnessed. You can't will yourself to be ignorant. Not if you have even a little bit of a conscience."

"That's where religion, or a spiritual life becomes useful for many people, I suppose," Sandra said. "As something that can help make sense of what on the surface seems senseless."

Suddenly, Mary felt the strange and compelling urge to speak about her religious past. For better or, she thought, most probably for worse. It was all the stupid gunman's fault.

"You know, I was raised in the Catholic tradition," she began, "and for a while, when I was little, I actually enjoyed parts of it. Getting dressed up on Sunday mornings; the pomp and ceremony of Christmas and Easter services; the dark romance of those old paintings and sculptures by the Italian Renaissance crew and the Netherlandish painters, every figure so overwrought with emotion or deep in spiritual ecstasy." Mary smiled. "I even loved the smell of incense until at about the age of twelve I suddenly found it repulsive. Conscious adoles-

cent rebellion or an uncontrollable shift in hormones? You decide."

"What happened to change things?" Amanda asked.

Mary thought for a moment before answering. "I'm not entirely sure, to be honest. All I know is that by the time I was a
sophomore in high school, I'd stopped going to church except
for a rare command performance, like a neighbor's funeral or
the wedding of a distant relative. I used to tell my parents that
I was meeting friends at the second Mass of the day—in those
days lots of people went to Mass regularly so there was a need
for several services—and instead, I'd go off to do something
else, sometimes with my friends and sometimes on my own,
anything really rather than having to sit and stand and kneel
and mumble words that had come to feel hollow and attempt
to choke down a dry wafer that had a tendency to stick to the
roof of your mouth. I never got found out, so maybe my parents trusted my word or maybe by that point they just didn't
care one bit for the sorry state of their daughter's soul. I used
to wonder if they ever bothered to say a prayer for their way-
ward daughter. Frankly, I thought it unlikely."

Mary's roommates sat in silence, perhaps as surprised as she
was that she had shared as much as she had shared. She wondered if she was she getting soft in her old age, losing her
finely tuned edge, that sharp instinct of self-preservation that
had kept her safe throughout an arduous and, at times, slightly
dangerous career.

"What about you, Sandra?" Mary asked, uneasy with the
lingering silence. "Would you describe yourself as religious?"

"I always find that a bit of a tricky question," Sandra admitted. "I'm a member of our local Episcopal church, but I consider myself not so much of a religious person as a spiritual
person. I guess for me, theology isn't as important as human
actions. I do believe in the power of prayer, if you pray with serious intent for the right sort of thing, such as the health and

happiness of others, or the ability to endure troubled times with dignity. Amanda?"

"I wasn't raised in a particular religious faith," Amanda told the others. "I suppose I consider my family vaguely Christian in that on occasion we'd attend a church service on Easter or Christmas, but we never actually belonged to a congregation, and rumor had it that some distant branch of the family was Jewish. Honestly, apart from a historical interest in the world's religions, I'm not at all drawn to spiritual practices. I suppose I find them all a bit—silly."

"Are you an atheist?" Patty asked, eyes wide.

Amanda shrugged. "Maybe. Probably. But I've never bothered to claim that label, so maybe I'm—nothing? Neither this nor that. Undecided. Uninterested."

"I just don't know how you can be uninterested in God." Patty shook her head.

Mary silently agreed with Patty, though she suspected that what Patty meant by being "uninterested in God" was something vastly different from what it meant to Mary.

"Patty?" she asked. "What's your story?"

Patty waved her hand and laughed a bit. "I have no story."

"I mean about religion," Mary pressed.

"Like I said, no story. Just, we grew up Catholic, you know."

"So, you were interested in God."

"Yes. I guess. Sure."

"And are you still interested in God?"

Patty frowned. "Of course."

After a moment of silence, Mary thought it unlikely that anything more was forthcoming from Patty. Before Mary could land on another topic of discussion—and why did she so often feel it was her responsibility to do so?—Amanda spoke.

"I know this is silly," she said, "but remember when I twisted my ankle and I couldn't think of anything I would choose as an indulgence? Well, I finally thought of something I'd consider an indulgence. Funyuns! I suddenly remembered having them once ages ago at a party given by one of the other teachers in my school. I had no idea what they were, just some sort of fried snack thing heaped in a bowl. I remember reaching out mindlessly, which is very unlike me, and taking one of the chips and popping it in my mouth. The taste kind of blew me away. I debated the wisdom of taking another chip and decided that as delicious as the chips were, no doubt they were exceedingly bad for your health and that it would be better not to indulge. That *is* very like me. So, I walked away from the table of snacks but in the back of my mind the taste sensation of that one chip lingered."

"I am truly grossed out," Mary said. "Funyuns, of all things. I'd have never suspected it from you. You just don't seem the type. Wow, that sounded bad."

Amanda laughed.

Sandra shrugged. "I've never heard of them. What are they?"

"They're a sort of fried onion snack," Patty explained. "I love Funyuns too, though I haven't had them in years and years. They might bother my stomach now."

"They can't be made with real onions, can they?" Mary asked, not surprised that Patty was a fan. But she would keep that snippy judgment to herself. "Whatever the case, I'm happy to bring you a party-sized bag, Amanda."

"You don't have to get anything for me. Now that my ankle is better I'm perfectly able to buy a bag on my own. But thanks."

Which was a good thing, Mary noted silently, as she really had no intention of being seen buying a bag of Funyuns, snack or party sized, for herself or for anyone else.

Boy, she could be a snob!

Still, Mary thought as she took the last bite of her broccoli, better a harmless snob than someone who violently murdered people just because they didn't agree with her opinions.

Chapter 59

"It's a terrible situation. Can you imagine?"

"Yes," Patty said to her sister Bridget. "Terrible."

Patty had come out to the front porch with one of Sandra's lifestyle and home decorating magazines, to while away a bit of the early afternoon. Until Bridget's call had come, Patty had been enjoying herself, if feeling a bit envious of the beautiful homes other people had, the sort of homes that she could never in a million years afford. Not at this point in her life.

"There's no money to care for Alice at home," Bridget went on, "the way she's going to need care, and with no close relatives to step in, well, there's no choice but for her to go into a home. A great-nephew, I think, or maybe it's a distant cousin, someone is going to sell the house for her, and that will help pay for the home, but what will happen when that money runs out I don't know." Bridget sighed. "Well, at least she *has* the house. I can't imagine where she'd be if she had nothing."

Patty felt slightly sick to her stomach. Her sister was speaking pointedly, of that she had no doubt.

"Patty?" Bridget said loudly. "Are you listening to me?"

"Yes," she said, staring blankly at a car passing slowly down the street. "I'm listening. Poor Alice."

"I just hope that nephew or cousin or whoever he is doesn't cheat her, and it would be easy to cheat Alice at this point. The poor woman doesn't know what day of the week it is, let alone how much her house might sell for in today's market."

Suddenly, Patty had had enough. "I've got to go," she said hurriedly. "I, uh, I'm doing an extra shift today at the shop, and if I don't leave now I'll be late."

She didn't care if Bridget suspected that she was lying. She had to get off the phone.

"Well, you don't want to be late," Bridget said crisply. "Should I tell Alice that you were asking for her?"

Why? Patty thought wildly. If Alice didn't know what day of the week it was, why should she remember Bridget's loser sister Patty? "Yes," she said, "fine, good-bye."

Patty immediately ended the call. If her sister thought her rude, so be it. Bridget already thought her stupid and selfish. Why not rude, as well? Rude and, at the moment, literally shaking. The call had upset her. Of course, she felt bad for the family's friend. But she also couldn't help but feel bad for herself, someone who might one day be in need of the kind of care only available in a nursing home. Bridget had said that Alice had no close relatives to help her. Well, Patty had her sisters. Maybe. To some extent. But what she didn't have was any equity, a house to sell that would help pay for a few years in a decent nursing facility.

And what would happen to her if Bridget and Teri left her to fend for herself in a system not exactly known to be an easy one to negotiate? And if she ran out of money before she ran out of life? What then? Would she wind up in a state-run facility, neglected, dirty, malnourished, tortured by underpaid aides? It was a terrifying thought.

Diverting magazine forgotten, glass of lemonade now mostly melted ice, Patty sighed. She thought about the conversation the other night at dinner, the one about the other women's experience of religion. She had avoided answering the questions

Mary had put to her as best as she could, sticking to the bare minimum of fact, that she had been raised in the Catholic faith. What she didn't say was that she still claimed, if quietly, to be a practicing Catholic, in spite of the fact that she had never been able to reconcile certain bits of her behavior—for example, her habit of being with married men—with the behavior of a God-fearing Christian woman.

Not that anyone in her family had ever used that expression. Patty thought "God-fearing Christian woman" might not be a term particularly favored by Catholics, but maybe she was wrong.

Anyway, it was about fifteen years ago now that Patty had undergone a sort of Paul on the road to Damascus moment. The wife of the man she had been seeing steadily for almost six months—a man Patty had really liked and hoped to marry— had confronted her husband with her suspicions that he was having an affair. Alan—that was his name—admitted to Patty that he had lied to his wife, sworn that he was innocent of any wrongdoing. But during that visit to Patty's apartment, he had broken down in copious tears and told her that he had no choice but to break off their relationship. He admitted his deep regret that he had ever cheated on his beloved wife, the mother of his children, his dearest friend. "I don't know what I would do without her. I don't think I could go on."

Patty had been so moved by Alan's seemingly genuine contrition and so concerned for his emotional well-being that she had temporarily forgotten to feel sorry for herself and sent him off with a hug and best wishes for the future of his marriage. It was only the next morning, when she woke after a night of restless sleep, that she fully realized what she had lost. Or, perhaps the truth was that she hadn't lost anything because she had never had anything in the first place. Alan had never been hers. Of course, he hadn't.

The unsettling experience had led Patty to spend much time soul-searching and finally, she had found the courage to go to confession in hopes that the sacrament would heal her guilty soul. Because she *was* guilty. She had attempted to tear asunder a union that God had wrought. She hadn't been to confession in years and hoped the formula had remained the same. "Bless me Father, for I have sinned" and so on. She hoped the priest would hear the sincerity in her voice and know that she was truly sorry for her sins. She told no one of her intentions.

Unfortunately, the experience had been a nightmare. Patty hadn't been met with even the smallest degree of understanding or compassion. On the contrary, the priest on duty at Saint Cyril's that day had verbally brutalized her, raised his voice in anger and disgust, only stopping short of actually condemning her to an eternity in hell. Before he could hand down her formal penance, Patty had bolted from the confessional booth and then from the church, mortified, too frightened and humiliated ever to go to confession again.

True, Father Hamilton, now deceased, had been old, a bit senile, and known to have a cantankerous nature, but still. He shouldn't have been abusive, calling her the whore of Babylon and a harlot—or had it been strumpet? If only there had been a way for her to confess to one of the younger, more liberal priests, maybe then she would have been able to gain something positive from the experience. But when she had drawn aside the heavy velvet curtain and stepped into the small, dark confessional booth, she had had no idea which priest of the parish was waiting for her on the other side of that intricate wooden screen.

She had spent the rest of that day and night in a state of extreme distress, wracked by feelings of guilt and shame. Finally, somehow, by the next morning she had managed to pull herself together enough to put on that pretty face and its welcoming expression and get on with the outward living of her life. But inside, Patty's conscience had continued to trouble her. She had vowed never again to get involved with a married man.

Patty picked up the glass of watery lemonade and took a sip. At least, she thought, it was liquid if no longer palatable. Her throat felt dry.

A few months after that dreadful experience in the confessional, Patty's resolve had been tested. She was introduced to a new guy at the office where she was working at the time. A few weeks later, this man, called Hamish, had asked her to go for a drink after office hours. He was good-looking, in a bland sort of way, and, like so many others before him, he was married to a woman who didn't understand him. Patty remembered sitting on the barstool next to this Hamish, listening to his tale of marital woe, trying to smile in a way that expressed sympathy but not too much of it, waiting for the moment when she could make her exit without arousing the man's annoyance or worse, his wrath. While he was not her immediate boss, he was a senior member of the company, a situation that left Patty vulnerable.

Patty had succeeded in extricating herself from the dalliance before it could become anything more than one drink. She had managed to keep the vow she had made to stay away from the husbands of other women, and for the past fifteen years she had continued to keep that vow. Well, to the best of her knowledge she had kept it. Lots of men lied; lots of married men didn't wear wedding rings. But she had tried her very best.

With a genuinely weary sigh, Patty went into the house, poured a fresh glass of lemonade, and went to her room. It felt stuffy, so she turned on the large standing fan Sandra had provided. Then she sat on her bed against the pillows, her legs out before her.

In spite of that horrible experience with Father Hamilton, she still sporadically attended Sunday Mass and services on holidays like Ash Wednesday and Good Friday. The most important event of the liturgical calendar for Patty (if not theologically) was Christmas, specifically, midnight Mass on Christmas Eve. Every year the Porter family dressed in their best, bundled against the cold, and walked together to the church in the highest of spirits, as if going to an old-fashioned fair or a neighborhood barn dance, looking forward to singing the traditional, well-loved hymns, to greeting longtime neighbors, to admiring the beautiful stained glass and colorful statues of saints.

But just last year, things had suddenly changed. Patty's sisters had announced they would no longer be attending midnight Mass. Bridget claimed it was easier to attend a Christmas morning Mass, whatever "easier" meant. Teri claimed that if she stayed up past midnight she would never get to sleep at all, and Christmas Day would be ruined. Midnight Mass just wasn't worth the trouble.

Patty didn't agree; she decided to go to the midnight service on her own. She had dressed with her usual care, even pinning a new brooch to her coat, a brooch she had kept hidden from Bridget, who would have asked how Patty had afforded such an unnecessary trinket. Thankfully, Bridget and Ed were already in bed when she left the house to begin the familiar walk to the church.

But before she reached the corner her spirits had started to lag. The journey seemed longer than it ever had, the darkness of the night a bit frightening. She had tried to focus on the strings of colored lights that festooned the houses she passed and on the distant sound of carolers making their rounds through the neighborhood. For a moment, she had been sorely tempted to turn back, to hurry home to her sister's house and the dubious comfort of the tiny room reserved for her visits, but she persisted.

Still, as Patty greeted people she knew in the vestibule of the church, she was aware that her smile was forced, her handshake limp. No one asked why her sisters weren't with her;

Patty thought that odd. Maybe people were just being polite, ignoring the glaring fact that Patty was on her own.

But she *was* on her own and had felt miserably isolated among the throng of parishioners. Everyone seemed to be with someone, a spouse, a parent, a friend. When it came time for the ritual kiss of peace, she had looked around helplessly for a moment for someone to greet, for someone to whom she could wish a merry Christmas, before the person behind her tapped her on the shoulder, prompting her to turn and receive her handshake. That brief interaction spurred Patty to turn to the person to her left and then to the person on her right, offering her hand in fellowship. But her heart hadn't been in it.

It had been a struggle to stay for the entire Mass, but it would have been rude to walk out, and she had hurried away as quickly as she could when it was over. She had cried a bit on the cold walk back to Bridget's house. Once there, she had let herself in with the key Bridget had given her earlier.

In the kitchen, Patty had found a plastic container of eggnog, and she had debated having a small glass with a drop of whiskey in it. The concoction might help her sleep. But she decided against both the eggnog and the whiskey and went upstairs to the room reserved for her visits. There was little furniture, only a single bed, an old armchair that had once sat in the living room, and a tall, narrow dresser that had belonged to her niece Colleen when she was a teenager. Over the bed was hung a large wooden crucifix. It had been a gift from her paternal grandparents to her parents on the occasion of their wedding. A bit of a grim object to give as a wedding present, but the senior Porters had been a grimly religious couple. Sleeping under a three-dimensional image of the near naked, dying Christ wasn't something Patty enjoyed in the least, but removing the crucifix for the duration of her visit seemed risky, like courting disaster.

Her cell phone rang, causing Patty to come back to the present with a start.

It was Phil. Patty felt suddenly nervous. She wondered if he was calling to tell her he didn't want to see her again. She wouldn't be surprised.

"Hello?" she said, aware that she sounded wary.

"Hello, Patty. How are you?"

Phil's tone sounded all right. Normal. "I'm okay," she said. "How are you?"

"I'm okay. But I'm sorry I haven't called before now. I've had this darn cold. Every year around this time it gets me."

"But you're better now?" Patty asked hopefully. She thought of Phil alone in his home and wondered if he had anyone in his life to take care of him when he was sick. She wondered if there had been anyone to bring him homemade chicken soup, or serve him tea with a spoonful of his honey, or offer him a cold cloth for his forehead.

"I'm just fine," Phil said with a laugh. "It takes more than a cold to lay me low. So, what's new with you?" he asked.

"Nothing," she said. "I just got off the phone with one of my sisters. She was telling me about a friend of ours who has to go into a nursing home."

Why, Patty thought, had she told Phil such a depressing bit of news?

"I'm sorry," he said, feelingly. "Seems every other day we hear some sad bit of news. But I guess that's life."

"I guess."

"Say," Phil went on, "I wonder if you'd like to go for a walk on the beach with me tomorrow. It's supposed to be a nice day."

Patty's mood lifted. She would not allow that phone call with her sister or those awful memories of Father Hamilton to ruin this day or any other day, especially not now that she had this nice man in her life. A nice man who didn't find her conversation depressing or boring.

"Sure," she told Phil, already planning what she would wear on their date. "I'd love to go for a walk with you."

Chapter 60

Amanda's ankle had healed nicely. She had proved to be a docile patient in spite of her initial resistance to accepting help from the others. An injured ankle coming just after being unceremoniously dumped by Liam just days before her birthday. Life tended to happen like that; bad things came in twos or threes to test a person's ability to bounce back from adversity. Amanda thought that after a shaky start she had bounced back nicely. At least, that she was in the process of bouncing back.

At the moment, she was sitting comfortably in the armchair in her bedroom, fighting off a feeling of guilt for doing nothing more than letting her mind drift. Poor Patty, Amanda thought now. She had seemed genuinely disturbed by the idea that Amanda might be an atheist. Well, some people thought of atheists as akin to devil worshippers, didn't they? What they didn't understand was that if a person didn't believe in the concept of God, it was pretty much assured they wouldn't believe in the concept of anti-God.

Anyway, the conversation had gotten Amanda thinking about the role formal religion had—or had not—played in her romantic life. None of the men she had been involved with, other than her long ago fiancé, had been particularly religious. The fiancé, Sam, had attended his Baptist church with some regularity, but he had cheated on Amanda, so what was the point of his kneeling and praying in church when his behavior outside of the church was antithetical to everything he pretended to inside? But God loved sinners, it was said, at least those who admitted their guilt and swore never to sin again. So, did it even matter if you went to church or not if all you had to do to get off the hook with God was apologize? See, Amanda thought? Silly. None of it made much sense, at least not to her.

Not that she went around criticizing people for whom a formal, organized religion was necessary. Live and let live. To each his own. As long as no one decided they had a right to compel other people to worship their version of God. Or god, lower case.

Inevitably, thoughts of God and church led to thoughts of weddings, with all of their fraught traditions. Amanda had always half assumed that her parents had wanted their daughter to marry, maybe even to have a family. Those hopes, however, must have died long ago. Maybe by now her parents had accepted that marriage would not be in Amanda's future, that a steady relationship with someone was just as good a fate.

Amanda reached for her cell phone. She owed her mother a call. They hadn't spoken since Amanda's birthday, and she knew she should tell her that Liam was no longer around. Mr. and Mrs. Irving had liked Liam well enough, though they hadn't seen all that much of him over the years.

"Mom?" she said when her mother answered on the second ring. "It's me."

"Amanda! Is everything okay?" her mother asked. "This is the first time you've called this summer."

"I know. I'm sorry. I should check in more often."

"It's fine," her mother said pleasantly. "I know how to reach you if we need to. And we did speak on your birthday."

"I called for a specific reason, actually," Amanda went on. "Not just to chat. I have something to tell you, Mom. Liam and I broke up. Actually, he ended things."

Mrs. Irving sighed. "Oh, Amanda, I'm sorry. Wait, are you calling me from Maine? Or have you come home?"

"No, I'm still in Maine," Amanda said.

"I don't understand. How did you and Liam . . . Did he come to see you?"

Amanda hesitated. The truth was so pathetic. "He sent me a text," she said finally. "We broke up by text."

There followed a moment of silence while Mrs. Irving took in this bit of information. "Not even a phone call?" she said finally. "What sort of a person does such a thing?"

In her mind, Amanda could see her mother's impressive frown.

"I won't pretend to ever having thought the man was the cat's meow," Mrs. Irving went on, "but to end an eight-year relationship in such a way! Amanda, did you suspect he was going to break things off? Is that why you went away at the start of the summer? Amanda, what's going on?"

Amanda almost laughed. Did anyone have the answer to that question? Certainly, she, Amanda Irving, didn't.

"Mom," she said, "what did you really think about my going away on my own for the summer?"

There was another moment of silence before Mrs. Irving spoke. "I don't really know how to answer that question," she said. "I guess I stopped trying to, well, to understand why you do what you do a long time ago. That doesn't mean I don't care about you," she added hurriedly. "I love you. You're my daughter. It's just that most times I don't know what to think about your choices."

"It's okay, Mom," Amanda said, and as she spoke she started to cry. She was acutely aware that the room wasn't soundproof and that one of the others might very well hear her crying, but she couldn't stop the tears from flowing.

"Honey, I'm so sorry. You must feel awful. Look, why don't you come and stay with us?" her mother urged. "Your father and I would love to have you here. You can sort of mend with us before you have to go back to work."

Amanda almost accepted her mother's invitation. How bad would it be, really, to be coddled by her parents like her housemates had been coddling her? But something held her back. She wiped the tears from her eyes.

"I'm okay, Mom, really," she said. "The other women here, my housemates, are, well, they're all really nice. One made me a cake for my birthday and when I twisted my ankle—"

"You twisted your ankle? Did you go to the hospital?"

"No, it was fine, it wasn't bad, and they, my roommates, took good care of me. I'm—I'm okay here."

I'm not alone, Amanda added silently. The realization of that fact felt terribly important.

"All right," Mrs. Irving said with a sigh. "But if you change your mind and want to come home before the end of the summer, your father and I will be very happy to see you."

"I know you will," Amanda said feelingly. "Thanks, Mom. Give my love to Dad."

Amanda laid her head against the back of the armchair. She was glad she had called her mother. She loved her mother. How many adults could say that and mean it?

Chapter 61

It was a cool and overcast day, both the sky and the ocean varying shades of gray and blue and silver. A person with a creative turn of mind, Sandra thought, might describe the scene as subtly ominous, or perhaps, as portentous of a celestial event.

"I'm sure this sort of weather makes some people feel depressed or sad or lonely," Mary said suddenly. "But I enjoy it. I always have, even as a child. I'm in my element in the fog, as it were."

"Maybe it's because of your Irish roots," Sandra suggested.

"How did you know my family is Irish?" Mary asked. "On both sides, too."

Sandra smiled. "Good guess."

"Is it my happy-go-lucky attitude that gave me away?" Mary laughed. "I'm not entirely besotted by doom and gloom, really. I *do* feel sad and lonely at times, not often, but it happens, and I don't like it very much."

"My family is all Irish," Patty announced, "and I don't like the fog, or being sad or lonely *at all*. I definitely prefer a nice sunny day and a smile on my face."

"Maybe you're an anomaly," Mary noted. "Never mind. It's

dangerous to stereotype any group of people as being either one way or the other."

"I wonder if a person ever outgrows the possibility of loneliness," Amanda said musingly. "I wonder if a person ever reaches a point of true self-sufficiency. Maybe it's possible only at the very end, just before dying. Nobody can help you then, and you know it, so maybe that's the only time you are fully self-sufficient. But how does it feel at that moment? Not very good, I would imagine."

Loneliness. It was something Sandra had thought about far too often since Emma had gone away. "Solitude," she mused aloud, "can be enjoyable if it's something you've pursued. Being alone with your own thoughts and perceptions, free to experience the world around you without the chatter of others, without their needs interfering with your own needs. That sounds a lot like heaven, to me. On the other hand, loneliness, which is not the same as being solitary, feels so empty."

"I read somewhere that people tend to benefit more from solitude as they mature. Supposedly, they've developed better cognitive and emotional skills over time to help them deal with solitude more constructively. That is, assuming they *do* mature, and not everyone does. Anyway," Mary went on, "from what I understand of the matter, in monastic life, all periods of silence have a purpose, the point being that without a purpose, without structure, solitude can feel intimidating rather than freeing."

"I guess you don't want the monks and nuns getting unduly depressed by all the silence and solitude, do you? I'm assuming that over the centuries the monastic orders have learned a thing or two about keeping their members sane." Amanda shook her head. "Can you even *imagine* what solitary confinement is like," she went on, "I mean, in prison? The idea is downright cruel. Maybe the rare person is so tough minded, so hardened against psychic distress, that he can tolerate it. Still, the idea is so inhuman. To be deprived of conversation, of touch, of any sort of real communication. Though maybe prisoners in solitary confinement are allowed letters or phone calls. I have no idea."

"There's no access to sunlight, I imagine, or very little access," Sandra said, at that moment very aware of her own personal freedom, and of the beauty of the world around her, a beauty she was free to enjoy. "And maybe no access to music, or even to books," she went on. "Nothing stimulating to look at, or soft to feel, or delicious to smell. I can't imagine a prisoner in solitary is given fresh flowers or fluffy pillows. And he probably isn't allowed to hang pictures on the wall, even photos of his family. And the food must be awful. I mean, everything else is awful so why wouldn't the food be, too?"

"Just enough to keep body and soul together," Mary said quietly, reaching into her beach bag and pulling out her phone.

Patty shook her head. "I wonder if the guards are allowed to make eye contact with the prisoner. Can you imagine being treated as if you weren't even *there*? It must be so humiliating and so frustrating. I'd crack up in a day, maybe less, maybe in an hour."

"It's inhuman," Sandra said softly.

"Okay," Mary said, looking at the screen of her phone, "I know, I spend too much time on my phone looking things up, but listen to this. It says here that fifteen days of solitary confinement are enough to cause permanent psychological damage. Anxiety, paranoia, inability to form coherent thoughts. Lord, it gets worse. Suicide, overdoses. And I imagine the long-term effects of solitary confinement must be far worse when a person is mentally ill in the first place. Although maybe if someone is declared mentally unfit he's not sent to solitary."

Patty frowned. "Remember how we saw those Mennonites or Amish or whoever they were? Groups like that practice, what's it called, when someone's done something against the rules and needs to be punished? Mary, you said the word, I think."

"Shunning," Mary said. "A casting out of a society. Ostracizing. What Catholics call excommunication. Banishment from the only world you've ever known."

"Like being put into solitary confinement in a way," Patty said.

"That's a good point, Patty," Sandra noted.

"Of course, there are some people who prefer solitude," Amanda said then, "deeply spiritual people who are so in tune with God they have no need for friends in the way the average person does. I wonder about the pope, though, and the other leaders of major religions. Those are political positions as well as spiritual ones, and politicians need friends to help keep them safe from their enemies."

"Are politicians capable of having genuine friends?" Mary wondered. "Aren't a politician's personal relationships more strategic alliances, quid pro quo arrangements, than real friendships?"

"That's pretty cynical," Sandra noted, "though quite possibly, true."

"What do we need friends for?" Mary went on. "We, as in human beings. I mean, it's clear we *do* need friends but why? What's the most common reason people give for needing a friend, in addition to family members and casual acquaintances?"

"Safety," Patty blurted.

"Fear of being alone with yourself?" Sandra suggested. "Boredom? Someone to talk to about the little things; someone with whom you can pass the time?"

"Or," Mary said, "someone with whom you can share every gory, embarrassing, intimate detail of your true self. Someone with whom you can talk about the big issues such as Life, Love, the Soul, Death, all that stuff."

"Maybe a bit of both. I don't know. I'm the last person to ask, frankly." Amanda shook her head. "It's finally dawned on me that all my life I've had acquaintances rather than friends.

I've been fairly close to some of them but not really close to any. It's never bothered me, not having a BFF or a series of BFFs. Maybe it should bother me. Aren't women supposed to have best friends? Aren't we predisposed to bond? I just don't know."

"All living creatures," Mary said, "as far as I know, create bonds, both within and sometimes outside of their species. No living creature is an island. Then again, I could be wrong. I'm not a natural scientist. There might very well be solitary creatures who only come together to perpetuate the species."

"I think koala bears are like that," Patty said. "I think they don't make friends. I think I saw that on television."

"Maybe," Sandra suggested, "we shouldn't bother questioning why we need friends and just go about making friends and keeping them."

Mary shrugged. "Sure."

"I don't feel at all lonely right now," Sandra said, after a moment of silence, "in this minute."

"Neither do I," Patty admitted. "It's nice, not feeling lonely."

Mary laughed. "The understatement of the year."

"I'm okay, too," Amanda added. "I mean, I don't feel alone."

"Neither do, I," Mary admitted.

Sandra looked with fondness on her summer roommates. It was certainly a good thing that no one in the group was of a radically different opinion on anything they had discussed thus far this summer. She didn't want to imagine having a group discussion about crime and punishment if one of the members of the group was in favor of bringing back the dreadful sentence of drawing and quartering.

"Anyone want something to drink?" Patty climbed to her feet. "I'm going to get a soda."

"Didn't you bring anything to drink with you?" Amanda

asked, squinting up at her. "It's a lot more economical to bring food and drinks from home than to buy them at a concession stand."

Sandra noted the expression of embarrassment that came to Patty's face. Amanda was right, of course, but forethought and planning were not Patty's strengths. Quickly, Sandra rose from her folding chair. Her beach bag contained a large reusable bottle of water, but it wouldn't go to waste.

"I'll go with you, Patty," she said with a smile. "I could use a soda, too."

Chapter 62

While the stylist worked on her hair, Mary's thoughts had firmly affixed themselves to the fact that it would soon be the one-year anniversary of her dear friend Judy's death. Not surprisingly, Mary had been having more trouble than usual falling asleep this past week. Several nights she had contemplated taking a sleeping pill, but each time, as she had on every occasion but one since she had been given the prescription, she had resisted. She was strong and could tough it out, she told herself. Things could be worse. She would save the pills for a really extreme case of insomnia.

The last time Mary had stepped inside a Catholic church had been for Judy's funeral. It had been an overcast day, appropriately gloomy. So many people had been dressed almost casually, even older people, though Mary had chosen to wear sober black, as had Judy's husband and the other three friends from her childhood, Maureen, Barbara, and Sheila.

There hadn't been a dry eye in the pews, and that included Mary. In some way, she had felt as if she were weeping for herself as well as for the loss of her old friend. Strangely, she had found some comfort there in the Catholic Rites for the Dead. First, the vigil, or wake, at the funeral parlor. Next, the liturgy, a full Mass in Judy's parish church. Mary had estimated that around a hundred people were in attendance. She hadn't even been bothered by the smell of the incense. In a way, she had found it comforting.

Finally had come the committal, the prayers recited at the open grave. It had been the most difficult part of the event for Mary and, she assumed, for most of the others present. The committal made the death so terribly final. If anyone had managed to fool themselves even a tiny bit about their loved one being dead, those moments in the cemetery, standing beside the flower-bedecked coffin waiting by the side of the grave that had been dug to receive it, head bowed and hands clasped, listening to the priest reading the prayers, and then, having to walk away, to leave the coffin and the person it contained alone at the edge of the grave . . . Well, it made it clear as glass that death had paid a visit.

Mary remembered enough of her religious schooling to know that this third aspect of the process, no matter how difficult, was intended to be an expression of the communion between the Church here on earth and the Church in heaven. Because Judy was no longer on earth, she no longer had need of faith. Now, she was face-to-face with God.

Though Mary had firmly rejected the religion in which she had been raised, every so often since Judy's death, she felt a twinge of loss and regret. She tried to dismiss those unpleasant feelings, put them down to nostalgia, an untrustworthy phenomenon at best. You could never go home, everybody knew that, and it was silly to try. The past was another country, one whose borders were permanently closed.

"All done," the stylist announced, bringing Mary back to the moment. "What do you think?"

Mary examined her reflection and nodded. "It's good," she said. "Very good. Thank you."

Finally, released from the salon chair, Mary went off to meet up with Patty. Truth be told, the last thing she had expected was for Patty to ask if she could come along for the ride to Portland that day. Patty had given no particular reason for asking, and, for some reason Mary couldn't fathom, she hadn't insisted on Patty's explaining the unusual request. So far that summer, the two hadn't spent much, if any, time alone together. Why start now?

"You know I'm going to be at the salon for a while, right?" Mary had said. "I mean, you'll be on your own for at least two hours."

"I know. I'd like to see the Old Port area. You could drop me off somewhere, and I'll meet you after your appointment."

"Yeah, okay," Mary had agreed after a moment. "I'm leaving at nine thirty on the nose. Don't make me late."

At exactly nine thirty Patty had been standing beside Mary's car, smiling brightly. She was wearing a pair of pale blue pants, a pale blue T-shirt dotted with tiny yellow flowers, and the pale pink jean jacket Mary had seen her in before. In her taupe linen pants and matching linen blazer, Mary felt that someone would be hard-pressed to find two more oppositely dressed friends, if they could be called friends.

The drive north to Portland had been painless, conversation light and sporadic, which had suited Mary entirely. When they had reached the city, and parked the car in a garage, Patty had set off in the direction of the Old Port with a spring in her step. Mary had watched her go for a moment before turning in the direction of the salon on Congress Street.

Now, Patty was right where she had said she would be, on the corner of Exchange Street and Fore Street. Mary had half expected her to be laden with shopping bags—she had gone on often enough about how she loved to shop—but Patty held only her purse.

"Your hair looks good," she said to Mary.

"Thanks. And it cost significantly less than what it costs me to have it cut and colored in New York. What did you get up to while I was getting beautified?"

Patty shrugged. "Nothing much. I just window-shopped. There are some really nice stores here."

"Yeah. It can be dangerous if you're not careful." Suddenly, Mary had an idea. "Hey, it's a beautiful day, how about we grab a drink and a bite to eat at the Regency's Garden Café before we head back to Yorktide? I read about it online. It sounds nice."

Patty blushed.

Mary could have kicked herself. Of course, Patty hadn't bought anything that afternoon. Of course, she couldn't afford a drink at one of the nicer restaurants in Portland. Everyone in the house on Spruce Street knew that Patty was hard up for cash.

"My treat," Mary said brightly. "As a sort of thanks for keeping me company on the ride. Besides, I'm starved."

Patty's face visibly brightened. "Okay. Sure. That would be nice. Maybe you can get French fries, the thin kind that you like."

So, they had gone to the shady outdoor café, and over a glass of wine and an appetizer (French fries were not on the menu) they had shared light conversation about nothing much: the weather so far that summer, how pretty Sandra's house was, what a good cook Amanda had proved herself to be. Patty had asked about Mary's apartment in New York City and admitted she had been to the Big Apple only two times in her life, many years ago. She hadn't liked it very much, she said. It was very large and very noisy. Yes, Mary agreed, New York City could be noisy, and it certainly was a large metropolis. But, she added, it was also a very stimulating place in which to make one's life, and she herself would never live anywhere else. Patty had shrugged. "It wouldn't work for me, city living," she said. Silently, Mary agreed that it probably would not.

Most interestingly to Mary, Patty had commented on the appearance of virtually every woman passing by the café. Mary wondered how much time Patty spent comparing herself to other women, analyzing their clothing, hairstyle, makeup, and physical shape in terms of her own. The exercise struck her as not only exhausting but also pointless. But, to each her own.

Afterwards, on the ride back to Yorktide, Mary realized with a bit of a shock that today had been one of the more pleasant days of the summer thus far. Thanks to Patty, she had managed to put all thoughts of Judy and her untimely death out of her mind for a few hours, and that was saying something.

She glanced at her passenger. Patty was humming under her breath. Mary smiled.

Chapter 63

Patty was propped up in bed, a cup of warm coffee in her hands. She wasn't due for lunch at Phil's until noon. There was plenty of time for just sitting in bed and doing nothing much of anything, one of her favorite pastimes.

She was thinking about the beach walk she and Phil had taken the other day. Phil had made her laugh with stories of some of the hijinks he and his friends had gotten up to when they were kids in Yorktide. They hadn't done anything really bad, and certainly nothing criminal, unless stealing peaches from the backyard of a grumpy neighbor could be considered criminal. It wasn't like the grumpy neighbor ate the peaches. He just left them to drop to the ground and rot.

Phil had also told her about a terrible storm that had hit Yorktide one winter when he was a young teenager. Six fishermen had been lost at sea. "The whole town was in mourning for months," he told her. "It felt to us that we had lost a part of ourselves when the men went down with their boat."

Patty hadn't known how to respond, other than to say that she was sorry for the families of the men. The town in which she had grown up had never experienced a tragedy like the one Yorktide had all those years ago.

In return, Patty had wanted to tell Phil a story or two about her own youth, but for some reason it hadn't been easy to call up anything that he might find interesting. Finally, she had told him about the Thanksgiving poster contest she had won in grade school. All on her own she had painted the image of a turkey—alive, not cooked—surrounded by images of autumn leaves, pumpkins, apples, and ears of Indian corn, with the words *Happy Thanksgiving* printed across the top of the poster. She had sprinkled gold glitter on the turkey's tail and stuck bits of red fabric into his colorful feathers.

"I won five dollars," she had told Phil, "which was a lot of money back then! I tried to save it like my older sister told me I should, but I spent it by the end of the week."

"Do you still make art?" Phil asked. "You must have been pretty good to win first prize."

Patty had felt herself blush. "No. No, I guess I just never stuck with it." Why, she had wondered? Why hadn't she pursued her early interest in art? Her life might have been very different from the way it had been. But no one had encouraged her, and Patty had never possessed the energy or the drive to . . . to push herself. To take a chance on herself.

Once or twice during the afternoon, Patty and Phil had accidentally touched hands. Neither had flinched or apologized.

Now, Patty's thoughts wandered to the afternoon she and Mary had spent in Portland. The truth was that Patty had figured she could save on gas if she went along with Mary. She had felt—and still did feel—a bit bad about her subterfuge, but no harm had come of it. She had brought her cell phone with her, of course, tucked safely in her bag, but had made a promise to herself not to use it unless there was an emergency. In fact, she had made a promise to herself not to spend one penny on the day-trip. Not one. And she had kept that promise.

Well, thanks to Mary. It had been very nice of Mary to treat her to a glass of wine and a hefty antipasto plate before the drive back to Yorktide. The prices at the café had been kind of high, definitely not within Patty's current budget, though in the past she wouldn't have hesitated to spend above her means. Well, look where that had gotten her.

Patty had especially enjoyed the time she had spent roaming the small Old Port district, chatting with the friendly sales people in the stores she had gone into in spite of having no money to spend. She had really liked D. Cole Jewelers, and Folly 101 (if only she had her own home to furnish!), and Abacus, a gallery of arts and crafts.

Oddly, the few hours she had spent roaming the Old Port had reminded her of how much she had liked the office environment, by which she meant, the presence of other people. She had never minded the noise of fingers tapping on keyboards and phones ringing and copy machines whirring. She had actually *enjoyed* these distractions, looked forward to them really, and had valued the opportunity to chat with coworkers about what they had watched on television the night before or what they were planning to make for dinner, without the necessity of having to form a close relationship that would exist outside of the office as well.

The problem with being alone, Patty had realized long ago, was that after a few minutes she started to think about her life and all of the mistakes she made along the way, and that led to her feeling seriously down. Sometimes those moods frightened her. They felt so heavy, so weighty, that it was easy to believe she would never ever have the strength to shift them.

So, it was a puzzle to Patty, even after all these years, why, being a person who needed to be around other people, she had virtually no friends. Well, not entirely a puzzle. For a long time, she had thought of herself as a man's woman. She had been taught that other women were rivals, not companions. They were determined to steal your job or your man. You could safely befriend a girl obviously less attractive; she would be no competition. But you should stay far away from other women as pretty or as smart as you, and be especially wary of those who were beautiful and brilliant.

Patty frowned. Her brothers-in-law, Ed and Kevin, had always been kind to and respectful of her, but often she had wondered what her sisters said about her to their husbands behind closed doors. She wondered if Bridget and Teri had ever viewed her as a threat to their marriages. Just because she was single didn't mean she was going to steal other women's husbands! Though that was exactly what she had done, too many times.

Anyway, as a result of this strange perspective on men and women, Patty had always felt a bit awkward with her brothers-in-law. A few times she had had to ask them for help with something in her apartment because she didn't have the money for a professional repair person. She had always gone through her sisters with her requests. The last thing she had wanted was for them to accuse her of trying to move in on their territory.

What nonsense that all now seemed, Patty thought, sipping her coffee. What damage that sort of cramped and suspicious thinking had done to countless generations of women like her.

There had been one bright spot, though, at least for a time, one relationship that she had been able to call a friendship, back when she was in her late thirties, and that had been with an across-the-hall neighbor by the name of Ross. Ross was gay, single, older than her by about ten years, and retired from an office job at a major utility company. Ross quickly became an avuncular figure to Patty, encouraging her to take better care of herself, to stop twisting herself into knots for men who were never going to come through for her.

They had been friends for five years when he passed away. At several moments over those years, Ross had hinted that when he died Patty would "not be forgotten." Patty naturally assumed this meant that Ross had left her something in his will. She was touched. She felt cared for.

But the funeral came and went, and Patty heard nothing from Ross's lawyer or the executor of his will, whomever that might have been. One day, about three weeks after Ross's death, someone showed up to empty out his apartment. Patty, who saw the man entering Ross's apartment through the peephole in her front door, ventured out and introduced herself.

The man was Ross's cousin. Awkwardly, Patty had asked if there had been a will. "You see," she said, "Ross kind of led me to believe that, well, that, I would, he said that he was going to . . ."

The cousin had laughed. "A will? No, Ross didn't have a will. He had absolutely nothing to leave other than the contents of this apartment. My wife and I paid for the funeral and burial. Frankly, from what I can see at first glance, there's nothing in this place of much monetary value."

Patty had felt both shocked and hurt. She had tried to say something witty to the cousin, something to make it clear that it didn't matter to her that Ross hadn't left her anything, but no words would take form. She had stood there, cheeks hot, miserable.

Then, the cousin seemed to take pity on her and suggested she go through the apartment and make a list of the things she wanted. He would review the list to be sure nothing *was* of real value (he didn't say this part aloud, but Patty wasn't entirely stupid) and then let her have the items she desired. Patty had thanked the man but was so depressed by the situation she could hardly see what she was looking at as she moved mechanically through the rooms. Everything seemed tainted now. Had Ross ever really cared for her? Had their friendship been real? Had he lied to other people as well? Maybe he just hadn't gotten around to writing his will. Maybe he had been planning to talk to a lawyer but then it was too late. How much had she really known about Ross Hamilton?

Fighting back tears, and very aware of the cousin not far away, keeping an eye on her no doubt, Patty had finally cho-

sen a wooden magazine rack. She didn't know why; she didn't
even particularly like it, but she was desperate to get out of
the apartment once and for all. The cousin raised an eye when
she pointed to the rack, as if in disbelief that anyone could
want such an ugly item, then had shrugged and said, "Sure."

A new tenant moved into the apartment a week later, a
woman about Patty's age, a nurse, never married, with no children. Though the woman was friendly when she met Patty in
the hall or on the elevator, even to the point once of asking
Patty to come for tea, Patty had rebuffed the woman's friendly
overtures.

That had probably been a mistake. They might have had a
lot in common; for all Patty knew, the woman might also have
been a collector. But Patty just hadn't been able to risk getting
hurt again. And the idea of stepping inside the four walls of
the apartment where she had spent so many pleasant hours
with a so-called friend who might never have really cared for
her, well, it didn't sound pleasant at all.

Patty put the empty coffee cup on the bedside table and
sighed. Would she *never* have a real friend? Would there never
be someone compatible and like-minded with whom she
could spend time just hanging out? The person didn't have to
be exactly like her. Maybe, in fact, they could be very different, someone like Sandra, for instance. She had been so nice
to Patty, so forgiving and always so pleasant. It would be nice
to count Sandra as a friend.

Suddenly, Patty looked at the traveling alarm clock on her
bedside table and gasped. What had she been doing, wasting all
this time thinking about the past and worrying about the future?
If she didn't hurry it up she would be late for lunch at Phil's
house, and that was the last thing she wanted. Patty threw back
the cover and raced to the dresser for fresh underwear.

Phil had described his house as a post and beam structure that
he had designed himself back in the early nineteen-eighties. It

had been built by local crafts people, most of them his friends. The house, the only one on Ridge Road, was situated on a large clearing at the edge of a wood.

Armed with this information, Patty still had no idea what to expect.

It wasn't difficult to find Ridge Road, or, of course, the only house on it. Patty climbed out of the car and pulled her blouse down as far as it would go over the waistband of her pants. Then she patted her hair, and, satisfied that she wasn't a mess, she looked up at the house.

It looked so alone. And isolated. Patty felt her mood dip. She couldn't help but wonder if the house was teeming with spiders, and bats, and mice. Patty was all for animals and for preserving their right to live a happy life, but creepy crawlies who had taken up residence in a human home without having been asked to do so struck her as just wrong.

Just then, the front door opened and Phil appeared.

"You found it all right, then?" he called as he walked toward her.

Patty nodded and smiled. "Yes. The directions were very clear."

"You looked a bit taken aback for a moment there."

"Did I?" Patty laughed awkwardly. "I guess I just—"

"Didn't expect something so rustic?"

Patty blushed. "Well, no, I mean, yes."

Phil laughed. "A lot of people have that same reaction. But come inside. I think you'll like it."

On the way to the house, Patty noted that the garden out front was nicely tended. She knew next to nothing about gardening, but she could tell that much. She could also see that there was a large deck on one side of the house, decorated with simple but attractive outdoor furniture.

"It's got all the amenities," Phil said once they were inside, "including a washing machine and dryer. I even got myself a microwave not long ago. I know a microwave is old hat to most people, but I'd never had one so I didn't know what I was missing."

"Do you know you can poach an egg in a microwave?" Patty asked.

Phil laughed. "Now I do. The locals call the house The Retreat," he went on to explain, "because of where it's located, all alone at the end of the road. I guess it is a bit of a retreat for me. I come home at the end of the day and here it is, ready to welcome me."

Patty looked around the room in which they stood, a combined living room and dining area. Her eye was immediately caught by a very impressive-looking woodstove. It probably was from the nineteenth century or something. To the right of the woodstove, a comfortable-looking couch was strewn with brightly colored throw pillows. On a low table in front of the couch there was a sculpture in wood. The form was a bit abstract but not enough to disguise its being in the shape of a bird.

"My father carved that," Phil explained when Patty noted it. "It's maple. He always had a way with wood."

"He was an artist," Patty said. "It's beautiful."

"He called himself a craftsman, nothing so lofty as an artist."

Patty continued her visual examination of Phil's house. A door led from the living/dining area onto a sun porch. From where she stood she could see that the walls and ceiling were a bright white. The floor was painted a sort of cerulean blue.

"The kitchen is off that way, as you can see," Phil told Patty. "The bedrooms are upstairs."

Patty realized that she felt a bit enchanted. "Your house is so charming," she said with a smile. "And, so neat and clean."

Phil laughed. "Did you expect to find a pigsty?"

"No," Patty said quickly, feeling herself blush yet again. "I'm sorry, no. I just—"

"Just teasing," Phil assured her. "I've always been a bit obsessive about neatness and cleanliness. When my wife was alive, I used to drive her crazy by straightening up after she'd already straightened. She thought I was criticizing her work, but I wasn't, honestly. Eventually, she gave up and let me handle all of the housework. We were both happier that way."

"I'm a very neat person, too," Patty said. "Neatness is important to me. Cleanliness, too. Gosh, I sound like a Girl Scout."

"They do have the best cookies, so I'd say that's a good thing."

"Oh," Patty exclaimed, "I love the mint cookies, the ones covered in chocolate."

"They're my favorite, too! Luckily, I know a family in town with a granddaughter in the Girl Scouts, so every year I'm able to buy a big supply."

Patty laughed. "Anything for a good cause, right?"

"Right. Now, all this talk of cookies has made me hungry. I hope you're hungry, too. I thought we'd have lunch on the deck if that's all right? It's right off the kitchen."

The table on the deck was set nicely with chunky white crockery that looked as if it might have been passed down through several generations. The heavy green glasses also looked old. In the center of the table was a milk glass vase containing a profusion of wildflowers. Patty felt as if she had been magically transported to another country or something. It was all so pretty.

When Patty had taken a seat, Phil offered iced tea, seltzer, or cranberry juice—"I love cranberry anything," he told her—and Patty chose an iced tea.

For lunch, there was clam chowder. "I didn't make it myself," Phil explained. "But I think you'll like this. It's homemade at this little place in town."

Patty took a taste. "It's delicious!" she exclaimed. "And so creamy. I love anything with cream. I probably shouldn't."

"Why not? If it makes you happy."

322 *Holly Chamberlin*

Phil's smile was so genuine, the look in his eyes so clear and honest, Patty knew without a doubt that he was not a man to criticize a woman's weight if it didn't fit his preconceived notion of female perfection. How many diets had she maintained over the years only to please a particular man? Too many to count.

There were also bread and butter and a small green salad. "The cucumbers are from my garden," Phil told her. Patty thought he seemed proud of this.

For dessert, there was a choice of vanilla or chocolate ice cream. "The classics," Phil said as he placed the cartons, bowls, and spoons on the table.

"I think vanilla ice cream is the best," Patty said. "But I like chocolate, too. Well, who doesn't?"

Phil smiled. "Then how about a scoop of each?"

"Why not?" Patty said.

"What's your home like, if I can ask?" Phil asked a moment later.

Patty swallowed hard. She knew she probably should have been expecting this question. "Well," she began with some hesitation, "to tell you the truth, I'm kind of in transition at the moment. I'm staying with my sister Bridget and her husband, Ed until I . . . until I figure things out. Until I decide where I want to be."

"It's good to have family when you're in between jobs or places," Phil said, with a firm nod.

"Yes," Patty said. "It is."

"Of course, friends can be just as good when things get tough."

Patty nodded. If you had friends, she thought. And she didn't have friends. Patty swirled what remained of the ice cream in her bowl. She would tell Phil the real truth at some other time. Maybe. It might never be necessary for Phil to know that she was broke, that if Bridget hadn't taken her in she would be living on the streets or just about.

"When my father was a young man," Phil was saying, "he hit a bad patch through no fault of his own. He was in rough shape, no money, only the clothes he wore on his back. His parents were gone, and the few other family members that were around were in no condition themselves to help him. But his best friend's family took him into their household, helped him get back on his feet. To the day he died, my father used to say that the Morrows saved his life, that he owed everything he achieved afterward to their care. He never forgot their kindness and repaid it when Mr. and Mrs. Morrow were old and in need of help. Their own son, my father's friend, had died, you see."

Listening to Phil talk about his father, Patty thought that Phil might very well be the sort of man to understand her and the choices she had made. Maybe he wouldn't judge her as so many others had. He seemed so kind and well, just really, genuinely *kind*. But she hardly knew him, not really.

It was already two thirty when Patty decided that she should go if she wasn't to overstay her welcome.

"I've had a lovely time this afternoon," she told Phil when he had walked her to the front door. "Thank you, Phil."

"Thank you for coming, Patty. I've really enjoyed our visit. I hope we can see each other again."

"I hope so, too," Patty said. Her stomach was tingling. She felt a bit like an awkward teen at the end of a first date, but it wasn't an entirely unpleasant feeling. There was a sense of anticipation and promise about it all that was very, very nice.

Phil stood on the front porch as Patty walked to her car. When she was behind the wheel, she glanced in the rearview mirror to see that Phil was smiling at her and waving.

Chapter 64

It was one of those perfect summer beach days, Amanda thought, if you were the sort to enjoy a mob scene. But every once in a while, it didn't hurt to join the crowd. The sand was packed with people and their gear: multicolored umbrellas, massive coolers, fancy reclining chairs, piles of plastic sports equipment. To avoid causing a disaster, it was necessary to dodge the hordes of laughing children racing or toddling toward the water's edge and then back, with their colorful plastic pails and shovels in tow.

"Children make me nervous," Mary said as she stepped aside to let a boy in neon swim trunks dash by. "They dart around like birds. You have to be vigilant when they're around."

Amanda laughed. "True, but they're having such fun. It kind of lifts the spirits, doesn't it, watching children at the beach?"

Mary didn't look convinced. "So, how are you?" she said. "I mean, about the Liam thing."

"I'm okay. It seems I have a lot to think about, but I'm not pining or anything."

"Good. Pining is a waste of time. Especially when it's for a guy who dumps you via text. Sorry. Maybe I shouldn't have said that."

"No, that's fine," Amanda assured her. "I agree completely."

It had been Mary's idea that the two go to the beach that afternoon for some fresh air and exercise. Amanda, a bit taken aback by Mary's offer, had nevertheless accepted. Now, she was glad that she had. Companionship was good, but it was something Amanda didn't know much about. The thing was, she had always been so good on her own, content and productive. But perhaps she had enjoyed solitude too much and it had ruined her for the possibility of a relationship of true reciprocity, for an intimate friendship. Now that she was thinking about such things, Amanda was realizing that on some level she had always viewed other people as intruders, forces that interfered with her life rather than contributed to it.

Amanda glanced at her companion. How did Mary view other people? Mary had chosen a single life as one best suited for her after an early, unsuccessful marriage. To choose a single life wasn't an easy choice; it wasn't the choice of a lesser existence; it didn't make a person a failure. She didn't really know Mary, but Amanda didn't think that she was in any way lacking in essential humanity.

"How was your trip to Portland with Patty?" Amanda asked suddenly.

"Okay," Mary said. "She chattered on the entire way north, but I managed to block out most of whatever it was she was saying. I don't really like talking while I'm driving. But we went to a nice café for a glass of wine and a bite to eat before heading back to Yorktide. She's not as silly as she appears, at least, not as silly as I assumed her to be. It was actually pleasant spending time with her, if she did go on about other women's clothes and hair color."

"I'm glad to hear that," Amanda said with a smile. "I mean, that you enjoyed her company. I'm afraid I've been pretty harsh in my assessment of Patty Porter." She had often been pretty harsh in her assessment of many women. That, Amanda promised herself, was going to change.

"You've heard of that expression, 'the golden years'?" Mary asked, seemingly out of the blue, as she dodged another running child with pail and shovel.

"Of course."

"Well, via my obsession with the Internet, I recently learned that the phrase came about in 1959 as part of the marketing for a new sort of retirement option. America's first large scale community, Sun City, located in Arizona on a big golf course, for people—get this—'55 and better.'"

Amanda shuddered. "How cheesy."

"The notion of retirement was being sold as the ultimate goal after years of toil and trouble. Retirement was meant to be an opportunity to travel, play golf, take up a hobby, be with the grandkids. How deeply stupid," Mary went on, with some vehemence, "the notion of putting your life on hold until you retire and then letting rip. Stupid or very sad."

Amanda sighed. "From what I've seen, too often retiring proves to be disappointing. People feel useless and worthless. I remember when my father retired. He was so down for months. I don't know exactly what happened to bring him around again. Maybe my mother said or did something to coax him back to life."

"It was the same with my father," Mary said. "So, why not cheerfully ignore all of those feelings of uselessness and worthlessness and go to live in a retirement village where you can slip into a state of carefree frolic with other older adults who . . . who what? Who need to pretend that it's all fun and games from here on out? Who want to isolate themselves with other retirees in retreat from the troublesome world?"

"Retirees," Amanda said, "who are painfully aware that they're redundant not only in the world of business but in the world entire. Retirees not wanting to be a burden on their children."

"The idea of the idyllic retirement community seems to entirely omit the very real possibilities of failing health and financial troubles. It omits, too, or at least, it did, those without spouses or families." Mary frowned. "I'm going to bet that the original notion of a retirement community was meant to cater only to white heterosexual couples who were legally married."

"We shouldn't assume that those early retirement communities weren't open to couples who weren't heterosexual and white and legally married," Amanda said.

"Retirement has become a privilege in this country," Mary went on, as if she hadn't heard Amanda's remark, "and it shouldn't be that way. Not everyone can afford to retire, but at some point, it's pretty likely that a person can no longer work at the job they've been performing because of ill health or sheer exhaustion or suddenly being dumped with grandkids to raise. So, they're forced to retire and what sort of life awaits them?"

What sort of life, indeed, Amanda wondered, aware of a gloomy mood approaching. "Look," she said then, "I'm usually not the one who says this, but I really think we ought to change the subject to something sunnier. Even if only for a little while."

Mary grunted what Amanda took to be her assent. Then, suddenly, Mary put a restraining hand on Amanda's arm. "Okay," she said quietly, "I really shouldn't be inflicting this on you, but check out the dude at three o'clock."

Amanda glanced to her right to see an old, very tanned man wearing nothing but a banana hammock. A red one. He was fairly fit, Amanda noticed. For a man who looked to be well into his seventies.

"That's so very wrong," she said, shaking her head. "So very, very wrong."

A fit of laughter overtook both women.

"Oh, my, God," Mary puffed finally, wiping tears from her eyes. "I never expected to see one of those men up here in Maine. I thought they preferred, I don't know, one of those swinging singles sort of beach resorts."

"What sort of man are we calling him?" Amanda said, struggling to take a deep breath. "Vain? A sex pest or predator?"

"To be fair—and I suppose we should be fair—maybe he just has a healthy sense of self-esteem. Or maybe we're just two prudish middle-aged women. Poor guy. Maybe he's madly in love with his wife and just enjoys getting an all-over tan."

"Don't give him any ideas," Amanda pleaded. "His almost all-over tan is quite enough for me!"

"And me! Hey, any interest in getting some ice cream before we head back to Sandra's?"

Amanda nodded. "Sure, why not? When we passed that ice cream shop earlier, the one at the top of the beach, I saw that they have cookies 'n cream on the menu. I haven't had that since I was a kid."

"Sounds pretty decadent. Let's go for it."

Decadence wasn't a thing Amanda usually did. Not until this summer, it seemed. Chocolate cake. Ice cream. Maybe her summer roommates were having a positive effect on her in more ways than one.

Chapter 65

Sandra was alone in the house with Clovis, who, since about two hours earlier, had been stretched out on a windowsill in the living room barely wide enough to accommodate him, soaking up the sun. No doubt when his internal clock announced that it was time for another meal, he would rouse himself and come howling to the kitchen.

In the meantime, Sandra was busy with small and relatively unimportant household matters. Taking stock of paper supplies. Dusting the frames of paintings and prints. Fetching the mail from the mailbox at the end of the drive.

Sandra sighed. Yet again, there was a letter from a real estate agency on the subject of her assumed desire to sell her house. Such advertisements had been coming at least once a week for months now. Did real estate agencies target all people over a certain age who were living on their own in homes? Sandra found this campaign very annoying. It even angered her a bit, and she wasn't one easily prone to anger.

The letter went into the recycling bin.

There was an advertisement from a major shoe outlet; glued onto the back was a card promising an extra ten percent off her purchase of fifty dollars or more if she shopped during a particular five-day period.

That, too, went into the recycling bin. Sandra didn't need new shoes. Besides, she had been to the outlet once and had rapidly discovered that the shoes on offer weren't designed for women over the age of fifty-five.

Finally, there was a good, old-fashioned itemized bill from one of the utilities. That went onto the small desk in the den at which Sandra paid her bills and used her laptop for Internet searches and FaceTime sessions with Emma and, on occasion, her children.

When was the last time, Sandra wondered, as she sank into a comfortable chair, that she had received an old-fashioned letter, the kind produced with a pen and paper and tucked into an envelope and then slipped into the maw of a corner mailbox? Sandra wasn't anti-technology, but she didn't see the harm in continuing a few of the now almost obsolete behaviors, such as letter writing and the sending of Christmas cards, another nice social practice that seemed to be seriously on the wane, in favor of group texts or Facebook posts.

Sandra sighed loudly. She was feeling grumpy. She wished Clovis would wake up. She was feeling lonely, too.

At least, some people still used the telephone for spoken conversation. She had just that morning learned from her son that he and Robbi were planning a trip to Greece in the fall. "It's one of the cradles of civilization," Jack had enthused, "and I've never even *thought* about going before now. What was wrong with me? And the food is supposed to be awesome, of course."

Well, Sandra thought, she couldn't argue with her son about Greece being an exciting vacation destination. But when had Jack last been to Maine to visit his mother? He and his wife had been around for a few days at the time of his father's death and had come back to Yorktide three months later for John's memorial. A year after that Jack had paid a short solo visit after having attended a work conference in Boston. Sandra had not seen her son since. Only that summer she had asked him if he had any plans to visit her that fall, and he had demurred. Now it was clear that ancient ruins in Greece had won out over Mom in Yorktide.

Maybe good ol' Mom should hop a plane to a foreign land and revel in outstanding cultural artifacts and delicious food. But the fact was that Sandra didn't want to travel, though once she had enjoyed even the less pleasant aspects, like careful packing, and had been able to tolerate the annoying but un-avoidable aspects like waiting on line at customs. Now, at this age, even great temptations like world-famous museums and stunning architecture couldn't quite convince her to update her passport.

Sandra had spoken to her daughter that morning, as well. The visit from Carrie's parents was going okay, according to Kate.

"Just okay?" Sandra had asked.

"It's the most to be expected. I swear I don't know where Carrie comes from. Maybe she was switched at birth. She's so different from the lot of them. A swan among ugly ducks."

Sandra had smiled. Kate was in full protective mode.

There was supposed to have been a FaceTime call with Emma, as well, but that had been canceled at the last minute. Sandra had been both disappointed and relieved. She never knew what to expect—Emma in a fairly lucid, convivial mood, or Emma in a deeply laconic or almost angry state.

"Mom's very agitated today," Millie had told Sandra. "I was hoping she wouldn't need to be sedated, but I finally agreed that it was in her best interest. She's so unhappy when she gets like that. I can't bear to think about what's happening in her mind in those moments."

Nor could Sandra. She was sorry that Millie had to make those sorts of decisions concerning her mother. But at least Emma had Millie, someone trustworthy, looking after her. So many people were alone at the end of their lives. That was nothing new, but it was still and always terrible.

And what about her summer roommates, all of whom lived alone? Would they, too, be isolated at the end of their lives? Or would each of them find some sort of companionship that would last until the final moments? Sandra sighed. What dark thoughts!

Still, it made her happy that her guests—could she call them her friends?—were voluntarily spending time together outside of the house. Mary and Patty had gone to Portland the other day and had returned wearing smiles, not the frowns Sandra had half expected. And earlier that very day, Mary and Amanda had driven to the beach. They had been gone for close to three hours, which probably meant that they were enjoying each other's company and in no great rush to go their separate ways.

The crunch of a car's wheels on gravel alerted Sandra to the return of one or more of her roommates. She felt a sense of relief.

"Someone is home, Clovis," she called out as she rose from her seat and headed toward the front of the house. A moment later she heard a thud. That was Clovis having jumped to the floor from the windowsill.

Soon, the house would feel alive again.

Chapter 66

One year ago, to this very day, Judy Strachey had been killed by a hit-and-run driver.

That morning, Mary had spoken to Maureen, Barbara, and Sheila. The calls had been short, also a bit awkward, almost as if each woman simply wanted to affirm that the other women were alive and no more. No one really wanted to chat or to reminisce. She wondered if next year they should arrange a group call on FaceTime. Make a sort of ritual of it, maybe even invite some laughter. She would suggest it to the others, see what they thought.

After speaking with her old friends, Mary had placed a call to Judy's husband. He hadn't picked up. Mary left a brief voice mail, encouraging Joe to call her at any time.

Poor Joe. Who would care for him when the time came? Would his children be able and willing to provide, or at least to organize, the support he might one day need? She hoped that they would step up to the plate, but in her experience, you never could tell how people would behave in times of crisis. Sometimes, they would behave in character. Sometimes, they would behave out of character. End of life concerns could wreak havoc with people's ability to act with forethought and reason.

Mary shook her head. She would think about such troubling things later. It was time for dinner, and she was hungry. She joined the others in the kitchen and took her usual seat at the table. "Patty," she said, noting the woman's beaming expression—how could she not?—"you look downright gleeful. Out with it."

Patty blushed and shrugged. "Okay," she said. "Well, maybe you should know, or at least maybe you'd like to know that I'm kind of dating Phil James. He's one of Sandra's friends. He's from Yorktide. He's lived here all his life."

"Oh," Amanda said, passing the bowl of fresh peas to Mary. "Well, that's nice. Good for you."

"It's nothing serious," Patty added hastily. "I mean, how can it be, we've only known each other a few weeks, but he's very nice and I enjoy spending time with him."

"At our age," Mary pointed out, scooping peas onto her plate, "there's no point in a lengthy courtship. You know—or you should know—what you want in a romantic relationship and should be able to recognize it if it comes along."

"It's not a courtship," Patty replied, eyes wide. "Nothing like that."

"Why not?" Mary asked.

"I don't know. It's just . . ."

"Whatever the situation," Sandra put in, "I'm glad Patty and Phil found each other as I'm sure we all are. Well, bon appétit, everyone."

There were several moments of silence during which Mary and her housemates loaded their plates with food. Mary had been pleased to discover that Sandra, Amanda, and Patty ate like normal people. No starvation diets in this house.

Suddenly, Mary wondered how Joe was eating. Judy had been the cook in the relationship. Joe had barely been able to boil the proverbial egg.

"What's on your mind?" Sandra asked. "Your face just darkened."

Mary shook her head. "I was just thinking about a friend of mine. He was widowed a year ago, and something made me wonder how he was getting along without his wife cooking his meals for him. He's not at all incompetent but . . ."

"But he's hopeless in the kitchen? John was the same way. It was almost funny how the only meal he could manage to fix was a bowl of cold cereal."

"So," Amanda asked, "is your friend totally on his own now? I mean, is there family?"

Mary nodded. "Kids. But he doesn't need care yet; he's healthy and only sixty-six. It's just, imagining him eating his dinner alone every night . . . It makes me sad."

"Maybe he likes being alone," Patty noted. And then she added, "I don't mean that he doesn't miss his wife. But maybe he's okay in his own company."

Mary didn't think that Joe *was* the kind of guy to be okay in his own company. But she smiled and said, "Maybe."

"Do you ever think about the language we use when we talk about helping each other?" Sandra asked. "Often, we say caretaking instead of caregiving. I prefer caregiving, especially when talking about caring for a loved one at home."

"It's never easy to care for someone old or ill at home," Amanda noted. "Too many people make the decision to do just that, only to realize that it isn't fair or even safe for anyone involved. Still, making the decision to transfer a loved one from his home and into a care facility is probably one of the most difficult decisions of all."

"I agree," Mary said. "And then there's the money issue, of course. What kind of facility can we afford? Will my husband or my mother get proper care there? Is the facility close to my home so that I can visit as often as I'd like to? Will I need to keep a close eye on my husband's or my mother's caregivers to ensure my husband and my mother are not ignored or abused?"

Patty nodded. "And will my loved one hate me for sending them away? Will they understand why I've done it? It's happening with a family friend at the moment. Alice. It's all such a nightmare. I seriously don't like to think about it."

"In the good old days," Sandra said, "generations of family lived together or on the same street or in the same neighborhood and took care of one another."

"In the good old days," Mary pointed out, "people didn't live as long as they do now. People popped off at sixty or seventy, not eighty-five or ninety. And who's to say that the quality of Great-Grandma's life was all that good if she was stuck alone in a bed twenty-four seven because everybody else was so busy working the farm or whatever, and there was no such thing as physical therapy which might have helped make her strong enough to get up and get dressed on her own and have a degree of independence?" Mary sighed. "It's just that it's dangerous to glamorize the past. For everything that appears better then than it is now, there's a whole bunch of things that were way worse."

"That's very true," Amanda said. "People tend to forget that and get all wrapped up in nostalgia, which only distorts the truth."

"I knew a woman years ago," Sandra said then, "who was determined to keep her husband at home after he'd had a major stroke. She was a tiny little thing, and he was well over six feet. Social services failed her; she wound up catering to the aides who were sent to help her, making them lunch while they sat watching game shows on television, giving her husband sponge baths while the aides talked on the phone with their friends. In the end, she had no choice but to put her husband in a care home. The situation was making her physically ill. She couldn't sleep, could hardly eat, was afraid of leaving her husband alone with the aides even for an hour so that she could get out of the house, take a walk, breathe fresh air."

"How did the husband fare in the home?" Patty asked.

"If such a story can have a happy ending," Sandra told them, "I'd say this one did. Mr. Fisher was well taken care of, made friends, and lived on for another four or five years. After he passed, Mrs. Fisher went to live at the home. The staff had gotten to know her well over the years, and she spent her final days safe and sound under their watch."

Patty smiled. "Whew."

"It's a beautiful idea," Mary said, "keeping our loved ones at home, but like Sandra's story illustrated, it can be unrealistic. For one, not everyone is cut out to be a caregiver. It's not a pretty job or an easy one, and people shouldn't be expected to take to it as if it was in their nature. I, for one, am not a caretaker at all. In fact, that's probably why I never married. Well, after that one stupid attempt, which only confirmed that I was better off on my own."

"But can you feel love?" Patty blushed. "I'm sorry. That sounds awful, I didn't mean—"

"Sheesh, Patty! Of course, I can feel love. I love my childhood friends like crazy. But my giving them a sponge bath or doling out their pills three times a day would not be to their benefit, believe me. I'd be sure to mess things up. Resentment would waft from me like garlic does from someone who's overindulged in, well, garlic. I'd much rather pay for someone qualified to be on the front lines."

"My parents," Amanda said then, "thank God, are still able to live on their own. They're very sharp and in good shape overall. But at some point, we might face a situation where one or both of them need full-time professional care. I certainly can't take them in, not with my job, and, honestly, like Mary, I'm not a natural caregiver. I'm not at all equipped to care for another adult in the way a nurse is equipped. Changing diapers? Making a bed around a patient? And all the other even less savory things a nurse is required to do for a patient? There's a reason I didn't go into a career in health care."

"I'm sure your parents don't expect you to take that sort of care of them," Patty said. "Do they?"

"No, they know me too well, but I'll certainly be there in any other way they need me to be."

"Hey, Patty, how old is Phil, this man you're seeing?" Mary asked.

Patty shook her head. "I don't know. The subject never came up."

Amanda smiled. "Maybe he's like you, doesn't like to reveal his age."

"Well, I know how old he is," Sandra said. "And it's no secret. Phil is seventy-five."

"Oh," said Patty. "Then he's older than me."

Mary bit back a smile.

"John was diagnosed with heart disease not too long before he died," Sandra said then, "so I never had the chance to take care of him, not in any significant way. Of course, I'm glad that in the last months of his life he wasn't plagued by trouble. But had he suffered, I'd like to think I would have been a good caregiver. I'm certainly not claiming to be a saint, but I enjoy taking care of people. It's why living alone these past five years has been . . . a strain. I need to be needed. I truly loved being a mother, and, growing up, I was very involved in meeting Jacob's needs. I would have done my best with John. Hopefully, I would have known when I was no longer capable of being his nurse and done the right thing, which would be to let him go into a care home."

"You would have known, Sandra," Amanda said with conviction. "I'm sure of it."

"As am I," Mary said firmly. "Anyway, kind of in the same vein, I was reading about this new movement. It's called living apart together, LAT for short. Basically, the partners in a relationship keep their own homes and provide each other with full emotional support, but, as they age and maybe fall ill, the physical care is provided by adult children, or friends, or paid caregivers. Personally, I think it's brilliant. I mean, women especially fear that a romantic relationship late in life will mean full-time caregiving, and, let's face it, lots of women have already gone through full-time caregiving with parents or spouses or both."

"Do you really think what's-it-called is becoming so popular because women don't want to get stuck being nurses?" Patty asked.

"That's partly the reason, yes," Mary answered. "And, for better or worse, as I said earlier, people are living longer. The old ways of aging aren't meeting the new needs of this aging population. Add to that what I find to be a shocking fact, that since the nineteen-nineties the divorce rate of people over the age of fifty has doubled. Suddenly, there are all these older people on their own."

Sandra shook her head. "That confuses me. On the one hand, if you're really unhappy and unfulfilled in your marriage, then there's no point in staying. If you can afford to leave, fine, you should go. But honestly, choosing to start over in your fifties or sixties seems so exhausting. I mean, unless you're married to an abuser, how bad can a marriage be? Boring maybe, routine, but so what? All the years of shared existence, all the good times and bad, to walk away for any reason less than a partner's atrocious behavior seems crazy."

"But again, people are living longer," Mary said. "Now, a person leaving a marriage at the age of say, fifty-five, can reasonably hope to live another twenty-five to thirty years. That's another lifetime in which to be happy in a new relationship. Okay, or to be miserable. The point is that fifty-five doesn't feel like the end; it feels like a gateway. At least, I guess it does for some."

Amanda laughed. "Turning fifty-five didn't feel like a gateway to me!"

"Nor to me, to be honest," Mary said with a smile. "Anyway, the point is that evolving social norms are allowing people to be together in whatever way they choose, and, hopefully, to feel good about it."

"It's no great shame anymore for a woman to be unmarried or never married," Patty said, a bit loudly. "And I'm not just saying that because of my own situation. At least, I try to remind myself of that."

"I think it shows great resourcefulness, this idea of living apart together," Mary said. "If a particular system doesn't work for you, build one that does. Of course, you have to be in a certain socioeconomic level to afford to keep two dwellings. So, once again, the rich make out better than the poor. And here's another interesting tidbit I came across in my reading. According to some expert or another, in general, wealthier people who are single later in life are more likely to find another partner."

Sandra frowned. "I wonder why that is. Maybe because wealthier people can afford to retire at a reasonable age and so have more time to date?"

"I don't know," Mary said. "But it must have something to do with money. Pretty much everything does."

"It's true, what you said before, Mary. Women have always been expected to serve as caregivers," Amanda said. "That's not necessarily bad, but caregiving takes a physical and an emotional toll. Sometimes it means a woman has to give up her personal life—her friends, even her job—to care for a sick relative. It happened to a colleague of mine. She was devastated, having to leave teaching way before she was ready to. It's not something I would ever accept for myself."

"The question is: What does love demand?" Mary said musingly. "What does it require? Those are very big questions, to which there are probably thousands of different answers. I've read that some social scientists have been wondering if the care expectation put on married people isn't too great."

"They might have a point. We vow to stick with our partner in sickness and in health, in good times and in bad. It doesn't seem like a reasonable promise to ask of anyone." Sandra smiled. "And I speak as someone who had a very happy marriage."

"According to the articles I've read, some couples living apart together are hiring elder-care lawyers to draw up caregiving agreements that clearly state what a person is willing to do and under what circumstances."

"It seems so cold," Sandra said. "'I love you but.' Then again, the idea of unconditional love, of total sacrifice for a partner, hasn't exactly proved all that workable in the real world, has it? I guess in every relationship there's a line that can't be crossed."

"Like," Patty said, "I'll stand by you no matter what, unless you cheat on me or murder someone."

Mary nodded. "Right. Or, the unspoken message from too many males: I'll stay with you unless you let yourself go and get fat. Yes," Mary went on, "you could look at the idea of a living apart together relationship as cold, or you could see it as a triumph of reason over sentiment. Older people have been through a lot, they know what they can handle and what they can't or simply don't want to handle. It's a very honest way to be together, I think, even if it might feel uncomfortable at first. I mean, if I were in one of those LAT situations, my mother would have a fit. Assuming she was still alive, of course. To her, it would just be further evidence of my selfishness. What sort of woman refuses to take care of her partner? A bad woman. An *unnatural* woman."

Sandra shook her head. "There are so many years—centuries—surrounding romantic relationships. What they should look like to the outside world, what they should look like on the inside. I think I would have a very difficult time agreeing to an LAT relationship, though I recognize the fact that it's a very sensible solution to a potentially unhappy situation."

Amanda looked to Patty. "Maybe one day you and Phil will have a living apart together relationship."

Patty's eyes went wide. "I hope not!" she declared. "It's marriage or nothing for me!"

Mary reached across the table and, with a smile, she patted Patty's arm. "Good for you," she said. "Stick to your guns." And then she realized that she felt a whole lot better than she had before she and her roommates had sat down to dinner. "I know we can't solve the world's aging problems while sitting around this table," she told the others. "We probably can't even solve the problem of what to have for dinner tomorrow. But at this moment I feel good about being here with you guys, trying, at least, to understand our lives."

"Me too," Sandra said.

Amanda and Patty agreed.

Chapter 67

The kitchen at Phil's house was well-ordered. It made sense. Things were where they should be; at least, things were where Patty, herself, would have put them if this were her kitchen.

It had been Patty's idea to cook dinner for Phil. She had decided to make one of her old specialties, chicken Parmesan, after, of course, ascertaining that Phil liked the dish. She had given him a list of ingredients, and he had shopped for her so that all was ready when she arrived at The Retreat. It was only when she picked up a knife to start chopping the parsley that she realized she had never once gone food shopping with a man, not even with one of her brothers-in-law, not even with her one-time friend and neighbor, Ross.

What a strange hole in her domestic experience.

"I told Sandra that we're, um, that we're spending time together," Patty said, keeping her eyes on the chopping board and the mound of parsley under her knife.

"And what does she have to say about it?" Phil asked. He was leaning against the counter, arms folded across his chest, ankles crossed.

Patty ventured to look up at Phil. "She seems glad. In fact, she said so. I told the others also, Mary and Amanda. They were okay with it, too, not that it really matters what they think, but still."

Phil smiled. "So, no secrets. Good."

Patty quickly looked away again. There *were* still secrets. For one, Patty knew Phil's age but she hadn't told him hers. And she had told Phil that she was living with one of her sisters but not the sordid details of how she had gotten there.

"This might sound like a funny question," Phil said, interrupting Patty's moment of guilt and unease, "but do you think you could be happy living here? I mean, you know, in a house like this, at the end of a lonely road?"

Patty felt herself blush. She hadn't expected this sort of question from Phil, certainly not so early in their relationship. "I don't know," she admitted, hoping her nervousness wasn't evident in her voice. "Maybe. I guess it would depend . . ."

"On certain factors?" Phil prompted.

"Yes. On certain factors."

"Like if were you living alone or with someone you liked."

"Right," Patty said. "Like that."

"Because living alone at the end of a road might become lonely."

"Yes. I imagine it might."

"And if the house was big enough for more than one person, it might get to feel—empty."

"Rather than spacious," Patty suggested.

"Exactly." Phil cleared his throat. "Well, I'd better check on that new watering system I installed out back."

When Phil had gone, Patty stared down at the mound of bright green parsley, only half chopped.

Living apart together.

It's marriage or nothing for me.

Was Phil going to ask her to live with him without, as it used to be said, the benefit of marriage? She hoped not. It was marriage or . . . or what? A romantic friendship? To be very honest, she didn't want that, either, not *just* that. She would almost

rather never have another man in her life than have another
"boyfriend," especially one who lived on his own. Was that
silly? Maybe, but it was how Patty felt.

But none of that mattered because in a few weeks she
would be returning to New Hampshire to finalize a plan for
her future, a plan that could not easily include a romantic relationship of any sort. Patty knew she would never feel comfortable bringing a man to her sister's home. She also knew
that neither of her sisters would ever feel comfortable with
her spending the occasional night at the house of this imaginary man.

It was all so ridiculous! She was almost seventy years old,
and to find herself in this embarrassing situation was . . . It was
intolerable. But she would have to find a way to tolerate it, and
quickly.

Briskly, Patty got back to preparing dinner.

Phil returned from his chores in the garden just as Patty was
about to bring the meal to the table. Phil hurried to help, and
soon they were seated. It pleased Patty to see Phil devour his
dinner. She liked that he was happy, and she liked that she
had been able to make him happy.

When they had reached the stage of coffee and dessert, Phil
leaned forward in his chair and rested his arms on the table.

"There's something I want to tell you, Patty," he said quietly.
"About my past. I've never told anyone the whole story, and I'm
pretty sure no one has found out about it in all these years."

Patty's stomach sank. Of course, it would be something bad,
something to make her continuing to date Phil impossible.
She had been stupid—yet again!—in thinking that a relationship of hers might turn out to be a success.

But what about his asking earlier if she would be comfortable living in a house like his?

"Oh," she said, utterly confused.

Phil looked down at his hands, clasped on the table before
him. "Before there was Nancy, my wife," he began, "I had a

sweetheart all through grammar school and high school. Everyone in Yorktide thought that Eileen and I would marry after graduation, settle down, start having kids. Especially me. I thought my life path was laid out before me, and I was truly happy."

"But?" Patty said softly after Phil had paused for a long moment. Maybe what Phil had to tell her was more sad than bad.

"Suddenly," Phil went on, looking up again at Patty, "people didn't see us at the coffee shop sharing a sandwich or walking along the beach hand in hand or heading out to the movies. No one knew what was going on, and no one asked us, not even our parents." Phil attempted a smile. "Good old-fashioned Yankee reserve. Anyway, at the end of that summer after graduation, Eileen left Yorktide for good. You can bet there were questions then, but I'd made a promise to Eileen, and I kept that promise. I refused to utter a word to anyone about what had happened, and Eileen's parents, who by then had learned the scoop, were equally silent. For years, people theorized about why Yorktide's golden couple had split, where Eileen had gone off to, why she never was seen again in Yorktide." Phil paused and attempted another smile. "Eventually, talk went cold. I'm sure Sandra could tell you all about what it was like back then."

Patty nodded and looked at Phil with sympathy. She didn't know what to say.

"There's more," he went on. "A few months after Eileen left town, I proposed to Nancy, a classmate of ours. I suppose people assumed it was a rebound proposal, that Eileen had broken my heart and that Nancy was my way of putting it back together. See, Nancy had always carried a torch for me, but I'd never paid her any special attention. When I proposed, well, Nancy knew she was my second choice, but she said yes."

"Did you love her?" It was a difficult question to ask, but Patty felt that she had to ask it.

"When Nancy said yes to my proposal, I vowed to be the

best husband that I could possibly be. I vowed to learn to love her for who she was and not to ever compare her to Eileen." Here, Phil paused. "But I can't help but believe that the fact of Nancy's being my second choice was the reason why only a few years into the marriage she was already turning her focus to the needs of everyone else in Yorktide but me."

After a moment, Phil went on, almost as if he were talking to himself. "There was no doubt in my mind that I was a good husband, but Nancy and I were just never able to connect on a certain level. And Nancy had to live with the sad truth that her love and devotion weren't returned in kind, no matter how hard I tried to do the right thing." Phil sighed. "My asking Nancy to marry me might not have been the wisest thing to do. It might have been terribly unfair to Nancy. But I can't turn back the clock now. What's done is done."

"But why did Eileen leave?" Patty asked softly. "What happened between the two of you? Can you tell me?"

Phil nodded. "Now that Eileen's parents are gone, I'm the only person in Yorktide who knows the truth. See, just after graduation, Eileen told me that she was attracted to women. She said that she genuinely loved me—and I believed her— but that she could no longer pretend to me or to anyone else. She swore me to secrecy, and I agreed. I was heartbroken, but I promised to keep her secret, and until this moment I have."

Patty felt her heart break for that long-ago young couple. "What happened when Eileen told her parents?" she asked, half-afraid to know the answer.

Phil shook his head and frowned. "They were devastated, and, though they didn't technically throw her out, they made it clear they didn't want her in the house. Eileen contacted a distant, older cousin who lived in New York City, a woman, also gay, who offered Eileen a place to stay and all the support she needed."

"Are you . . ." Patty shook her head. No. She would not ask that question. *Are you still in love with Eileen?* "Do you know what's happened to Eileen?"

Phil smiled now, a genuine smile. "I've heard from Eileen over the years. It's always she who contacts me, not the other way around. I'm very glad to say that she's well, still happy in her decision to leave Yorktide. She's been in a solid relationship for more than thirty years now. I'm sorry that she felt forced to leave her home, but I'll always admire her courage in being honest with herself, and with me."

Patty reached for Phil's hand and clasped it in her own. "Eileen sounds like an extraordinary person. Thank you for telling me all this. About Eileen and about your marriage."

"I wanted you to know in case . . . in case it makes a difference for you, seeing me again."

Patty smiled and squeezed Phil's hand. "It makes a difference," she said. And then, boldly, Patty leaned over and kissed Phil on his cheek. It was the right thing to do.

On her way home to Sandra's house a little while later, Patty thought about all that Phil had told her. She was deeply moved by the story. She thought she could understand how Phil's marriage might have been a lonely one for both husband and wife. Marriages were complex, and each one was so very different. And marriages might be fairly easy for people to get into, but they weren't all that easy to get out of. She could point to all of the married men she had been involved with as examples of husbands who couldn't or wouldn't walk away from their wives and children. Fear of financial reprisal was probably at the top of the list of reasons, or very near. But the strength of habit and daily routine—maybe boring at times but also comforting and reliable—couldn't be ignored. Neither could a genuine love for a spouse, or a deep sense of responsibility for the well-being of a spouse and children.

It had been brave of Phil to share with her the story of his love for Eileen and his marriage to Nancy. Patty felt honored that Phil had taken her into his confidence.

Honored and very, very happy.

Chapter 68

Amanda sat on the front porch, a mystery novel unopened on her lap. Everyone else was out, Sandra on an errand, Mary for a drive, and Patty was at work. It was nice sitting there on the porch, with a view of the few houses on the other side of Spruce Street, all of which were very similar to Sandra's, neat, large, and charming.

Earlier, Amanda had received a text from Liam letting her know that he had mailed his keys to the landlord, and that he had filed a change of address request with the post office. If mail continued to show up at Amanda's address, would she let him know? Thanks.

What if she *didn't* let him know that some of his mail was still coming to her apartment? What if she lied to him, told him there was no mail, when in reality she had thrown out what items had arrived?

No. Amanda knew that she would never do such a mean and stupid thing. Revenge of any sort wasn't her style. Besides, throwing away someone else's mail was probably a federal offense, and she was not a lawbreaker.

Liam Sexton. They had had some good times over the eight years of their relationship. When she had turned fifty, Liam had taken her to Chicago for the weekend. They had wandered through the Art Institute, tried deep-dish pizza, spent an afternoon at the Shedd Aquarium, gone out one night to hear a jazz band. That was a nice memory. And the next year, they had gone to New Orleans for a three-day vacation. Last year they had . . . In fact, they hadn't gone anywhere together in the past *three* years except to dinner at a local pub once every few weeks.

Yes, Amanda's feelings for Liam had truly waned and then, pretty much had died, to be replaced not by hatred but by a sort of lethargic lack of concern. It seemed that Liam's feelings for her had undergone much the same journey.

Had the eight years they had spent together been a total waste? If she allowed herself to believe that, she would be depressed for the rest of her life. She had to salvage something from her time with Liam, a lesson learned, a bit of wisdom gained, a grain of self-knowledge discovered. Anything!

Suddenly, Amanda found herself reaching for the pen she always carried in her fanny pack. Then, she opened the book on her lap, turned to the back cover, and, almost without conscious intent, began to write.

I know myself when I'm on my own. At least, I get closer to knowing myself when I'm on my own. I don't know myself when I'm with someone. I don't recognize myself. Is the answer, then, that I need to be on my own in order to be true to myself?

The pen dropped from Amanda's hand. She let it remain on the floorboards of the porch. Silently, she read the words she had written so hurriedly, so surely.

Where had the words come from? What had made her write them down? She had never been in the habit of keeping a journal, or of engaging in dedicated self-reflection. But she had come to Maine this summer specifically to take a long, close look at her life, and, just maybe, she was beginning to accomplish a bit of that task.

It was odd, Amanda thought now, but Clovis might just be

playing a role in her search for answers on how to go forward with her life. Just the other day she had experienced a moment of intense, uncanny communication with Sandra's cat. She had been sitting in a corner of the couch in the den with a book when Clovis had jumped up next to her and settled almost against her leg. Amanda was startled and a tiny bit worried. Was he going to attack her? Warily, she returned his steady gaze until, after a while, she felt her wariness fade away. And then, Clovis had reached out his paw and placed it on Amanda's leg, all the while holding her gaze. After that, Clovis had let Amanda stroke him. It had been very soothing to run her hand gently down his silky back.

The experience had been entirely new to her. Until that moment, she had had virtually no contact with animals of any sort. She had never had a pet growing up—she had never asked for one—and none of the men she had lived with had come with an animal. A roommate in college had kept some sort of lizard for a while, maybe an iguana, but it had freaked Amanda out, and she had avoided even glancing at the reptile's terrarium.

But now, she was beginning to see how it might be very nice to live with a cat. They were interesting creatures. Some people believed that a particular animal came into a person's life for a specific reason, to ease a difficult passage or to open one's eyes to an unsuspected truth. Could Amanda's truth be that she was an animal person after all? The idea of cleaning litter didn't bother her. What was the big deal? Hair balls and occasional vomit? Whatever. Clipping nails? Well, that might take some practice, but there were always veterinary services to help with the tough stuff, and some vets even offered at-home care. She had the income to provide for an animal, and she kept a spotless home. She doubted that a shelter would turn her down as an adoptive parent.

Amanda reached down to retrieve the pen that had fallen from her hands. She decided that she would go inside and check on Clovis. Even if he was sleeping—and he did a lot of sleeping—maybe she would just sit by him, watch to see if he twitched, which Sandra said meant that he was chasing mice in his dreams. Amanda wasn't sure she believed that, but it really didn't matter if she did or not. She enjoyed watching Clovis in his kitty sleep.

And maybe he would wake up and put his paw on her again.

Chapter 69

Sandra and Mary were sitting in the backyard. They had dragged two Adirondack chairs to the shade of one of the large maple trees on the property.

"It's more breathable now that the sun is going down," Mary noted, though her tone wasn't convincing. "I never expected sultry weather in Maine."

"We used not to get these terribly humid days," Sandra said. "But all that's changed and, I suppose, will continue to change. Poor planet. Mother Earth is angry, I'm afraid, and she has good reason to be."

Mary grunted what Sandra took to be her assent. She noted that Mary looked pensive.

"Penny for your thoughts," she said.

Mary laughed darkly. "You really want to know?"

"Yes. If you want to tell me."

"Okay. A few days ago, it was the anniversary of the death of an old friend. A dear friend. I mentioned her husband, the guy who can't even boil an egg. Anyway, it's been one year now, but sometimes it still feels as though I've just gotten the news. In fact, Judy's death was part of the reason I decided to retire when I did."

Sandra could understand the loss of a friend. In some ways, Emma, her own dear friend, might as well be dead.

"Mary," she said, "I'm so very sorry for your loss. Do you want to tell me what other reasons played a part in your decision to retire? I've been told I'm a good listener."

Mary sighed. "Sure, why not? My firm was sued for negligence. I'd rather not go into the details, if you don't mind. We were completely innocent of any wrongdoing, and that was proved in the end, but the experience really took it out of me. I was completely blindsided by the feelings of exhaustion, panic, and fear that overcame me. I guess I always thought of myself as pretty much indestructible. I had this story about myself, a persona I'd built up over all the years of fighting for the rights of my clients. A warrior, that was me, Boadicea. But the very idea that someone would cast doubt on my colleagues and me, that someone would threaten to destroy what we'd worked so hard to achieve, well, maybe it shouldn't have, but it threw me off my feet. I never saw it coming, that sort of personal breakdown. All my defenses were breached."

Sandra shook her head. "I honestly can't imagine what that must have been like. I'm so sorry."

"Then," Mary went on, "only days after we were cleared of any wrongdoing, Judy was killed. She was on her way to the hospital to see her youngest daughter, who'd just given birth to her first child, when she was killed in a hit-and-run. When I got the news . . . Anyway, it was like I didn't have a moment to breathe, to enjoy the relief of knowing that the practice was no longer in jeopardy, before I was hit by this loss. Now, I'm not saying I'm the major victim here. Judy's the one who lost her life and there's Joe, her husband, their kids and grandkids. But her awful death hit me before I'd had time to pick myself up and rebuild that tough-as-nails persona."

Mary shook her head. "One day, I realized I'd had enough. All I wanted to do was . . . stop. Do nothing. Money was—is— no problem, thank God, not that I didn't work hard for it, so I didn't have to bother coming up with a plan for future earnings. I just wanted *out*. So, I got out." Mary smiled strangely. "I'm a dropout. I never thought I, Mary Ann Fraser, would have a reason for saying that."

"I'd hardly choose the term 'dropout' to describe you," Sandra said with a smile. "But tell me more about Judy, your friend. If you'd like to."

"I would," Mary said with some enthusiasm. "I'd welcome the chance to talk about her. Like me, Judy left Rivervale to go away to college, and like me, she never went back. But I should start at the beginning. There was a group of us from the first grade, right through high school. Maureen, Barbara, Sheila, Judy, and me. We were inseparable, the Five Musketeers, BFFs before such a term existed. Maureen was always pretty religious, the one people assumed would go into the convent one day, which, by the way, she never did, though she eventually married an ex-priest. Barbara was the tomboy of the bunch, though now we'd just say she was the most athletically gifted. Sheila was the homebody sort, very much her mother's mini-me, always talking about how many kids she was going to have when she grew up. Five, if you're curious, three boys and two girls. And I was the troublemaker, the smart aleck, the one most likely to do something I shouldn't be doing and get caught doing it."

"And Judy?" Sandra asked.

Mary smiled. "Judy was the perfect one. And she was by far the prettiest of the five of us. She had that peaches-and-cream complexion people used to go on about, and the loveliest blond hair, almost golden. Her eyes were dark brown, so big they were like saucers. I remember thinking when we were about twelve or so, why is she still hanging out with us? Boys were crawling all over her, but she had no interest in them or in abandoning us for the cooler girls." Mary smiled a bit. "That attitude is dating me, isn't it? Back then it was still a world in which young girls were told that appearance held the most value. To wonder why your good friend stayed your good friend when all the boys wanted her attention is really dreadful. But I needn't have worried. Judy had her head screwed on right, as my father used to say. She, of all of us, best knew what was really and truly valuable. Her friends."

Sandra thought of Emma. She, too, had always known what was truly valuable in life. "Judy sounds like a special person, indeed," Sandra said feelingly.

"She was. When I got married—briefly—I asked her to be my maid of honor. She was fantastic, handled everything calmly and efficiently, and when, less than a year later, the marriage failed, Judy was great then, too, the proverbial rock. She was always so kind, rescuing baby birds that had fallen out of the nest, befriending the new kid in school, remembering how you'd said in passing that you liked something, a book or a silly little piece of plastic jewelry, and then getting it for your birthday." Mary smiled. "You could hate someone like that, so good and sincere. You could suspect them of being self-righteous or attention-seeking, except that Judy was so unaffected, so quiet about her kind acts. She never sought the spotlight, yet she wasn't at all a pushover. When she married Joe, we all sighed with relief. He really understood her, genuinely appreciated her, unlike so many other guys before him who'd made the stupid assumption that anyone so beautiful and kind had to be easy to take advantage of."

"No wonder her death, especially in such a sudden and awful way, hit you hard," Sandra noted gently. "You experienced a trauma and all the misery and challenge that goes with that."

"I suppose so," Mary said after a moment. "Not that I'm claiming to be suffering from PTSD or anything, though maybe a psychiatrist would differ. But yeah, Judy's dying in the way she did, being treated so vilely by the hit-and-run driver, her life being so carelessly tossed away, regarded as worthless . . ." Mary took a deep breath. "Sometimes I still feel so bloody angry about it. Prison is too good for that creep, though he'll be there for a long time, and maybe he'll get what he deserves from the other inmates. I shouldn't say that, I certainly shouldn't think it, but it's what I hope for."

"So, the driver was caught."

"Yeah. There's some consolation in that, but not much, not for me and certainly not for Joe or their children."

Sandra sighed. "Aside from the loss of both of my parents in that car accident I told you about, I've been very lucky in my life. After that tragedy, I never lost a loved one in a brutal or unexpected way. Even Jacob's death wasn't entirely unexpected, and the same was true with John. We had some little time in which to prepare for the possibility that he wouldn't live to a ripe old age. Still, it was horrible when he died, but it didn't come out of the blue. I guess I'm grateful for that small mercy."

Mary nodded. "We take what we can get and make the best of it. Lemonade out of lemons. A tad grim but practical advice."

"Do you see your old friends often?" Sandra asked.

"No," Mary admitted. "Last time I saw the old gang was the week of Judy's funeral. We all stayed in the same motel so we were able to spend some time together. It was pretty much how it always is when we're in the same room. All the years drop away, and we're back to being the bunch of kids we once were, totally accepting of one another because we bonded before we became aware of things like judgment and actually choosing people to be friends. It doesn't seem to matter that Maureen and Barbara and Sheila don't know a lot about my daily life since I left Rivervale, or that I don't know much about theirs. It's . . . it's amazing, really. That feeling that there's no need to explain anything, the decisions you've made, good and bad, the reasons that took you away or that brought you back. I'm just Mary, the kid who lived at 23 Canon Street. Maureen's just Maureen, Barbara's just Barbara, and Sheila's just Sheila. End of."

Sandra smiled. "You're lucky to have one another."

"Don't I know it! Even though I have no idea when I'll see them again, it hardly matters. We're tight. We'll always be friends. But listen to me carrying on. What about you? Do you have friends from your childhood?"

"Not from my childhood, no," Sandra told her. "A fair number of my peers left Yorktide after high school or college, and that meant I lost touch with them and they with me. My dearest friend, Emma, she recently moved away . . . Well, it's complicated."

"Tell me," Mary urged. "You listened to me. I'm happy to listen to you."

Chapter 70

The sun had almost fully set by then, and the temperature had dropped. The air felt drier, for which Mary was grateful. She was also grateful for Sandra's having listened to her so intelligently.

"Emma," Sandra began now, "was my closest friend for years, more like what I imagine a sister would be like, one you love and can rely on. We raised our children side by side, helped each other through the deaths of our husbands, and maybe most important, we shared a sense of humor."

"And then?" Mary asked.

Sandra attempted a smile but it failed. "And then, Emma was diagnosed with dementia. For a while things were okay, she was able to function safely on her own, but too soon, things began to get bad, as they always do. It became clear that it was too risky for Emma to live on her own, so her daughter brought her to live with her in Illinois. That worked well for a little while, but then Emma's decline seemed to speed up, and Millie and her husband, both of whom work full-time, weren't able to provide the round-the-clock vigilant care Emma needed." Sandra sighed before going on. "Things came to a head when Emma went missing early one morning, still in her nightgown and slippers. Luckily, a neighbor spotted her and called Millie and her husband, who set out immediately. They found Emma telling this neighbor all about something that had happened when she was little, as if it had just taken place that day."

Mary sighed. "I'm so sorry. Dementia is such a cruel disease."

Sandra nodded. "It tore Millie apart to put her mother in a facility with a memory care unit, but she knew it was the kindest thing to do. When you're the caretaker, you have to think of the sick person first and foremost, not of your own feelings. That's not easy, particularly when the person for whom you're deciding is someone you love."

"It certainly isn't easy," Mary agreed. "It's why I've never had a pet. I love animals but I'm too weak to make the decision to send a pet to Heaven. Too weak and too selfish."

Sandra laughed. "Mary, do you really mean you've deprived yourself of the company of an animal because you're worried you won't be able to make a tough end-of-life decision? That's a little extreme. You're not alone when that time comes. Your vet helps you through the decision-making process. And before that time comes, you'll have the joy of loving and being loved."

"If you say so. So, what's Emma's situation now?"

"Not good," Sandra admitted. "Some days she doesn't recognize me at all. Other days, I think she realizes I'm someone she used to know or should know, and still other days, she seems to know exactly who I am. She asks about my children though she refers to them as if they were still little kids. And she talks as if our husbands were still alive. But she knows my name and smiles at me, and it both lifts and breaks my heart."

"I'm sorry," Mary said. "You know, my father was showing a few signs of the disease when he died of something else entirely. At least my mother was spared the trial of trying to take care of him as he lost his mind—and he was spared the inevitable disaster of her playing nurse."

"And your mother?" Sandra asked. "What about her state of mind as she aged?"

"She was as sharp as a tack until the moment she gave up the ghost. Mean, cantankerous, judgmental. I know I shouldn't speak ill of the dead, but she spoke ill enough of the living, both to their faces and behind their backs, and I deem *that* a far worse crime. Don't get me wrong," Mary said hurriedly, "I loved my mother, you know, the way you have to love your parents. But I never liked her. I don't know how my father tolerated living with her for forty-some-odd years. I used to hope he had a secret life that made him happy, but I know he didn't. He wasn't a courageous or a particularly curious man. Maybe he just learned how to block her out at some point. Well, I'll never know. He took his secrets, assuming he had any, to the grave."

Sandra smiled. "As do we all."

The two women were silent then, and Mary found herself remembering how not long ago, the four housemates had talked briefly about the need for friendship and why it was so vitally important in a person's life. Right then, she decided that she would not like to let Sandra slip out of her life when the summer was at an end. She hoped Sandra felt the same, that she would like to keep Mary as a friend, even if that only meant as someone who might enjoy a long phone conversation or e-mail exchange every few months.

"Look," Sandra said suddenly, "this is not something I ordinarily do, but since we've shared so much this evening and we're both of legal drinking age, how about we go into town and get a glass of Prosecco?"

Mary raised her eyebrows. "A glass? Make it a bottle, and it's on me. We'll take an Uber home."

Chapter 71

It had been raining steadily since late morning. Patty was glad she had worn her old, olive-green rain slicker, even though it wasn't very attractive. Maybe, she thought now, if she could find a pink slicker at a resale shop, she would buy it. Resale was probably a smarter way for her to shop.

Patty and Phil were sitting on the deck of a clam shack not far outside of Yorktide. At two thirty in the afternoon, they were the only lunch patrons left, the only two watching the rain over the marsh from a table under a large canopy, sipping coffee, and finishing thick slices of blueberry pie. The pie had been made on the premises. The crust was definitely not store bought; Patty had always been able to tell the difference.

Phil had already paid the bill. Patty had thanked him for that, and Phil had replied that he was an unrepentantly old-fashioned guy. "A man pays for a woman. It was how I was raised, and I don't want to think what my dear departed mother would say if she knew I'd ever let a woman pay for my meal."

Patty felt very peaceful, and, oddly, very safe, somehow protected not only from the rain but also from, well, from everything that might tear her down, such as all the pointed reminders of the mistakes she had made in her life. Like spending money on a new fairy figurine when there was an outstanding utility bill to be paid.

The thought of unpaid utility bills made her think of her sister's child Jim, who worked for the gas company in Massachusetts. This made her realize that she and Phil had never talked about children. She realized that she had just assumed that Phil had no kids of his own; he had never mentioned a child, and neither had Sandra. But a person should never assume.

"Do you have children?" Patty asked then. "I'm sorry. I know that's a question I should have asked before now."

"No children," Phil said promptly. "Nancy and I would have liked a family, but it wasn't in the cards for us. And you?"

Patty hesitated, wondering how to word her answer. Finally, she said: "Same. I mean, I wanted a family but since I never married . . . I know lots of people have a child on their own, but it wasn't what I wanted."

"I'm sorry."

Patty shrugged. "It's okay. I mean, what are you going to do, right? Anyway, I have three nephews and three nieces. They're grown-up now, but it was fun being their aunt when they were little."

"I bet you were a wonderful aunt, and still are."

"Well, they don't need me anymore," Patty admitted. "That's okay. That's what happens. Now, they try to give me advice, like how I should update my computer skills. Well, back when I was still working in an office."

Phil sighed. "It's all about the darn computer and the Internet. And the phone! It's as if people are surgically attached to the things."

"I know, right? Sometimes I wish the computer would just go away!"

The rain had almost stopped by then, and Patty saw that there was a silvery mist like a pretty shawl over the marsh. Phil had told her about his unhappy marriage. Now, Patty wanted to match that act of bravery and trust. Phil seemed like the sort of person who deserved the truth—or as close as she could come to it.

"There are some things about me I want you to know," she began, fiddling with her paper napkin. "Well, to be honest, I really don't want you to know them, but I think that I have to tell you a few things about me."

Phil nodded. "I'm listening," he said.

"The thing is, I haven't made the best choices in terms of romance. See, I always wanted to be married. Since I was a little girl I fantasized about the beautiful dress I would wear at my wedding and the shiny ring my husband would give me. I was obsessed with all that went along with getting married, like choosing a china pattern and picking out a wardrobe for the honeymoon, and selecting the first song my husband and I would dance to as a married couple. And then, after we were married, there would be all the evenings entertaining other married couples with the new china and glassware, and then, after a year or two, there would be a perfectly behaved little child." Patty swallowed hard. She didn't want to cry, not now. "But I never even got close to the real thing," she went on. "Once or twice I thought I was close. But . . . but nothing ever happened. I don't blame anyone else. Not much, anyway. It was just my bad luck, I guess."

"Luck shouldn't be underestimated," Phil said gravely, "good or bad."

"No. It was more than bad luck with me," Patty went on, suddenly determined to tell all. "I consciously did things I shouldn't have done. I sabotaged my chances for happiness. I said yes to seeing men who were married when I knew it was wrong. I don't know why I thought something good would come of those relationships. It was ridiculously stupid of me. Things could have been different if only I . . ."

"Don't drown in 'if only,'" Phil said, reaching across the table for Patty's hand. She let him take it and hold it.

"It's hard not to look back and be angry with myself," Patty admitted. Her hand felt so nice in Phil's. "Some days I just can't . . . I feel as though my whole life has been a huge waste."

Phil leaned forward across the table and looked intently into her eyes. "I won't hear you talk that way, Patty Porter. I won't. It hurts you, and it hurts me, too. You're a good person, and I won't hear otherwise."

The sincerity on Phil's face was unmistakable. Patty thought her heart would burst with happiness.

"There's something else I haven't told you," she said, this time with a bit of a smile. "My age." Patty took a deep breath. This would be the first time since she turned twenty-nine that she had ever correctly stated her age (to anyone but a doctor, of course, not that she went to the doctor all that often). "I'm sixty-nine," she said bravely. "I'll be seventy on December twelfth."

Phil smiled. "So that means you're a Sagittarius! I've always gotten along very nicely with you folk."

"That's right, I'm a Sagittarius. And what are you? I mean, when's your birthday?" She thought it was a good sign that Phil knew a little about astrology. Astrology was fun.

"I'm a Leo. Another sun sign. "

"We're compatible." Patty blushed. "I mean, our signs are compatible."

"Well, that's good to know." Suddenly, Phil looked around the dining area. "I guess we'd better get going," he said. "Looks like the staff wants to start prepping for the dinner crowd."

Patty looked at her watch. "Is it really almost three thirty? I had no idea."

"Time flies when you're having fun."

Patty smiled. "It really does." And in spite of the heavy nature of much of the conversation, she had enjoyed herself that afternoon. Being with Phil James was good. Really good. He liked and respected her for who she was, not for a person he wanted her to be.

Suddenly, Patty noticed that the rain had ended. The air felt fresh. She could hear a bird singing.

Together, Patty and Phil left the clam shack, hand in hand.

Chapter 72

It was a lovely afternoon to sit on a park bench and read.

Earlier, Amanda had stopped in Yorktide's independently run bookstore and bought three recently published cozy mysteries. One was by an author new to her, and she was curious to get acquainted with the author's heroine, the owner of an old, family-run jewelry store in a small New England town. Solving mysteries around poison rings, memorial brooches stuffed with the woven hair of a dead relative, and stolen rubies with a curse upon them sounded like fun.

Don't let me hear you say life's taking you nowhere, Angel.

There it was again, that line of lyric, running through her head! She hadn't actually heard the David Bowie song in years, so where had it come from? And for that matter, where *was* life taking her? Wasn't she the one who should be *leading* her life, taking it somewhere, making it into something? So much came back to that old question of fate versus free will. To what extent did Life happen to us and to what extent did we happen to it?

Sometimes, Amanda supposed, an earworm was just an earworm.

She was just about to open one of the new books when a

figure appeared in her peripheral vision. She turned her head to the left. A woman was walking along the path, coming toward the bench on which Amanda sat. She looked tall, almost elongated, but that was probably just a trick of the light or . . .

Suddenly, as Amanda continued to watch the woman approach, she realized that she felt almost terrified by the idea of an encounter. But that was insane. Why should she be frightened of nodding a greeting to another woman in the middle of a quaint little park in a quaint little town like Yorktide, with people nearby walking their dogs or pushing their children in strollers or, like Amanda, sitting placidly on a bench, face turned up to the sun or down to a book?

The woman, now closer to Amanda, suddenly seemed— vague. Amanda shut her eyes and kept them that way for a long moment, as if believing she had somehow conjured the woman and if she closed her eyes it would make the apparition or whatever it was disappear. When Amanda finally opened her eyes, the woman was still there on the path, not a figment of Amanda's imagination.

Amanda gripped the book she held in her hand and wondered if she had time to dash off before the woman reached her. But the question was irrelevant. Something was holding Amanda in place. Try as she might she could not make herself stand up. Her heart was racing. She felt slightly sick to her stomach.

And then the tall woman, no longer vague, very tangible, was taking a seat at the other end of the bench. She turned her head to look directly at Amanda. Her eyes were a strange pale brown, almost tawny, like those of a lion. Amanda could not look away.

The woman smiled kindly. "You are whole and complete within yourself, Amanda," she said. "You know that, don't you?"

Amanda swallowed hard. She realized that she was trembling from head to foot. The feeling wasn't entirely unpleasant, though it was disconcerting. How in the world did this woman know her name?

Without uttering another word, the woman rose and walked off in the direction from which she had come. Amanda squeezed her eyes shut again—she didn't know why—and when she opened them she saw no one. No one at all. Amanda twisted on the bench, looked over her left shoulder, and then her right. No one. How could the woman have disappeared from sight so quickly?

Suddenly, Amanda realized that she couldn't recall what the woman had been wearing or what color her hair had been, or how old she had seemed. All she could recall was the woman's strange, pale brown eyes. And the fact that she had known Amanda's name. And the fact that she had seemed to disappear into thin air.

Could the woman have been an angel?

Amanda dropped the book she still held and put both hands over her eyes. What a ridiculous thought! She was losing her mind. The woman was just a woman, nobody in particular, insignificant.

No. It felt wrong to dismiss what had just happened, whatever it was, or to belittle the woman.

Suddenly, Amanda became aware that she was crying. What had she done to deserve the care she had been receiving from her summer roommates? What had she done to deserve a kind word from a complete stranger?

Amanda took a deep but wobbly breath. She felt that she was somehow changed. She also suspected that the meaning or the message of the encounter she had just experienced would only be fully revealed to her over time.

Where had all this—this what?—this willingness to believe, where had it come from? Until that summer, until almost that moment, Amanda had never been open to anything remotely spiritual. She had always prided herself on being an entirely grounded human being, immune to the fanciful and to wild imaginings.

I don't know myself when I'm with someone. I don't recognize my-self. Is the answer, then, that I need to be on my own in order to be true to myself?

She had written those words just the other day. Rather, the words had seemed to write themselves, to be a message sent to her. And what the woman had just told her. *You are whole and complete within yourself, Amanda. You know that, don't you?*

Do I? Amanda asked herself. *Do I know that?*

Yes. She thought that maybe, at long last, she did.

Chapter 73

Clovis was dozing at the exact center of the couch in the den. It was amazing how cats seemed to instinctively know about geometry and interior design. Amazing and a little scary.

Sandra wondered why she didn't spend more time in the den. It was a very comfortable and pleasant room, especially on a rainy day like today. Amanda had really appreciated the time she had spent there recuperating from the twisted ankle. And, after all, it had been John's favorite room in the house.

Emma, too, had enjoyed spending time in the den, having tea in the afternoon or a glass of wine at cocktail hour. It was strange that they had never spoken of setting up house together; even Jack had thought the idea a good one. Could Emma have known, five years ago, that her mind was beginning to fail, that before long she would be in no condition to live interdependently with a friend?

Maybe. Still, it would have been so nice to share a home with Emma, even for a little while. They were so compatible in so many ways. They were both early risers. They enjoyed the same sorts of books and movies and music. They had even traveled well together, which wasn't always a given even in the closest of relationships.

And, like Sandra, Emma had always been vocal about not liking the idea of living in a community of only her peers. It seemed unnatural, and, very possibly, boring. How restrictive were those retirement places, anyway? Certainly, as long as a person was in good health and her right mind, she could get in her car each morning and drive anywhere she liked. A retirement home wasn't a prison. Though there might be restrictions concerning visitors. No overnight guests? No children under twelve? Sandra had heard of such rules and regulations, and she could understand the need for a sense of order—hadn't she put rules and regulations in place this summer?—but the idea of someone she didn't know imposing strictures on her social life felt wrong. She was a mature adult. Surely, she could be trusted not to bring a burglar or a rapist into the community! Was her common sense to be doubted simply because she was over the age of fifty-five?

Enough speculating, Sandra thought, slightly irritated with herself. She went over to her desk and opened her laptop. She decided to search for information on independent living options for older adults in the state of Maine.

It didn't take long for Sandra to find the sort of thing she was looking for. The population was aging. People needed safe homes in safe—and expensive—communities. The prices of the homes Sandra found listed online started at around three hundred thousand dollars. It was interesting, in a cynically amusing sort of way, how many of these communities referred to themselves as "villages," "cottages," or "estates." No bland house farms these. No, these communities were places of charm. At least, they sold themselves as places of charm.

And, of course, these were communities for people entering the final phase of their lives. The "golden years."

In many of the houses or apartments, there was an open-concept floor plan; in as many, the home was laid out on one floor. No potentially dangerous stairs for elders to fall down. Kitchens invariably featured a breakfast bar, which seemed to have replaced the old-fashioned breakfast nook. Many homes featured a back deck. Sandra wondered if there were rules about what sort of furniture or decorations one might use on those decks. Maybe such rules only applied to places that could be seen from the road. Charm could only exist with some degree of agreed-upon uniformity.

Living rooms had gas fireplaces. There were no logs to haul around, and therefore, no mess to clean up. Each condominium had a primary suite—the word *master* was no longer used; her rental agent, Marcia Livingston, had told Sandra that—some with a walk-in closet and many with attached bathrooms of a size and shape to allow the use of a walker or wheelchair.

Many of the communities offered a clubhouse and a fitness center; sometimes this also meant an indoor pool. One "village" advertised a communal kitchen. There were probably several good reasons for a communal kitchen but at that moment, no really excellent reason sprang to Sandra's mind.

Some communities were adjacent to a golf course. That meant nothing to Sandra, who had never picked up a golf club in her life and had no interest in doing so now. But for many people, a golf course was probably a big draw.

The condominium communities had a homeowners' association, run by a board of directors elected by the homeowners to handle all matters concerning common property, including setting and enforcing rules and managing the community's finances.

All of the communities—villages, cottages, and estates—claimed to be located close to a beach or a state park or a wilderness trail; to health care providers, grocery stores, and cultural hubs.

Importantly, pets were allowed in the communities, with certain restrictions regarding dogs. Sandra thought there might be some objection should a homeowner decide to raise chickens in the backyard. Lots of people raised chickens; it had become a popular thing to do. But maybe raising chickens in a fifty-five and older community was not considered charming.

Sandra sighed and closed the computer. In truth, she really didn't want to leave her home, but one day it was sure to become too much for her to handle on her own. It was probably better to get out while she still had the luxury of choosing another way of living. And what had happened to her thoughts about putting together a small community of her own under this roof? In many ways, the idea still held appeal; in other ways, not so much. Forming such a community would require a lot of hard work, and Sandra had come to realize she really didn't want to put in the effort. If that made her lazy, so be it. Now, if someone else should decide to spearhead such an enterprise, well, she wouldn't be opposed to listening.

But, nothing had to be done at the moment. Sandra turned in her chair and looked to the couch, on which Clovis was now washing his face.

"Right, Clovis?" she said. "For now, we're okay just as we are."

In reply, Clovis opened his mouth and yawned.

Chapter 74

Dinner that evening consisted of three pizzas the summer roommates had ordered from Yorktide's surprisingly good Italian restaurant. One mushroom; one sausage and onion; and one margarita. Mary had found a delicious and inexpensive red wine in a shop in town, and all but Patty were happy to partake of a glass or two. Patty preferred light white wines, like Vinho Verde and Pinot Grigio.

"This sausage and onion is seriously good," Mary said. "And I'm fussy about my pizza."

Patty nodded. "Very good crust. And the sauce is delicious. Homemade, I think."

"And the wine is excellent, Mary," Sandra said.

"You know how sometimes mushroom pizza can be kind of bland?" Amanda noted. "Not this. I don't even need to add red pepper flakes."

"So, what did everyone get up to today?" Mary asked.

"Well, I can't say it was terribly exciting," Sandra replied, "but I spent a bit of time online researching retirement villages. The kind where you buy your own home and have access to communal resources. Not inexpensive, by the way."

"Mary," Amanda said, "do you remember what you told me

about the first large-scale retirement community in the United States? The marketing campaign used the term 'golden years' to sell the idea of a secure community for, get this, people 'fifty-five and better.' Speaking for myself, I'm not convinced that being fifty-seven is better than being fifty!"

"There's a distinction," Mary pointed out, "between what we mean by the golden years and what we mean when we refer to a golden age. The golden age is a past period of perceived prosperity and excellence. We talk about the golden age of cinema, fashion, painting, democracy. The golden age is only determined to be so after the fact of its passing. You know, 'those were the good old days.'"

"I'm sure that at some point in everyone's life they consider 'the way things were' better than the way things are in the present," Sandra noted. "Nostalgia is unavoidable, and waxing nostalgic can serve as a pleasant way to pass an evening with an old friend. But it can also be very dangerous. It can poison the present if a person lets nostalgic thinking get out of hand."

"Very true," Amanda said.

"The sunset years. The twilight years. Is anyone supposed to be happy about entering that final phase?" Mary wondered aloud. "Why does it need to be emphasized? I know I'm never going to see sixty again. Don't rub it in!"

"Do you know that the state of Maine has a huge population of people over the age of sixty-five?" Sandra said.

"Really?" Mary replied. "Do you think older people are coming to Maine on purpose? Who comes to a cold climate to grow old? Maybe the population over sixty-five was already here. Maybe most young people have been leaving Maine for opportunities elsewhere. Maybe the old people are in effect being left behind."

"You're not actually being left behind if you don't want to leave," Amanda pointed out.

"Perspective. Still, I'd be curious to know the answer to the question of why Maine has so many senior citizens."

"I never liked that term, senior citizen," Sandra admitted. "We don't have junior citizens. Why, then, do we need senior citizens? Besides, I'd bet that most people wouldn't describe themselves as a citizen before, say, describing themselves as a father or wife or lawyer or construction worker."

"Around the world," Mary informed the others, "the population sixty-five and over is the fastest growing. Low birth rate and increasing longevity seem to be the biggest reasons for that."

"Why aren't people having more children than they are?" Patty wondered.

"I don't know. Poverty? Financial strain on every level of society? A sure sense that the world is a freakin' mess and that to bring a new life into it would be cruel?"

Sandra shook her head. "I don't believe that having a sense that the world is in big trouble—no matter how true and terrifying that may be—is a strong enough reason for masses of people to stop having children. Species procreate. It's what they do."

"Okay, the masses are mindless then. They don't know, and they don't want to know."

"That's not what I mean," Sandra said a bit sharply. "What I mean is that people are terminally optimistic."

Mary laughed. "Terminally is right."

"They, we, have the need to nurture, to love."

"Adopt a pet."

Sandra frowned. "Now you're just being annoying."

Mary sighed. "I know. Sorry. I get that way."

"Listen to this," Amanda said, looking up from her phone. (Mary was pleased that she wasn't the only information junkie in the house.) "By 2030, one in five Americans will be sixty-five or more. Our time has come. We old people—and I will be one shortly—are in ascendancy."

"Whoop-de-do. So?" Mary said.

"So," Amanda went on, "maybe our growing numbers will

compel there to be more intelligent and compassionate care and better, more affordable services than there used to be in the past. Maybe it will be easier to be old than it was for our parents."

Mary shook her head. "Aging is still aging. It's never been for sissies, and it never will be. And if you put your faith in bureaucracy to achieve any sort of meaningful, lasting change for the good, you're kidding yourself badly."

"Is there nothing to look forward to then?" Patty said with a bit of a desperate laugh. "I mean, for us, at this point in our lives?"

"I didn't say there wasn't anything to look forward to," Mary replied. "Personally, I look forward with great anticipation to my evening cocktail. Every single year I look forward to the first snowfall as if I were still a kid. I look forward to the next book in my favorite series and the next episode in my favorite television series."

Sandra nodded. "The small things."

Mary nodded. "Exactly. Never knock the small things."

"I can't tell you what pleasure I derive from rewatching my favorite old movies or from buying a small bouquet of fresh flowers every Monday morning," Sandra went on. "Habits, routines. They provide a structure, maybe even more so when you've stopped going to the office every day or doing whatever it was you did to support yourself and your family all those years."

"When you live alone," Patty said, "habits and routines become things you can rely on, like a friend. Gosh, that sounds pathetic."

"Not at all," Mary said. "I agree with you."

Amanda sighed. "I guess I'm going to have to get used to living on my own again. It's been a while, but I think I'm going to enjoy it. At least, I hope I will. I've always been good on my own. Why should that have changed?"

"You might go through a transition time, though," Sandra noted. "You know, adjusting to Liam's being gone. You'll find an old sock he forgot to pack and have a moment of sadness or anger. You'll forget to take out the garbage one night because it was Liam's job to do that and you'll feel foolish for having forgotten. Little things like that will take you by surprise. My transition to living alone after John's passing is in some ways still going on. But I suspect yours will be far briefer, not because your relationship wasn't important, but because it didn't last most of a lifetime."

"I hope you're right," Amanda said. "I want to get on with my life, not waste time looking back."

"You're wise," Mary said, quite seriously. "Sometimes even the unhappy parts of the past get colored more brightly when we let nostalgia sneak in. We start to miss times or people we once were very eager to be rid of." Mary raised her wineglass. "I say, here's to the future and to heck with the past!"

"To the future!" chimed the others.

Chapter 75

When the light had turned green, and not a split second before, Patty moved the car ahead. She was on her way to meet Phil at the marina, though she didn't feel particularly happy about it.

The summer was coming to an end, and she would soon have to say good-bye to Phil and to her summer roommates and go back to living with her sister and brother-in-law. A wave of sadness threatened to engulf her but Patty fought it off. She was determined to enjoy every moment she and Phil had together.

Suddenly, Patty found herself wondering what Nancy, Phil's wife, had had to say about her husband to friends and neighbors. Had she ever spoken ill of him, rolled her eyes when his name was mentioned, shaken her head and said things like, "That man will be the death of me"?

Had Nancy been the way she had been—the way both Sandra and Phil had described her: excessively devoted to good deeds—because she couldn't have children? Had being a good and selfless person in the community served as a distraction from the pain of her lonely marriage? Maybe, Patty thought, being "selfless" was, in fact, Nancy's way of being selfish, of punishing Phil for not loving her as she loved him. Or maybe it had never occurred to Nancy that Phil might feel left out of her life of service and alienated from his wife.

Patty had arrived at the marina, no wiser to the mystery that had been Nancy James. As she made her way toward the pier, she passed a woman who looked vaguely familiar. Maybe she had seen her here before. The woman smiled and said hello to Patty, who greeted her in return.

Yorktide was a friendly place, from what Patty had been able to tell this summer. The locals she had encountered— most important, Sandra and Phil—had welcomed her with open arms. Even Michelle, although a bit intimidating, had proved to be a nice person. No wonder Phil loved living here. Who wouldn't?

"You made it!"

Patty smiled and hurried her pace toward Phil, who, when she had reached his boat, helped her on board.

"Did you think I wouldn't?" Patty asked, wondering at the exuberance of his greeting.

"No, I'm just glad you're here."

Patty thought that Phil seemed nervous, a bit jumpy. She had never seen him anything but laid-back, mellow. Maybe he, too, was thinking about the summer's ending so soon.

Suddenly, Patty's eyes widened. "What's this? Champagne?" On a small table, a bottle sat in a silver-toned ice bucket.

"Yup."

"I don't understand," Patty said. "Are we celebrating something?"

"I hope so."

And then, Phil was down on one knee.

Patty's heart began to thump uncomfortably in her chest. There was no way that what she thought might be about to happen was actually going to happen. Was there?

Phil looked up at her, his eyes shining with sincerity. "Patty

Porter," he said, "would you do me the honor of becoming my wife?"

Only now did Patty notice that he held a small, white velvet box. Carefully, he opened the box to reveal a diamond engagement ring. Tears sprang from Patty's eyes when she saw the stone glittering and flashing in the sunlight.

She had waited almost all of her seventy years for this moment. No, she thought, not for this moment. *This* moment, here with Phil James, was unimaginable. This was beyond her wildest dreams. This was heaven.

But heaven was something she would have to say no to.

"Phil," she said, her voice wobbly and thin, "I can't marry you, as much as I want to, and I really, really do, because I love you, but . . . I have no money."

Phil, still kneeling, holding the ring box aloft, looked genuinely puzzled. "What does money have to do with our becoming husband and wife? I'm not looking for a meal ticket. Besides, I have plenty of money to take care of the two of us."

"But I don't want you to think I'm taking advantage of you and . . ."

Finally, Phil climbed to his feet. "Patty," he said firmly. "I don't think that. At all."

"All I can bring to a marriage is, well, me."

Phil smiled. "That's all I'm asking, Patty, that you share my life with me and let me share your life with you. It's pretty simple, really." Now, Phil removed the ring from its slot in the velvet box and reached for Patty's left hand. The ring fit her finger perfectly. How, Patty wondered, had he known her size?

"Then, yes, Phil," she said, tears streaming down her face— and no doubt ruining her makeup—"yes, I will marry you."

And then, Phil kissed her on the lips and Patty kissed him back.

"So, we would live in your house, The Retreat, I mean?" she asked, wiping her eyes with the back of her hand.

"Of course. If that's okay with you."

"Oh, yes," Patty assured him. "It's a lovely house. I can't believe my good luck. . . ."

"Of course, the house could use some sprucing up, a woman's touch, so . . ."

Patty smiled. "And I'd like to keep my job at Crystal Breeze, or if that isn't possible, I'm sure I haven't been the greatest employee, then maybe I could get a job somewhere else in town. Part-time. It would help me feel . . . It would help me feel better about myself."

"You can do whatever you want to do, Patty. You're in charge of your life, not me, not anyone else."

Phil was right, Patty realized. Finally, she was taking charge of her life, showing herself the respect she had always deserved as a decent human being.

"So, when can we have the champagne?" she asked with a smile.

"Right now!" Phil opened the bottle of champagne. Instead of glass flutes they drank from plastic cups, which, honestly, suited Patty just fine.

Suddenly, Phil turned and waved his arm in the air, calling out to passersby: "She said yes! She said yes!"

There were calls of congratulations from every direction, and Patty put a hand to her face. "Phil, I can't believe you did that!"

"Why shouldn't I announce our news to the world?" he countered. "I'm the happiest man alive."

For the first time in her life, Patty felt like a celebrity. She liked the feeling a lot. And right there and then she resolved not to tell her sisters how bad they had made her feel through the years, especially the last few years when things had really begun to fall apart. It was water under the bridge. Instead, she would thank her sisters from the bottom of her heart for coming to her aid when she needed them most.

Also, Patty decided, she wouldn't share the exciting news of her engagement with her summer roommates until she had told her sisters. Family was family, after all, and family took precedence. At least, that was what she had been raised to believe. As much as it would make her crazy, she would hide the engagement ring from Sandra and the others until then.

"To the future," Phil said then, lifting his plastic cup and calling Patty back to the moment.

"To *our* future," she amended. "I know it will be a beautiful one."

Chapter 76

The sun was setting. It wasn't the most spectacular sunset Amanda had ever witnessed, the pinks weren't as pink as they could be, but really, any sunset could be considered glorious. She should never forget that fact.

She thought about finding the unbroken sand dollar, a discovery she had deemed meaningful in some way, a gift from the Universe.

She thought about encountering that woman in the park, the woman with the strange colored eyes, the woman who had known her name.

Before this summer, she had never believed in anything other than the material. Now, she was becoming susceptible to the power of the intangible.

Maybe, Amanda thought, continuing along the shore, it was best not to question her belief. Maybe it was better simply to accept that she did believe in *something*.

And maybe that belief in something as yet unnamed was helping her to recover her passion for teaching. At the start of the summer Amanda had been genuinely concerned that her students would suffer because of her lack of motivation. Now, things felt different. Now, *she* was different.

Maybe the summer spent in Yorktide with Sandra, Mary, and Patty, along with the end of her relationship with Liam, had freed her from distractions. She felt rejuvenated somehow, focused, ready to engage with the more important things in life.

Another solitary walker, a man about her own age, passed Amanda going the opposite way. She wondered what he was thinking, if he was happy with his life, or if, like her, he was at a moment of crisis, a moment of possibly profound change.

And then she realized that she was probably not so unusual, just one of the millions, maybe billions, of people who found themselves "going along for the ride" as it were, letting life happen to them. Luckily, she had been given the opportunity to realize that it was time to move to the driver's seat before she was too old to effect major changes for the better.

Soon, she would go home to a newly empty apartment and reclaim it for her own. Already, she had a few decorating ideas. Liam had hated the idea of the walls painted any color but white. Now, freed from his opinions, Amanda thought she might paint the walls of her bedroom in soothing tones of blue and green. She could do the painting on her own. It would be a challenge.

She wondered if her cat—the one she would be adopting—would like to sleep in bed with her, in the blue and green room. Maybe she would buy a cat bed just in case he liked his own space, though she had heard that a blanket folded into a cardboard box would work as well as an expensive bit of feline furniture. She still had to research the best brands of litter available; maybe the people at the shelter would have some advice about that. And catnip. Some cats didn't like it, she had learned. It made some cats aggressive and others, goofy.

Amanda stopped and gazed up at the darkening sky. It was so very beautiful. Tears pricked at her eyes. She had come to realize that she had wanted this result all along, but hadn't had the nerve to bring it about. She had wanted to leave Liam, to be on her own. In a way, she had to thank him for making the break. Not that cheating on her had been the most mature way to go about things but . . . Well, it was in the past now. She hoped that Liam's new girlfriend—and the child—had better luck with him. Liam wasn't a bad person. He just hadn't been the special person with whom she was meant to spend the rest of her life.

That special person, Amanda knew now, smiling up at the sky, was Amanda Irving.

Chapter 77

"I'm glad that you were home," Millie said. "Moments like these don't come all that often these days. I knew I had to call you right away."

Sandra smiled at the screen of her laptop. "I'm glad, too," she told Millie, who was sitting in a chair next to her mother, her hand resting lightly but protectively on Emma's arm. Millie looked tired.

Emma's hair was neatly combed, and her skirt and blouse were, as far as Sandra could tell, clean. She had lost weight this summer, though. Sandra wondered if her old friend had any real interest in food these days. Many people lost their appetite as they grew old or ill. Maybe the food in the nursing home just wasn't very appetizing.

"Hello, Emma," Sandra said.

Emma nodded.

"How are you today?" What a ridiculous question, Sandra thought. Why had she asked that of Emma? What could Emma possibly reply? Had she even understood the question? It was so difficult to talk to a person suffering from dementia. There were guidelines of course, but often, in the moment, Sandra—

and presumably many others—forgot what to say and what not to say in order not to cause distress.

"Mom," Millie said, taking her mother's hand. "Here's Sandra. Can you see her?"

Emma turned to her daughter. "Of course I can see her. She's on the screen."

Sandra smiled. "I thought of you this morning, Emma," she said. "I had a cup of tea with honey and I thought of how much you like your tea with honey."

Emma looked back to the screen and smiled. "Honey," she said. "Yes."

Encouraged, Sandra quickly searched her mind for a bit of light gossip that might possibly amuse her friend. "I saw Tatti Brown the other day, Emma. She was still carrying that big old straw bag she's been toting around forever. The bottom's falling out, but I bet there's nothing that will induce her to throw it away."

"She always was an odd one," Emma said with a ghost of her once wicked grin.

Then suddenly, as if a switch had been flipped, Emma's expression turned to one of confusion followed rapidly by an expression of blankness.

"Mom?" Millie put her hand on her mother's shoulder and then looked to Sandra. "I think Mom's tired now."

"Yes," Sandra said. "Thank you, Millie. Thank you for making this moment happen for us."

Millie smiled a bit. "Talk soon, Sandra."

"Good-bye, Emma," Sandra said. But Emma made no reply.

A moment later the screen was blank.

Sandra sat back in her chair. Suddenly, she felt very low. But she knew the moments of lucidity were fleeting. She couldn't allow herself to focus on the negative. The fact was that she was very glad to have shared one of the precious lucid moments with Emma and Millie.

And, she was glad that she had been able to share a bit of Emma with Mary the other evening. Mary was a good and sensitive listener. Sandra would like to keep in touch with her after the summer. In some ways, they were very different people—certainly, their paths through life had been distinct—but they connected in some easy way that was not always available in relationships.

Slowly, Sandra got up from the chair and headed for the kitchen. A nice cup of tea was in order, with a spoonful of honey in honor of Emma. People, Sandra reflected, lived on in the memories of those who knew and loved them. Emma—who she had been—lived on in Sandra's memory, no matter her present state.

That was how legacy really worked.

Chapter 78

Mary was seated on a wooden bench in the charming little park in the center of downtown Yorktide. Though it was a fine day, there were few other people in the park, and, for this, she was grateful. She felt that she needed a degree of privacy for this call; it was why she had left the house and come to the park. Not that she suspected Sandra, Amanda, or Patty to be the eavesdropping types. Still.

After her conversation with her brother, Mary had decided that she wanted to help her nephew, Bill Junior, in his career. But that would only be possible if they developed a relationship. Which meant that Mary needed to call her nephew, even if she was nervous about the prospect. She hoped he wouldn't be annoyed with her suddenly reaching out after all the years of neglect. She would just have to take her chances.

"Hey, Bill," she said when he had answered. "It's Mary. Your aunt."

"Oh, hey." His tone, Mary noted, was friendly. "I didn't recognize the number but something made me pick up. I don't usually do that."

Of course, he wouldn't have recognized the number, Mary

thought. She had never called him before. Not once in twenty-four years.

"Thanks. I mean, I'm glad you did answer. Is this a good time to chat? If not, I—"

"No, it's fine. I'm between meetings. If you hear chewing it's because I'm finishing a sandwich."

"What kind?" Mary had no idea why she had asked that. Did it matter?

"Turkey with lettuce and tomato on white toast with mayo. I have the same sandwich every day. Boring, I know, but it saves me the trouble of actually having to consult my appetite."

Mary laughed. "I know just what you mean. When I was working, I ate pretty much the same thing every day, a plain bagel with butter for breakfast and a tuna salad sandwich for lunch. On automatic pilot so I could focus my energy on important matters."

"Exactly. So, what's up?"

His tone was not only friendly, Mary thought. It was welcoming. Mary forged ahead. "Well, your father told me about your graduating summa cum laude and about your winning the Hirsch Prize. He also told me that you're working in a legal aid office, which is pretty impressive. I just wanted to offer my congratulations."

"Yeah, thanks. Dad's more excited about it all than I am. Mom, too. But you know how parents are."

Not good parents like Bill and Stacy Fraser, Mary thought. She couldn't recall one instance in which her own parents had shown excitement about any of her achievements. But that was all in the past.

Mary suddenly felt tongue-tied. What sort of questions was an aunt supposed to ask of her twenty-something nephew, a person she barely knew? What are your hobbies? What kind of movies do you like? Did you enjoy school? She should have asked all of those questions and more years ago.

"Um," she said, "are you in a romantic relationship?" She hoped she had phrased the question properly, in an inoffensive and not presumptive way.

"Not at the moment," Bill replied. "I figure that it's better I keep free of commitments until I get settled, make a good start in my career. But," he went on, with a bit of a smile in his voice, "if you're curious, I'm heterosexual. I know that sexual identity is not something anyone can assume these days."

"Oh," Mary said. "Thanks." Sheesh, she thought. How old was she? Old. "I'd like you to visit me in New York," she went on. "I know we hardly know each other, but you're welcome to stay with me. I've got a guest room, but if you'd rather stay in a hotel or an Airbnb, that's fine, too. People need their independence."

Bill laughed. "People also need to save what little money they have! I'll bunk down at your place if you really don't mind. And I'd love to see as much of the city as I can in a few days."

Mary realized that she felt genuinely excited about the prospect of her nephew's paying her a visit. "You'd better make a short list," she suggested. "New York can be overwhelming even for those of us who live there. Pick one neighborhood to explore, or a few museums or gallery shows to catch, a restaurant to try. It might be your first visit to New York, but it definitely won't be your last."

"Good advice. Thanks, Aunt Mary."

Aunt Mary. The idea of being this young man's aunt was fine; it was more than fine. But the idea of being addressed with the title just didn't feel right. It made Mary feel too distanced in time from Bill. Was that the right way to put it? It made her feel old. That was what she meant.

"If you feel comfortable doing so," she said then, "I'd like you to just call me Mary."

"Sure," he said. "No worries."

They chatted for a bit longer before Bill—having finished his sandwich—had to dash off to his next appointment.

Mary remained seated on the wooden bench. She wasn't sure how big of a commitment she was willing or able to make to her nephew in terms of time and energy. Then again, maybe the size of the commitment didn't much matter. Bill was no longer a child; he was an independent young adult who didn't need his hand held by his aunt. Still, make a commitment she would, a commitment to get to know her brother's only child, the only one left to carry on the family name (if that meant anything particularly good, and Mary wasn't sure that it did).

It felt nice, she realized, to have a connection with a person of another generation. She could learn a lot and maybe teach a little. Maybe, just maybe, they could become friends.

That would be a good thing, Mary thought, as she got up and headed back to her car. A really good thing.

Chapter 79

Patty's engagement ring was nestled in its white velvet box, out of sight for the moment. Patty didn't want the ring to speak for her. She wanted to be the one to give her sisters the big news. No doubt they were expecting to hear something awful from their middle sister, like that she had spent all of her money on tourist stuff and now couldn't afford the gas to drive back to New Hampshire. Or that she had totaled Kevin's car. Or that—

"I'm so nervous," Patty admitted, turning to Phil. They were seated side by side at his kitchen table. "What if they—"

"Object?" Phil smiled. "You don't need their permission to marry me, you know."

"I know. But I would like their blessing. See, I'm not sure they have any faith in me. They might not believe that I know what I'm doing."

Phil looked at her steadily. His expression was serious. "It doesn't matter what they do or don't believe," he said. "*We* know that we love each other and that we want to be married."

Patty took a deep breath. "Okay," she said. "Make the call."

Phil opened his laptop. Patty had asked both of her sisters

to join in this call. It had been decided that Teri was to go to Bridget's house, as Bridget's computer screen was larger.

Suddenly, the connection came live. When Patty saw her sisters, sitting shoulder to shoulder at Bridget's kitchen table, she felt a wave of emotion wash over her. She loved her family very much, and she was happy that she would no longer be a burden on them. Not that she was marrying Phil to spare her sisters. No, she was marrying Phil because she loved him and because he loved her.

"Hi," she said, possibly a bit too brightly. She wondered if her sisters could tell that she was very nervous.

Her sisters mumbled a greeting. Clearly, they were anxious about what was to come.

"Thanks for being here. I want to introduce you to someone," Patty went on. "Bridget, Teri, this is Phil James. Phil, these are my sisters."

Neither woman said a word. Their expressions were wary, as well they might be.

"Phil and I met this summer," Patty went on, "here in Yorktide. Phil keeps bees, and one day he brought a case of honey into the store where I've been working, I told you about my job, and well, we got to know each other after that and . . ."

Suddenly, Patty froze. Her sisters, silent and still stony faced, were not making this easy. She felt Phil take her hand, and it gave her the courage to go on.

"And we're getting married," she said. "Isn't that wonderful?"

The silence continued. The grim, wary expressions on the screen didn't waver.

"Aren't you . . . Aren't you happy for me?" Patty's voice broke, and tears pricked at her eyes.

Beside her, Phil cleared his throat. "Now, I know this is sudden," he said, "but I'm not a spring chicken, and I don't have time to waste. I'm in love with your sister, and, more to the point, I love her and I'll take good care of her as my wife for the rest of my life. She's the kindest, warmest-hearted woman, and she makes me smile and well, we have fun together. You can ask anyone here in Yorktide, where I've spent every day of my life since the day I was born, and they'll tell you I wouldn't hurt a hair on your sister's head. And I own my home straight out, and I have a boat, and my bees produce enough honey for me to sell, and I make candles from their wax, too. It all does very nicely in the shops around here. Your sister won't be wanting for anything."

Phil had finished speaking, and Patty squeezed his hand in gratitude. For a long moment, neither of Patty's sisters said a word. Finally, Bridget and Teri came to life. They exchanged a glance and then turned back to Patty and smiled, if a bit cautiously.

Bridget was the first to speak. "I have to say this was the last thing we expected to hear from our Patty at this point in her life, but if she says that she's happy, well, then we're happy for her, and for you, Phil. Congratulations."

"Congratulations, Patty," Teri added. "Looks like you got what you always wanted at long last."

Patty smiled at her fiancé and wiped her eyes. "I did," she said. "The love of a good man. I'll call you soon to tell you our plans and to arrange to get my things sent to Maine. Oh, and to get your car back to New Hampshire, Teri. But I'd like to know now if you would both be my maids of honor."

Bridget looked thoroughly surprised. "Okay," she said after a moment. "Just don't make us wear fancy gowns. I can't be spending money on frivolities."

"And no high heels," Teri added. "My bunions won't allow it."

"And no pink," Bridget went on. "I look ridiculous in pink."

"It's a deal," Patty promised, though she had been considering pink as a wedding color. Wasn't pink always a good idea? And as for gowns . . . Oh, well. You couldn't have everything you wanted in life.

"Hey, wait a minute," Bridget said suddenly. "Is there a ring? Is this thing really official?"

"Oh!" Patty exclaimed. "I almost forgot." She reached for the white velvet box in which her engagement ring was nestled, opened it, and slipped the ring on her finger. "Here it is," she said.

"Why were you hiding it from us?" Teri queried. "Unless you didn't want to blind us. Mother of God, that is some ring!"

"You'll take good care of our Patty, won't you?" Bridget said huskily.

"I will," Phil assured her solemnly.

The call ended soon after.

"You did it," Phil said, kissing the tip of Patty's nose. "I knew that you could."

"Phil, have you ever gone to midnight Mass on Christmas Eve?" she asked him.

"Can't say that I have," Phil admitted. "But what's that got to do with anything?"

"It's one of my favorite things to do. Would you come with me this year?"

"And every year after that. Oh," Phil said then, "you know, I was thinking. Those collectibles you told me about, the fairy figurines. If you want I can build a special display cabinet for them in our living room. Or they could be in the bedroom, or maybe you want to put them throughout the house, you know, on shelves. Whatever you think is best."

Patty literally felt her knees go weak and thanked God that she was sitting and that Phil was holding her hand. Every other man in her life had laughed at her love of the figurines, belittled her taste in "art." Only Phil accepted her hobby as valid, as truly important to her. Only Phil respected her, Patty Porter, for who she was.

"Thank you, Phil," she said, her voice catching, her heart overflowing. "I would like a special display cabinet very much."

Chapter 80

Amanda had made polenta with mushroom sauce and cod filets for dinner. At the start of the summer she had never expected to have so many opportunities to indulge her love of cooking. She would miss not having other people to feed once she was back home. Maybe she could get in the habit of inviting a few of her colleagues for dinner every now and then. It was something to think about.

Once the women were seated around the table, Patty cleared her throat rather loudly.

"I have something important to tell you all," she said.

"Well, go on," Mary urged, helping herself to a hefty spoonful of polenta. "Don't keep us waiting."

A smile broke out across Patty's face as she pulled her left hand from under the table. "Phil asked me to marry him, and I said yes."

Mary whistled. "Nice ice!"

Sandra put a hand to her mouth, her eyes wide. "Patty," she said, "it's absolutely beautiful."

"Wow. I had no idea things were getting serious with you two," Amanda said. "You swore there was no courtship."

"I wasn't sure that there was," Patty admitted, with a shy smile.

Amanda nodded. "Congratulations then. I wish you both the best."

Patty looked to Sandra. "I know it's all been very fast, but I guess that old saying is true. You know when you know."

"I think it's fantastic," Sandra said warmly. "Phil's a lucky man. And he has very good taste in jewelry. And in women, of course."

Patty held out her hand and looked at the ring. "I thought that maybe it was a bit too big but then I said to myself, *oh, why not?* If Phil wants me to have a diamond like this, it would be rude not to accept it!"

Mary smiled. "Way to go, Patty. I wish the both of you the best. So, what was it that sealed the deal? Those cobalt Capri pants?"

"Don't be silly," Sandra scolded. "It was Patty's goodness that caught Phil's attention."

"And her cooking?" Mary ventured with a smile.

"Phil does like my cooking."

"So, did you tell your sisters the good news yet?" Amanda asked.

Patty nodded. "I did. I mean, Phil and I did, on FaceTime."

"What did they say?" Mary asked. "I'm dying to know."

"After they came to?" Patty laughed. "Really, they looked like they would pass out or something. But then they congratulated me and agreed to be my maids of honor. And you know what? I don't care if they're not really happy for me as much as happy for themselves, having me taken off their hands. What they think doesn't matter. It never should have, I guess, but it did, for a long time."

"Well," Amanda said, "cheers to the happy couple. Let's lift our glasses to Patty and Phil." She was genuinely happy for Patty, pleased that Patty was getting what she had wanted and been denied for so long.

As a conversation about wedding details unfolded, Amanda, never one much interested in things like flower arrangements and processional marches, allowed her thoughts to turn once again to the woman she had met in the park, maybe an angel in human form, come to give her an important message. Maybe she would tell the others about her strange encounter. She would like to know what Sandra, especially, had to say. But she decided to stay silent on the matter. She decided she wanted to savor the special, if still confusing, moment on her own for a while longer. Maybe forever. Maybe moments like the one in the park weren't meant to be shared. She just didn't know. Besides, she didn't want to spoil Patty's moment in the spotlight.

"Amanda? Will you come?"

Amanda startled and looked to Patty. "Come where?"

"Haven't you been listening at all?" Sandra asked with a bit of a smile.

"Sorry. My mind wandered. What did I miss?"

"I just asked you and Mary and Sandra to come to the wedding. I'd really like you to be there. It will be here in Yorktide, of course."

Amanda realized that she was touched by Patty's invitation. "I'll do my best, Patty," she said. "That's a promise."

"Okay, Patty," Mary said now, leaning forward over the table. "How about it? How about you finally tell us exactly how old you are?"

Amanda nodded. "Really, Patty, what does it matter?"

Patty looked from one woman to the other and then sighed. "Okay," she said. "I'm sixty-nine. I'll be seventy on December twelfth. I'm a Sagittarius, and my moon is in Scorpio."

"See? Was that so bad?" Amanda smiled.

"I guess not," Patty admitted, looking again at the sparkly diamond ring on her finger. "I guess it wasn't so bad at all."

Chapter 81

Sandra and Clovis were alone in the house. She was in the kitchen, arguably her favorite room, and Clovis was in one of his zoomie modes, tearing from one end of the house to the other, knocking things over as he went. When he tired of being insane, Sandra would right the items he had knocked off tables in his race to nowhere.

Mary had gone to a gallery to view an exhibit by a local painter who had caught her eye when she had seen some of her work in a magazine a few weeks back. She herself might be a lousy artist, Mary had said, but she would continue to be as much of an artists' patron as she could afford to be.

Amanda was taking a walk, prepared against the sun, ticks, and speeding cars. She had told Sandra that she was planning to adopt a cat once she was back home. Clovis, she said, had opened her eyes to what she had been missing all her life. Sandra had been pleased and surprised. She hadn't been aware that Amanda was spending time with Clovis. But he was pretty special. Maybe he had worked his magic with just a few winks of a golden eye.

And Patty was out with Phil. They had plans to make. There was talk of their driving down to New Hampshire the following week to meet Patty's family, return the car Patty had borrowed, and load up Phil's truck with Patty's personal items, including of course her collection of fairy figurines.

Sandra believed that Patty and Phil would be good together. And she remembered yet again how Patty almost hadn't been given the chance to come to Yorktide this summer. Certainly, Marcia Livingston had been against the idea. But something in Sandra had sensed that Patty should be a guest at number 12 Spruce Street. In some way, Sandra felt that she might be considered responsible for bringing the lovebirds together. It was a nice thought.

Was that someone coming up the drive? Sandra cocked her head as if that might help her discern the source of the sound she thought she had heard. No, she decided. There was no car in the drive. She realized that she felt disappointed.

At the start of the summer, being alone in her home was the norm and had been for the past five years. She had become used to—mostly—the sound of the silence since John's passing. Now, at the end of this special summer, it felt a bit strange, not quite right, the lack of human voices, the absence of human presence. Very soon she would have to readjust to being under this roof alone with Clovis. Well, she thought, things could certainly be worse.

The landline rang then. It was Kate's number, and Sandra smiled as she picked up the receiver.

"Are you sitting down, Mom?" Kate said, without preamble.

"Do I need to be?"

"It might be wise."

Sandra frowned but took the phone to the table and sat. "Please, Kate," she said. "What's this about? You're scaring me."

"Sorry, Mom. Are you ready?"

Sandra said that she was, though ready for what she didn't know.

"Carrie and I are having a baby. We didn't want to say anything earlier in case things went wrong, but it's okay now. Carrie is twelve weeks pregnant, and we couldn't be happier."

Sandra felt the tears spring from her eyes and she laughed. "Oh, my God, this is such wonderful news! Oh, Kate, I'm so happy for you both!"

"And for yourself, too, am I right?" Kate asked. Sandra thought she sounded anxious.

"Of course!" she said. "Gosh, if you knew how much I've wanted a grandchild . . . But I couldn't say anything, could I?"

"No," Kate agreed, "and you were very good about keeping silent on the subject. I appreciated it; really, we both did. And now I'm happy that Carrie and I can give you what you've wanted for so long."

"Please don't say you're doing this just for me!" Sandra cried.

Kate sighed. "Mom, of course not. But it's nice to know that a grandchild will make you happy."

Sandra hesitated a moment before saying: "Um, may I ask about the father? Is it someone you know? I'm sorry. It's probably not my business."

"It's okay that you asked," Kate told her. "And no, we don't know anything about the birth father but what we learned from the sperm bank we used, and that's a fair amount actually. Donors used by the company we chose are vetted in every way you can think of, from screening for hundreds of genetic conditions to criminal background checks. Carrie and I feel confident we did the right thing in going with a donor. We debated for some time about it, Mom, believe me. We have a good friend who might have agreed to be the father of our child but . . ."

"Kate, you don't have to justify your choices," Sandra said firmly. "I trust that you and Carrie made the right choice for you."

"I know I don't have to justify my behavior, but I'd like you to know the truth. We just didn't want any conflict in the future, and conflict might have come about if the father was someone we knew. We've seen it happen to friends. Maybe we were being overly cautious but . . . Anyway, what's done is done, and we're fine about it. Mom, there's something else," Kate went on. "Now, if you have any hesitations whatsoever about what I'm about to propose, you need to be honest about them, okay? This will only work if all of us are comfortable with the idea."

Sandra laughed a bit. "Okay, I promise. But I have no idea what you're talking about."

"Okay, here goes. Carrie and I have been doing a lot of thinking about the idea of 'communal living' for some time now. What with your experiment this summer, and all the news about the growing trend of people living together in new sorts of communities, well, it all began to come together for us."

"Okay," Sandra said, now a bit confused as well as anxious. Were Kate and Carrie planning to merge their little family with another little family?

"The thing is," Kate went on, "well, Carrie and I would like to suggest that we three move in with you and that all four of us live together. Now," Kate went on hurriedly, "we think it could work well for all of us, but as I said, you would have to be one hundred percent into the idea as well. The three of us would have to sit down and agree on some rules and work through the financial stuff so that everything is clear and no one ever feels taken advantage of. So—what do you think?"

Sandra stared into space. She was shocked. She was thrilled. She was wary. Suddenly, she recalled Kate's saying, on her last visit to Yorktide, that interdependence, rather than total independence, should be a person's goal.

"I thought you couldn't wait to get out of Maine all those years ago," Sandra said. Maybe that wasn't the best thing she might have said at the moment, but it was what came out.

"You're right," Kate admitted, "I couldn't. But I'm older now. My idea of what's really important has changed. Now, I know it's where I want to be. Carrie, too. Maine is where we want to raise our child, Yorktide, specifically. Consider it a compliment to you and Dad. In a way, I want to recreate for *my* child my own pretty great childhood."

Sandra took a deep breath before speaking. "To be honest, Kate, this feels very sudden. I know you and Carrie have been discussing this, and I know that I've been toying with the idea of merging households but . . ."

"I want to assure you that Carrie and I are making a genuine commitment to you, Mom. We're not going to change our minds and move away in a year or two. I'm not suggesting we need a signed legal contract to that effect, but if you'd feel more comfortable with everything spelled out, let's get ourselves a lawyer and make it all legal."

The thought of signing a legal contract with her daughter, her own flesh and blood, seemed—strange. "No," Sandra said quickly. "Well, maybe. There's time for that later." She took a deep breath. "I think the idea of our all living together under one roof is lovely, Kate, really. A very good idea for us all. Thank you."

Kate exhaled loudly. "Whew. You had me worried there for a moment. Are you really, one hundred percent sure?"

"One hundred percent," Sandra assured her. "Are you going to want to make any changes to the house? It was fine for children back in the old days, but I understand if you and Carrie want to make some improvements for the sake of safety. Things are so much more . . . I can't think of the word!"

"Things are so much more hyper-anxiety-ridden these days," Kate said, "maybe too much so. No, I think the house is just fine the way it is. But we can talk about any adjustments once we've settled in. Again, all three of us will need to be in agreement before any important decisions are made. This is going to be *our* home, belonging to all four of us. Um, Carrie is here. Do you want to say hello?"

Sandra laughed. "Of course, I do!"

Kate put the call on speaker mode.

"Congratulations to you both," Sandra said. "I'm so happy for you. And for me!"

"Thank you, Sandra. Kate and I couldn't be more thrilled."

"Did you mention this development to your brother, Kate?" Sandra asked.

"No. We wanted to talk to you first about both the baby and the living arrangements before we told Jack and Carrie's family. And Mom? A big part of our thinking is that we want to be there for you as you age. There might come a time when you need help, and we'll be right there to provide it."

"Thank you," Sandra said feelingly. "And don't worry. I vow to abide by the rules of the parents when it comes to the child. There must be a united front."

"I agree. We agree, I mean!"

The call ended soon after, leaving Sandra feeling a bit overwhelmed. Wow, she thought. Her life had changed drastically in a matter of minutes. Her future had been decided in the space of a phone call. So much was about to change. Sandra had no doubt that some of that change would be daunting. She also knew that other aspects of that change would be thrilling.

Suddenly, it occurred to her that relocating to Maine would greatly affect Kate's career. She had passed the bar in Maine, Massachusetts, and New Hampshire, as well as in New York, but might she need to be recertified or something? Well, Kate would figure that out. She was nothing if not smart and resourceful.

As for Sandra, there were plans she could begin to make. She would relinquish the master suite to Kate and Carrie and move into the second largest bedroom, the one Mary was occupying that summer. The next largest room, Amanda's, could be the child's. The smallest room, the one Patty was currently occupying, would be perfect for Carrie's at-home office. Kate could set up at the desk in the den, the room in which Amanda had healed after her accident, John's favorite room.

To think that there had been times this summer when Sandra had thought about selling the big house and buying a house or a condo in a fifty-five and older community! She far preferred the idea of three generations of family living together. Once again, the house would be filled with the laughter of a child, maybe more than one child someday. But she would have to wait and see.

A vivid memory of her dear brother Jacob came to Sandra then. She wondered if Kate and Carrie would consider naming a child Jacob (if a boy, of course), but she knew she didn't have the right to make such a request. Maybe Carrie wanted her baby to be named after someone in her birth family, or maybe the mothers had already chosen a name that resonated with just the two of them.

Well, whatever her grandchild was to be called, the fact remained that the summer had been a success. Sandra felt both pleased and proud that she had been brave enough to open her home to three strangers. As a result, if indirect, of her having chosen Patty Porter as a summer roommate, she would be gaining a new neighbor. It was true that she probably would never have chosen Patty as a friend had they met in other circumstances. But after having spent the summer under the same roof with her, Sandra was truly pleased that Patty would be part of her life going forward. And that Patty would get to know Sandra's first grandchild!

It was like something her Aunt Kitty used to say, Sandra thought. If you were waiting around for a miracle to happen, stop waiting and take action. Leave the house and go for a walk. Smile at someone you pass on the street. Chat with the people behind the counters at the local shops. Invite opportunities for connection. Because miracles were really about humans interacting with humans; at least, many of them were. Some miracles were about humans interacting with members of other species.

As if to prove this point, Clovis came pacing into the kitchen, stopped at Sandra's feet, and howled. Clearly, zoomie time was over.

"Lunch time, is it?" she said with a smile, rising from her chair and heading toward the fridge. "What will it be today? Chicken or tuna?"

Clovis announced that he would prefer chicken.

Chapter 82

Mary was in her room, prepacking for her departure in a matter of days. She had bought a few interesting items this summer, some of which needed to be packed with special care, including a small oil painting by a local woman who had a bit of a reputation in New England. She knew the perfect place for it at home.

Of course, there was the wonderful book about L.S. Lowry she had discovered, along with the rather ragged but perfectly readable paperback copy of Truman Capote's *In Cold Blood* she had stumbled upon at a yard sale.

In a dingy little antique shop—often, the best kind of antique shop—she had been captivated by a sage-green Jasperware brooch by Wedgwood. The brooch, set in sterling silver, wasn't worth much monetarily, but it spoke to her, and that was what mattered most. And, the brooch would work well with a good many pieces in her wardrobe, especially those that were gray or black.

Mary had bundled the art supplies she had bought earlier that summer and now tucked them into her bag, next to the painting. She had decided that she would ask her sister-in-law if she was interested in the supplies. She would text

Stacy photos and descriptions of the items—including that ten-dollar drawing pencil—and see what she thought. It might be a start to mending their messy relationship.

Mary closed the suitcase. She suddenly remembered the to-do list she had compiled at the start of the summer. It had been an ambitious list, and she had accomplished very little of the projected tasks. For one, she hadn't made it to the Farnsworth Museum in Rockland, though she had managed to spend an afternoon at the Ogunquit Museum of American Art. Still, though she had been uncharacteristically lazy, she had enjoyed this summer so very much.

Thanks to Patty's influence, and to Sandra's, too, Mary was going forward with a vow to be—at least, to try to be—less negative and pessimistic and cynical. She would try not to be rude to strangers, particularly to men, the way she had been to Sandra's friend Pete at the Fourth of July party. And, she was truly determined to be less annoying, as Sandra had once accused her of being.

Maybe the most important aspect of the new Mary was the relationship she was building with her nephew. She had decided to give Bill a hefty check as a sort of cumulative graduation present (she had missed them all, grammar school through law school), and she was determined to bully him into accepting it if he put up a fuss. She had the money to spare, and she owed him. He was her nephew, her only brother's only child, and she had neglected him for too long. Money wasn't everything, but it was helpful. No one could argue with that.

Finally, she had gotten it through her thick skull that going back to work was what she was meant to do. So what if she was a workaholic? There were far worse things to be. There were many possibilities open to retired lawyers. She could volunteer to run or even to start a charity. If she didn't want to step into a leadership role, she could offer to head up special limited projects for a nonprofit organization.

One thing was for sure: going forward she would dedicate

her skills and talents to working for a worthy cause, one that appealed to her sense of justice. She was not meant to be a lady of leisure. Hell, she wasn't meant to be a *lady* at all. Maybe she was that old-fashioned (and definitely un-woke) thing, a dame. Certainly, she was a strong woman, one who always got too hungry for dinner at eight.

Patty Porter, Mary thought with a smile. Patty was a good kid, as people used to say. She deserved some happiness at long last. And Phil, who Mary had recently met, was a really solid guy. He couldn't hide that fact if he wanted to. They would be okay. And, they would have Sandra to keep an eye on them, should they ever need assistance.

Sandra. Mary wondered what would change for her when her houseguests left in a few days. Maybe Sandra would find herself feeling lonely. Maybe, instead, she would find herself feeling grateful for the reestablishment of her solitude. Maybe she would feel a bit of both emotions.

Whatever the case, Mary had every intention of keeping in touch with Sandra. And if her new work commitments, whatever they might be, prevented her from spending an entire summer at her leisure, certainly she might swing a week or even a long weekend in Yorktide the following year. If Sandra's house was no longer open for business, Mary would find a place at a hotel or bed-and-breakfast. She had resources.

As for Amanda, she was going home to a very new life. Mary had trouble imagining what it would be like to return to a home that was now vacant of the person with whom you had shared the space for eight years. Strange, at the very least. Hopefully, Liam's absence would feel to Amanda like a thoroughly good thing. And, Amanda had said something about adopting a cat from her local shelter. A cat, even a nasty one, had to be a better living companion than "dump 'em by text" Liam.

Mary, hands on hips, cast a glance around the lovely room in which she had been privileged to live for the past few months. And what a few months they had been! The summer had proved to be a time of self-reckoning. She had absolutely no regrets about having come to Yorktide to live under Sandra Pennington's roof. Like each of her roommates, she had taken a risk, set out on an adventure, perhaps without being fully prepared for what she might find along the way. But what was the point of life if you didn't take a leap of faith now and then?

Yes, Mary thought. She was all for taking another leap of faith.

Chapter 83

Patty had started to pack her things in preparation for leaving Sandra's house. It was very unlike her; she had always been a last-minute sort of person. But somehow, it felt important to take a real step closer to her new life. She would be moving into Phil's house in a matter of days. At first, the couple had talked about asking Sandra if Patty could continue to rent her room until the wedding in early October, but then they had decided not to stay apart one more moment longer than was necessary. Life was too short. They were getting on. What harm could it do, living together before marriage? Phil had become not only Patty's fiancé but also, as important, her friend.

And because Phil was her friend, Patty had told him about the times she had messed up this summer, about how she had been late with the rent and about how she had intended to feed Sandra's cat a bowl of cream when she had promised not to give him any people food.

Phil had been so kind, especially about the Clovis incident. "Your intentions were good," he had told her. "You just didn't think things through before acting."

"That's always been my problem," she said ruefully.

Phil had pulled her to him in a hug. "You're human, Patty. We all are."

Like Phil, Sandra also understood that humans might try their best and act with all good intentions, and still make mistakes. Patty felt comforted by the fact that Sandra would be there to help her adjust to Yorktide, so that she wouldn't have to rely solely on Phil. Patty had never been a member of a community before. She literally had no idea of how to go about becoming one.

Well, she had some idea. For one, she had spoken to Michelle at Crystal Breeze, and Michelle had agreed to let Patty keep her job at the shop after the summer, except for the months of January and February when the shop closed up. Michelle was very fond of Phil James, and Patty suspected that fondness might be the reason Michelle had been okay with keeping Patty on the payroll.

Phil was completely supportive of Patty's continuing to work. And Patty wanted to help Phil with the honey and candle business, too. It sounded like fun. She had never been part of a team before, at least, not in her romantic life. She had never been a true, equal partner, both trusting and trusted. It might take some getting used to, but she felt game to try.

Suddenly, Patty decided that she had done enough packing for the moment, and went to join the others in the den, a room that over the course of the summer had become a favorite place for the women to gather. There was a pot of tea and a plate of sugar cookies on the coffee table. Patty helped herself to a cookie and took a seat in the plushy armchair that she preferred.

Sandra looked from one woman to the other, a smile on her face. "Patty, now that you're here I can share the big news with you all. Kate and her wife, Carrie, are going to be moving in here with me permanently. They're expecting a baby in

February and have decided they want to raise the child in Yorktide."

Amanda raised her eyebrows. "Now that *is* big news. And congratulations on becoming a grandmother."

"I wish Sandra could be my grandmother," Mary said with a laugh. "You know what I mean. She'll be perfect in the role."

"Wow," Patty said. "Was it your idea, Sandra? Did you offer Kate and Carrie a home?"

"No," Sandra said. "Kate suggested the arrangement; it seems she and Carrie had been talking about it for some time. Frankly, I was totally surprised at first, but then I gladly accepted the idea. We won't go into the situation blindly or with unrealistic expectations. We might even hire a lawyer to help us negotiate any sticky questions about finance. A lot will change for all of us, forming this new family unit. But I hope with all my heart it will work out."

"And that Clovis will like the baby!" Mary said, glancing at Sandra's sidekick.

"He's sure to be jealous, at least for a while," Sandra said with a shrug. "But cats are often very taken with babies, so you never know. I hear the Internet is rife with cats and their baby friends. So, Mary, any thoughts about what comes next for you?"

Mary smiled. "Plenty of thoughts. I'm never short of thoughts. I've come to accept that I needed to retire when I did, but I've also come to realize that retirement wasn't meant to be a permanent state. I needed to recharge my batteries, as it were, and I think I'm just about ready to get out there again. And I'm serious about getting to know my brother and his family."

"Wonderful," Sandra said. "What about you, Amanda?"

"Well," Amanda said, a bit musingly, "I've been doing a lot of thinking this summer, and while there are still questions for which I have no answers, I do know for sure that, going forward, I have no interest in allowing myself to fall into another romantic relationship. That's what I've done in my past, fall into relationships in a sort of lazy way without any genuine consideration of whether or not I really want to be there. It hasn't been fair to me, and it hasn't been fair to my partners, either. It's been a no-win situation, and I'm tired of it."

"Won't you be lonely?" Patty asked. "I mean, now that Liam is gone." Maybe it was the fact that she was newly engaged, but the idea of anyone's living alone suddenly seemed scarier than ever to Patty.

Amanda shook her head. "No. I mean, there will probably be moments when I feel lonely, but not for Liam's company. Besides, you know that I'm adopting a cat. That will keep me busy! And, I also plan on spending much more time with my parents. I want to just enjoy being with them while I can."

"That sounds like an exceptionally good plan," Sandra noted with a smile. "Every bit of it."

"I agree," Mary said. "Brava, Amanda. So, Patty, what's next? I mean, besides planning the wedding."

"I have a lot to do," Patty told them. "Phil says I should feel free to make changes to the house so that it really feels like ours, and not just his."

"Any ideas so far?" Sandra asked.

"Yes! I'm going to totally redecorate the bedroom. Right now, the walls are a sort of drab gray, but I'm going to paint them something sunny, yellow maybe. Well, *I'm* not going to paint the walls, we're going to hire someone to do that, but still, I get to choose the new color scheme. And the carpet is old and threadbare so that's going too, though I'm not sure what I want put down in its place. It's all so exciting. Of course, I'll be working to a budget so it will be challenging, but I'm looking forward to that part, too! Phil says you're never too old to learn new things, and maybe he's right!"

"Of course, he's right," Mary said firmly.

Patty smiled and looked from one of her summer roommates to the other, Sandra, Mary, and Amanda. And then, of course, there was Phil, not present in the room but present in her heart. All these good people! Patty realized that she was happier now than she had ever dreamed she would be. Maybe she didn't have a right to this happiness, but it had been given to her, and she would cherish it for as long as it lasted.

Chapter 84

Amanda had completed her packing, the sand dollar wrapped carefully in tissue paper and tucked safely in her handbag, a memento of this very special summer when things had begun to come clear to her.

The school semester would be starting in less than a week, and there was preparation to see to. The staff would spend two days in meetings, and then there would be a half day of school, an introduction to the fall semester, during which there would be an assembly of all students and a special welcoming program for the freshmen and their parents.

Amanda felt excited, even energized, by the prospect.

So much in her life had changed this summer, and so much was still changing. For every one of her summer roommates, really. Take Sandra, for instance. She seemed genuinely happy that she would be sharing a home with her family again after five long years on her own.

As for Mary, Amanda wasn't in the least bit surprised that she had decided to go back to work. It was clear that she had talent, and talent shouldn't be wasted. And Mary had spoken excitedly about connecting with her family.

And then there was Patty. Though Amanda had only met

Phil once, after the announcement of the couple's engagement, once had been enough for her to determine that Phil was the proverbial salt of the earth type. She truly hoped that Patty and Phil would be happy together. She suspected that they would be.

The summer roommates would see one another next at Patty's wedding, scheduled for the first weekend in October. It would be a quick visit for Amanda; she would leave Boston Friday after school got out and return to Boston Sunday evening. Of course, she would also need to buy an outfit for the wedding, and that prospect frightened her more than a little. Who could she ask to help her shop? Would one of her fellow teachers be willing to spend an afternoon at Copley Place mall going through racks of dresses and fancy pantsuits? It seemed a big favor to ask. Her mother, though, might be willing to help. Yes, she would ask her mother, who always dressed well, to spend an afternoon at the mall, and she would take her mother for a nice lunch as a thank you.

Suddenly, Amanda remembered that she had promised her summer roommates that she would watch a few episodes of *The Golden Girls*. She wondered now if her mother had enjoyed the show. Maybe they would watch it together.

Amanda reached for the purple gift bag that sat on top of the dresser. It was a special parting gift for Clovis, a package of bright crinkly balls she had bought only after checking with Sandra as to his likes and dislikes. Clovis was responsible for opening Amanda's eyes to the possibility of life with a cat companion, and, for that, she owed him thanks. She had already placed a call to her local animal shelter and made an appointment to visit the day after her return home. There was one cat she had seen on their website that particularly interested her. Something about his face. He looked intelligent. Maybe also wise. Most interestingly, his eyes reminded her of the strange, lion-like eyes of the woman in the park. He was already nine years old, but that didn't bother Amanda. She really wanted to bring this cat home. Maybe she did possess some of that mythical maternal instinct she had dismissed for so long. The cat had been given a name by the shelter workers—he had been one of dozens rescued from a hoarding situation—but Amanda felt that the name didn't suit him. His new name would be Ranulf, after one of those old warring dukes of Aquitaine. She believed that he would like it.

Amanda took a final look around the room that had been hers this summer. A room that had been a haven, a safe and nourishing place in a safe and nourishing home.

Now, it was time to make her farewells to her fellow golden girls, her summer roommates, her friends. She would try not to cry too much.

Epilogue

"Are you playing that song again?" Kate rolled her eyes in mock annoyance. "It's the fifth time this morning!"

Carrie shrugged. "It's my favorite Christmas song. Who doesn't like 'I'm Dreaming of a White Christmas'?"

"I love it," Sandra said, robustly. "And it beats those chipmunks Kate is so fond of."

"Come on, the chipmunks are cute!"

"No," Carrie and Sandra said in unison, "they are not."

Carrie was, by her own admission, a fanatic fan of Christmas, so had set out to decorate every inch of the house. There were garlands of pine boughs wound around the banister of the central staircase and fresh pine wreaths on the front and back doors and the doors of the garage. With Sandra's permission, Carrie had set out a crèche that had once belonged to John's grandmother. Handmade in Italy, the crèche was a true work of art, the baby Jesus cradled in a bed of straw, the expression on the face of his mother both tender and joyous.

More garlands were draped across the mantelpiece of the fireplace. Little glittery snowmen and women peeked out from behind the greenery. Red and green candles had replaced the usual white candles Sandra kept around the house. A dish of old-fashioned ribbon candy sat on the coffee table in the living room, next to a vase of candy canes stood on end. An Advent calendar on the theme of Santa's workshop hung in the kitchen. The three women took turns opening each day's little flap to reveal an elf or a wrapped present or one of Santa's reindeer.

The den had been transformed into a blue-and-silver-themed winter wonderland. In Sandra's opinion—one she kept to herself—the scheme wasn't entirely successful. The fairly sophisticated color palette didn't quite "go" with the room's casual chintz vibe, but it was the effort that mattered.

The tree, of course, was huge. Kate and Carrie had chosen it at a tree farm and brought it home tied to the roof of their car. Together the three women had wrangled the tree off the car's roof, up the stairs to the porch, through the front door, and into the living room where it had pride of place. They had proceeded to decorate the lovely fir with a combination of family heirloom ornaments, silver tinsel, and glass balls in red, blue, and gold. An eight-inch-tall angel figurine in gold and silver robes served as a topper.

The tree skirt had been made by one of Carrie's great-grandmothers and featured images—pine trees, Santa Claus, angels—cut from felt and sewn on by hand. It had a distinct folk art feel to it, and Sandra imagined her grandchild—a boy, it had been announced—playing under the Christmas tree in years to come, finding the skirt a familiar friend. That Clovis hadn't chosen to throw up on it yet seemed another sign of the skirt's special place in their family.

Clovis, who had been a bit unsettled by what he no doubt saw as yet another invasion of his territory with the permanent arrival of Kate and Carrie back in October, had by late December accepted the situation and had even become fast friends with Carrie who, being a warmhearted person, tolerated Clovis's periodic attacks on the tree's lower hanging branches.

Christmas gave Sandra the perfect excuse for using her

good china and glassware. She and Carrie had shared the tasks of ironing the linen tablecloth and napkins, polishing the silverware (though it had been properly stored, it still needed a touch-up), and filling the cut-glass salt and pepper shakers. For dinner, they would be serving roast turkey, mashed potatoes, green beans, crescent rolls (everyone's favorites from Pillsbury), and homemade cranberry sauce, one of Carrie's specialties. For dessert, there would be Sandra's famous apple pie, made from a recipe that had been handed down through her family, and a deliciously moist fruitcake made by a member of Sandra's book group. That would be served with a brandy hard sauce. There was red and white wine and sparkling cider to drink, and the coffee pot and teakettle were ready to go at any time.

The day would be perfect, Sandra thought, if only Jack and Robbi had been able to join them, but they had promised a lengthy visit the following spring. They had enjoyed their trip to Greece and had promised a good old-fashioned slide show, something to which Sandra, Kate, and Carrie were looking forward.

At precisely two o'clock, the doorbell rang. "That's Patty and Phil," Sandra announced, going to the door to let them in. "They're always exactly on time."

Sandra opened the door to the couple. Standing there wearing matching red and white Santa hats and big happy smiles, they looked so suited for each other that Sandra felt a twinge of what might be termed jealousy, but what was really a sweet sorrow for the loss of her own beloved spouse.

"Merry Christmas!" Patty cried as she presented Sandra with a massive tray of homemade cookies. Phil explained that there were classic chewy chocolate chip cookies, butter crescents rolled in powdered sugar, decorated gingerbread people, and spicy German pfeffernuesse.

"I'm getting fat living with this lady," Phil said as he removed his coat and patted his stomach. He didn't seem in the least bit concerned about this.

Sandra ushered the pair into the living room where Kate and Carrie were settled by the tree. Sandra and the other summer roommates had attended Patty and Phil's wedding back in October, and what a lovely day that had been. Patty had been touchingly shy throughout the entire experience, almost as if she still couldn't quite believe that her lifelong dream was coming true. She had worn a white skirt suit with a pale pink silk blouse that Sandra had helped her find at a small boutique in Portland. Her bouquet was composed of lush, pale pink roses and green ferns. After years of not being able to afford a decent haircut and color and a professional manicure, Patty was thrilled to be able to pamper herself. She had looked beautiful. She had looked like herself.

Of course, Patty had worn the truly magnificent diamond ring Phil had given her, a two-carat cushion-cut, colorless diamond in a classic and simple eighteen-karat yellow gold setting. In her ears, Patty wore diamond studs, another gift from her husband. Her wedding ring was a simple gold band, matching Phil's.

Sandra had met Patty's family at the wedding, including all of the nieces and nephews. She couldn't say she had exactly taken to either Bridget or Teri, but Sandra had been able to conclude that their love for Patty was genuine enough, if slightly tainted with judgment. But Patty was free of her sisters now in a way she never had been before, and she would remain free, even should Phil pass before her.

After the ceremony, there had been a big party at Phil's favorite family-style restaurant to which it seemed most of Yorktide had been invited. For their wedding song, Patty and Phil had chosen an old standard, "Smoke Gets in Your Eyes."

At one point in the festivities, according to custom, Patty had tossed her bouquet over her shoulder toward the group of single females, young and old, gathered in hopes of catching it. In a remarkable moment, the bouquet was caught by Mildred Price, a notoriously old-fashioned, man-hating battle-axe who had surprised everyone in Yorktide by accepting the invitation to the wedding in the first place. That Mildred had actually been interested in reaching for the bouquet astounded the guests so deeply that no one managed to laugh or to applaud or to react in any visible way when she stood there, bouquet in hand, a smug and triumphant smile on her face.

Mary had looked sleek and stylish as always that day, in a dark purple sheath dress, a black leather clutch, and black heels, her hair perfectly cut, and her jewelry simple yet striking. Her work as legal advisor for a Brooklyn-based food bank and shelter was keeping her busy, and she had talked excitedly about a flying visit her nephew had made to visit her. Mary was thriving; Sandra had had no doubt about that. She had looked more upbeat than she had back in the summer when she had been wrestling with the new reality of being retired. She had even accepted an invitation to dance by Sandra's friend Pete. Sandra had a photograph to prove it.

Amanda, too, had seemed far more relaxed than she had back in the summer, more content in herself, and had said as much to Sandra. She had been wearing a silver and peridot pendant along with the ubiquitous silver hoop earrings, and her outfit, a fitted taupe pantsuit, was surprisingly stylish. Amanda had told the others that she had bought a bag of Funyuns and found that she still loved them, and that she and her mother had watched several seasons of *The Golden Girls* together. Also, she had announced that she was living happily with a cat companion she adored; her phone was crammed with photos of Ranulf, a brown tiger with strangely beautiful eyes. "He's so grumpy," Amanda enthused. "I adore him! Did you see this photo? Just look at him! Could he be any cuter?" While Sandra agreed that Ranulf was, indeed, cute, in her mind he was not half as cute as Clovis.

Since the wedding, Sandra had been in touch with both Mary and Amanda. The week before she had received a good, old-fashioned Christmas card from each woman, complete with a handwritten note. Of course, Sandra had sent cards of her own.

But the wedding hadn't been the only big event of the autumn. Only weeks after Sandra celebrated her seventy-fifth birthday on November twenty-second, Patty had celebrated her seventieth with Phil in Quebec. It was the first time that Patty had been out of the country, so the excursion had been extra exciting for her. Upon the couple's return, Sandra had had them over for dinner and a cake. The evening had warmed her heart. The truth was that she and Patty were becoming real friends. Each week they might go for a walk on the beach, browse through an antique market, or attend an afternoon concert at the library. The last time Sandra had been to The Retreat for dinner, Patty had proudly shown her the beautiful cabinet Phil had built to display Patty's collection of fairy figurines—which included two new members, Moonstone Fairy and Fairy with Harp.

"Phil and I went to midnight Mass at the Catholic church," Patty was telling the others gathered around the Christmas tree. "It was Phil's first time. It was like being in a fairy tale, not one of the scary ones, but one where only good things happen. It was all so beautiful, the music and the candlelight. We loved it, didn't we, Phil?" Patty turned adoring eyes on to her husband.

"We sure did," he replied, taking her hand. "To think I'd been missing out on such a wonderful experience all my life until Patty came along."

Kate, sitting next to Sandra on the couch, leaned in to whisper: "They're too cute for words. I might just be sick."

"Whoa!" Carrie suddenly cried, hand on her belly. "The baby just threw a punch! Anyone want to feel? Whoa, there he goes again!"

Sandra gently placed her hand on her daughter-in-law's belly and smiled. "We'll have our work cut out for us with this one!"

"Any thoughts on a name?" Patty asked. "Or is it going to be a surprise?"

Kate looked to Carrie, who nodded. "Well, we were going to let it be a surprise, but Carrie pointed out that Christmas was the perfect time to make the announcement."

"Well," Sandra said. "Don't keep us in suspense."

Kate reached for her mother's hand. "The baby's name is Jacob," she said. "After Mom's brother. My uncle. I never got to meet him, and I wanted to honor him in some way."

Sandra didn't bother to hide the tears that had sprung to her eyes. "I can't tell you how much this means to me," she said, squeezing Kate's hand and with her free hand, reaching for Carrie's. "Truly. Thank you, both."

Phil raised his glass. "To Jacob! To both Jacobs!"

"To all of us!" Patty added. "To the summer roommates and their families!"

"No more toasts. I'm hungry." Carrie rose from her chair. "And so is Jacob. Let's have dinner."

"Agreed." Phil helped Patty to her feet, and Sandra led the way into the dining room, proud and honored to be at the center of this group of family and friends.

Acknowledgments

Love and thanks to John Scognamiglio, friend, colleague, and editor for thirty years. Where did the time go?

And my deepest appreciation to everyone at Kensington Publishing Corporation who has made my journey from in-house New York editor to Maine writer possible.

I would like to make it known that I am forever grateful for my four years at The Academy of Mount Saint Ursula in the Bronx, New York. Thank you to the teachers, both lay and religious; to the wonderful friends I made; and most important, to my parents for having had the wisdom to choose the school for me.

This is in memory of Judith and William Sowa, beloved friends.

Please turn the page
for a very special Q&A with
Holly Chamberlin!

Q. This is a question often asked of writers of novels: Is there any of you in a particular character featured in *Summer Roommates*?

A. In the past, I've never consciously inserted aspects of myself into any of my characters, though of course unconsciously, bits and pieces have made their way into various characters. That's hard to avoid. While writing *Summer Roommates*, however, I found myself consciously drawing on several aspects of my personality as well as on recent incidents in my life to bring the four main characters to life. For example, not long after I began the book I found a perfect sand dollar on the beach and gave that nice experience to Amanda. Like Patty, I have an addiction to "things"—accessories, jewelry—and am not always as careful as I should be with spending. Like Sandra, I love living with cats. Like Mary, I am intensely interested in art. I recently discovered the work of British painter L.S. Lowry and gave an interest in him to Mary. There's also a correspondence on a deeper level between two of the four heroines and me. But I won't say any more about that! Too personal!

Q. The characters talk a lot about various forms of communal living and new ways of being together as a couple, like, for example, the idea of living apart together. What's your thinking on these topics?

A. Much like Sandra, I'm drawn to the idea of interdependent living. It seems eminently sensible. I'm super sociable, but it takes a lot out of me. Home is a refuge, the one place I can be my own weird, antisocial self. To share a home with anyone other than, let's say, my brother when younger (poor guy!), or my husband now (ditto!), seems deeply unattractive. The idea of LAT relationships is a bit of a difficult one for me, as well, having been raised with fairly old-fashioned assumptions of what a committed relationship is supposed to look like and of what the woman's role is supposed to be. That said, I think LAT is a very good idea, and I hope that people who chose and choose that format thrive in it. I suspect that they do.

Q. You mentioned "old-fashioned assumptions" about relationships. Your character Patty seems to have been seriously damaged by the old stereotypes of men and women, and her behavior hasn't always been without serious blemish. It seems to me, though, that you present Patty in a very sympathetic way. Is she your favorite of the four summer roommates?

A. I really don't have a favorite character. I like all four women! It's true, however, that as Patty came to life I found my heart breaking for her. I mean, in terms of the messages I received about what was possible and not possible for women, my own early upbringing wasn't so terribly far removed from the sort that Patty experienced. But poor Patty really was sacrificed on the altar of—I don't even know what to call it—sexism? So, in a sense I guess I have more sympathy for her than for the others. I mean—her fairy figurines!!! They mean so much to her, and, until she meets Sandra and Phil, no one has shown her carefully amassed collection any respect. I know I made it all up, but I still find it so sad! Having to go to midnight Mass on her own? Come on! No one should have to do that.

Q. How did you go about creating the particular mix of personalities for the house on Spruce Street? Did you have a plan or did the different characters just sort of show up?

A. A bit of both, actually. Obviously, there had to be a central figure, the woman who owned the home to be shared for the summer. She needed to be steady, and I wanted her to be nurturing as well, not just the homeowner but a bit of a matriarchal figure. The other three sort of showed up, as you put it, each one portraying a different part of me as I find myself in the present, at the age of sixty. Of course, Mary, Amanda, and

Patty then took on fuller lives of their own. They are not me—for example, none of them has been married for twenty-six years, as I have!—and I am not them. To be honest, Amanda was the slowest to evolve. Months into the writing I still had very little idea of who she was. It was a bit scary not to be able to get a grip on her. Finally, she showed up! But that's Amanda: elusive, secretive, a mystery even to herself.

Q. You've been writing women's fiction for many years. Have you ever wanted to try your hand at another genre?

A. I've dabbled with the idea of developing a cozy mystery series. A few years ago, I went so far as to make about forty pages of very preliminary notes about the setting, heroine, tone, et cetera. But honestly, I ran out of energy before I could go any further! I think I'll stick to reading mysteries written by other people. After all, there are so many wonderful writers already producing fantastic work.

SUMMER ROOMMATES

ABOUT THIS GUIDE

The suggested questions are included to enhance
your group's reading of
Holly Chamberlin's *Summer Roommates*!

DISCUSSION QUESTIONS

1. Have you ever considered the idea of some form of communal or interdependent living as a viable option for yourself? If the answer is yes, what about the idea appeals to you? If the idea doesn't appeal, why doesn't it? Sandra and the others think and talk about many issues surrounding the idea of adults who are not members of the same family and not necessarily friends choosing to cohabitate. Can you think of other issues the characters might not have considered?

2. Sibling relations play an important part in the lives of Sandra, Mary, and Patty. What is your take on Bridget and Teri's relation to and treatment of Patty? Mary and her brother, Bill, seem open to reknitting a bond that unraveled when Mary went off to college. How might Mary's nephew and sister-in-law play a part in this regeneration of family ties? Sandra still mourns the early passing of her brother, Jacob. Kate and Carrie's decision to name their child Jacob is a gift to Sandra. Do you think Sandra feels badly that her own children, Jack and Kate, aren't closer to each other? As for Amanda, she claims never to have missed what she never had—a brother or a sister. Pretend you're writing a different version of Amanda's story, one in which she had a sibling. How might that have made Amanda a different person in the story's present?

3. At one point in the book, Amanda wonders why a single life—a life lived on one's own—has yet to be presented to women as a viable option. She comes to believe that a life consciously lived without a romantic commitment is not a lesser life than one lived with a romantic commitment. And it's certainly not an easier one. Mary, we

know, would agree. Do you think things have changed to any great extent for today's young women? Are options for how to live one's life presented in a viable way? Does our culture really respect and support those who live on their own?

4. Amanda declares herself to be a totally earthbound person, but during the course of her story, she begins to find herself open to thoughts, feelings, and experiences she would, in the past, have ignored or ridiculed. By the end of the summer, she feels she has begun to change for the better, and that, going forward, she will be able to live a more authentic life. What are your thoughts about Amanda's experience with the woman in the park? Have you ever had a similar experience, one in which a stranger offers a kind word that effects a real change for the better in your life?

5. Patty regrets that she has never cultivated female friendships. By her story's end, she is in the process of building a genuine friendship with Sandra. In your opinion, just how important are a woman's female friends at various times of her life? Historically, the idea of women's friendships has been presented in a largely negative light, as fraught with bitchiness, jealousy, and competition. (Think, for example, of Amanda's habit of judging other women harshly, and her lack of close friends.) In your experience, how has that notion changed? *Has* it changed?

6. Mary has always styled herself a warrior—tough, dedicated, unstoppable. But the combination of the lawsuit against her legal practice and the sudden death of her childhood friend in a hit-and-run accident seriously rattled her sense of competency and self-assurance and

led directly to her taking an early retirement. We've all experienced events in our lives that have challenged every notion we've held to be true about ourselves. Who among the summer roommates—Sandra, Amanda, and Patty—do you think most helps Mary as she works through the aftereffects of the traumas she's suffered?

7. The loss of Sandra's friendship with Emma—and the particular way in which it was lost—leads her to the decision to open up her house for the summer to other women. Her daughter, Kate, worries that her mother will be overworked and taken advantage of. The real estate agent, Marcia Livingston, warns against accepting a woman like Patty Porter, who is financially insecure. Only Sandra's son, Jack, is one hundred percent enthusiastic, hoping that having other people around the house will ease his mother's loneliness. Clearly, Sandra takes an enormous leap of faith in setting up a temporary *Golden Girls*-like situation as a sort of trial run for a future permanent, interdependent community. Do you think you would ever attempt the same?

8. A fun question: Who is your favorite summer roommate and why?